TIDES OF THE HEART

TIDES OF THE HEART

EMMA DREAMWEAVER

Copyright © 2024

Disclaimer of Liability

Contents

Preface

Love is rarely a straightforward path. It winds, it twists, and it leads us down roads we never expect to travel. In *Tides of the Heart*, I wanted to explore not just the joy and beauty of love, but its complexities—the decisions we make that change the course of our lives, the choices we hesitate to make, and the deep emotional scars we carry with us.

Isabel's story is one of rediscovery, not only of the island she once called home but of herself. Through her journey, she confronts the unresolved questions of her past, the raw feelings of loss, and the powerful connections that linger long after we believe they've faded. Like the tides that shape the shorelines of Rosemere Isle, her story is about the pull of the heart and the choice to stay, to heal, and to love again.

In writing this novel, I found myself reflecting on the importance of home—not just as a place, but as a feeling, a connection, and sometimes, a person. The characters of this book are shaped by their relationships, their past, and the way they interact with the island that forms the backdrop of their lives. It is my hope that their emotional journeys resonate with you, and that *Tides of the Heart* offers a story that speaks to the deep, enduring power of love and the courage it takes to open one's heart again.

Thank you for joining Isabel, Gabe, and the others on this heartfelt journey. I hope you find within these pages not only a story of love but a reminder of the strength it takes to rediscover yourself and follow the tides of your own heart.

Warmest regards,

Emma Dreamweaver

1

Chapter 1: Homecoming to the Island

Isabel Thorne stood at the bow of the ferry, the wind whipping through her dark hair as Rosemere Isle slowly came into view. The island was just as she remembered it—a sliver of land rising from the sea, surrounded by jagged cliffs and crowned with emerald-green forests. The lighthouse, standing tall and weather-beaten on the eastern tip, was the first familiar structure she could make out. It had always been a beacon of safety for the island's fishermen and travelers. For Isabel, though, it was a reminder of the place she had been avoiding for the past ten years.

She inhaled deeply, the salty air filling her lungs, grounding her in the present moment. Rosemere Isle had never really changed. The air still carried that wild, briny scent, and the waves still crashed relentlessly against the rocky shores. But everything inside her felt different, heavier, laden with a sense of finality she couldn't shake.

As the ferry's engine hummed beneath her feet, she tightened her grip on the railing. She wasn't ready to come back. Not to the place where so many memories—good and bad—were etched into every inch of the landscape. But her mother's death had forced her hand. Matilda Thorne had passed away unexpectedly, and now the estate and her mother's long-untouched belongings awaited Isabel. It felt wrong, as though she was returning to something that didn't belong to her anymore. And yet, here she was.

When the ferry pulled into the small harbor, she saw a handful of locals waiting on the dock. Rosemere Isle wasn't a place where you could come and go unnoticed. Word traveled faster than the ocean breeze, and surely by now, everyone knew that Isabel Thorne had returned. Their gazes followed her as she disembarked, carrying nothing but a small leather bag slung over her shoulder and a camera tucked inside. She had been a photographer in the city—still was, technically—but she hadn't picked up her camera for weeks. Not since her mother's death. The camera now felt like a weight she didn't know how to carry.

She nodded at the dockworker as he tossed the rope to secure the boat, but she avoided making eye contact with the others who were undoubtedly whispering about her return. Isabel didn't want to face the curiosity or the well-meaning condolences. Not yet. Maybe not ever. She wanted to slink into the shadows and process her grief alone, to tuck herself away inside the walls of her childhood home and drown out the noise. But that was impossible here. Rosemere Isle was a community, and solitude was not something you could easily find.

"Isabel! You're back!"

The voice cut through her thoughts, bright and warm. She turned to see Eliza Carrington hurrying toward her, arms outstretched. Her best friend from childhood. Eliza had always been a burst of color in Isabel's grayscale world, with her vibrant scarves and jangling bracelets. Even now, her smile was as wide as ever, though the years had softened her features and added new lines around her eyes.

"Eliza," Isabel murmured as they embraced, though the hug felt awkward, forced even. She was out of practice with affection, out of practice with people in general. "It's good to see you."

Eliza pulled back, holding her at arm's length as if to assess her. "You look different. Thinner, maybe. And sadder," she said, her tone softening. "I'm sorry about your mom."

The words hung in the air between them, and Isabel swallowed the lump that rose in her throat. She had no idea how to respond to that, so she simply nodded. "Thanks."

"Are you staying at the house?" Eliza asked, tilting her head toward the hill that led up to the old Thorne estate. The house was a looming Victorian, its gray stone walls blending into the cliffs behind it. Isabel could see the rooftops from here, just barely peeking over the trees.

"Yes, for a while," Isabel said, though even that felt uncertain. She hadn't decided how long she would stay. Just long enough to settle her mother's affairs and figure out what to do with the house. Sell it, probably. There was no reason to hold on to it. Her life was in the city now, far from the slow, suffocating rhythm of island life.

"I'll come by later. We can catch up properly," Eliza said, squeezing her arm before waving a quick goodbye. "Don't be a stranger!"

Isabel watched her disappear into the small crowd that had gathered at the harbor, feeling the familiar pull of isolation tug at her. Eliza's offer was genuine, and Isabel knew she'd have to take her up on it at some point. But not today. Today, she needed the quiet.

She started the walk up the hill, her boots crunching on the gravel path that wound its way through the village. The island was small—small enough that she recognized nearly every face she passed. Old Mr. Finley, the fisherman who had once taught her how to tie a proper knot, gave her a brief nod as he mended his nets by the dock. Mrs. Jennings, the baker, stood outside her shop, dusting flour off her apron and giving Isabel a sympathetic smile. Everyone knew. Of course, they knew. That was how things worked here.

As Isabel continued up the path, her gaze shifted toward the landscape that surrounded her. The island had always been beautiful, in a rugged, untamed sort of way. The cliffs were jagged, as though the earth itself had cracked open to let the sea in. The forests were thick with pine trees, their branches swaying gently in the wind. And the ocean, ever-present, was a deep, endless blue, stretching out to the horizon in every direction.

This place had once felt like home to her, but now it felt foreign. Like a part of her past she no longer knew how to connect with. Ten years was a long time to be away, and the distance had grown not just in miles but in her heart as well.

When she reached the Thorne estate, the sight of the house made her pause. It was grand and imposing, perched on the edge of the cliff like a sentinel watching over the sea. The stone walls were weathered, and ivy climbed up the sides, curling around the windows like fingers. The house had always felt too big for just the two of them—her and her mother. Now, it felt even more cavernous, the silence inside stretching out like a shadow.

Isabel hesitated at the front door, her hand resting on the worn brass handle. She wasn't ready for this. Not for the memories that would come flooding back the moment she stepped inside. But there was no avoiding it. She had to face this, sooner or later.

The door creaked as she pushed it open, the sound echoing through the empty halls. The air inside was cool and musty, the scent of old wood and dust filling her nose. She stepped inside, closing the door behind her with a soft click. The house had been locked up for weeks since her mother's death, and it felt as though time had stood still. Everything was just as her mother had left it—books stacked neatly on the shelves, a vase of dried flowers on the table, and her mother's favorite armchair positioned near the window overlooking the sea.

Isabel walked through the house slowly, her footsteps muffled by the thick carpet beneath her feet. Each room held memories, and each memory carried a weight she wasn't ready to bear. The kitchen, where her mother had taught her how to bake bread. The study, where her mother had spent hours painting and sketching, her creative energy filling the room. And Isabel's old bedroom, still decorated with the same faded wallpaper and worn-out furniture from her childhood.

She paused at the doorway to her mother's studio, her hand resting on the frame. The door was slightly ajar, just as her mother had left it. Isabel hadn't stepped foot in here for years. Not since she had left the island for good. The studio had always been her mother's sanctuary, a place where she could escape the world and lose herself in her art. Isabel had never understood that. She had never shared her mother's passion for painting, preferring instead to look at the world through the lens of her camera.

Pushing the door open, Isabel stepped inside. The studio was just as she remembered it—light-filled, with large windows overlooking the sea. Canvases were stacked against the walls, some finished, others only partially complete. Her mother's easel stood in the center of the room, a painting still perched on it. Isabel walked over to it, her eyes scanning the image. It was a lighthouse—familiar, yet different from the one on the island. There was something about it, a small symbol painted in the corner, that caught her attention. She leaned closer, squinting at the detail, but couldn't make sense of it.

Isabel stepped back, shaking her head. She wasn't ready to dive into whatever mystery her mother had left behind. Not yet. Right now, she needed space, distance from the memories and the emotions that threatened to overwhelm her.

Leaving the studio, she made her way to the back of the house, where the garden stretched out toward the cliffs. The wind was stronger here, tugging at her hair and clothes as she stood at the edge of the property, staring out at the vast expanse of the ocean. It was a view she had seen a thousand times before, but today it felt different. Today, it felt like the ocean was calling her back—back to a time when things had been simpler, when the world hadn't felt so heavy.

But things weren't simple anymore. Isabel wasn't the girl who had left Rosemere Isle all those years ago, full of dreams and ambitions. She had grown up, hardened by the world and by the walls she had built around herself. And now, standing here on the edge of the island, she wasn't sure if she could ever tear those walls down.

The sound of footsteps on the gravel path behind her pulled her out of her thoughts. She turned to see a man approaching—a tall figure with broad shoulders and a familiar face. Ethan West. He hadn't changed much, though there was a new seriousness to him, a weight to his presence that hadn't been there before.

"Isabel," he said, his voice low and steady. "Welcome home."

Home. The word felt foreign on her tongue, but she forced a small smile. "Thanks, Ethan."

They stood there for a moment, the wind carrying the silence between them. Ethan had been her closest friend once, maybe even more than that, but time had put a distance between them that she wasn't sure could be bridged.

"I'm sorry about your mom," Ethan said after a long pause. "She was a good woman."

Isabel nodded, her throat tightening again. "Yeah, she was."

He shifted, as if searching for the right words, but none seemed to come. Instead, he simply stood there, offering his quiet presence as the waves crashed below.

And for the first time in a long while, Isabel didn't feel entirely alone. But she wasn't ready to admit that to herself just yet.

Isabel turned back toward the ocean, letting the rhythmic crash of the waves fill the silence between her and Ethan. She wasn't ready to face whatever emotions their meeting might stir up. It had been years since she had seen him last—since she had seen anyone from Rosemere, really—and yet here he was, standing beside her as if no time had passed. The man had always been steady, grounded like the cliffs that lined the island. But Isabel had left that stability behind when she'd escaped, and she wasn't sure if she could allow it back into her life now.

Ethan remained quiet, giving her space. It was something he had always been good at, sensing when she needed solitude and when she was ready to talk. For a fleeting moment, Isabel almost appreciated his presence—almost. But she pushed the feeling aside, reminding herself that she had come back to Rosemere for one reason only: to settle her mother's affairs and leave again. Quickly. Permanently.

"I didn't expect to see you so soon," she finally said, breaking the silence but still not looking at him. She could feel his eyes on her, though—steady, observant, waiting.

"Well, news travels fast around here," Ethan replied, his voice calm but not without a hint of warmth. "You know that."

Isabel nodded, wrapping her arms around herself to shield against the wind, though the chill she felt wasn't entirely from the breeze. "I guess some things never change."

Ethan took a step closer, his boots crunching against the gravel beneath him. "Some things don't. But you... you've changed."

She finally turned to face him, the corners of her mouth tightening into a faint smile. "It's been ten years, Ethan. People change."

He met her gaze, his dark eyes soft but unwavering. "Yeah, I suppose they do."

Isabel swallowed hard, feeling the weight of his words settle deep in her chest. She had changed—more than he could probably imagine. Life in the city had hardened her, and the years of isolation had built walls she wasn't ready to tear down. Not for anyone. Not even for Ethan.

"I should probably get going," she said, more abruptly than she intended, taking a step back from him. "I have a lot to go through at the house. It's... overwhelming."

Ethan's expression shifted, concern crossing his features, but he didn't push. "Of course. If you need anything, you know where to find me."

Isabel nodded, grateful for his understanding even as she turned away from him. She wasn't ready for the conversations that being back on the island would inevitably bring. Not with him. Not with anyone.

As she made her way back toward the house, the weight of Rosemere Isle's communal nature pressed down on her. She could feel the invisible strings of the island's social web tugging at her from every direction. People here knew everything about each other—what you ate for breakfast, what time you went to bed, who you talked to, and why. Privacy was a luxury that didn't exist on Rosemere, and that fact gnawed at her. After years of living anonymously in the city, where no one cared who you were as long as you stayed out of their way, the thought of being scrutinized again made her skin crawl.

The estate's stone walls loomed in front of her as she reached the house, the overgrown garden brushing against her legs as she walked toward the door. She hesitated before entering, glancing one last time down the path where Ethan still stood, a solitary figure against the backdrop of the sea. He watched her, but he didn't move, and for that, she was grateful. She needed to be alone right now, to figure out how to navigate the chaos of her own emotions before she could even consider letting someone else in.

Inside the house, the silence was thick and oppressive. Isabel closed the door behind her, resting her forehead against the cool wood for a moment before straightening up. The house seemed bigger than she remembered, the vastness of the empty rooms amplifying the loneliness she felt inside. Her mother had been a quiet woman, but her presence had always filled the house with a sense of life. Now, it felt hollow—like a shell left behind after the tide had pulled away.

Isabel walked through the hallway, her fingers trailing along the familiar wainscoting as she made her way into the kitchen. The room still smelled faintly of her mother's lavender sachets, a scent that tugged painfully at Isabel's chest. She didn't linger there. Instead, she moved upstairs to her mother's bedroom, the place where she knew she had to start, no matter how much she dreaded it.

The bedroom door creaked as she pushed it open, revealing a room that had remained untouched for weeks. The bed was neatly made, the quilt her mother had sewn by hand lying folded at the foot of it. The curtains were drawn, casting the room in a soft, muted light. Everything was in its place, just as it had always been—except for the absence of her mother, whose presence had once felt so constant.

Isabel walked slowly toward the dresser, her hand hovering over the old wooden jewelry box that sat on top of it. She opened the lid carefully, revealing the collection of trinkets and treasures her mother had amassed over the years. There were no expensive pieces, just small things—an old locket, a silver ring, a seashell bracelet—that held sentimental value. Isabel's fingers brushed over the locket, the cool metal against her skin stirring a flood of memories she wasn't prepared to face.

Her mother had worn that locket every day. Isabel could still remember the feel of it against her cheek when her mother hugged her goodnight as a child. She had never opened it, never asked what was inside. Now, holding it in her hands, she felt an urge to finally see the secret her mother had kept hidden for all these years.

She pressed the tiny clasp, and the locket popped open with a soft click. Inside was a faded photograph of a man—her father, she realized with a jolt. He had left them when she was just a child, disappearing without a word. Her mother had never spoken much about him, and Isabel had long ago stopped asking. But here he was, tucked away in the locket her mother had worn close to her heart every day. A man she barely remembered, but who had somehow remained a part of her mother's life, even if only in secret.

Isabel closed the locket, her heart heavy with the unanswered questions that now surfaced. Why had her mother kept this all these years? Why had she never said anything? The locket felt like a key to a door Isabel had never known existed, one that led to parts of her mother's life she had never been allowed to see.

She placed the locket back in the jewelry box, closing the lid with a quiet snap. There was no point in dwelling on it now. Her mother was gone, and whatever secrets she had kept would stay buried with her. Isabel had enough ghosts to deal with—she didn't need to chase after the ones her mother had left behind.

As the afternoon light began to fade, Isabel made her way back downstairs, her head throbbing from the strain of sorting through her mother's belongings and the weight of her own grief. She found herself wandering into the study, the room where her mother had spent countless hours painting. The easel was still set up in the corner, a half-finished landscape of the island stretching across the canvas. The strokes were bold, confident, just like her mother had been when she was working.

Isabel stood in front of the painting for a long time, her eyes tracing the familiar lines of the cliffs and the sea. It was as if her mother had captured the very essence of Rosemere, its wild beauty and untamed spirit. And yet, there was something in the painting that felt different—something Isabel couldn't quite put her finger on. It was as if her mother had been trying to say something through her art, something Isabel had never been able to understand.

The realization hit her suddenly, like a wave crashing against the shore. She had spent so much of her life trying to escape this place, to escape the weight of her mother's expectations and the isolation she had felt growing up. But now, standing here in the house that had been her mother's world, Isabel realized that Rosemere had been more than just a home for her mother. It had been a canvas, a place where she could pour all of her hopes, dreams, and sorrows into her art.

For the first time since returning to the island, Isabel felt a flicker of something she hadn't expected—a connection to the place she had once called home. It wasn't enough to make her stay, but it was enough to make her pause, to consider the possibility that maybe there was more to Rosemere than she had allowed herself to see.

The thought was fleeting, though, as the weight of reality settled back in. She wasn't here to reconnect with the island or to rediscover her roots. She was here to finish what needed to be done and then leave—just like she had always planned. The island wasn't her home anymore. It never had been, not really.

But as Isabel stood in the fading light, staring at the unfinished painting, she couldn't shake the feeling that maybe—just maybe—her mother had been trying to show her something all along. Something she hadn't been ready to see until now.

And maybe, in the quiet spaces of Rosemere Isle, Isabel might begin to uncover what that was.

2

Chapter 2: Reconnecting with the Past

T he next morning, Isabel awoke to the soft sound of rain tapping against the window, the familiar scent of sea salt lingering in the air. For a brief moment, she forgot where she was, her body still attuned to the city's relentless hum. But as her eyes adjusted to the dim light filtering through the lace curtains, the weight of Rosemere Isle settled back into her chest, heavy and unavoidable.

She sighed, pulling herself out of bed, and padded across the wooden floor to the window. Outside, the sky was a soft gray, the rain casting a delicate mist over the island. The cliffs were shrouded in fog, and the ocean beyond them seemed to merge with the sky, creating a landscape that was both beautiful and eerily still.

Isabel wrapped a shawl around her shoulders and made her way downstairs. The house was as quiet as it had been the night before, the silence punctuated only by the occasional creak of the old floorboards beneath her feet. She wasn't sure what she had expected—that somehow, in the light of day, the house would feel different? More welcoming, perhaps. But the emptiness persisted, a stark reminder that she was alone.

She moved into the kitchen, setting a pot of water on the stove to make tea. As she waited for the water to boil, her mind wandered back to the previous day—back to Ethan. His presence had stirred something inside her, a feeling she had spent years trying to suppress. Seeing him again, after all this time, had made her realize just how much of herself she had left behind when she'd fled Rosemere. He had been a part of her world once, a constant in the life she had turned her back on. Now, he was a reminder of everything she had chosen to forget.

But it wasn't Ethan who occupied her thoughts as the water began to steam. It was Gabe.

She hadn't expected to run into him, not so soon, and certainly not in the way she had. The encounter had been brief—too brief, really—but it had stirred memories she hadn't been prepared to face. Gabe had always been different from the others in Rosemere. While the rest of the island's inhabitants had embraced its tight-knit community, Gabe had always kept a part of himself separate, much like Isabel. There had been a shared understanding between them once, an unspoken bond forged in their mutual desire for solitude.

But that was years ago. People changed, and Isabel had no reason to believe that Gabe would be any different.

Still, something in the way he had looked at her—the quiet intensity in his eyes, the way his shoulders had tensed ever so slightly when he'd seen her—had unsettled her. He had always been guarded, but there was a vulnerability in his body language that she hadn't expected. A vulnerability she hadn't known how to respond to.

The sound of the kettle whistling broke her thoughts, and she poured herself a cup of tea, taking it with her into the study. The rain outside had softened to a gentle drizzle, casting a grayish hue over the room. She stood by the window, sipping her tea and letting the quiet settle over her.

Her mind wandered back to the past—to the nights she and Gabe had spent walking along the cliffs, the wind whipping through their hair, their conversations deep and winding, yet never quite touching the emotions simmering beneath the surface. They had always been careful with each other, cautious not to cross the invisible line between friendship and something more.

But now, as Isabel stood in her mother's house, her cup of tea growing cold in her hands, she couldn't help but wonder if maybe they had missed something back then. Something that had lingered, unspoken, between them all these years.

The rain eased off by mid-morning, and Isabel decided to take a walk, hoping the fresh air might clear her head. She wrapped herself in a long coat and stepped outside, the cool mist kissing her skin as she made her way down the path toward the village. The island was quiet, the streets still wet from the rain, the air thick with the smell of damp earth and saltwater. As she walked, her mind kept returning to Gabe, to the way he had looked at her with that quiet intensity, his emotions carefully masked but not entirely hidden.

Isabel had never been good at reading people's feelings. She preferred the simplicity of solitude, where she didn't have to navigate the complexities of human interaction. But with Gabe, there had always been something different. Something that made her want to understand him, to dig beneath the surface of his calm exterior and uncover the emotions he kept so carefully hidden.

As she approached the village, Isabel saw him standing by the docks, his back to her. He was talking to one of the fishermen, his tall frame relaxed but alert, as though he were constantly on guard, even in this familiar setting. His hands moved as he spoke, gesturing toward the boat tied to the dock, but his body language was tense, as though he were holding something back.

Isabel hesitated for a moment, unsure if she should approach him. She wasn't ready for a conversation—not yet. But something pulled her toward him, a magnetic force that she couldn't quite explain.

Before she could decide, Gabe turned and saw her. His eyes met hers, and for a brief moment, the tension in his body seemed to melt away. He gave her a small nod, acknowledging her presence without saying a word.

Isabel took a deep breath and walked toward him, her heart beating a little faster than she would have liked. "Morning," she said, her voice sounding more composed than she felt.

"Morning," Gabe replied, his gaze steady but guarded.

The fisherman tipped his hat to Isabel and excused himself, leaving her alone with Gabe. The air between them was thick with unspoken words, the weight of their shared history hanging in the space between them.

"Out for a walk?" Gabe asked, his tone casual but his eyes searching hers, as though he were trying to gauge her mood.

"Yeah," Isabel replied, glancing out at the water. "Needed some fresh air."

He nodded, his hands slipping into his pockets. "It's good to get out. Clears the mind."

Isabel turned back to him, studying his face. He had always been difficult to read, but now, as she stood in front of him, she could see the tension in the way his jaw tightened, the way his shoulders seemed to hold a weight he wasn't willing to share. There was something on his mind, something he wasn't saying.

"How are you?" she asked, the question coming out more softly than she had intended.

Gabe shrugged, his eyes flickering away for a moment before meeting hers again. "I'm fine."

But Isabel could see that he wasn't. His body language told a different story—the slight shift of his weight from one foot to the other, the way his hands stayed buried in his pockets, as if he were trying to shield himself from the world.

"You don't look fine," Isabel said, her voice gentle but firm.

Gabe's lips twitched, almost as if he were about to smile, but it never quite reached his eyes. "You've always been good at seeing through people."

Isabel smiled faintly, surprised by his honesty. "Only when they let me."

For a moment, Gabe didn't respond. He looked out at the water, his expression unreadable, and Isabel wondered if she had pushed too far. But then he sighed, his shoulders relaxing ever so slightly. "I guess I'm still getting used to the idea that you're back."

Isabel felt a pang of guilt at his words. She hadn't thought about what her return might mean to the people she had left behind, the people who had remained on the island while she had built a life elsewhere. Gabe had been a part of that world, and her absence had undoubtedly left its mark.

"I didn't think I'd stay long," Isabel admitted, her voice barely above a whisper.

Gabe turned to her, his eyes searching hers. "Is that still the plan?"

She hesitated, unsure of how to answer. The truth was, she didn't know. She had come back to Rosemere with the intention of leaving as soon as her mother's affairs were settled, but now that she was here, something was holding her back. Something she couldn't quite put into words.

"I don't know," she finally said, her voice quiet. "I thought it would be easier."

Gabe nodded, his expression softening. "It never is."

For a moment, they stood in silence, the sound of the waves filling the space between them. Isabel watched as Gabe's gaze shifted to the horizon, his face pensive, as though he were lost in thought.

"You know," he said after a long pause, "I used to think about leaving, too."

Isabel looked at him in surprise. Gabe had always seemed so rooted in Rosemere, so connected to the island in a way that she had never been. The thought of him wanting to leave had never crossed her mind.

"Why didn't you?" she asked, her curiosity piqued.

Gabe shrugged, his eyes still fixed on the water. "I don't know. Maybe I was afraid of what I'd find out there."

Isabel studied his face, the way his brow furrowed ever so slightly as he spoke. There was something in his voice—something vulnerable and uncertain—that tugged at her heart.

"You would've been fine," she said, her tone soft but certain. "You're stronger than you think."

Gabe turned to her, his eyes locking onto hers. For a moment, Isabel felt as though the world around them had disappeared, leaving only the two of them standing on the edge of the dock, suspended between the past

As the rain continued to fall in a steady drizzle, Gabe and Isabel stood together on the dock, the intimate quiet of their surroundings creating a cocoon around them. The mist rising from the water seemed to soften the edges of the world, making everything feel both distant and immediate. Isabel could sense the weight of Gabe's presence, his subtle shifts and the way he glanced at her from time to time, betraying emotions he struggled to keep in check.

The silence between them was neither uncomfortable nor oppressive; instead, it was filled with a sense of shared understanding, an unspoken acknowledgment of the complexity of their past. Isabel shifted slightly, drawing her coat tighter around her, and turned her attention back to Gabe. She noted how the rain beaded on his weathered jacket, dripping off the brim of his hat in a steady stream.

Gabe cleared his throat, breaking the silence. "You remember how we used to come out here during storms? Just sit and watch the waves?"

Isabel smiled, her gaze softening. "I do. We'd sit in that little shelter by the lighthouse and talk about everything and nothing."

Gabe chuckled softly. "Yeah, I remember. It was our way of escaping the world."

The nostalgia in his voice was palpable, and Isabel felt a pang of regret for the years they had lost. She hadn't realized how much she had missed these small, seemingly inconsequential moments until now, standing here with Gabe. She wondered if he had felt the same emptiness, the same sense of loss that she had.

"There's something about this place," Gabe continued, his voice thoughtful. "It has a way of holding onto memories, doesn't it? Like it never really lets go."

Isabel nodded, her eyes scanning the landscape. "It does. Sometimes I think that's why I left—to escape those memories. But now that I'm back, it feels like they're all coming back at once."

Gabe's gaze met hers, his expression serious. "I guess we all have our ways of dealing with the past. Some people leave, some people stay."

Isabel considered his words, her mind drifting back to the reasons she had left Rosemere in the first place. It hadn't been just about escaping the island; it had been about escaping the pain and disappointment that seemed to cling to her like a shadow. But now, as she stood here with Gabe, the lines between escape and confrontation were blurring.

"Do you ever wish you'd left?" Isabel asked, her voice barely more than a whisper.

Gabe's gaze was steady, unwavering. "Sometimes. But then I think about everything I'd miss. This place, the people. Even the memories."

Isabel could see the depth of his connection to the island in the way he spoke, the way his eyes softened as he looked around. It was a stark contrast to her own feelings of detachment and conflict. She wondered if this was the reason she had always felt so drawn to him—because he embodied everything she had tried to leave behind.

"I'm not sure I'm ready to stay," Isabel admitted, her voice tinged with uncertainty. "I came back to settle things, but I didn't expect to feel so... conflicted."

Gabe's eyes narrowed slightly, a flicker of something passing over his face—concern, perhaps, or curiosity. "What's making you conflicted?"

Isabel hesitated, the weight of her own feelings almost too heavy to articulate. "I thought coming back here would give me clarity, but instead, it's made me question everything. My life, my choices, and what I really want."

Gabe nodded, his expression thoughtful. "Sometimes it's hard to find answers when you're surrounded by everything that reminds you of what you left behind."

There was a long pause, during which Isabel felt the enormity of their conversation sinking in. The rain had slowed to a gentle patter, and the atmosphere between them seemed charged with unspoken possibilities. Gabe's presence, so steady and grounded, felt like an anchor in the turbulent sea of her thoughts.

"What about you?" Isabel asked after a moment. "Do you ever question your choices?"

Gabe's gaze remained fixed on the horizon. "Sometimes. But I've learned to find peace in the choices I've made, even if they're not always the ones I expected."

The sincerity in his voice made Isabel's heart ache. It was as if Gabe had found a form of contentment that she was still searching for, and that realization both comforted and unsettled her. She wanted to ask more, to understand how he had come to terms with his own decisions, but the words seemed to escape her.

"Well," Gabe said, breaking the silence, "I should get back to work. The storm's let up, but there's still a lot to do."

Isabel nodded, her heart sinking slightly at the thought of ending their conversation. "Of course. I should probably get going, too."

As Gabe turned to leave, Isabel hesitated for a moment, then spoke up. "Gabe, do you ever... think about what might have been?"

Gabe paused, looking back at her. His eyes were searching, as though he were trying to decipher her question. "All the time," he said finally. "But thinking about it doesn't change anything. Sometimes you have to just accept what is and move forward."

His words resonated deeply with Isabel, echoing her own internal struggle. She knew that she needed to confront her past, to reconcile with the choices she had made and the person she had become. But standing here, on the brink of this old connection, she felt a glimmer of hope that maybe, just maybe, she could find a way to move forward.

"Thanks, Gabe," Isabel said softly. "I appreciate you talking with me."

Gabe offered her a small, genuine smile. "Anytime, Isabel. You know where to find me."

As he walked away, Isabel watched him go, feeling a mix of emotions swirling within her. The conversation had been both enlightening and unsettling, a reminder of the depth of their shared past and the complexity of the present. She knew that she had to face her own fears and uncertainties, but for now, the brief connection with Gabe had given her a sense of clarity, however fleeting.

Isabel turned and began walking back toward the village, her mind racing with thoughts of what lay ahead. The path was still wet from the rain, the air crisp and cool against her skin. She felt the weight of her decisions pressing down on her, but she also felt a newfound resolve to confront them head-on.

The village seemed quieter than usual as she walked through it, the rain having driven most of the townsfolk indoors. The familiar sights—the quaint shops, the old bakery with its enticing smells, the small, community-centered feel of the place—were all wrapped in a comforting sense of nostalgia. But even as she took in the sights, her mind kept returning to Gabe and their conversation.

She knew that she had a lot to process, and that her return to Rosemere was far from over. The questions she had about her future and her past were still very much unanswered. But for the first time since her arrival, she felt a small flicker of hope, a sense that maybe she could find her way back to a place she had once called home.

As she approached her mother's house, the rain having stopped and the sky beginning to clear, Isabel took a deep breath. She was ready to face whatever lay ahead, to confront the past and the present, and to find a path that was truly her own. The journey was far from over, but with each step, she felt a little more certain that she was moving in the right direction.

Isabel's footsteps echoed softly against the cobblestone streets as she walked towards her mother's house. The rain had ceased, leaving behind a fresh, earthy scent that filled the air. The clouds were breaking up, allowing the sun to peek through and cast a warm glow over the village. The weather seemed to be mirroring her internal shift, as if nature itself were hinting at the possibility of renewal.

She approached the old house with a mix of apprehension and nostalgia. The place seemed to hold its breath, waiting for her to unlock the door and re-enter the world she had left behind. As she turned the key in the lock and pushed the door open, the familiar creak greeted her, and she was met with the musty smell of disuse and memories.

The interior was much as she remembered—comfortable but somewhat faded, like a photograph that had seen better days. Dust had settled over the surfaces, and the furniture was draped in white sheets, giving the place an almost ghostly appearance. Isabel moved through the rooms slowly, taking in the remnants of her mother's life.

Her mother's presence was still palpable in every corner—the faint scent of lavender, the delicate china cups on the kitchen shelves, and the myriad of framed photographs that adorned the walls. Each picture seemed to whisper a story, and Isabel couldn't help but feel overwhelmed by the weight of her mother's memory.

She paused in front of a large, old-fashioned mirror that hung in the hallway, its surface fogged with age. As she gazed into it, she saw not just her reflection but the echoes of the past, of a younger Isabel who had once walked these very floors with her mother. The sight was both comforting and disconcerting, reminding her of the years she had missed and the life she had left behind.

Isabel decided to start her task by tackling the attic, which was where she suspected her mother had kept her personal belongings and perhaps some unfinished projects. Climbing the creaky steps, she felt a sense of anticipation mixed with trepidation. The attic was cluttered with old furniture, dusty boxes, and forgotten treasures.

She began sorting through the boxes, finding old letters, family albums, and mementos that spoke of a life once vibrant and full of love. As she rifled through the contents, she came across a box marked "Personal." Her heart raced as she opened it, revealing a collection of journals and sketchbooks. She pulled out one of the sketchbooks and opened it to find her mother's intricate drawings—landscapes, portraits, and abstract designs that reflected a talent she had never fully known about.

Among the sketches, Isabel found a series of drawings of the lighthouse, each with a different view and angle. One in particular caught her eye—a detailed rendering of the lighthouse with an unusual symbol etched into the side. It was a design she didn't recognize, and its presence stirred a sense of curiosity and unease within her.

She set the sketchbook aside and continued to explore the attic, finding an old, dusty easel and several canvases that had been abandoned. There was an air of unfinished business about the room, as though her mother had left it in the midst of a creative burst. Isabel's heart ached at the thought of her mother's unfinished dreams and the life she had left behind.

As she worked, she heard the faint sound of footsteps on the stairs, followed by a knock on the attic door. She turned to see Eliza standing there, her expression a mix of concern and curiosity.

"Hey, Isabel," Eliza said, stepping into the attic. "I thought I'd check in on you. How's it going?"

Isabel offered her a tired smile. "It's... a lot. There's so much here, so many memories. I didn't realize how overwhelming it would be."

Eliza walked over and glanced around the attic, her eyes taking in the scattered items and the air of neglect. "I can imagine. It must be tough going through everything."

"It is," Isabel admitted. "I've found some of her artwork and journals. It's like piecing together a part of her I didn't know."

Eliza picked up the sketchbook Isabel had set aside and opened it to the drawings of the lighthouse. Her eyes widened slightly as she studied the unusual symbol. "This is fascinating. I've never seen this symbol before."

"I haven't either," Isabel said, feeling a spark of excitement mixed with confusion. "I wonder if it has any significance."

Eliza nodded thoughtfully. "It could be something important. Maybe it's connected to something in her past or something she was working on."

As they examined the sketches together, Isabel felt a sense of camaraderie with Eliza, who had always been a steady presence in her life. Eliza's support was a comfort, and Isabel appreciated her willingness to share in the discovery of her mother's secrets.

"We should try to find out more about this symbol," Eliza suggested. "It might lead us to something meaningful."

Isabel agreed, her curiosity piqued. "Yes, I think you're right. It's a piece of the puzzle I need to understand."

As the afternoon wore on, Isabel and Eliza continued to explore the attic, uncovering more of Isabel's mother's hidden life. The sun had begun to set, casting a golden glow over the room as the light filtered through the small attic window.

Eventually, Isabel decided it was time to take a break. She and Eliza descended the stairs, leaving the attic behind for the moment. They made their way to the kitchen, where Eliza offered to make some tea.

As they sat at the kitchen table, sipping their drinks, Isabel felt a sense of relief in the presence of her friend. The warmth of the tea and the companionship of Eliza were comforting, offering a brief respite from the emotional turmoil she had been experiencing.

"I'm glad you came by," Isabel said, her voice filled with gratitude. "I could use the support."

Eliza smiled warmly. "Of course. I'm always here for you, no matter what."

They chatted about lighter topics, sharing stories and laughter, which helped ease the heaviness of the day. Isabel appreciated the distraction, though her mind kept returning to the mystery of the symbol and what it might reveal about her mother's life.

As the evening progressed, Eliza stood up to leave, her expression thoughtful. "If you need any help with the symbol or anything else, just let me know. I'm here to help."

Isabel thanked her again, and Eliza left with a promise to check in soon. Isabel remained in the kitchen, her thoughts swirling around the day's discoveries. She felt a sense of resolve to delve deeper into her mother's past, to uncover the secrets that lay hidden within the attic and within herself.

She knew that reconciling with her past would be a difficult journey, but with the support of her friends and the strength she found within herself, she felt a glimmer of hope. As she looked around the kitchen, filled with the memories of her mother's life, Isabel made a silent promise to herself—to uncover the truth, to heal, and to find a way forward.

As she cleaned up the remnants of their tea, Isabel felt a renewed sense of purpose. The path ahead was still uncertain, but with each step, she was moving closer to understanding her past and finding her place in the present. The mystery of the lighthouse symbol was just the beginning, and Isabel was ready to face whatever came next.

As Isabel finished tidying up the kitchen, the warmth of the tea still lingering in her chest, her thoughts turned again to the symbol from her mother's sketches. The unusual design seemed to taunt her, a silent enigma beckoning her to uncover its meaning. The more she thought about it, the more determined she became to solve the mystery, feeling it might hold the key to understanding her mother's hidden side and perhaps her own.

Her resolve was momentarily interrupted by the sound of the doorbell ringing through the quiet house. Isabel's heart skipped a beat, her initial thought being that it might be Eliza returning. However, when she opened the door, she was greeted by a figure that made her breath catch—Gabriel "Gabe" Marshall stood on her doorstep.

Gabe's presence was both unexpected and unsettling. His strong frame and rugged demeanor contrasted sharply with the soft warmth of the evening light. He looked as if he belonged to the island itself, his features weathered by time and the elements, yet his eyes held a depth that seemed to pierce through Isabel's guarded exterior.

"Evening, Isabel," Gabe said, his voice low and steady. "I thought I'd drop by and see how you're settling in. Didn't expect to catch you at home."

Isabel struggled to mask her surprise and the rush of conflicting emotions that his appearance stirred. "Hi, Gabe. I wasn't expecting visitors, but come in. It's nice to see you."

Gabe stepped inside, his eyes briefly scanning the familiar surroundings of the house. Isabel noticed the slight tension in his shoulders and the way his gaze lingered on the photographs of her family on the walls. It was as if each image was a reminder of the past they shared and the distance that had grown between them over the years.

"Thank you," Gabe said, his gaze finally settling on her. "I brought some of the old records from the island's history. I thought you might find them useful, especially if you're going through your mother's things."

Isabel was taken aback by the thoughtful gesture. "That's very kind of you. I'm sure they'll be helpful."

Gabe handed her a small box, and as their fingers brushed against each other, a jolt of electricity ran through Isabel. She noticed how his eyes lingered on her hand for a moment longer than necessary before he looked away, a subtle sign of his lingering feelings and the connection they once shared.

They moved to the living room, where Isabel took a seat on the couch, and Gabe sat opposite her. The silence between them was filled with an unspoken tension, and Isabel could feel the weight of their shared history pressing down on them. Gabe's presence was a reminder of everything she had left behind, and she was unsure whether to embrace the comfort of old memories or to keep her distance.

"So, how are you finding everything?" Gabe asked, breaking the silence. His tone was casual, but his eyes were observant, studying her closely.

Isabel sighed, trying to maintain a composed exterior. "It's been overwhelming. There's so much to go through, and it feels like every corner of this house holds a memory I'm not ready to confront."

Gabe nodded, his expression sympathetic. "I can imagine. It must be tough coming back after so long, especially with everything you've been through."

She appreciated his understanding but couldn't shake the feeling that he was holding something back, a sentiment she couldn't quite place. "Yes, it is. But it's also oddly comforting in a way. I'm reconnecting with parts of my past I thought I'd lost."

Gabe's eyes softened as he listened, and for a moment, Isabel saw a flicker of the tenderness that had once been a part of their relationship. "You always had a way of finding beauty in the past," he said quietly. "I remember how you used to see the island as a canvas, capturing its essence in your photographs."

Isabel smiled faintly, touched by his words. "I used to think of it as a magical place, full of stories waiting to be told. But I've been away for so long that I've forgotten some of that magic."

Gabe's gaze lingered on her, and Isabel could feel the weight of his unspoken feelings. She noticed how he seemed to hesitate before speaking, as if choosing his words carefully. "Maybe the island still has a few stories left to share. Sometimes, you just need to listen."

The remark seemed loaded with a deeper meaning, and Isabel found herself wondering if Gabe's words were meant to imply something about their own past. She could see the way he shifted slightly, his body language revealing a vulnerability that he was trying to hide.

"Maybe," Isabel replied, her voice thoughtful. "I suppose we'll see."

Gabe glanced around the room, his gaze falling on the box of records he had brought. "If you want, I can help you go through these. There might be some interesting bits of history in there that could shed light on your mother's artwork."

Isabel's heart warmed at the offer, and she felt a sense of relief that Gabe was willing to assist her. "That would be great, actually. I'd appreciate the help."

They spent the next few hours sorting through the records, Gabe's presence a steady and reassuring anchor amidst the whirlwind of Isabel's emotions. As they worked, they fell into a comfortable rhythm, their conversation drifting between memories of the past and updates about their lives since Isabel's departure.

Gabe's gestures were subtle but meaningful. He would occasionally brush against her hand as they reached for the same document, and each touch sent a shiver down Isabel's spine. His body language, though restrained, spoke volumes—he was careful to maintain a respectful distance, yet his eyes revealed the depth of his emotions.

Isabel found herself increasingly drawn to Gabe, not just by his physical presence but by the kindness and understanding he offered. She couldn't help but remember the years they had spent apart, the reasons for their separation, and the lingering feelings that seemed to resurface with each shared glance and gentle touch.

As the evening wore on, the room grew darker, the only light coming from the lamp on the side table. The atmosphere was cozy, with the soft glow casting a warm hue over the room. Isabel felt a sense of contentment in Gabe's company, though she was acutely aware of the unresolved tension between them.

Gabe finally closed the last box, his hands brushing dust off his jeans as he stood up. "I think we've made some progress. There's definitely a lot to explore here."

Isabel looked up at him, her heart aching with a mix of gratitude and longing. "Thank you for helping. It means a lot to me."

Gabe's eyes met hers, and for a brief moment, the world seemed to stand still. "Anytime, Isabel. I'm here if you need anything."

As Gabe prepared to leave, Isabel felt a pang of regret. She had grown accustomed to his presence and the comfort it brought. The silence of the house seemed to close in on her as he headed for the door.

"Gabe," she said, her voice faltering. "I... I didn't expect to see you again, not like this."

Gabe turned to face her, his expression softening. "Neither did I. But sometimes, things have a way of working out in unexpected ways."

Isabel nodded, her eyes searching his face for a hint of what lay beneath his composed exterior. "I guess we'll see where this leads."

Gabe offered her a small, reassuring smile before stepping out into the night. Isabel watched him walk away, his figure disappearing into the darkness. She closed the door with a sigh, her thoughts a jumble of emotions and unanswered questions.

The evening had left her feeling emotionally raw, caught between the comfort of the past and the uncertainty of the future. As she sat alone in the dimly lit room, the weight of the day's discoveries and the unresolved feelings for Gabe pressed heavily on her. The island, with all its secrets and memories, seemed to hold her in a delicate balance between solitude and connection.

With a deep breath, Isabel resolved to face whatever lay ahead, knowing that her journey was only beginning. The symbol from her mother's artwork, the fragments of their shared history, and the feelings stirred by Gabe were all threads in the complex tapestry of her return to Rosemere Isle. As she prepared for bed, she felt a renewed sense of determination to unravel the mysteries of her past and find her place in the present.

Isabel spent the remainder of the evening alone, the stillness of the house punctuated only by the occasional creak of the floorboards and the distant call of an owl. Despite the comfort of having made some progress with Gabe's help, she couldn't shake the sense of unease that had settled in her chest.

Her mind replayed the moments of their interaction, each nuance of Gabe's body language vivid in her memory. The way he'd looked at her, the almost imperceptible hesitations in his voice, and the warmth of his touch—all these details seemed to weave together a tapestry of unspoken feelings and unresolved tension.

She wandered through the house, trying to distract herself with the mundane tasks of sorting through her mother's belongings. As she sifted through old letters and photographs, the weight of her memories and the presence of Gabe's shadow loomed large.

The old photographs of her and Gabe from their younger days, captured in candid moments of joy and laughter, seemed to speak to her from the past. She paused to study one where they stood on the beach, their faces alight with youthful exuberance. It was a stark contrast to the strained emotions she felt now, and she couldn't help but wonder how things had changed so drastically.

Isabel sighed, placing the photograph down gently. She felt an ache in her heart as she thought about the years that had passed since she'd left the island, years filled with challenges and changes that had molded her into the person she was today.

The clock ticked steadily on the wall, each second stretching into what felt like an eternity. The solitude of the house, once a sanctuary, now felt like a prison, each shadow and creak a reminder of the emotional walls she had built around herself.

With a weary glance at the disarray of her mother's belongings, Isabel decided it was time for a change of pace. She grabbed her camera, the one she had brought with her as a link to her past and a tool for her present. Photography had always been her escape, a way to capture the beauty of the world and the emotions she often kept hidden.

Stepping outside, the cool night air greeted her with a refreshing chill. The moon cast a silvery glow over the island, illuminating the path she walked as she headed toward the beach. The rhythmic sound of the waves crashing against the shore provided a soothing backdrop to her turbulent thoughts.

As she walked along the beach, Isabel's thoughts drifted back to her conversation with Gabe. The subtle way he had watched her, the brief touches of their hands, and the genuine concern in his eyes—all of it had left her feeling more vulnerable than she cared to admit.

She paused at the edge of the water, the gentle ebb and flow of the tide mirroring her inner conflict. She raised her camera and began to snap photos, focusing on the play of moonlight on the waves, the distant silhouette of the lighthouse, and the scattered seaweed that decorated the shore. Each click of the shutter was a small release, a way to channel her emotions into something tangible.

As she continued to photograph the night, her mind kept returning to Gabe. The memory of his presence, his kindness, and the depth of his feelings stirred something within her—a longing for a connection that she had buried deep within herself.

The sound of footsteps on the sand pulled her from her reverie. She turned, her heart racing, and saw a familiar figure approaching. Gabe's silhouette against the moonlight was unmistakable, and he walked with a purposeful stride toward her.

"Isabel?" Gabe's voice called out softly as he reached her side.

She lowered her camera, her surprise evident. "Gabe, what are you doing here?"

He looked around at the beach, taking in the serene beauty of the scene. "I couldn't stop thinking about our conversation earlier. I figured you might need some company."

Isabel's heart skipped a beat. His presence was both comforting and unsettling, and she wasn't sure how to react. "I'm fine. Just needed some time to clear my head."

Gabe took a few steps closer, his gaze fixed on her with an intensity that made her pulse quicken. "I understand. But I thought maybe we could talk a bit more. There's something about this place that makes it easier to open up."

Isabel nodded slowly, her resolve wavering in the face of his earnestness. "Sure, we can talk."

They walked along the shoreline, the moonlight casting a soft glow around them. The silence between them was filled with unspoken words and unresolved feelings. Gabe's presence was a constant reminder of the past, a past that she had been trying to navigate with mixed emotions.

Gabe glanced at her, his expression thoughtful. "You know, I've always admired how you see the world through your camera. It's like you have this special way of capturing moments that others might miss."

Isabel looked at him, surprised by the sincerity in his voice. "Thank you. Photography has always been a way for me to make sense of things, to find beauty even in difficult times."

Gabe nodded, a small smile playing at his lips. "I remember when you used to take photos of the island. You'd always find the most unexpected angles and details."

A sense of nostalgia washed over Isabel. "I used to think the island was full of hidden stories. It's funny how returning here feels like opening up a chapter I thought was closed."

Gabe's gaze lingered on her, his eyes reflecting a mix of sadness and hope. "I think sometimes the past has a way of catching up with us, whether we're ready for it or not. But it's also an opportunity to heal and find new paths."

Isabel felt a lump form in her throat at the depth of his words. It was as if Gabe had somehow understood the internal struggle she had been facing, a struggle she had barely articulated even to herself.

They continued walking in silence, the rhythm of the waves a steady companion to their thoughts. Gabe's presence was a comforting one, yet it stirred up a storm of emotions within Isabel. She found herself drawn to his quiet strength, his unwavering support, and the way he seemed to understand her in a way no one else did.

After a while, they stopped near a large rock, sitting down to rest. The ocean stretched out before them, its vast expanse a reflection of the unknown future that awaited Isabel.

Gabe turned to her, his expression earnest. "Isabel, I know it's been a long time, and things have changed. But if you ever need someone to talk to, or just someone to be there, I'm here."

His words, simple yet profound, struck a chord with Isabel. She looked at him, her heart aching with the weight of her feelings. "Thank you, Gabe. I appreciate that."

Gabe reached out, gently touching her hand. The contact was brief but charged with an emotional intensity that made Isabel's breath catch. "I mean it, Isabel. You're not alone."

Isabel's heart swelled with a mix of gratitude and longing. The connection she felt with Gabe was undeniable, yet she was still grappling with her own fears and uncertainties. The past was a complex web of emotions and memories, and she wasn't sure if she was ready to unravel it all.

As they sat together on the beach, the night air cool against their skin, Isabel felt a sense of clarity begin to emerge. Gabe's presence was a reminder of what she had left behind, but it was also a beacon of hope for what might be possible.

The hours passed unnoticed, and eventually, they stood to leave. Gabe's hand remained on hers for a moment longer, a silent promise of support and understanding.

As they walked back to the house, the silence between them was filled with a newfound sense of connection. Isabel was beginning to see the possibility of healing and reconciliation, though she knew that the journey ahead would be fraught with challenges.

When they reached the door of the house, Gabe paused, turning to her with a gentle smile. "I'll let you get some rest. Tomorrow, we can continue with the records if you'd like."

Isabel nodded, feeling a surge of warmth at his thoughtfulness. "That sounds good. Thank you for tonight, Gabe."

With a final, lingering look, Gabe turned and walked away into the night. Isabel watched him go, her heart a mix of hope and apprehension.

As she closed the door behind her and made her way back inside, she felt a sense of resolve settling within her. The past was no longer something to be feared or avoided—it was a part of her, and it was time to confront it, to understand it, and to find her way forward.

The night was quiet once more, but for Isabel, it was filled with the promise of new beginnings and the potential for healing. As she prepared for bed, her mind was filled with the memories of the evening and the emotions that had surfaced. She knew that her journey was just beginning, and the path ahead would be both challenging and rewarding.

With a deep breath, Isabel turned off the lights and settled into bed, the echoes of Gabe's words and the beauty of the island's night still lingering in her heart. She was ready to face whatever came next, armed with the hope that, with time and patience, she might find the peace and connection she had been searching for.

As Gabe finished explaining how the boat business had picked up after the old ferry had been decommissioned, Isabel noticed something in his stance, a subtle tension that belied his calm exterior. His arms, though relaxed, occasionally tightened at the sides. His eyes lingered on hers just a fraction longer than necessary when she spoke, and the faintest shadow of a smile played at the corner of his lips when she glanced away.

Isabel's gaze softened as she allowed herself to study him in these moments of silence. The sun caught in his brown hair, now streaked with strands of gold and silver she hadn't remembered from their younger days. His hands, calloused from years of working with wood and rope, rested on the edge of the workbench in the boatyard. Those hands had always been steady, even when everything else around them had shifted. She remembered them—strong, dependable, the hands that had once helped her when she was trying to fix her bike during high school, a rare smile crossing his face as he effortlessly solved the problem that had been plaguing her all day.

She had always admired his quiet competence, how he could say so little yet make her feel safe. It was disarming now, as it had been then, but now that safety carried a weight she wasn't sure she was ready to accept.

"You've done well for yourself," she said, her voice quiet but steady, gesturing toward the neatly crafted boats. "I can see the island's lucky to have you."

Gabe didn't reply immediately. He stood a little straighter, his lips pressing together as if debating whether to speak. The wind ruffled the loose fabric of his shirt as he turned to look at the boats, then back at her, his expression unreadable. "The island's always been home," he finally said. "I couldn't leave it. Not like some people."

The words stung more than she expected. There was no malice in them, but the truth of what he left unsaid hung between them. Isabel had left. She had abandoned the island, her mother, and him. And now she was back, and he was still here—unchanged, steadfast, and part of a world she had run from.

"I needed to leave," she whispered, almost to herself, as if saying it aloud might make the truth more palatable. "I thought I needed something else."

Gabe's eyes softened, but he didn't say anything. Instead, he moved closer, just enough that she could feel the warmth radiating from his body, but still kept a careful distance. The closeness wasn't threatening—it was grounding. Isabel realized she had been holding her breath.

"You were always searching for something," he said quietly. "I never blamed you for it. But...you never looked here. You didn't see what you had."

Isabel swallowed, suddenly aware of the tightness in her throat. His words stirred something in her—an aching regret she had tried so hard to bury. She hadn't seen what she had. She hadn't allowed herself to feel it, because feeling meant attachment, and attachment meant the risk of being hurt.

Her gaze drifted to the boats again, the rhythm of the waves providing a lull in the tension between them. "Do you ever wonder what might've happened if things had been different?" she asked, more out of curiosity than expectation.

Gabe chuckled softly, shaking his head. "I've had ten years to think about that, Izzy. More than enough time to wonder." He turned toward her, and his expression softened again, the corners of his lips curling into a sad but understanding smile. "But there's no use living in 'what ifs,' is there? Life moves forward, whether we're ready for it or not."

Isabel found herself nodding, the weight of his words settling heavily in her chest. He was right, of course. The past was behind them, but the echo of it still lingered in her heart, pulling at her in ways she hadn't fully understood until now. She had always been running—away from the pain of her mother's illness, away from her broken engagement, and away from this island that held more memories than she was prepared to face.

And yet here she was, standing before the one person who had never stopped being part of her story.

"I thought leaving was the answer," she admitted quietly. "But maybe I was just too scared to stay."

Gabe's gaze held hers for a moment longer before he let out a soft breath. "Everyone's scared of something, Izzy. It's what we do with that fear that matters." He paused, as if choosing his next words carefully. "You've come back, though. That's something."

Isabel nodded, her fingers tracing the worn surface of the bench beside her. She didn't know if returning was the right decision, or if staying was even an option. But Gabe's presence, his steady, unspoken understanding, made her feel like perhaps—just perhaps—there was more to be found here than she'd allowed herself to believe.

The silence stretched between them again, but this time it wasn't heavy with the weight of things unsaid. Instead, it felt...comfortable. Like an old sweater you hadn't worn in years but still fit perfectly, despite the time.

Gabe shifted, clearing his throat. "Anyway," he said, breaking the silence gently, "I should get back to work. These boats don't build themselves."

Isabel smiled, grateful for the reprieve from the emotional intensity that had been building. "Of course. I'll get out of your way."

But before she could turn to leave, Gabe spoke again, his voice soft but deliberate. "Izzy."

She turned, caught off guard by the sudden vulnerability in his tone.

"I'm glad you're back," he said, his eyes locking with hers. "No matter what happens. I'm glad."

Isabel's breath caught in her throat, her heart thudding in her chest. The sincerity in his words washed over her like the tide, leaving her unsure of how to respond.

All she could manage was a small nod, her voice failing her in that moment. Then, without another word, she turned and walked away, the weight of his admission settling in her chest.

As she made her way back down the path toward her mother's house, she couldn't shake the feeling that something significant had shifted between them—something she wasn't sure she was ready to confront.

But there was no denying it.

The island was already beginning to stir her emotions in ways she hadn't expected, and Gabe was at the center of it all.

3

Chapter 3: Dylan's Return

The sound of seagulls overhead and the familiar scent of salt-water greeted Isabel as she walked along the narrow dirt road leading to the island's main pier. The day was bright, with a cloudless sky stretching above, and the gentle rhythm of the waves lapping against the shore filled the air. It had been a few days since her conversation with Gabe, but the emotional undercurrent of their exchange still lingered. She couldn't shake the feeling that something between them had changed—yet, she wasn't sure what it meant, or if she was ready to confront it.

As she neared the docks, a figure appeared in the distance. Tall, with a confident stride, the man moved with an air of ease and familiarity. Isabel squinted against the sunlight, the shape growing clearer. Her heart skipped a beat.

Dylan.

She hadn't expected him to be back so soon. It had been years since she last saw him, and even then, their interactions had always been a mix of easy friendship and something more—a charged energy that neither had fully acknowledged. While Gabe had been the steady, quiet presence in her life, Dylan was the spark, unpredictable and alluring.

He caught sight of her just as she reached the pier. His lips curled into a slow, easy grin, and his dark eyes sparkled with a mischievous glint that Isabel remembered all too well. His hair, wind-tossed and unruly, fell into his eyes as he approached her with a loping gait.

"Isabel Prescott," Dylan drawled, his voice carrying over the sound of the water. "Back from the mainland and looking as stunning as ever."

Isabel's cheeks flushed slightly at the compliment, but she forced herself to meet his gaze with a cool smile. "Dylan. I wasn't expecting to see you here."

He shrugged, his smile widening. "Thought I'd make a surprise visit. You know me, I can't stay away from this place for too long."

Isabel couldn't help but chuckle at that. Dylan had always been a wanderer, never staying in one place for too long, and yet somehow, he always found his way back to the island. It was as if this place had a pull on him, just like it did on her.

"It's good to see you," she said, her voice softening. "How've you been?"

Dylan leaned casually against one of the wooden posts, his eyes never leaving hers. "Oh, you know. Life's been...interesting. Travel, work, the usual. But I heard through the grapevine that you were back, and I couldn't resist coming to check if the rumors were true."

Isabel raised an eyebrow. "The island gossip mill is still going strong, I see."

"Stronger than ever," Dylan replied with a laugh. "But, hey, they weren't wrong. Here you are, in the flesh."

For a moment, the two of them stood there, the weight of their shared history hanging between them like an invisible thread. Memories of late-night conversations, stolen glances, and the thrill of the unspoken swirled in Isabel's mind. She remembered how they used to sit on the pier, just like this, talking for hours about everything and nothing at all. There had always been an unspoken attraction between them, but it had remained just that—unspoken.

Until now.

"So," Dylan began, his tone shifting slightly, "how does it feel to be back? You sticking around this time, or is this just a pit stop before you disappear again?"

Isabel hesitated, unsure how to answer. She hadn't really made a decision about staying or leaving. Part of her wanted to embrace the simplicity of life on the island, while another part still felt the pull of the life she'd built elsewhere. And then there was Gabe—his words and his presence making her question everything.

"I'm not sure yet," she admitted, her eyes drifting to the horizon. "It's...complicated."

Dylan studied her for a moment, his expression thoughtful. "Complicated, huh? Sounds like there's more to that story."

"There always is, isn't there?" she replied with a small smile, trying to deflect the weight of the conversation.

But Dylan wasn't so easily deterred. He took a step closer, his voice dropping slightly. "I always thought you'd come back eventually, Isabel. You belong here. We both do."

Isabel's heart fluttered at his words, though she wasn't sure if it was the sentiment or the way he said it that affected her. Dylan had a way of getting under her skin, making her feel things she wasn't ready to face. But the island wasn't the only thing that tied them together—there was history, unfinished conversations, and the lingering tension of what could have been.

As if sensing her hesitation, Dylan smiled again, this time more gently. "But hey, no pressure. I'm just glad you're here, even if it's only for a little while."

Isabel nodded, grateful for the reprieve, though she could still feel the tension simmering beneath the surface. There was something about Dylan—something magnetic, almost dangerous, in the way he made her question everything. The years apart hadn't dulled that effect. If anything, it seemed more potent now.

Just then, a gust of wind blew in from the sea, rustling the leaves of the nearby trees and sending a chill down Isabel's spine. She wrapped her arms around herself, suddenly feeling exposed, vulnerable. Dylan noticed and quickly shrugged off his jacket, draping it over her shoulders with a quick, effortless motion.

"Here," he said softly. "Can't have you catching cold."

Isabel pulled the jacket tighter around her, the warmth of it enveloping her in more ways than one. The scent of Dylan—familiar and grounding—mixed with the crisp ocean air, and for a brief moment, she allowed herself to sink into the comfort of it. The moment felt intimate, like stepping into a memory she hadn't realized she'd missed.

"Thanks," she murmured, glancing up at him.

Dylan met her gaze, his expression unreadable. "Anytime."

The silence between them stretched, neither of them moving to break it. Isabel could feel the weight of everything they weren't saying pressing down on her—memories of the nights they spent together, the laughter they shared, and the way things had always seemed on the verge of something more but had never quite crossed that line.

She could see it in his eyes now, too. The unspoken feelings that had been tucked away for years. But she wasn't sure if she was ready to confront those feelings, not after everything that had happened—especially with Gabe's presence looming in the background. Gabe, with his steady, reassuring presence, and Dylan, with his fire and unpredictability. They represented two very different parts of her life, two very different choices.

Dylan shifted, breaking the spell. "You know, I was thinking," he said casually, though there was a deeper undertone to his words, "maybe we should catch up. For old times' sake. Have dinner or something. It's been a long time, after all."

Isabel hesitated. The idea of spending more time with Dylan stirred something inside her—a sense of nostalgia, maybe even longing—but there was also a caution she couldn't ignore. Things between them had always been intense, and she wasn't sure if diving back into that intensity was what she needed right now.

"I don't know, Dylan," she replied slowly. "It's...a lot."

Dylan nodded, his expression surprisingly understanding. "I get it. No pressure. But the offer's on the table if you change your mind."

He gave her a soft smile, one that didn't quite reach his eyes, before stepping back and shoving his hands into his pockets. The air between them felt lighter, but Isabel could still sense the tension lurking beneath the surface. There was so much left unsaid, so many emotions that hadn't been fully explored.

"I should probably get going," Isabel said, suddenly feeling the need to retreat, to distance herself from the swirling confusion inside her. "I promised my mom I'd help with some things around the house."

Dylan nodded, his gaze lingering on her for a moment longer. "Of course. Don't be a stranger, Isabel."

"I won't," she promised, though the uncertainty in her voice made her wonder if she was lying to herself.

As she turned and walked away, Dylan's jacket still draped over her shoulders, Isabel couldn't shake the feeling that Dylan's return had stirred something deep within her—something unresolved, something that made her question not only her feelings about him, but also the choices she'd made in her life.

The past wasn't as distant as she had once believed. It was right here, standing on the pier, watching her walk away.

Isabel walked briskly down the dirt road, Dylan's jacket still wrapped tightly around her shoulders. The warmth of it was a comfort, but the weight of the encounter settled uncomfortably in her chest. The air felt different now, thick with the unspoken words that hung between them. Dylan's easygoing charm, the way he could slide so effortlessly back into her life, was something she'd always both admired and feared. He had the power to shake things up, to remind her of a time when things were simpler, but also more complicated.

As the familiar sight of her childhood home came into view, Isabel's thoughts drifted back to the past, to the late-night conversations they'd shared under the stars, sitting on the old porch swing. They used to talk about everything—dreams, hopes, even their fears—but they'd never quite talked about each other. There was always an unspoken line that neither of them had been willing to cross. Now, she wasn't sure what that line even was anymore.

She opened the gate and stepped onto the path leading to the front door. The scent of freshly mowed grass and the sea breeze greeted her, but her mind was still back at the pier with Dylan. The way his eyes had softened, how he'd carefully draped his jacket over her shoulders—small gestures, but they carried weight. Was he trying to rekindle something? Or had she been reading too much into it?

Inside, her mother's voice floated from the kitchen, humming softly to a tune that Isabel didn't recognize. It was comforting, grounding her as she stepped through the threshold, leaving behind the confusing whirlwind of emotions.

"Isabel, honey, is that you?" her mother called, her voice warm and inviting.

"Yeah, it's me," Isabel replied, pulling off Dylan's jacket and hanging it by the door. She paused, staring at it for a moment. It seemed out of place here, in the neat and orderly confines of her mother's home.

"I thought you'd be out longer," her mother said as she emerged from the kitchen, wiping her hands on a dish towel. "Everything okay?"

Isabel forced a smile, but it felt tight. "Yeah, just ran into Dylan at the pier. He's back."

Her mother raised an eyebrow, the expression laced with subtle concern. "Dylan, huh? It's been a while since he's been around."

"I know," Isabel said, rubbing her hands together absently. "It caught me off guard."

Her mother gave her a knowing look, the kind that only a mother could give, as if she understood more than Isabel was letting on. "How was it, seeing him again?"

Isabel sighed and sank into the couch, feeling the weight of the day pressing down on her. "It was...weird. Familiar, but also strange. It's like nothing's changed, but everything has, you know?"

Her mother sat beside her, folding the dish towel in her lap. "That's often how it is with people from the past. They remind us of who we were, but we're not the same anymore."

Isabel nodded, her mother's words striking a chord. That was exactly how it felt. Dylan wasn't just another person from her past—he was a symbol of the girl she used to be, the girl who dreamed of the world beyond the island but also loved its simplicity. And now, seeing him again, she felt that pull, that yearning for something that was no longer within reach.

"I just don't know what to think," Isabel admitted quietly. "I don't know if I'm ready for him to be back in my life."

Her mother gave her a gentle smile, placing a hand on her arm. "You don't have to figure it all out right now. Take it one step at a time. If Dylan's back, it doesn't mean you have to dive right into anything. Let yourself feel what you feel, and the rest will come."

Isabel leaned into her mother's embrace, grateful for the moment of comfort. Her mother always had a way of making things seem less overwhelming, of reminding her that she didn't have to have all the answers. Still, the thought of Dylan being back on the island, of the inevitable interactions that would follow, made her stomach twist in knots.

Later that evening, after dinner, Isabel found herself outside again, sitting on the porch swing that had been a part of her home for as long as she could remember. The sky was painted in hues of deep purple and orange as the sun dipped below the horizon. The rhythmic creak of the swing was soothing, a constant in a world that seemed to be shifting around her.

She thought about Dylan—how his presence on the island was already affecting her, stirring up emotions she thought she'd buried long ago. But she couldn't forget about Gabe either. The quiet strength of his presence, the way he'd always been there, solid and unwavering. The thought of him brought a sense of calm, but also confusion. Gabe had been so supportive, so patient. He'd told her that whatever decision she made, he would understand. But even in his words of reassurance, she could sense the unspoken—he didn't want her to leave.

It was that contrast between Dylan and Gabe that unsettled her. Dylan was unpredictable, magnetic, a reminder of a part of her that craved excitement and freedom. Gabe was steady, dependable, a reminder of the life she could have here, rooted and real.

The sound of approaching footsteps broke through her thoughts, and Isabel turned to see Gabe walking toward the porch. He moved with a quiet confidence, his familiar silhouette easing the tension in her shoulders.

"Hey," he greeted softly, his voice warm as he climbed the steps. "Mind if I join you?"

"Of course not," Isabel said, smiling as she scooted over to make room for him on the swing.

Gabe sat down beside her, his proximity bringing a comfort that she hadn't realized she needed. For a moment, they sat in silence, the only sound the gentle creak of the swing and the distant call of the ocean. Isabel felt herself relax, the tightness in her chest easing as she soaked in the peacefulness of the evening.

"I saw Dylan today," she said after a while, her voice barely above a whisper.

Gabe's expression remained calm, though his eyes flickered with something she couldn't quite read. "I heard he was back."

Isabel glanced at him, trying to gauge his reaction. But as always, Gabe was hard to read. His face was serene, betraying none of the emotions she had been grappling with since running into Dylan.

"Is it weird?" she asked, almost afraid of the answer.

Gabe took a deep breath, leaning back slightly on the swing. "I wouldn't say weird. I knew he'd come back eventually. Dylan's never really been the kind to stay away for long."

Isabel nodded, grateful for his steady presence. Gabe had always been pragmatic, able to accept things for what they were without getting lost in the emotional whirlwind like she sometimes did. Still, there was a part of her that wondered how he truly felt about Dylan's return—if it stirred up any old insecurities or made him question their fragile dynamic.

"You don't have to worry about me," Gabe said suddenly, as if reading her thoughts. "Dylan being back doesn't change anything between us."

Isabel exhaled a breath she hadn't realized she was holding. His words were comforting, but she couldn't ignore the way her heart fluttered with uncertainty. She wasn't sure if anything between them had changed—she wasn't even sure what "them" meant anymore. All she knew was that with both Gabe and Dylan now in her life, things were bound to get more complicated.

They sat together, the quiet stretching between them as the stars began to appear in the darkening sky. The familiar constellations above reminded her of all the nights she'd spent on this porch, gazing up at the same stars, trying to make sense of the world and her place in it.

And now, here she was again, torn between two men, two paths, and the part of her that still hadn't figured out who she truly was or where she belonged.

"Thanks for being here, Gabe," Isabel said softly, turning to face him. "I don't know what I'd do without you."

Gabe smiled, his eyes warm as they met hers. "You don't have to thank me, Isabel. I'll always be here. You know that."

As the night deepened and the island settled into its quiet rhythm, Isabel leaned her head against Gabe's shoulder, finding solace in the simple act of being close to someone who understood her—someone who would never pressure her or rush her to make decisions she wasn't ready to make.

But even as she sat there, feeling the comfort of Gabe's presence, her mind drifted back to Dylan—to the way he'd looked at her, the memories they shared, and the unspoken promise of something unfinished.

The past had returned to the island, and with it, the tangled emotions that Isabel had thought she'd left behind. And though she wasn't sure what the future held, she knew one thing for certain: Dylan's return had changed everything.

Isabel stayed pressed against Gabe's shoulder for a long time, her eyes half-closed, lulled by the rhythm of the ocean and the warmth of his presence. There was comfort here, a simplicity that had been missing ever since Dylan's reappearance stirred up old feelings, old wounds. But even in Gabe's quiet steadiness, Isabel's mind wandered to the complexities of the past, to the places where the two men in her life had marked her heart in different, indelible ways.

Eventually, she pulled back slightly, lifting her head to meet Gabe's gaze. His eyes were soft and full of understanding, as though he could see through the layers of her turmoil without her saying a word. That was Gabe—he never pushed, never pried. He simply waited, giving her the space she needed to work things out on her own. But sometimes, that patience only made things harder. It made her feel like she had to have all the answers, that she had to make a decision she wasn't ready for.

"Do you ever think about leaving?" Isabel asked suddenly, her voice quiet, almost drowned out by the soft rustle of the wind through the trees.

Gabe's brow furrowed slightly as he looked out toward the horizon. "Leaving the island, you mean?"

"Yeah," she said, her eyes following his to the dark expanse of the sea. "Starting over somewhere else. Somewhere that isn't tied to the past."

Gabe was silent for a moment, his jaw tightening as though weighing his words. "I used to, when I was younger. I thought there was something out there that I couldn't find here. But the more I thought about it, the more I realized it wasn't the place that mattered. It was the people."

Isabel bit her lip, the weight of his words settling over her like a heavy blanket. She had always thought of the island as both a sanctuary and a prison. It held so much of her history, so many memories, both beautiful and painful. And now, with Dylan back, it was as if the past had become inescapable, something she couldn't outrun no matter how hard she tried.

"I don't know if I can stay here," she whispered, the confession slipping out before she could stop it. "Not with everything that's happened. Not with Dylan back."

Gabe's eyes flickered with something—hurt, maybe—but it was gone so quickly that she couldn't be sure. He leaned forward, resting his elbows on his knees, his hands clasped together as if in deep thought.

"You don't have to make any decisions right now," he said, his voice steady, but she could hear the strain beneath it. "You've only just come back, Isabel. Give yourself time to figure things out."

Isabel nodded, but the uncertainty gnawed at her. Time. That was what everyone kept telling her. Time would make things clearer. But the truth was, time hadn't healed anything. It had only blurred the lines between what she wanted and what she was afraid of wanting.

Gabe straightened up, his tone softening as he reached out and took her hand. "You're not alone in this. Whatever you decide, I'll be here."

His words were a lifeline, something solid to hold on to in the swirling sea of emotions that threatened to pull her under. She squeezed his hand in return, grateful for his presence, even as the weight of her indecision pressed harder against her chest.

"I don't deserve you, Gabe," Isabel said, her voice barely audible.

He smiled, that gentle, understanding smile that always seemed to break through her defenses. "I think that's for me to decide."

They sat there for a while longer, the silence between them comfortable, but heavy with the unspoken. As the night grew darker, Isabel felt the chill of the evening air creeping in, and reluctantly, she stood, pulling the jacket tighter around herself.

"I should get some sleep," she said, her voice tinged with fatigue. "It's been a long day."

Gabe stood as well, his eyes lingering on her face as though he wanted to say something more, but he didn't. Instead, he simply nodded. "I'll walk you back."

They walked in silence, the familiar crunch of gravel underfoot the only sound that punctuated the quiet. When they reached her door, Gabe hesitated, his hands tucked into his pockets as he rocked back on his heels.

"Goodnight, Isabel," he said softly, his gaze lingering on her for a moment longer than usual.

"Goodnight, Gabe," she replied, her heart aching with the weight of everything unsaid between them.

As she closed the door behind her, Isabel leaned against it, closing her eyes and letting out a long, shaky breath. The night had left her with more questions than answers, her emotions tangled in ways she didn't know how to untangle. She wanted to let Gabe in, to let him be the anchor she so desperately needed, but something inside her held back. Something that she couldn't quite name, but that was undeniably tied to Dylan's return.

The next morning, Isabel woke to the sound of gulls crying overhead and the soft murmur of the ocean in the distance. She stretched, feeling the ache in her muscles from a restless night's sleep, her mind still swirling with the events of the previous day.

As she made her way to the kitchen, she found her mother already up, sitting at the table with a cup of tea in hand, her eyes fixed on the window as if lost in thought.

"Morning, Mom," Isabel greeted, stifling a yawn as she poured herself a cup of coffee.

"Morning, sweetheart," her mother replied, her gaze never leaving the view outside. "You've got a visitor."

Isabel's stomach tightened, and she followed her mother's gaze to see Dylan standing outside, leaning against the fence with that same easy smile on his face. His presence brought a surge of emotions—excitement, anxiety, confusion. She wasn't ready to face him again, not after everything that had happened last night with Gabe.

But it seemed she didn't have a choice.

With a deep breath, Isabel grabbed her mug and headed outside, her heart pounding in her chest. As she approached, Dylan straightened up, his eyes lighting up as he caught sight of her.

"Morning, Isa," he greeted, using the old nickname he'd given her when they were kids.

"Morning," she replied, her voice guarded, unsure of where this conversation was going.

"Hope I'm not interrupting anything," Dylan said, his tone casual, but there was an edge to his words that made Isabel's pulse quicken.

"No, just... having coffee," she said, gesturing to the mug in her hand. "What brings you by?"

Dylan leaned against the fence again, his hands resting on the top rail as he looked out toward the water. "I've been thinking about what you said last night. About the past, about how things never really change around here."

Isabel felt a lump form in her throat. The way he spoke, so casually, so effortlessly, stirred something inside her. He had always had that effect on her, making her feel like they were the only two people in the world, even in the middle of a crowd.

"I wasn't sure what you meant by that at first," Dylan continued, his voice softer now. "But I've been thinking... maybe you're right. Maybe the past is still here, lingering. Maybe that's why I came back."

Isabel swallowed hard, her heart racing. She wasn't sure if she was ready for this conversation, for the memories that were already bubbling up to the surface. The way Dylan looked at her, with that familiar intensity, made her feel like she was standing on the edge of a cliff, one wrong step away from falling into something she wasn't sure she could climb back out of.

"I didn't come back to stir things up, Isa," Dylan said quietly, his gaze locking with hers. "But I can't pretend like nothing's changed between us. You feel it too, don't you?"

Isabel's breath hitched in her throat, the weight of his words crashing over her. Of course, she felt it. She'd been feeling it ever since she saw him standing on the pier, that pull, that magnetic connection they'd always shared, but never acknowledged.

But where did that leave her? Where did that leave Gabe?

"I don't know what I feel, Dylan," Isabel admitted, her voice trembling. "Everything's so complicated now."

Dylan took a step closer, his hand reaching out as if to touch her, but stopping just short. "It doesn't have to be. Not with us."

Isabel's pulse quickened as his words hung in the air between them. She felt the familiar tug of their shared history, the memories of stolen glances and unfinished conversations. But she also felt the weight of the present, the reality of her life now, with Gabe, with the island, with all the unresolved feelings she'd carried with her for so long.

"I need time," she whispered, stepping back, her heart pounding.

Dylan's face softened, and for the first time, she saw something vulnerable there, a crack in the mask he always wore. "I get it, Isa. I'll give you all the time you need. Just... don't shut me out."

As he turned to leave, Isabel stood there, her heart aching with the enormity of it all. Dylan's return had reopened wounds she hadn't realized were still there, and now, standing at the crossroads of her past and present, she wasn't sure which path to take.

And as she watched him walk away, the only thing she knew for certain was that no matter what she chose, nothing on this island would ever be the same again.

Isabel stood there for what felt like hours, her mind racing as she watched Dylan disappear down the path. The lingering tension in the air was palpable, leaving her with a profound sense of disorientation. Her heart was torn between two worlds—one she thought she had moved beyond, and the other she wasn't sure she was ready to face.

The sound of the waves lapping against the shore drew her back to the present. She took a deep breath, trying to steady herself. The island had a way of anchoring her, of reminding her that no matter how turbulent her emotions became, life here continued in its slow, steady rhythm.

Isabel's thoughts drifted to Gabe, to the comfort she found in his quiet, steady presence. He had been there for her when she returned, offering her a kind of peace she hadn't known she needed. But now, with Dylan's return, that peace felt fragile, like something that could easily be shattered if she wasn't careful. How could she even begin to explain to Gabe the storm that was raging inside her?

The sky was beginning to turn the soft hues of dusk, casting long shadows across the island as she made her way back inside. Her mother glanced up from her book, but didn't ask any questions, sensing Isabel's need for space. Isabel gave her a small nod and headed upstairs, feeling the weight of the day pressing down on her.

Once in her room, she sank onto the edge of the bed, staring out the window at the familiar landscape. The island had always been her refuge, her safe haven when life got too overwhelming. But now, even the serenity of the place couldn't quiet the turmoil inside her.

Dylan's words echoed in her mind. *You feel it too, don't you?* She did. She felt it in the pit of her stomach, in the way her heart skipped a beat whenever she saw him, in the memories that flooded her every time they were in the same space. But it was more than just old feelings resurfacing. It was the unresolved nature of their relationship, the unfinished business that neither of them had been brave enough to face back then.

Her phone buzzed, snapping her out of her thoughts. She glanced at the screen and saw a message from Gabe.

Gabe: *Hey, just checking in. You okay?*

Her heart squeezed a little at the sight of his name. Gabe always knew when something was off, even when she tried to hide it. She hesitated for a moment, not knowing what to say. She didn't want to lie to him, but she wasn't sure how to explain what was happening inside her.

Isabel: *I'm okay, just... a lot on my mind.*

She set the phone down, unable to bring herself to type anything more. The truth was, she didn't know how to begin that conversation. How could she tell Gabe about the pull she felt toward Dylan, the confusion swirling inside her every time he was near? How could she admit that she wasn't sure if she was ready to let go of the past, even though she had been trying to move forward with him?

A knock on her door startled her. Isabel looked up to see her mother standing in the doorway, her expression soft but concerned.

"Mind if I come in?" her mother asked gently.

Isabel shook her head, motioning for her to enter. Her mother sat down beside her on the bed, her eyes full of the quiet wisdom that only years of life experience could bring.

"You seem troubled, sweetheart," her mother said softly, reaching out to tuck a loose strand of hair behind Isabel's ear.

Isabel let out a shaky breath, feeling the knot in her chest tighten. "It's Dylan," she admitted. "Him being back... it's stirred up so much."

Her mother nodded, her eyes never leaving Isabel's face. "I figured it might."

"I thought I was over it," Isabel continued, her voice trembling slightly. "I thought I had moved on, that I could come back here and start fresh. But now that he's here, everything feels... complicated."

Her mother sighed, her expression both understanding and sad. "The past has a way of holding onto us, especially when things were left unresolved. It's not surprising that seeing Dylan again would bring all those feelings back to the surface."

Isabel bit her lip, trying to hold back the tears that were threatening to spill over. "I don't know what to do, Mom. I don't want to hurt Gabe. He's been so good to me, and I care about him so much. But with Dylan... it's like there's still something between us. Something unfinished."

Her mother reached out and took her hand, giving it a reassuring squeeze. "It's okay to feel conflicted, Isabel. You don't have to have all the answers right now. But I will say this—don't make any decisions out of fear. Whatever path you choose, make sure it's the one that feels right for you."

Isabel nodded, her mother's words sinking in. It was a reminder that she didn't have to rush to figure everything out. She could take her time, sort through her feelings, and eventually, the right path would become clear.

"I just don't want to mess everything up," Isabel whispered, her voice barely audible.

"You won't," her mother said softly, her eyes full of love. "You're stronger than you give yourself credit for, Isabel. And no matter what happens, you'll find your way."

They sat together in silence for a while, the quiet presence of her mother a comfort in the midst of the emotional storm. When her mother finally stood to leave, she pressed a gentle kiss to Isabel's forehead.

"Get some rest," she said, her voice tender. "Everything will look a little clearer in the morning."

Isabel nodded, grateful for the reassurance, even if she wasn't sure she believed it yet.

After her mother left, Isabel lay down on the bed, staring up at the ceiling. Her mind was a tangled web of emotions—her feelings for Dylan, her connection with Gabe, the unresolved past that seemed to be creeping back into her life no matter how hard she tried to keep it at bay.

She thought about the way Dylan had looked at her earlier, the intensity in his eyes, the unspoken words that hung in the air between them. It had always been like that with Dylan—so much left unsaid, so many moments that felt like they were on the brink of something more, but never quite getting there.

And then there was Gabe. Sweet, patient, reliable Gabe. He had been her rock ever since she returned, offering her a sense of stability that she hadn't realized she craved. But now, with Dylan back, she couldn't help but wonder if Gabe was the right choice for her, or if she was holding onto him because he represented safety in a world that suddenly felt unpredictable.

The thought of hurting Gabe made her heart ache. He deserved so much more than being someone's second choice, and the last thing Isabel wanted was to string him along while she sorted through her complicated feelings for Dylan.

But what if it wasn't just about choosing between them? What if it was about choosing herself, about finding her own sense of peace before she could fully commit to anyone?

As the night stretched on, Isabel found herself tossing and turning, her mind too restless to find sleep. The familiar creak of the old house, the soft rustle of the wind through the trees, even the distant sound of the waves—all of it felt like a reminder that this island held so much of her history. And yet, it was also where she had the chance to create something new, to rewrite the story of her life in a way that felt true to who she was now.

But to do that, she knew she had to face the past head-on. She had to confront the feelings she had for Dylan, the unresolved tension between them, and decide if there was a future there worth exploring. And she had to do it without losing sight of the fact that she deserved happiness too, regardless of what that looked like with either man.

With that thought in mind, Isabel finally closed her eyes, her heart heavy but resolute. Tomorrow, she would talk to Dylan. She would try to find some closure, some understanding of where they stood, and from there, maybe—just maybe—she could start to untangle the mess that her emotions had become.

But for now, she would rest, knowing that whatever came next, she had the strength to face it.

4

Chapter 4: Secrets in the Studio

Isabel woke up the next morning with a gnawing sense of restlessness. The encounter with Dylan lingered in her mind, but something deeper tugged at her, something she couldn't quite place. It wasn't just about Dylan or Gabe—this was different. It felt like an invisible thread pulling her toward something that had been hidden for far too long.

The house was quiet when she made her way downstairs, the familiar creaks of the floorboards a comforting reminder of the life she had once known here. Her mother was already outside in the garden, her soft humming floating through the open window. Isabel was grateful for the momentary solitude. She needed to think, to breathe, to figure out what exactly was making her feel so unsettled.

She poured herself a cup of coffee and stood by the window, staring out at the shimmering waves beyond the cliff. The island was always so beautiful in the mornings, bathed in a soft golden light. But today, the beauty felt like a distraction, like a veil over something much more profound.

Her gaze drifted, almost unconsciously, toward the old studio at the far end of the garden. The small, weathered building had been her mother's sanctuary for as long as she could remember. Growing up, Isabel had always been curious about what went on inside, but the studio had been off-limits, a private space that her mother guarded fiercely. Isabel hadn't been inside since she was a child, when her mother had painted whimsical landscapes and abstract shapes to calm the restlessness of a mind that was always racing with creative ideas.

But something about the studio called to her now. It was as if the very air around it had shifted, becoming heavier, more charged with meaning. She set her coffee down and, almost without thinking, began walking toward it. The closer she got, the more she felt the weight of something unspoken hanging in the air, as if the studio held secrets not only of her mother's past, but of her own.

When Isabel reached the door, she hesitated for a moment. She hadn't been inside for years. Would her mother mind if she went in now? Something in her gut told her that this was different, that she needed to see what was inside, that whatever was in that studio was meant for her.

She pushed the door open, her heart pounding in her chest as she stepped inside.

The air was thick with the smell of oil paint and turpentine, and the dim light filtering through the dusty windows gave the room an otherworldly glow. The studio was cluttered but in a way that suggested organized chaos—brushes, canvases, and sketchpads were scattered across tables, along with jars of paint and palettes smeared with every color imaginable.

It was a time capsule, frozen in place, as if her mother had stepped out for a moment and would return any second to resume her work. But it was the large, covered canvas in the center of the room that immediately drew Isabel's attention.

She approached it slowly, her breath catching in her throat. There was something about it—something about the way it sat there, shrouded in cloth, that felt like it was waiting for her. Her fingers trembled slightly as she reached for the edge of the covering.

She pulled it back.

The painting beneath took her breath away.

It was a portrait, but not just any portrait. It was of her mother—young, vibrant, eyes alight with an intensity that Isabel had never seen before. But that wasn't what shocked her. It was the fact that she wasn't alone in the painting. There was a man standing beside her, his arm draped loosely around her shoulders, his expression warm and intimate.

Isabel stared at the man's face, a chill running down her spine. She didn't recognize him, yet there was something familiar about him, something that stirred the deepest parts of her memory. Her mother had never mentioned anyone like him, had never spoken of a past relationship with this kind of intimacy. Who was he? And why had her mother kept this hidden?

The more Isabel looked at the painting, the more unsettled she became. There was something almost haunting about the way her mother's eyes seemed to follow her, as if challenging her to uncover the truth. The vibrant colors, the fluid brushstrokes—it all felt so alive, so charged with emotion.

Her mind raced with questions. Why had her mother painted this? Why had she hidden it away? And, most importantly, what did it mean?

Isabel stepped back, her gaze still locked on the portrait. She could feel her heart pounding in her chest, her pulse quickening with a sense of urgency. This was more than just a painting. It was a piece of her mother's soul, a glimpse into a life that had been kept secret from her.

But it was more than that, too. Isabel realized, with a start, that it wasn't just her mother's secrets she was uncovering. It was her own. She had always sensed that there was something missing, some part of herself that she had never been able to fully access. And now, standing in front of this painting, she knew she was on the verge of finding it.

The realization was almost too much to bear.

She took a step back, her hands trembling. The room felt too small, too claustrophobic. She needed air. She needed space to think, to process what she had just discovered.

Isabel hurried out of the studio, the door slamming behind her as she stumbled into the garden. The cool breeze hit her face, but it did little to calm the storm inside her. She leaned against the side of the house, her chest rising and falling in rapid breaths as she tried to make sense of it all.

Who was the man in the painting? And why had her mother hidden this part of her life from her? Isabel had always thought she knew her mother, but now she realized how little she truly understood.

And yet, there was something else, something even more unsettling. As she stood there, the wind swirling around her, she couldn't shake the feeling that this wasn't just about her mother's past. This was about her. The painting had awoken something deep within her, something that had been buried for so long she had forgotten it was even there.

Memories began to surface—fragmented images of her childhood, moments she had long since pushed to the back of her mind. She remembered the way her mother would sometimes disappear for hours, lost in her art, leaving Isabel to play alone in the garden. She remembered the way her mother's eyes would glaze over when she asked too many questions about the past, as if she were guarding a treasure too precious to be shared.

But now, standing on the brink of discovery, Isabel realized that the answers had been there all along, hidden in plain sight. Her mother's art had always been her refuge, her way of expressing the things she couldn't say out loud. And now, through this painting, she was speaking to Isabel in a language only they could understand.

Isabel knew what she had to do.

She took a deep breath and headed back inside, her feet moving almost of their own accord as she made her way to the bookshelf in the living room. Her mother had kept journals for as long as Isabel could remember, always scribbling down thoughts and sketches in worn leather notebooks. If there were answers to be found, they would be there.

She scanned the shelves, her fingers brushing over the spines until she found the one she was looking for—a battered old journal, the cover soft and worn from years of use. She pulled it out and sat down on the couch, her hands trembling slightly as she opened it.

The pages were filled with sketches and notes, but it wasn't until she reached the middle of the journal that she found what she was looking for. There, tucked between the pages, was a letter, written in her mother's familiar handwriting.

Isabel,

If you're reading this, then you've found the painting.

Isabel's heart skipped a beat as she continued reading, her breath catching in her throat.

There are things I've kept from you, things I wasn't ready to share. But now, it's time. The man in the painting... his name is James. He was a part of my life long before you were born, and I loved him in a way I can't explain. But we were never meant to be. Our paths took us in different directions, and I thought I had let him go. But I never really did.

Isabel's hands shook as she turned the page.

You are more like me than you know. There are parts of yourself you haven't yet discovered, parts of your heart that you've hidden away, just as I did. But now, it's time for you to find them. Don't be afraid of what you uncover. The truth, even when it's painful, is always worth finding.

Isabel felt a lump form in her throat as she read the final words.

You are my greatest masterpiece, Isabel. Never forget that.

Love, Mom.

Isabel closed the journal, tears streaming down her face. She felt like a dam had broken inside her, releasing years of pent-up emotions and unanswered questions. The painting, the journal, her mother's letter—it was all connected, all part of a story that she had never fully understood until now.

She wiped her eyes and took a deep breath. She wasn't sure what to do next, but one thing was clear: her mother had left this painting for her to find, to help her uncover the parts of herself she had kept hidden for so long.

And now, it was up to Isabel to finish the story.

Isabel sat in silence for what felt like hours, her mother's letter resting on her lap, the weight of its words pressing down on her. The revelation had stirred something deep inside her, a mix of grief, longing, and an inexplicable sense of relief. Her mother had known her better than Isabel had ever realized. She had known that Isabel, like her, had been keeping parts of herself hidden—guarded, perhaps out of fear, or maybe out of habit. And now, the painting, the letter, and the secrets in the studio were all invitations to face those hidden parts.

But what did it all mean? The man in the painting—James—was a figure Isabel had never heard of, and yet her mother had loved him deeply enough to immortalize their connection in art. Isabel could only imagine the kind of love that would inspire such a portrait. She glanced over at the painting again, feeling a strange connection to it, as though it held answers not just about her mother's past but also about her own future.

Her thoughts swirled, tangling into knots she wasn't sure how to unravel. But one thing was clear—her mother had wanted her to find this. She had wanted Isabel to understand that love, even when it doesn't last in the way we expect, leaves a lasting mark.

Isabel closed her eyes, letting the silence of the room settle over her like a blanket. She could hear the faint rustling of the wind outside, the creak of the house as it adjusted to the weight of time and memory. Her breath slowed, her mind drifting back to the time when she used to sit and watch her mother paint. The way her mother's brush would move across the canvas, with such focus, such intention. Isabel had always admired that—her mother's ability to create something beautiful out of nothing.

But now, as she sat there, Isabel realized that the studio held more than just artistic memories. It was a space of secrets, a place where her mother had come to confront her own demons, her own past loves, and perhaps even her own fears. Isabel felt the weight of that realization, the sense that she was about to embark on a similar journey—one where she would have to confront the parts of herself she had long buried.

With a deep breath, she rose to her feet, her mind buzzing with questions she wasn't sure she was ready to answer. She needed more. The painting and the letter were just pieces of a larger puzzle, and she wasn't sure where it would lead her, but she knew she couldn't stop now.

She carefully folded the letter and tucked it back into the journal before placing it on the table beside her. Then, with a renewed sense of determination, she turned toward the studio once more, her eyes scanning the space for anything she might have missed. The air in the room felt charged, as if it held the remnants of her mother's energy, her thoughts, her struggles.

Isabel's gaze lingered on a small table in the corner, one she had barely noticed before. It was cluttered with old photographs, paint-stained brushes, and a stack of sketchpads. Something about the table called to her, the way the studio had earlier. She approached it slowly, her heart thudding in her chest, a sense of anticipation building within her.

As she reached the table, she picked up the first sketchpad, flipping it open with careful hands. The pages were filled with rough, quick sketches—some landscapes, others abstract shapes and figures. But as she neared the end of the sketchpad, she paused, her breath catching in her throat.

It was a sketch of her mother and the man from the painting—James. But this time, the sketch was different. The lines were softer, more intimate, and there was something in their expressions that stirred a sense of longing in Isabel's chest. The way they looked at each other, the way their hands almost touched but didn't—it spoke of a love that had been left unfinished, a love that had been interrupted by something beyond their control.

Isabel's fingers traced the outline of the sketch, her mind whirling with thoughts. Who was James? And why had her mother kept him a secret for so long? The more Isabel stared at the sketch, the more she realized that there was a story here, one that her mother hadn't been ready to share while she was alive.

But now, that story was Isabel's to uncover.

She set the sketchpad down, her pulse quickening. She needed to know more. There had to be more clues, more pieces to this puzzle. Her eyes scanned the studio again, and then they fell on an old chest in the corner, half-hidden beneath a stack of canvases.

Isabel's heart skipped a beat. The chest had always been there, tucked away in the shadows, but she had never given it much thought before. Now, though, it seemed to take on a new significance. With a sense of trepidation, she walked over to it, her hands trembling slightly as she knelt down and lifted the lid.

Inside were more sketchpads, more photographs, and a small, velvet-bound journal. Isabel's breath caught in her throat as she reached for the journal, her fingers grazing the soft fabric. She opened it slowly, her heart pounding in her chest as she flipped through the pages.

The journal was filled with her mother's handwriting, but this time, the entries were different. They were more personal, more raw. The words spoke of a time before Isabel was born, a time when her mother had been in love with James. The entries were filled with longing, with heartache, with a sense of inevitability that they couldn't be together.

Isabel's hands shook as she read the final entry.

"I loved him. I loved him in a way that I've never loved anyone else. But it wasn't meant to be. Our lives were too different, our paths too far apart. And now, I'm left with only memories, only these sketches and paintings to remind me of what could have been."

Isabel's breath hitched as she closed the journal, her mind reeling. Her mother had been in love with this man—James—but for some reason, they hadn't been able to be together. It was a story as old as time, but somehow, it felt different. It felt personal. And it left Isabel with more questions than answers.

She set the journal aside, her thoughts racing. What had happened between her mother and James? Why hadn't they been able to be together? And why had her mother kept all of this hidden from her for so long?

The air in the studio felt thick, oppressive, as if it were weighing down on her with the weight of all these unanswered questions. Isabel stood up, pacing the room as she tried to make sense of it all.

Her mother had been a woman of secrets, a woman who had kept her past hidden even from her own daughter. And now, Isabel was left to pick up the pieces, to uncover the truth that had been buried for so long.

But what did that mean for Isabel? What was she supposed to do with this knowledge? How was she supposed to reconcile the mother she had known with the woman who had loved a man she had never even heard of?

Isabel's mind spun with possibilities, with questions that she wasn't sure she would ever find the answers to. But one thing was clear—her mother had left this studio, this painting, and these journals for her to find. She had wanted Isabel to uncover the truth, to confront the parts of herself that she had been hiding for so long.

And now, standing in the middle of her mother's studio, surrounded by the remnants of her past, Isabel realized that she couldn't run from it anymore. The secrets, the hidden parts of herself—they were all intertwined, all connected in ways she had never imagined.

She took a deep breath, her resolve hardening. She wasn't sure what the next step was, but she knew she couldn't turn back now.

The secrets in the studio had opened a door, and she was going to walk through it, no matter what she found on the other side.

Isabel stood frozen, the journal heavy in her hands, the weight of the discoveries pressing on her chest. She wanted to believe she had uncovered enough—enough of her mother's secrets, enough of the buried past—but something inside her urged her to keep going. The studio was a shrine to her mother's hidden life, and it felt incomplete, as though there was more to be revealed.

Her eyes were drawn back to the painting of James. His face, so delicately rendered in her mother's brushstrokes, held a calmness that contrasted the emotional storm brewing inside Isabel. How could someone from her mother's past—someone Isabel had never even heard of—have inspired such powerful work? She stepped closer to the painting, examining it in greater detail.

The longer she looked, the more she noticed—the soft shadows under James's eyes, the slight tilt of his head, as though he were in the middle of a thought, something just on the edge of being spoken but never voiced. Isabel could almost imagine the conversations that had taken place between him and her mother, filled with unspoken desires and unresolved tension.

Isabel's fingers grazed the edge of the canvas, wondering if this man had understood her mother in ways that no one else had. And what about her father? Had he known? Her parents' relationship had always seemed so solid, so built on mutual respect, but now Isabel wondered if there had been fractures in that foundation that she had never noticed.

As her thoughts swirled, Isabel's gaze fell on a small box at the base of the easel. She hadn't seen it before, partially obscured by the scattered canvases leaning against the wall. It was old, wooden, with a delicate latch that looked like it hadn't been opened in years. Without thinking, she knelt down and pulled the box closer.

Her heart raced as she opened the lid, half expecting to find another letter or sketchpad filled with more of her mother's secrets. But instead, inside were small trinkets—things that must have meant something to her mother. A dried flower, brittle and fragile, tucked inside a small envelope. A tarnished silver bracelet, its charm shaped like a star. A faded photograph of her mother, smiling in a way Isabel had never seen before, standing next to a man who must have been James.

Isabel's breath hitched. The man in the photograph was younger than the one in the painting, his hair darker, his eyes more vibrant, but there was no mistaking it—this was him. The two of them stood together, their shoulders barely touching, but there was an intimacy in their stance, a closeness that spoke of history. Isabel could feel it—the connection between them, the way her mother had loved him.

Her fingers traced the edges of the photograph, and a sudden wave of sadness washed over her. She had never seen her mother look so... alive. There was a lightness in her expression, a joy that had seemed absent in Isabel's childhood memories. Her mother had always been loving, but she had also been reserved, as though part of her had always been somewhere else—somewhere unreachable.

Isabel set the photograph down, her emotions swirling with a mix of longing and confusion. She couldn't reconcile the woman in the photograph with the mother she had known. It was as though she were seeing a different side of her—a side that had been kept hidden, even from those closest to her.

The bracelet caught her eye again, and she picked it up, holding it in her palm. It was delicate, worn from years of use, but the star-shaped charm still glimmered faintly in the dim light of the studio.

As she turned it over in her hand, she noticed an engraving on the back: *To C., with all my love—J.*

Her breath caught in her throat. James had given this to her mother—Catherine. The inscription was simple, but the words carried so much weight. Isabel could almost feel the depth of their relationship in that single sentence, the way love and loss had been woven into the fabric of their lives.

She placed the bracelet back in the box, her mind racing. Her mother had never mentioned James—not once. But now, it was clear that he had been a pivotal part of her life, someone who had shaped her in ways Isabel was only beginning to understand.

She sat back on her heels, staring at the contents of the box, feeling both overwhelmed and strangely comforted. The pieces were starting to come together—slowly, painfully—but they were coming together. Her mother had loved deeply, had experienced heartache and joy in ways Isabel had never imagined.

And yet, her mother had chosen to keep that part of herself hidden. Why? Was it shame? Regret? Or was it something else—a desire to protect Isabel from the complexities of her own life? Isabel couldn't be sure, but the more she uncovered, the more she realized that her mother had been far more complicated than she had ever let on.

Isabel closed the box gently, her fingers lingering on the lid for a moment before she stood up. The room felt different now, heavier with the weight of everything she had learned. But it also felt more familiar, as though she were finally seeing it for what it truly was—a reflection of her mother's inner world, a place where she had come to grapple with her own emotions, her own struggles.

As Isabel stood there, taking it all in, she realized that this wasn't just about her mother's secrets. It was about her own. The parts of herself that she had kept hidden, the emotions she had refused to confront. The studio, the painting, the journal—they were all reminders that life was messy, that love was complicated, and that sometimes, the most important things were the ones we tried to bury.

Isabel walked over to the window, her mind still racing with everything she had discovered. The view outside was peaceful, the island bathed in the soft light of the setting sun. But inside, Isabel's heart was anything but calm. She felt as though she were standing on the edge of something—a precipice—and she wasn't sure what lay on the other side.

For so long, she had kept herself guarded, closed off from the world. She had built walls around her heart, around her emotions, afraid of what might happen if she let herself be vulnerable. But now, standing in the studio, surrounded by her mother's art, her mother's secrets, she realized that those walls were starting to crack.

Her mother had loved James, but she had also loved Isabel's father. She had lived with the tension of those two truths, and somehow, she had found a way to carry both with her. Isabel wasn't sure if she could do the same, but she knew she had to try. She couldn't keep running from her emotions, from the people who mattered to her.

The island had always been a place of solitude, a refuge where Isabel could hide from the world. But now, it felt different. It felt like a place where she might finally confront the things she had been avoiding for so long.

She turned away from the window, her gaze falling on the painting of James once more. His eyes seemed to follow her, filled with a quiet understanding. Isabel took a deep breath, letting the air fill her lungs, grounding her in the moment.

There was still so much she didn't know, so much she had yet to uncover. But for the first time in a long time, Isabel felt ready. Ready to face the secrets, the emotions, the parts of herself she had kept hidden for far too long.

With one last glance at the painting, she left the studio, closing the door softly behind her. The path ahead was uncertain, but Isabel knew that she couldn't turn back now. The secrets in the studio had opened a door, and she was ready to walk through it.

Isabel stepped out of the studio, the door creaking softly behind her, but the weight of what she'd uncovered seemed to follow her. The cool evening breeze kissed her skin, a stark contrast to the warmth of the sun that had bathed the island earlier. The air smelled of salt and the faintest hint of flowers from the garden her mother had once so carefully tended.

The island's familiarity felt both comforting and alien. Now that she had unearthed parts of her mother's life she never knew existed, even the landscape appeared different—steeped in mystery. She walked slowly, her feet moving of their own accord, leading her down a well-worn path toward the cliffs. It was a place she used to visit often as a child, a place where the sea's roar drowned out everything else, where she could lose herself in the sheer power of nature.

As she walked, her mind drifted back to the box she had found in the studio—the trinkets, the bracelet, the photograph. Her mother had never spoken of James. Isabel wasn't sure how to reconcile the woman in that photo—vibrant and full of life—with the mother she had grown up with, who had always seemed so composed, so restrained.

Her thoughts spun in circles, returning again and again to that engraved bracelet: *To C., with all my love—J.* The message was clear—her mother had been loved deeply by this man. But why had she kept it a secret? Why had she chosen to stay with Isabel's father instead? The questions weighed heavily on her, pressing down like the thick evening fog that had begun to roll in from the sea.

When she finally reached the cliffs, she stood at the edge, staring out at the horizon where the sky met the ocean. The sun was sinking lower now, casting long shadows over the water, turning the waves a deep shade of indigo. It was beautiful—so achingly beautiful that it made her chest tighten.

Isabel closed her eyes and breathed deeply, willing herself to focus on the present, to let go of the confusion, the uncertainty, if only for a moment. But the image of the painting—the way her mother had captured James's likeness with such tenderness—refused to leave her mind. What had their relationship been like? Was it a passionate love that had burned out, or had it been something quieter, something that lingered even after they had parted ways?

And what about her father? Did he know? A knot of guilt twisted in Isabel's stomach at the thought. If her father had been aware of James, if he had known that her mother's heart had once belonged to another man, how had he lived with it? How had he stayed, knowing he wasn't the only one she had loved?

The breeze picked up, whipping strands of hair across Isabel's face, but she didn't move to brush them away. She stood there, letting the wind and the sea envelop her, as if the elements could somehow cleanse her of the weight she carried. For so long, she had been running—running from her own emotions, from her memories, from the parts of herself she didn't want to face. And now, she realized, she had been running from her mother's past as well.

Isabel's eyes opened, drawn back to the waves crashing against the rocks below. The sound was deafening, the force of the ocean relentless. And yet, in its fury, there was also a kind of peace—a reminder that nature, like life, was unpredictable and uncontrollable. No matter how much she tried to bury her emotions, to keep them hidden away like her mother had done, they would always find a way to resurface.

As the sky darkened, a familiar voice pulled her from her thoughts.

"Isabel."

She turned slowly, her heart jumping in her chest at the sight of Gabe standing a few feet behind her. His face was partially shadowed in the dim light, but she could see the concern in his eyes, the way his brows furrowed as he looked at her.

"I figured I might find you here," he said, his voice soft but steady. "This was always your spot."

Isabel didn't respond at first. Her emotions were too raw, too close to the surface, and the last thing she wanted was to unravel in front of him. But as Gabe stepped closer, his presence so solid, so familiar, she found herself unable to keep the wall up.

"I found something," she said quietly, her voice barely audible over the roar of the ocean.

Gabe moved to stand beside her, his eyes searching her face. "What is it?"

Isabel hesitated, her gaze falling to the ground. She hadn't planned on telling anyone—not yet, not until she had more time to process everything. But now, standing here with Gabe, she realized she didn't want to carry this burden alone.

"It's about my mother," she said, finally looking up at him. "There was someone else. Someone she loved before my father."

Gabe's expression didn't change—no shock, no surprise. He simply nodded, as though he had expected this, or perhaps he understood better than anyone that life was full of hidden truths.

"James," she continued, the name feeling foreign on her lips. "I found a painting of him in her studio. And there was a bracelet... a photograph." She paused, struggling to find the words. "I don't know what to make of it, Gabe. I don't know who she really was anymore."

Gabe was silent for a moment, his gaze drifting out to the horizon before returning to her. "Your mother was a complex person, Isabel. People... we're not just one thing. We carry all these different parts of ourselves with us. Sometimes we show them, sometimes we don't."

Isabel's throat tightened. "But why didn't she tell me? Why didn't she tell *anyone*?"

"Maybe she thought it was easier that way," Gabe said gently. "Or maybe she was trying to protect you. From what, I don't know. But I think sometimes people hide things because they're scared of what will happen if they don't."

His words settled over her, and Isabel felt the sting of unshed tears at the corners of her eyes. She hated how vulnerable she felt, how exposed, but there was something about Gabe's presence that made it easier to let go. He wasn't judging her, wasn't asking for explanations. He was just there, offering her the space to feel everything she had been holding back.

"I thought I knew her," Isabel whispered. "But now, I'm not sure I did."

Gabe's hand reached out, his fingers brushing against hers, and for a moment, Isabel felt the urge to pull away—to retreat back into the safety of her emotional walls. But she didn't. Instead, she allowed herself to take comfort in the warmth of his touch, to lean into the connection between them that had always been there, even when they had been apart.

"She was still your mother," Gabe said softly. "That hasn't changed."

Isabel nodded, but her heart was heavy with the weight of the secrets she had uncovered. Yes, her mother was still her mother, but the woman she had discovered in the studio was a stranger in many ways—someone with a life, a love, and a passion that Isabel had never known.

They stood in silence for a long while, the wind whipping around them, the ocean crashing below. Isabel's thoughts drifted back to the painting, to James's face, and to the realization that there was so much more she still didn't understand.

But perhaps that was part of it—the not knowing, the acceptance that some things would remain hidden, no matter how deeply she searched. And maybe, just maybe, that was okay. Life wasn't about having all the answers, after all. It was about learning to live with the uncertainty, with the complexity of love, loss, and everything in between.

Gabe squeezed her hand gently, grounding her in the moment. "You'll figure it out, Isabel," he said, his voice filled with quiet assurance. "Whatever it is, you'll figure it out."

Isabel took a deep breath, letting his words sink in. She wasn't sure she believed him—not yet. But standing here, on the edge of the cliffs, with Gabe by her side, she felt a small flicker of hope. Maybe she didn't have to have all the answers right now. Maybe it was enough to just be here, to feel the wind, to hear the sea, and to know that she wasn't alone.

For the first time in what felt like forever, Isabel allowed herself to let go—just a little. The weight of the secrets she had uncovered still pressed down on her, but now, they felt a little lighter, a little less overwhelming. There was still so much to unravel, but she didn't have to do it all at once.

And maybe, just maybe, she didn't have to do it alone.

Isabel and Gabe remained at the edge of the cliffs for a while longer, the silence between them growing more comfortable as the sun dipped below the horizon. The sky was now a canvas of twilight blues and deep purples, the first stars beginning to twinkle faintly above.

The sound of the waves crashing against the rocks below seemed to carry away some of the heaviness Isabel had been feeling. It was as if the ocean, with its relentless ebb and flow, was reminding her of the natural rhythms of life, where moments of turmoil were always followed by moments of calm.

As the sky darkened, Gabe finally broke the silence. "I should probably get going. It's getting late, and I've got some work to finish up at the shop."

Isabel nodded, reluctantly breaking the peaceful spell of the evening. "Thank you for coming out here. I didn't expect... well, I didn't expect to talk about this."

Gabe gave her a reassuring smile. "Anytime. If you need to talk more—or if you just need some company—don't hesitate to call. I'm around."

Isabel appreciated his offer more than she could express. "I will. Thanks, Gabe."

They made their way back along the path in silence, the soft crunch of gravel under their feet the only sound between them. As they approached the edge of the garden, where Gabe's old truck was parked, Isabel felt a pang of sadness that their time together was coming to an end. It was surprising how comforting his presence had been, even amidst the chaos of her emotions.

Gabe hesitated before getting into his truck. "Isabel... about the painting and the studio. I know it's a lot to process. If you want, I could help you go through some of that stuff. Just to make it a bit less overwhelming."

Isabel looked at him, her heart swelling with gratitude. "I'd like that. I think it would help. Maybe this weekend?"

"Sounds good," Gabe said with a nod. "I'll give you a call. Take care."

He climbed into his truck, and Isabel watched as the vehicle's headlights cut through the encroaching darkness. The truck rumbled to life, and as Gabe drove away, Isabel felt a bittersweet pang. It was reassuring to know that Gabe was there, but part of her still longed for the clarity she desperately sought.

With Gabe gone, Isabel made her way back to her mother's house. The night air was cooler now, and the familiar creak of the front door as she opened it was oddly comforting. The house was quiet, save for the gentle hum of the refrigerator in the kitchen. She flicked on the lights, casting warm pools of illumination that seemed to push back against the encroaching shadows.

Isabel's gaze was drawn immediately to the studio door, which was slightly ajar. She had left it open earlier, but now it seemed to beckon her back, its secrets still waiting to be uncovered. She walked over, her footsteps muffled on the old wooden floor, and pushed the door open fully.

The studio looked almost exactly as it had when she first entered—except now, with the knowledge of the hidden paintings and the secrets they held, it felt different. The room seemed to pulse with untold stories, the very walls saturated with the echoes of her mother's past.

Isabel approached the easel where the enigmatic painting of James had been displayed. The painting was still covered by the sheet she had placed over it, but she could see its shape and the hint of its colors through the fabric. She reached out tentatively, her fingers brushing the edge of the sheet before she pulled it away.

The painting was even more captivating in the dim light of the studio. The lighthouse was depicted in muted blues and grays, with a faint glow emanating from the beacon. The figure of James stood on the shore, looking out at the sea, his expression a mix of longing and melancholy. The obscure symbol, partially obscured by shadows, seemed to pulse with a hidden meaning that Isabel couldn't quite decipher.

She leaned in closer, examining the details. The brushstrokes were delicate, almost fragile, conveying a deep sense of emotion. It was clear that her mother had poured her heart into this painting, but what was the message behind it? Why had she chosen to paint James this way, and what was the significance of the lighthouse and the symbol?

Isabel's fingers traced the outline of the lighthouse on the canvas, her touch light as though she feared disturbing the memories embedded in the paint. The symbol seemed to call to her, inviting her to uncover its meaning. But where to begin?

Her eyes wandered around the studio, settling on the assortment of materials and objects that filled the space. Paintbrushes, tubes of paint, and sketches were scattered haphazardly on the tables and easels. Each item seemed to hold a piece of her mother's life, a fragment of the woman who had kept so many parts of herself hidden.

She noticed a small drawer in one of the desks, its handle slightly tarnished with age. Without thinking, Isabel reached for it and pulled it open. Inside were various sketches and studies—some of them incomplete, others showing intricate designs and details. She rifled through them, her heart racing with each new discovery.

One particular sketch caught her eye. It was a rough drawing of the lighthouse, but with the same obscure symbol from the painting prominently featured. There were notes scribbled around the edges, but the handwriting was difficult to read. Isabel's eyes strained to make out the words, but it was clear that they were written in a hurried, almost frantic scrawl.

The sketch and the notes suggested that her mother had been working on something significant, something that went beyond mere art. It was as if the lighthouse and the symbol were keys to unlocking a deeper truth, one that Isabel was only beginning to grasp.

She pulled out the sketch and carried it over to the light of the desk lamp, trying to decipher the notes. The writing was fragmented, filled with incomplete sentences and erratic punctuation. But one phrase stood out clearly: "The light will reveal what's hidden."

Isabel's heart skipped a beat. The phrase seemed to resonate with her, echoing the sense of revelation she had experienced when she uncovered the studio. It was as if her mother had left behind a clue, a guide to understanding the mysteries she had hidden away.

With a sense of determination, Isabel decided to explore the connection between the lighthouse and the symbol further. She knew that if she wanted to understand her mother's past—and her own—she would have to delve deeper into the mysteries that had been left behind.

As she worked late into the night, Isabel felt a renewed sense of purpose. The studio, once a place of hidden secrets, was now a beacon of discovery. The painting, the sketches, and the notes all pointed to something greater, something that was waiting to be uncovered.

By the time the first light of dawn began to seep through the windows, Isabel had a plan forming in her mind. She would return to the lighthouse, the physical and symbolic heart of her mother's work. There, she hoped to find more clues, to piece together the puzzle that had been left behind.

But as she closed the door to the studio and prepared for bed, she couldn't shake the feeling that the journey ahead would be more challenging than she had anticipated. The lighthouse held the promise of answers, but it also represented the unknown—a place where the past and present would collide.

Isabel's thoughts were a whirlwind of emotions as she drifted off to sleep. The weight of her discoveries and the anticipation of what lay ahead filled her dreams with fragmented images of the lighthouse, the painting, and the mysterious symbol. It was a restless night, but in her heart, she knew that she was on the cusp of something significant.

As the sun rose on a new day, Isabel was ready to face whatever challenges lay ahead. The secrets of the studio were just the beginning, and she was determined to unravel the full story of her mother's past, no matter where it led her.

5

Chapter 5: The First Real Conversation with Gabe

The afternoon sun stretched across the horizon, casting warm hues over the beach where Isabel found herself walking aimlessly. The sand shifted beneath her feet, offering the familiar resistance of a landscape that had shaped her childhood, yet felt foreign now. Rosemere Isle held memories in every grain, and with each step, those memories seemed to pull her further into her past, whether she wanted to confront it or not.

The sound of waves crashing against the shore was soothing, yet the weight of all she had discovered—the studio, the paintings, her mother's unspoken life—pressed on her. She glanced at the sea, thinking about how her mother had likely stood here, looking out at the same expanse, burdened by her own secrets.

A figure emerged in the distance. Gabe.

Isabel's heart gave a faint tug, a recognition of something unspoken between them. He walked with his usual steady, grounded pace, his presence solid like the island itself. He was carrying a fishing net over his shoulder, the kind of simple, everyday task that had always defined him, and yet, as he approached, the tension between them felt anything but ordinary.

"Hey," Gabe greeted, his voice as steady as the waves. He stopped a few feet away from her, seemingly uncertain whether to step closer.

"Hi." Isabel's reply was almost a whisper, caught somewhere between hesitation and anticipation.

For a moment, they stood there, two figures on the edge of the ocean, both grappling with the weight of their own histories. Gabe adjusted the net on his shoulder, clearly trying to find the right words. Isabel waited, her gaze flickering between the horizon and Gabe's face, tracing the lines of tension that softened when he caught her eye.

"How's the house?" he asked finally, his voice carrying the ease of familiarity but also the weight of concern.

"It's... more than I expected," she said, her fingers curling into the hem of her shirt. "I found a studio. My mom's. It had these paintings I never knew about."

Gabe's brow furrowed, and he took a step closer, closing the physical gap between them. "What kind of paintings?"

Isabel hesitated, trying to find the right words to explain the strange and emotional discovery. "There's one of the lighthouse... but there's something more to it. A symbol I don't understand. It feels like she was trying to tell me something, but I don't know what."

The mention of the lighthouse seemed to stir something in Gabe, though his expression remained unreadable. "That place has its own mysteries," he said softly, his voice tinged with the weight of the island's unspoken history. "You think she was trying to leave you a message?"

"I don't know," Isabel admitted, her voice breaking with the uncertainty that had been gnawing at her since the discovery. "Maybe... I was never close to her. I don't even know why she kept all of this hidden from me. And now, it feels like... like I'm too late to understand."

Gabe studied her face, the vulnerability in her eyes that she seemed desperate to hide. For a moment, he didn't say anything, letting the quiet of the beach settle around them. Then he set the net down on the sand and stepped even closer, his presence offering a kind of stability she didn't realize she needed.

"You're not too late," he said, his voice low but firm. "Sometimes, we find things when we're ready to see them. Even if we don't realize it at the time."

Isabel met his gaze, the sincerity in his words hitting her in a way she hadn't expected. There was something comforting about his certainty, even if she wasn't sure she believed it herself.

They stood there for a while, letting the silence stretch between them, broken only by the rhythm of the waves. Isabel felt the tension in her chest ease, just a little, in Gabe's presence. She hadn't allowed herself to feel this kind of quiet comfort in years—perhaps not since they were kids, sitting together on this very beach, before life had complicated everything.

"Do you ever think about what could've been?" she asked suddenly, the question surprising even herself. It was a bold question, a risky one, but the weight of the past few days made her want to know. She needed to know.

Gabe's jaw tightened slightly, a subtle shift that revealed more than his words ever could. His gaze drifted to the horizon before returning to her, a flicker of something deep, something unspoken, lingering in his eyes.

"Yeah," he admitted, his voice barely audible over the sound of the waves. "More than I should."

Isabel's heart clenched at his words, and for the first time in years, she allowed herself to think about the possibility of 'what could have been'—not just with Gabe, but with the life she had left behind on the island.

"Why didn't you say anything?" she asked, her voice softer now, almost afraid of the answer.

Gabe's eyes darkened with a mixture of regret and something more difficult to name. "Because you were always meant for something bigger. At least, that's what I told myself."

His words hung in the air, heavy with the truth of what they had both lost. Isabel's breath caught in her throat. She had always thought that leaving the island had been her decision alone, that it was what she needed to do to find herself. But now, standing here with Gabe, she realized that maybe she had been running—from the island, from him, and from herself.

"I'm not so sure about that anymore," Isabel whispered, her voice trembling with the weight of the confession.

Gabe's eyes softened, and for a moment, the space between them seemed to collapse. Isabel could feel the pull of something old, something familiar, and yet something entirely new building between them.

But before either of them could say anything more, Gabe took a small step back, breaking the moment. His gaze fell to the sand, as if the intensity of what had just passed between them was too much.

"I should probably head back," he said, his voice suddenly distant.

Isabel nodded, feeling the same hesitation gnawing at her. The emotional walls she had spent years building were still there, even if they were starting to crack. "Yeah, me too."

They stood there for a moment longer, neither of them moving, the weight of unspoken words and lingering emotions still hanging in the air.

"Take care, Izzy," Gabe said softly, using the nickname he hadn't called her in years. The sound of it caught her off guard, and for a brief second, she was transported back to a time when things between them were simpler—before all the heartbreak, the distance, and the walls they had built around themselves.

"You too, Gabe," she replied, her voice quieter than she intended.

With one last glance, Gabe picked up his net and started to walk away, his footsteps slow and deliberate. Isabel watched him go, feeling a strange mix of relief and longing. The conversation had left her more unsettled than she had expected. But it had also opened a door she wasn't sure she was ready to walk through.

As she turned to head back toward her mother's house, Isabel realized that the past wasn't something she could keep running from forever. Not when it was woven into the very fabric of the island, into the faces of the people she had left behind, and most of all, into the lingering connection between her and Gabe.

For the first time since returning to Rosemere Isle, she felt the tug of something deeper—a pull toward the life she had left behind, and maybe, just maybe, the chance to build something new.

As she walked, Isabel's mind raced. The lighthouse, her mother's paintings, Gabe—everything was swirling together in a way that felt both overwhelming and inevitable. There was so much left unsaid, so much that she had to figure out. But for now, she let the sound of the waves fill the silence, allowing herself to take it one step at a time.

This moment marks the beginning of a deeper emotional connection between Isabel and Gabe, as their first real conversation hints at shared regrets and unspoken feelings.

Isabel's footsteps grew slower as she made her way back from the beach, her mind still tangled in the conversation with Gabe. The breeze was cooler now, the day slipping into early evening, and yet her skin felt warm, flushed with the emotions swirling inside her.

His words echoed in her mind. *Because you were always meant for something bigger.*

Had she been running all these years because of that belief? That there was something beyond Rosemere Isle, something bigger waiting for her out there? Or had she been running because staying meant facing the past, facing the depth of her feelings—feelings for her mother, for this place, and most of all, for Gabe?

She shook her head as if trying to clear the thoughts, but they clung to her, a reminder that she couldn't escape her past, not anymore. Gabe had opened a door, one she wasn't sure she was ready to walk through. Yet she couldn't deny the pull toward him, the way his presence had always grounded her, even when she felt untethered in her own skin.

The walk back to the house felt longer than usual, and when she finally reached the front porch, she hesitated at the door. Stepping inside meant confronting more than just the quiet of her mother's home. It meant confronting herself—the person she had become while she was away, and the person she had always been, shaped by the island and its people.

With a deep breath, she pushed the door open and stepped inside. The house greeted her with its familiar stillness, the air thick with the scent of salt and aged wood. Her mother's house, her house now, was full of memories and ghosts she hadn't yet begun to understand. But tonight, there was something else here—a weight she hadn't felt before.

Isabel moved slowly through the rooms, trailing her fingers along the worn banister of the stairs, feeling the rough texture of the walls beneath her hand. The house had been lived in, and every corner seemed to hold a story. Some she knew, but many she had yet to uncover.

Her mind drifted back to the studio, to the discovery of her mother's paintings, and the cryptic symbol that seemed to hold a secret Isabel hadn't yet unlocked. The lighthouse—the painting haunted her in the same way her conversation with Gabe lingered. Both held pieces of her past she was only beginning to understand.

She entered the living room and stood in the center of the space, her arms wrapped around herself as if trying to ward off the chill that had nothing to do with the air. Everything felt different now, sharper, more intense, as if the island itself was stirring something within her.

She hadn't expected to feel this unsettled. The studio, Gabe, her mother's secrets—it was all converging, demanding her attention. But what scared her most wasn't the mystery of the lighthouse or the painting. It was Gabe's words, the way he had looked at her, the unspoken tension that had simmered between them.

Isabel sank onto the couch, her gaze drifting toward the window, where the sky had turned a deep, dusky blue. The sun had set, and the stars were beginning to appear, scattered across the sky like distant memories. She stared at them, feeling the weight of the day pressing down on her.

How long had it been since she had truly talked to someone about her feelings? About her regrets, her fears?

What could have been?

The question had hung in the air between her and Gabe, and now it hung in her mind, refusing to be ignored. There had been a time, years ago, when she thought her future might include Gabe. When the possibility of *what could have been* had felt real, tangible, just within reach. But she had left. She had chosen a different path, one that had taken her far from Rosemere Isle, far from Gabe.

And yet, standing on that beach with him, it had felt as if no time had passed at all. The connection between them was still there, humming just beneath the surface, waiting to be acknowledged.

But acknowledging it meant more than just confronting her feelings for Gabe. It meant confronting everything she had left behind—the life she had walked away from, the people she had hurt, and the parts of herself she had buried along the way.

Isabel leaned her head back against the couch and closed her eyes. She was exhausted, not just physically but emotionally. The weight of her mother's secrets, the mystery of the lighthouse, and the unresolved tension with Gabe—it was all too much.

She hadn't expected to feel this way when she returned to the island. She had come back for closure, to put the past behind her, to make peace with her mother's memory. But instead, it felt like the island was pulling her deeper into its grip, forcing her to confront the very things she had been running from.

A soft knock on the door startled her, pulling her from her thoughts. She sat up, her heart skipping a beat. Who could it be at this hour?

Slowly, she rose from the couch and made her way to the door. When she opened it, she found Gabe standing on the porch, his expression unreadable, his hands shoved into the pockets of his jacket.

"Gabe?" Isabel's voice was quiet, uncertain.

"I didn't mean to bother you," he said, his voice low, "but I wanted to make sure you were okay."

She blinked, surprised by the gesture. "I'm fine," she said, though her voice wavered slightly, betraying her emotions.

Gabe stepped closer, his eyes searching hers. "Are you?"

Isabel hesitated, the vulnerability she had been holding back all day threatening to spill over. She opened her mouth to speak, but the words caught in her throat. She wasn't fine. She was far from fine.

But admitting that felt too raw, too exposed.

"I don't know," she whispered, her voice barely audible.

Gabe didn't say anything. He just stood there, his presence solid and steady, offering her the comfort she hadn't realized she needed. There was something in his gaze—something unspoken, but deeply understood. It was as if he knew what she was going through, even without her having to say it.

And maybe that was what scared her the most.

"I keep thinking about what you said earlier," she admitted, her voice shaky. "About what could have been."

Gabe's expression softened, and he took a small step closer. "So do I."

The honesty in his voice hit her like a wave, and for a moment, she felt the urge to step back, to retreat into the safety of her emotional walls. But something stopped her. Maybe it was the way he was looking at her, or maybe it was the fact that for the first time in years, she didn't feel so alone.

"Why didn't we ever talk about it?" she asked, her voice barely above a whisper. "Back then?"

Gabe's jaw tightened, and he looked down at the ground for a moment before meeting her gaze again. "Because we were young.

And scared. And we both had dreams that took us in different directions."

Isabel swallowed hard, the weight of his words sinking in. He was right. They had been young, and they had been scared. But that didn't make the regret any less painful.

"Do you think things would have been different if I had stayed?" she asked, her voice trembling with the weight of the question.

Gabe's eyes softened, and he took another step closer, closing the distance between them. "Maybe," he said quietly. "But we'll never know."

The truth of his words hung in the air between them, heavy and bittersweet. Isabel felt a lump form in her throat, and she blinked back the tears that threatened to spill over.

"But that doesn't mean we can't figure it out now," Gabe added, his voice soft but steady.

Isabel's heart skipped a beat, and for the first time in years, she allowed herself to imagine the possibility of a future—not just for herself, but for her and Gabe. The thought scared her, but it also filled her with a sense of hope she hadn't felt in a long time.

"I don't know if I'm ready for that," she admitted, her voice shaking with uncertainty.

Gabe reached out and gently took her hand, his touch warm and grounding. "You don't have to be ready," he said softly. "But I'm here. Whenever you are."

The simplicity of his words hit her like a balm to her soul, and for the first time since returning to Rosemere Isle, Isabel felt a sense of peace. Maybe she wasn't ready yet, but she didn't have to do this alone.

Gabe's hand was still wrapped around hers.

Isabel's hand remained in Gabe's, and the weight of his presence was both comforting and terrifying. She wasn't used to this—being so close to someone, physically and emotionally, and she wasn't sure she was ready to let herself sink into it. But the warmth of his skin against hers grounded her, anchoring her to the moment in a way that felt both familiar and new.

"Gabe," she whispered, her voice barely audible as her gaze remained locked on their hands, "I don't know how to do this. I've been running for so long, I don't know if I can stop."

Gabe's thumb brushed over the back of her hand in a slow, reassuring motion, and he stepped just a little closer, enough that she could feel the subtle warmth radiating from him. His proximity was both a comfort and a reminder of what she had spent years trying to avoid—connection, vulnerability, the rawness of truly being seen by someone who mattered.

"You don't have to figure it all out right now, Isabel," he said gently. His voice was a quiet, steady thing in the evening air. "But you don't have to do this alone either."

Isabel looked up at him then, her eyes searching his face. There was no judgment in his gaze, no pressure. Just understanding, the kind that made her chest tighten with emotion. For years, she had been used to putting on a front—strong, independent, invulnerable. But Gabe saw through that. He always had.

"I'm scared," she admitted, the words falling out before she had time to think. Her voice trembled, and she immediately regretted the confession. It felt like too much, too soon, too raw.

But Gabe didn't flinch. Instead, his expression softened even further, a deep empathy settling into his features. "What are you scared of?"

Isabel exhaled slowly, a bitter laugh escaping her lips. "Everything. Scared of staying, scared of leaving. Scared of letting people in, but also terrified of being alone." Her hand tightened around his without her even realizing it, as if her body was clinging to the only stable thing in the whirlwind of her thoughts.

Gabe didn't let go, didn't pull away. "I think that's normal," he said softly. "After everything you've been through... it makes sense. You've been carrying a lot on your own for a long time."

Isabel nodded, her throat tightening with emotion. "It just feels like... like the island has always had a hold on me. And now, with my mother's death, and everything I've found in the studio... it's like it's pulling me back, but I don't know if I'm ready to face all of it."

Gabe's eyes flickered with understanding. "You're allowed to feel that way, Isabel. You don't have to have all the answers right now."

She swallowed hard, her chest constricting as the weight of his words sank in. For so long, she had been convinced that she needed to have it all figured out. That she couldn't afford to show weakness, especially not to someone like Gabe, who had seen her at her most vulnerable before she had built up her walls.

But here he was, still standing in front of her, holding her hand, offering her the space to be uncertain. To be scared.

Isabel blinked back the tears that threatened to fall. She hadn't expected to feel this emotional, but the weight of everything she had been carrying was suddenly so much heavier. She hadn't realized how much she had needed someone to be there with her, to understand.

"Do you remember that night?" she asked, her voice barely a whisper. "The last one, before I left for the city?"

Gabe's expression shifted slightly, his eyes darkening with the memory. "Of course I do," he said quietly. "I've thought about it more times than I can count."

Isabel let out a shaky breath, her heart pounding in her chest. She had never talked about that night—not to anyone, not even to herself. But now, with Gabe standing so close, it felt like the unspoken words between them were finally surfacing, demanding to be acknowledged.

"I always wondered... what would have happened if I'd stayed," she said, her voice barely above a whisper.

Gabe's hand tightened around hers, just for a moment, before he let out a long, slow breath. "I wondered that too," he admitted. "For years. But we were both so young, Isabel. I don't know if either of us would have been ready for what that would have meant."

Isabel nodded, her heart heavy with the truth of his words. They had been young, and the world had felt so much bigger than the island, bigger than the lives they had been living. She had craved more—more adventure, more freedom, more of something she couldn't even name at the time. And Gabe... well, Gabe had always been steady, content with the life he had built on the island, the roots he had put down.

But that hadn't made leaving any easier.

"I still regret it sometimes," she admitted, her voice thick with emotion. "Leaving. Not giving us a chance."

Gabe's eyes softened, and he took another small step toward her, closing the distance between them. "You don't have to regret it, Isabel. You made the choice that was right for you at the time. And maybe... maybe it wasn't the right time for us back then."

She looked up at him, her eyes searching his face. "And now?"

Gabe's gaze held hers for a long moment, his expression unreadable. But there was something in his eyes, something that made her heart flutter with a mixture of fear and hope. "I don't know," he said softly. "But maybe it's worth figuring out."

Isabel's breath caught in her throat, her chest tightening with the weight of his words. Could it really be that simple? After everything that had happened, after all the years that had passed, was it possible that they could still have a chance?

"I don't know if I can, Gabe," she whispered, her voice trembling with uncertainty. "I don't know if I'm ready to let someone in like that again."

Gabe's expression softened, and he reached out with his free hand, gently cupping her cheek. His touch was warm, grounding, and for a moment, Isabel closed her eyes, leaning into it, letting herself feel the safety of his presence.

"You don't have to decide anything right now," he said softly. "But just know... I'm here. And I'm not going anywhere."

Isabel opened her eyes, her gaze locking with his. There was something so honest, so raw in the way he looked at her. It scared her, but it also made her feel something she hadn't felt in a long time—hope.

For a long moment, neither of them said anything. The world around them seemed to fade, leaving only the two of them standing on her porch, the weight of their shared past and the possibility of a future lingering in the air between them.

Isabel wasn't sure what would happen next, but for the first time in a long time, she didn't feel like she had to run away. She didn't have to have all the answers right now. For now, it was enough to stand here, in this moment, and let herself be seen.

"Thank you," she whispered, her voice barely audible. "For being here. For not giving up."

Gabe's hand slipped from her cheek, but he didn't let go of her hand. "I could never give up on you, Isabel. Not then, not now."

Isabel's heart swelled, and for the first time in years, she allowed herself to believe that maybe—just maybe—things could be different this time.

It wasn't a promise of forever, but it was a beginning.

Isabel stood there for a long moment, her breath shallow, trying to make sense of the emotions swirling inside her. Gabe's words echoed in her mind, reverberating with a resonance that struck her deeply. He had never given up on her—not then, not now. The magnitude of that realization felt heavy, like a weight pressing down on her chest, but at the same time, it was oddly comforting. In a world where she had always been running, Gabe had remained—steady, constant.

Her instinct, as always, was to retreat, to put up walls and distance herself. She had spent years perfecting the art of emotional distance, keeping people at arm's length to protect herself from the inevitable pain of getting too close. And yet, here she was, standing inches from Gabe, the one person who could see right through those defenses, the one person who seemed to understand her without the need for explanations.

"Isabel?" Gabe's voice was quiet, almost tentative, as if he could sense her internal struggle. His hand remained loosely intertwined with hers, offering her the choice to stay or pull away.

She inhaled slowly, letting the cool evening air fill her lungs, grounding her in the present. For so long, her life had been defined by movement—leaving the island, forging a new life in the city, staying on the move so she wouldn't have to face the ghosts of her past. But now, standing here with Gabe, she felt something she hadn't allowed herself to feel in a long time.

Stillness.

It was terrifying.

"I... I don't know if I'm good at this," she admitted, her voice barely above a whisper. She hated how vulnerable she sounded, how exposed she felt. But there was no point in pretending anymore, not with Gabe.

"Good at what?" Gabe's brow furrowed slightly, his gaze soft and patient as he waited for her to find the words.

"Letting someone in," Isabel said, her voice thick with emotion. "I've spent so many years building these walls, Gabe. It's how I've survived. But now... now I don't know how to tear them down."

Gabe's expression softened, and he took a small step closer, closing the space between them. "You don't have to tear them down all at once, Isabel," he said gently. "It's not about breaking everything apart. It's about making space, little by little, for someone else."

Isabel blinked, feeling the sting of unshed tears prick at the corners of her eyes. She wasn't used to this, to the idea that it didn't have to be all or nothing. For so long, she had believed that vulnerability meant exposing herself entirely, leaving herself open to pain. But maybe Gabe was right. Maybe it was about finding moments, small pockets of trust, where she could let someone in.

"I'm scared," she admitted again, her voice wavering. It was the only thing she could say, the only truth that seemed clear amidst the confusion in her mind. "I'm scared that if I let you in... I'll get hurt again."

Gabe's hand, still holding hers, tightened just slightly in a reassuring squeeze. "I'm scared too," he said, his voice low and honest. "But I'm more scared of not trying. Of losing the chance to see what we could have, if we just gave it a shot."

Isabel's breath caught in her throat, her heart pounding as she looked up at him. His words were so simple, yet they carried a weight that she wasn't sure she was ready to bear. But at the same time, they offered her something she hadn't expected—hope. A future that wasn't defined by her past mistakes, by the pain she had carried for so long.

Could she really do this? Could she trust Gabe enough to let him in, even just a little?

Her mind raced with a thousand thoughts, doubts, fears. But then she looked into Gabe's eyes, saw the steady, unwavering patience there, and something inside her shifted. It wasn't a grand epiphany, nor a sudden flood of confidence. It was quieter than that—a small, fragile thing that felt like the first step toward something new.

"I don't know what this is," she said softly, her voice trembling with uncertainty. "But... I want to try."

The words hung in the air between them, a tentative offering of trust, of vulnerability. It wasn't a promise, not yet. But it was a start.

Gabe's lips curved into a gentle smile, the kind that made her heart flutter despite the fear still gnawing at the edges of her resolve. "That's all I'm asking for," he said quietly. "Just a chance."

For a moment, they stood there in silence, the weight of their shared history and the fragile hope for a future unspoken between them. The evening air was cool against Isabel's skin, the sound of the waves in the distance a constant, soothing backdrop. And for the first time in a long time, she allowed herself to breathe—really breathe—in the stillness of the moment.

"You're different than I remember," she said softly, her gaze tracing the lines of his face, the way his eyes crinkled at the corners when he smiled.

Gabe chuckled lightly, his grip on her hand never faltering. "I'd hope so. It's been, what, eight years?"

"Yeah," she breathed, her mind drifting back to those younger, simpler days. But the truth was, neither of them was the same. Time had changed them, shaped them in ways neither could have predicted.

"Do you ever regret it?" she asked before she could stop herself. "Not... not pursuing whatever this was, back then?"

Gabe's smile faltered for a brief second, his eyes darkening with memories. "I think about it sometimes," he admitted. "But I don't regret how things turned out. You needed to go, to find yourself in the city. And I needed to stay, to figure out what this island means to me."

Isabel nodded, though a part of her still ached with the weight of that lost time. She had always wondered, in the quiet moments when the city felt too loud, what might have happened if she had stayed. If she had let herself fall for Gabe, for the life they might have built together.

"But now," Gabe continued, his voice steady, "we have a second chance. And maybe that's all that matters."

Isabel looked at him, her heart pounding in her chest. A second chance. It was a terrifying thought, and yet, it stirred something inside her that she hadn't felt in years. Possibility.

"Maybe you're right," she whispered, more to herself than to him. The fear was still there, a constant presence in the back of her mind. But alongside it, there was something else now—something that felt like hope.

Gabe released her hand then, but not before brushing his thumb gently over her knuckles one last time. "You don't have to decide anything right now," he said softly. "Take your time, Isabel. I'll be here."

His words were a quiet promise, one that settled into her chest like a lifeline. And for the first time in a long time, Isabel believed him.

As Gabe turned to leave, the warmth of his presence lingered, even after he had disappeared into the night. Isabel stood there on the porch, her hand still tingling from where his had been, her mind racing with everything they had said, everything left unsaid.

She didn't know what the future held—whether she could truly open herself up to Gabe, to the life she had once run away from. But for now, in the stillness of the evening, she let herself hope that maybe, just maybe, she could find her way back.

To Gabe. To the island. To herself.

And that, she realized, was enough for tonight.

Isabel remained on the porch long after Gabe had left, her mind replaying their conversation over and over, like the waves constantly lapping at the shore. She had always thought of herself as someone who lived with one foot out the door, never fully committing to any place or person. But Gabe's quiet, steady presence, and his offer of a second chance, unsettled something deep inside her.

Her gaze drifted toward the horizon, where the dark outline of the lighthouse stood against the night sky. The sight of it, usually a comforting symbol of home, now seemed to mirror her inner turmoil. She had returned to this island for solitude, to escape the pressures of the city and the demands of her past, but it felt like the island was drawing her back into everything she had tried to leave behind—old memories, old wounds, and now, old loves.

The wind picked up slightly, rustling the leaves in the trees, and Isabel wrapped her arms around herself as if to hold everything together. Her thoughts strayed back to the studio and the painting she had discovered. The hidden message in her mother's sketches,

"The light will reveal what's hidden," kept echoing in her mind. What was it supposed to mean? Was it about the lighthouse, or was it about something more personal, something her mother had never told her?

Isabel sighed, pulling herself out of her thoughts, and made her way inside. The house was quiet, but not in a comforting way. It felt almost too quiet, like the calm before a storm. She wandered into the living room and absentmindedly picked up the photo of her and her mother from the mantle. They were smiling, standing in front of the lighthouse, the wind blowing their hair in wild directions. Her mother had that free-spirited look in her eyes, the one that had always made Isabel feel like her mother had secrets she would never fully understand.

Isabel put the photo down and walked to the window, staring out at the lighthouse again. What had her mother been trying to reveal with her art? Was it about her past, or was it about Isabel's? And why, after all these years, did it feel like everything was converging at once—her mother's mysteries, Gabe's reappearance, Dylan's return?

The past had a way of catching up with you, Isabel thought. No matter how fast or far you ran, it always found you.

She was about to head upstairs to bed when she heard a faint knock at the door. Her heart skipped a beat—could Gabe have come back? But when she opened the door, it wasn't Gabe. It was Sarah, standing on the porch with her arms crossed, a concerned look on her face.

"Hey," Sarah said, her voice soft but firm. "Can I come in?"

Isabel stepped aside, letting her friend in. Sarah had a way of appearing exactly when Isabel needed her most, even if she wasn't ready to admit it. They sat down in the living room, and Sarah looked at her with an expression that said she knew something was up.

"Gabe told me you two talked," Sarah began gently, leaning forward slightly. "How are you feeling about all of this?"

Isabel exhaled, leaning back into the couch, suddenly feeling the weight of everything. "I don't know, Sarah. I really don't know. It's like... I came back here to get away from everything, to figure myself out. But now it feels like everything's closing in on me."

Sarah nodded, listening intently. "It sounds like you're feeling overwhelmed. But, Isabel, maybe this is exactly what you needed. To face these things instead of running from them."

Isabel looked at her friend, the bluntness of her words cutting through her like a knife. Sarah had always been able to see through her, past the walls Isabel tried to build.

"I don't know if I can, Sarah," Isabel said softly. "It's easier to just... not deal with it."

"But is that really easier?" Sarah pressed, her voice full of concern. "You've been carrying this weight for years, Isa. Maybe it's time to finally let it go."

Isabel stared at the floor, her hands gripping the edge of the couch. "How do I do that? How do I just let go of everything when I don't even know where to start?"

Sarah reached out and took her hand, squeezing it gently. "You don't have to do it all at once. Just one step at a time. Like tonight, with Gabe. You let him in, even just a little. That's a start."

Isabel swallowed hard, thinking back to the conversation with Gabe, the vulnerability that had scared her but also made her feel alive in a way she hadn't in so long. "I'm afraid, Sarah. I'm afraid that if I let him in, I'll get hurt again. That I'll lose everything."

Sarah's eyes softened, and she gave Isabel's hand another squeeze. "I get it. I do. But life isn't about never getting hurt, Isa.

It's about finding people who are worth taking the risk for. And I think Gabe... he might be one of those people."

Isabel felt her heart tighten at the truth of Sarah's words. Gabe was someone worth taking the risk for. But could she really do it? Could she let go of the past enough to embrace whatever this was, this connection that had always lingered between them, waiting for the right moment?

As they sat there in silence, Isabel thought about all the times she had tried to outrun her feelings, only to end up back here, on this island, facing the very things she had tried to leave behind. Maybe Sarah was right. Maybe it was time to stop running.

"I don't know if I'm ready," Isabel admitted, her voice small.

"That's okay," Sarah said softly. "You don't have to be. But just know, Isa, you're stronger than you think. And whatever happens, you don't have to go through it alone."

Isabel felt a lump form in her throat as Sarah's words sank in. She didn't have to do this alone. Gabe had shown her that tonight. And now, Sarah was reminding her again. Maybe she didn't have to carry the weight of the past all by herself anymore.

"Thanks, Sarah," Isabel whispered, her voice thick with emotion.

Sarah smiled gently, standing up and giving Isabel a hug. "Anytime. You know I'm here for you."

As Sarah left, the house felt a little less heavy, a little less quiet. Isabel walked back to the window, staring out at the lighthouse again. The light from it was steady, illuminating the dark waters below, just as it always had.

For the first time in a long time, Isabel allowed herself to wonder if she could find that kind of steadiness in her own life. She had come back to this island searching for solitude, but maybe what she needed was connection. Maybe what she had been running from all these years wasn't the island, or her mother's secrets, or even Gabe.

Maybe she had been running from herself.

With a deep breath, Isabel turned away from the window and headed upstairs. She didn't have all the answers, not yet. But tonight had been a step, a small one, toward something new. Toward healing, maybe even love. And for the first time in a long time, she felt like she could let herself take that step.

Even if it scared her. Even if it meant opening up in ways she never had before.

She wasn't ready yet—but maybe she didn't have to be. Maybe, for the first time, it was okay to be a little uncertain.

Isabel climbed into bed, her thoughts still lingering on Gabe's words, on Sarah's quiet support, and on the mysteries still waiting for her in the studio. Tomorrow would come with its own challenges, its own questions. But for now, she allowed herself to drift into sleep, with the faintest flicker of hope in her heart.

The following morning, Isabel awoke to the soft glow of the sun filtering through her bedroom window. The familiar sounds of the island—birds chirping, waves crashing, wind whispering through the trees—seemed more vivid today, as if the world outside was urging her to rise and face what lay ahead.

She lay there for a while, staring at the ceiling, her mind circling back to her conversation with Gabe the previous night. His quiet sincerity, his ability to see through her defenses, had left her feeling raw and exposed in a way she hadn't anticipated. The idea that someone could look at her—really look at her—and still want to be there, still care for her, was both terrifying and comforting.

Isabel didn't know how long she had been lost in her thoughts before she heard the soft knock at her front door. Her heart raced. Maybe it was Gabe again, coming by for another talk. A part of her hoped it was, though the other part—still guarded—wasn't quite ready.

She threw on a light sweater and made her way downstairs, her bare feet padding softly against the wooden floor. When she opened the door, it wasn't Gabe. Instead, she found Dylan leaning casually against the doorframe, a mischievous smile tugging at his lips.

"Good morning," Dylan greeted, his tone playful yet subdued.

Isabel blinked in surprise. She hadn't expected to see him again so soon, not after their somewhat strained conversation at the pub.

"Dylan," she said, pulling the door open wider to let him in. "I didn't expect to see you this early."

He stepped inside, his gaze wandering briefly around the room before settling on her again. "I figured we didn't really finish our conversation last night."

Isabel gave him a tentative smile, unsure of where this was going. "You're not wrong."

He followed her into the kitchen, where she instinctively began making coffee, the scent of freshly ground beans filling the air. They stood in silence for a moment, the weight of unspoken words hanging between them.

Dylan finally broke the silence. "Look, Isa, I know I've been distant. And I know that coming back here after all this time is probably stirring up a lot of things for you." He paused, his voice softening. "It's stirring up a lot for me, too."

She looked at him then, really looked at him. There was something in his eyes—regret, maybe? Or was it something more? The easy charm he had always worn so effortlessly seemed to have slipped away, leaving him vulnerable in a way she hadn't seen before.

"I'm not the same person I was when I left," Isabel admitted, her voice barely above a whisper. "I thought I'd changed. I thought coming back here would be easy. But it's not."

Dylan nodded, his expression serious. "None of us are the same, Isa. Time changes us, whether we want it to or not."

Isabel poured two mugs of coffee and handed one to Dylan, who accepted it with a grateful nod. She took a sip of hers, the warmth of the drink grounding her as she gathered her thoughts.

"You were always good at running from things," Dylan said, his voice gentle but pointed. "But you can't run from yourself, no matter how far you go."

His words struck a chord, hitting too close to home. Isabel set her mug down, her gaze drifting toward the window. She could see the lighthouse in the distance, its silhouette stark against the brightening sky.

"You sound like Sarah," she said with a small, humorless laugh.

"She's not wrong," Dylan replied. "And neither am I."

Isabel sighed, running a hand through her hair. She didn't want to admit that he had a point. That everyone seemed to have a point lately. But the truth was, she had been running—from her past, from her feelings, from everything. And now, it was all catching up with her.

"I've been back for a few days, and already everything feels so... complicated," Isabel confessed, her voice low. "I came here for solitude, to clear my head, but now it feels like I'm being pulled in every direction."

Dylan stepped closer, his expression softening. "You don't have to figure it all out right now. You don't have to make any big decisions. Just... take it one day at a time."

Isabel looked up at him, meeting his gaze. There was something comforting in his words, in the way he seemed to understand the turmoil she was feeling without pushing her for more than she was ready to give.

"Thanks, Dylan," she said quietly. "I mean it."

He gave her a small smile. "Anytime."

For a moment, the tension between them eased, the awkwardness of their earlier interactions giving way to something more familiar. But there was still a distance there, an unspoken understanding that while they had once shared something deep, time had changed them both.

"Are you planning to stick around the island for a while?" Isabel asked, trying to steer the conversation toward safer territory.

Dylan shrugged. "For now, yeah. I'm not in any rush to leave."

She nodded, unsure of how she felt about that. A part of her was relieved, knowing that she wouldn't have to face the ghosts of her past alone. But another part of her was wary—wary of what Dylan's presence might stir up, wary of the memories that still lingered between them.

Dylan set his mug down and glanced at the clock. "I should get going. Got some things to take care of."

Isabel walked him to the door, and as he turned to leave, he hesitated for a moment, as if he wanted to say something more.

"Isa," he began, his voice softer now, almost hesitant. "I don't know what's going on with you and Gabe, but... just be careful, okay?"

Isabel felt a pang of defensiveness rise in her chest. "Careful of what?"

Dylan met her gaze, his expression serious. "Just... don't let history repeat itself."

With that, he turned and walked away, leaving Isabel standing in the doorway, her mind racing. What had he meant by that? Was he warning her about Gabe, or was he warning her about herself?

Isabel closed the door and leaned against it, her heart pounding. Dylan's words echoed in her mind, but it was Gabe's face that filled her thoughts. The way he had looked at her last night, the quiet intensity in his eyes, the way he had made her feel seen in a way she hadn't in years.

She didn't want to admit it, but she was scared. Scared of getting hurt again. Scared of letting someone in, only to lose them. Scared that no matter how hard she tried to protect herself, the past would find a way to repeat itself.

But as she stood there, alone in the quiet of her house, Isabel realized something else—she was tired of running. Tired of holding back. Maybe, just maybe, it was time to stop being so careful. Time to take a risk, even if it meant getting hurt.

Isabel's thoughts drifted to the studio, to the painting she had uncovered the night before. The message, "The light will reveal what's hidden," seemed to take on new meaning now. Maybe it wasn't just about her mother's secrets. Maybe it was about her own.

With a determined breath, Isabel pushed herself off the door and headed toward the studio. There was more to uncover, more to learn. And maybe, just maybe, the answers she was searching for would help her make sense of the tangled mess of feelings she had for both Gabe and Dylan.

She wasn't sure what she would find, but for the first time in a long time, Isabel felt ready to face whatever was waiting for her.

As she opened the door to the studio, the faint scent of oil paint and dust greeted her, familiar and comforting. The painting stood on the easel, still unfinished, still mysterious. Isabel stepped closer, her eyes tracing the brushstrokes, searching for answers.

Maybe the light really would reveal what was hidden.

Isabel stood in front of the painting, feeling its weight settle over her like an invisible shroud. She stared at the delicate brushstrokes, the muted colors that hinted at something more, something just beyond reach. Her mother's artistry had always been a mystery to her—so layered, so subtle, like her emotions, never fully exposed.

She raised her hand to touch the canvas but stopped just short, letting her fingers hover millimeters from the surface. The memory of her mother flooded her mind, the soft cadence of her voice, the way she'd work in silence for hours in the studio, creating worlds with her hands.

A sudden knock at the door jolted Isabel from her reverie.

She turned, startled. Her heart skipped a beat as her mind immediately went to Gabe. Since their last conversation, she'd felt a tug, a quiet need to continue what they'd started, to peel back more layers of the silence between them. Maybe this was him—coming back, offering a bridge to what they'd both avoided for so long.

She opened the door, her breath catching slightly when she saw Gabe standing there. His expression was soft, but there was something in his eyes—a vulnerability she hadn't seen in years.

"Hey," he said, his voice low, almost tentative.

"Hey," she replied, stepping back to let him in.

He entered the studio slowly, his gaze immediately drawn to the painting. His brow furrowed as he studied it, then he looked back at her, a silent question in his eyes.

"I found it last night," Isabel explained, her voice barely above a whisper. "It's one of my mother's. She never finished it."

Gabe stepped closer to the painting, his fingers brushing the edge of the frame. "It's beautiful. There's something about it... like it's hiding something, you know?"

Isabel nodded, surprised at how easily he'd put her own feelings into words. "That's exactly how I feel. Like there's something underneath all of it—something I'm supposed to find."

He turned to her, the intensity in his gaze making her breath hitch. "Maybe it's not just about the painting."

Isabel blinked, her throat tightening. His words had struck a chord she wasn't ready to acknowledge. "What do you mean?"

Gabe hesitated, his eyes scanning her face as if trying to gauge how much to say. Then, with a deep breath, he spoke. "You're not just looking for your mother's secrets, Isabel. You're looking for yourself."

The truth of it hit her like a wave, and she had to steady herself, leaning against the edge of the table. She hadn't expected him to see that, to understand the depth of what this was doing to her. But he always had, hadn't he? Even when they were younger, Gabe had this way of cutting through the layers she wrapped herself in, finding the heart of what she was too afraid to confront.

Isabel's defenses began to crumble, and before she knew it, words were spilling out of her.

"I don't know who I am anymore, Gabe," she confessed, her voice trembling. "Coming back here—it was supposed to help, but all it's done is bring back everything I tried to bury."

Gabe stepped closer, his hand hovering near hers, but not quite touching. "What are you afraid of?"

Isabel swallowed hard, the weight of her fears crashing down on her. She'd spent years running, avoiding, hiding from the pain, from the past. But now, here with Gabe, with the painting, with her mother's legacy all around her—there was no more running.

"I'm afraid of being vulnerable," she whispered, her eyes fixed on the floor. "I'm afraid that if I open up, if I let people in, they'll see how broken I really am."

Gabe's breath hitched, his hand finally finding hers, his touch warm and grounding. "You're not broken, Isabel. You've been through a lot, but that doesn't make you broken. It makes you strong."

Isabel felt her eyes sting with unshed tears. She hadn't cried in so long, hadn't allowed herself that release. But here, now, with Gabe standing so close, she felt the walls inside her cracking.

"Do you ever regret it?" she asked suddenly, her voice thick with emotion. "Leaving the island... leaving me?"

Gabe's expression tightened, and for a moment, she thought he wouldn't answer. But then, with a heavy sigh, he spoke. "I didn't want to leave, Isabel. But I felt like I had to. I thought maybe if I got away, I'd find a way to be enough for you. But the truth is, I was running too—just like you."

Isabel stared at him, her heart aching. She had always wondered what had driven him away, had always assumed it was something about her that hadn't been enough. But now, hearing him admit that he had been just as lost, just as scared, made her see things differently.

"Why didn't you tell me?" she asked, her voice soft but urgent.

Gabe looked away, his jaw tightening. "Because I was a coward. I didn't want you to see how messed up I was. I didn't want to drag you down with me."

Isabel shook her head, a sad smile tugging at her lips. "We could've helped each other, you know."

Gabe finally met her gaze, the vulnerability in his eyes mirroring her own. "I know that now. But back then... I didn't see it. All I saw was my own fear."

They stood there in silence for a long moment, the weight of their shared history filling the space between them. Isabel could feel the shift—something was changing between them, something deep and unspoken. And it scared her, but it also felt right.

She looked at Gabe, her heart pounding. "What now?"

Gabe's eyes softened, and he took a step closer, closing the gap between them. "I don't know. But I do know that I don't want to run anymore."

Isabel felt her heart swell at his words. She didn't want to run anymore either.

"I don't either," she whispered, her voice barely audible.

For the first time in what felt like forever, she allowed herself to be vulnerable. She allowed herself to feel, to hope, to believe that maybe, just maybe, there was a way forward.

Gabe reached out and gently cupped her cheek, his thumb brushing against her skin. "You don't have to do this alone, Isabel. I'm here. I've always been here."

And in that moment, with the weight of their past hanging between them and the promise of something new lingering in the air, Isabel felt a glimmer of hope.

Maybe this was where healing began.

Maybe this was where they both found their way back to each other—and to themselves.

For a long time, they stood there in the studio, the unfinished painting behind them, the world outside fading away. In that small, sacred space, the walls they'd built around themselves began to fall.

And as they shared that quiet moment of understanding, Isabel knew that this was only the beginning. There would be more hard conversations, more painful truths to confront, but for the first time in a long time, she wasn't afraid.

She wasn't alone.

And maybe, just maybe, she was finally ready to let someone in.

6

⚜

Chapter 6: The Storm

The first rumble of thunder rolled in from the horizon as Isabel stood at the edge of the pier, staring out into the darkening sky. The wind whipped her hair around her face, and the scent of rain hung thick in the air. She could feel the storm coming, its energy pulsing through her like a live wire, but she made no move to seek shelter. Instead, she welcomed it. The storm outside seemed to mirror the turmoil inside her, the unrest that had been building since her return to the island.

Behind her, she heard Gabe's familiar footsteps approaching. She didn't turn to greet him, but his presence was steady, grounding her in a way she hadn't expected. She felt him stop just beside her, close enough that his shoulder brushed hers. For a moment, neither of them spoke. The only sound was the wind and the distant growl of the approaching storm.

"You're not going to stay out here, are you?" Gabe finally asked, his voice low and calm, though laced with concern.

Isabel shook her head, though she didn't move. "It feels like the storm is what I need right now."

Gabe didn't respond immediately, but he stayed beside her, his silence a quiet acceptance of whatever she was feeling. There was something about his wordless presence that gave her space to breathe, to let the storm in her soul settle, if only for a moment.

The first drops of rain fell, light and scattered at first, then heavier as the sky opened up. Gabe glanced at her again, his brows furrowed slightly in question, but when she didn't budge, he simply stood there, letting the rain wash over them both.

Isabel finally turned to look at him. His hair was damp, and the droplets clung to his skin, but his eyes held that steady warmth, the same quiet strength she'd come to lean on without even realizing it.

"Come inside," he said softly, not as a command but as an invitation.

For a moment, Isabel considered refusing, but there was something in the way he said it—like the storm wasn't just outside anymore but part of the space between them. The vulnerability they'd shared in the studio was still raw, hanging in the air like the storm clouds above them. Isabel wasn't ready to face it all, but she couldn't turn away either. Not from him.

She nodded slowly, and Gabe didn't wait for her to change her mind. He took her hand, his fingers strong and sure as they wrapped around hers, and gently guided her back toward the house.

Inside, the storm battered against the windows, the rain drumming in a constant rhythm as the wind howled through the cracks in the old wooden walls. The electricity flickered, casting brief shadows across the room, before plunging them into darkness. The dim light from the fireplace was the only source of warmth now, and Isabel couldn't help but feel the intimacy of the moment—the quiet, the storm, the proximity of Gabe beside her.

"Looks like we lost power," Gabe murmured, his voice soft as he moved to stoke the fire, bringing the flames back to life.

Isabel watched him, the flickering light casting warm hues across his face. She sat down on the old, worn couch, pulling her knees up to her chest, her gaze following the dance of the fire as the room filled with a quiet, soothing heat.

Gabe turned and sat beside her, not too close but close enough that she could feel his presence like a protective barrier against the storm outside. The silence stretched between them, but it wasn't uncomfortable. Instead, it felt like a moment of shared peace, a respite from everything that had been swirling around them since her return to the island.

The storm raged on, the thunder growing louder, but inside the cottage, everything felt still, calm. For the first time in what felt like ages, Isabel wasn't drowning in her thoughts. The quiet was no longer oppressive; it was... comforting.

Without thinking, Isabel leaned slightly into Gabe, her shoulder pressing into his arm. It was such a small gesture, but it felt like a massive step for her—allowing herself to be this close to someone, to trust that she didn't need to carry all her burdens alone.

Gabe didn't move. He didn't need to. The weight of his silence was enough. There was no need for words, no need to fill the space between them with explanations or reassurances. Just being there, together, was enough.

Isabel closed her eyes, letting the sound of the rain lull her into a state of calm. The fire crackled, the warmth seeping into her bones, and she allowed herself to relax for the first time since she'd come back to the island.

Gabe shifted beside her, and Isabel opened her eyes to find him watching her, his expression soft, unreadable. There was something about the way he looked at her that made her heart stutter—an unspoken understanding, a connection that went beyond words.

"You okay?" he asked quietly, his voice barely above a whisper.

Isabel nodded, not trusting herself to speak. She wasn't okay—not entirely—but for the first time, she felt like she could be. Like maybe, in this moment, with Gabe sitting beside her, she didn't have to have all the answers. She didn't have to be anything more than what she was right now—just Isabel.

Gabe smiled faintly, and for a brief second, Isabel allowed herself to wonder what might happen if she let go. If she allowed herself to lean on him, to let him in. The thought scared her, but it also thrilled her in a way she hadn't expected.

"I used to love storms," Gabe said suddenly, his gaze drifting to the window. "When we were kids, remember? We'd sit on the porch and watch the lightning."

Isabel smiled at the memory. "Yeah. I remember."

They used to stay up late on nights like this, daring each other to see who could stay outside the longest, watching the lightning crack across the sky. It had been one of the few things they shared back then, a strange but comforting ritual between them.

Gabe leaned back against the couch, his arm resting along the top of it, close to Isabel's head. The gesture was so familiar, so simple, but it stirred something deep inside her. She glanced at him out of the corner of her eye, watching the way the firelight danced across his face, highlighting the strong lines of his jaw, the softness in his eyes.

"What changed?" she asked softly, not sure if she was asking about him or herself—or maybe both.

Gabe didn't answer right away. He seemed to be searching for the right words, but when he finally spoke, his voice was gentle.

"I think we both did. Life changes you, you know? Sometimes, in ways you don't expect."

Isabel nodded, her throat tight. She knew that better than anyone. Life had changed her in ways she still wasn't sure she fully understood.

They lapsed into silence again, but this time, it was a different kind of quiet. It wasn't the tense, uncomfortable stillness that had often hung between them since her return. It was... peaceful. Almost like they were finding their way back to each other, slowly, without needing to force it.

The fire crackled, the storm continued its furious assault on the island, but inside, everything felt safe. Isabel leaned into Gabe a little more, testing the waters, and when he didn't pull away, she allowed herself to rest her head on his shoulder. It was such a small gesture, but it felt like a monumental leap for her.

For a moment, Gabe didn't move. Then, slowly, he lifted his arm and wrapped it around her shoulders, pulling her closer. His warmth enveloped her, and Isabel felt a quiet sense of relief wash over her.

They didn't speak. There was no need. The storm outside was loud enough, filling the space with its power, but inside, they were cocooned in their own little world, a world where words were unnecessary.

The storm would pass, Isabel knew that. But for now, in this moment, she let herself stay here, in the quiet, in the safety of Gabe's presence. The weight of the past, the uncertainty of the future—it all seemed distant, irrelevant. All that mattered was now.

Isabel closed her eyes, her body relaxing into Gabe's as the storm raged on, and for the first time in a long time, she felt something close to peace.

She didn't know what would come next. There were still so many questions, so many unresolved feelings, but for tonight, she allowed herself to simply be.

The storm outside had calmed to a steady rhythm, with the wind no longer howling but whistling softly through the cracks in the windows. The rain fell in a light, constant drizzle, and the occasional roll of distant thunder echoed across the island, a fading reminder of its earlier fury. Inside the cottage, the fire still crackled, casting a warm glow that danced along the walls. Isabel remained nestled against Gabe, her head resting on his shoulder. The quiet between them felt like an unspoken agreement, a shared peace that neither wanted to disturb.

Isabel had never been one to let her guard down easily, but something about this moment—about being here with Gabe—felt different. For the first time in years, she allowed herself to enjoy the stillness, to feel comfort in someone else's presence without the fear of being judged or misunderstood.

She could feel the steady rise and fall of Gabe's chest beneath her cheek, his breathing slow and calm, as if he were content to sit there in silence with her for as long as she needed. It was a strange feeling, this quiet intimacy, one that Isabel wasn't used to but found herself craving more and more.

"I missed this," Gabe said softly, his voice barely louder than the crackling of the fire. His arm, still wrapped around her, gave her a gentle squeeze as if to emphasize his words. "Not just this moment, but... being close to you. Being able to sit like this, without needing to say anything."

Isabel didn't reply right away, unsure of how to respond. The truth was, she had missed it too, though she hadn't allowed herself to admit it until now. She had spent so long keeping people at a distance, building walls around herself to keep from getting hurt again, that she had forgotten what it felt like to simply be with someone. To share a moment without expectation, without the fear of what might come next.

"I missed it too," she finally whispered, her voice soft but honest.

Gabe didn't say anything, but the way he shifted slightly, pulling her just a bit closer, told her that he understood. They stayed like that for a long while, the fire crackling softly in the background, the rain tapping lightly against the windows. It was as if the storm had washed away some of the tension between them, leaving behind only the quiet comfort of being near one another.

But even as Isabel allowed herself to relax in Gabe's arms, she couldn't ignore the thoughts swirling in the back of her mind. The questions, the doubts. She had come back to the island hoping to find some answers, to reconnect with the pieces of herself that she had left behind, but now that she was here, everything felt more complicated than she had expected.

Gabe's presence stirred something deep inside her, something she hadn't allowed herself to feel in years. But it also made her question whether she was ready for it—ready for him, for what they might become. The storm outside had passed, but the storm inside her was just beginning.

"I used to think I'd never come back here," Isabel admitted suddenly, the words slipping out before she had a chance to stop them. She didn't know why she was saying it, why she was opening up to Gabe in a way she hadn't opened up to anyone in years, but once she started, she couldn't seem to stop. "I thought I could leave this place behind. Leave everything behind. But... it's harder than I thought."

Gabe's hand rested gently on her arm, his touch steady and reassuring. "Sometimes it's not about leaving things behind," he said quietly. "Sometimes it's about coming back to face them. To see what's left and figure out what still matters."

Isabel swallowed hard, her throat tight with emotion. She had spent so long running—from the island, from her past, from herself—that she wasn't sure how to stop. How to face the things she had buried deep inside.

"Do you think that's why you're here?" Gabe asked, his voice soft but probing. "To face whatever it is you left behind?"

Isabel turned her head slightly, her gaze shifting to the flickering flames in the fireplace. The warmth of the fire seemed to mirror the warmth of Gabe's presence, but it didn't chase away the cold knot of uncertainty in her chest.

"I don't know," she admitted. "I thought I came back to... I don't even know. To find closure, maybe. To make sense of everything that happened."

Gabe's hand gently traced a path down her arm, his touch grounding her, reminding her that she wasn't alone in this. "And have you?" he asked softly. "Found what you were looking for?"

Isabel closed her eyes, letting out a slow, shaky breath. "I don't know," she said again, her voice barely above a whisper. "I don't even know if I know what I'm looking for."

Gabe was silent for a moment, and when he spoke, his words were thoughtful, measured. "Sometimes we don't know what we're looking for until we find it. And sometimes... it's not about finding answers. It's about accepting the questions."

Isabel didn't respond right away, but Gabe's words resonated with her. She had spent so much time searching for answers, for something to explain the emptiness she had felt for so long. But maybe Gabe was right. Maybe it wasn't about finding answers. Maybe it was about accepting that some things couldn't be explained, that some parts of her past would always be messy, unresolved.

The fire crackled softly, and Isabel leaned into Gabe a little more, allowing herself to find comfort in his presence. For the first time in a long time, she didn't feel the need to run, to push him away. Instead, she allowed herself to simply be—to exist in this moment, without worrying about what it meant or what would come next.

They sat in silence for a while longer, the storm outside fading into the distance, leaving only the gentle sound of rain tapping against the windows. Isabel's thoughts drifted, but for once, they didn't feel overwhelming. She wasn't drowning in them the way she usually did. Instead, she felt like she was floating, anchored by the steady presence of Gabe beside her.

Eventually, Gabe shifted, breaking the silence but not the connection between them. "I should probably get going," he said quietly, though his tone was reluctant. "The storm's letting up."

Isabel hesitated, not wanting the moment to end, but she nodded. "Yeah. You're right."

Gabe stood, offering her a hand to help her up from the couch. Isabel took it, her fingers lingering in his for a moment longer than necessary. When she looked up at him, she saw something in his eyes—something unspoken, but undeniable.

"Thanks for staying," she said softly, her voice carrying more weight than just gratitude for his company during the storm. It felt like she was thanking him for more than that—for being there, for not pushing her, for understanding her in a way that no one else seemed to.

Gabe's lips quirked into a small, almost sad smile. "Anytime, Isabel."

For a moment, they stood there in the soft glow of the fire, the air between them charged with something Isabel couldn't quite name. She felt her heart beat a little faster, her pulse quicken, and for a split second, she wondered if he felt it too.

But then Gabe stepped back, his hand slipping from hers as he moved toward the door. Isabel watched him go, her heart heavy with something she couldn't quite define—regret, maybe, or longing. Or maybe both.

"I'll see you around," he said, his voice quiet but steady.

Isabel nodded, watching as he opened the door and stepped out into the night. The rain had slowed to a light drizzle, the storm a distant memory now, but the weight of their conversation lingered in the air.

As the door closed behind him, Isabel stood in the silence of the cottage, the warmth of the fire still flickering, but the absence of Gabe's presence felt almost palpable. She wrapped her arms around herself, feeling the weight of everything they had shared settle over her.

The storm had passed, but the questions remained.

And for the first time, Isabel wasn't sure if she wanted to find the answers—or if she was content to simply live with the uncertainty.

Isabel stood in the doorway for what felt like minutes, though it could have been longer. The soft patter of the rain outside was the only sound now, a steady hum that contrasted with the stillness inside the cottage. Gabe's absence left a strange, empty space around her. She could still feel the warmth of his presence, the echo of their shared silence, but now she was alone again.

Closing the door quietly behind her, Isabel walked back toward the fire, which had started to die down, its embers glowing softly. She crouched in front of the hearth, stoking it gently to bring the flames back to life. The light danced on the walls once more, but the cottage felt different—quieter, as if the energy Gabe had brought with him had left along with him.

Sitting cross-legged in front of the fire, Isabel stared into the flickering flames, letting her mind wander back to the conversation they'd had. It wasn't the words themselves that stuck with her but the feeling behind them—the vulnerability she hadn't expected to feel, and the quiet understanding in Gabe's eyes. He hadn't pushed her to explain herself, hadn't demanded answers or forced her to confront the tangled mess of emotions she'd buried for so long. Instead, he'd simply been there, steady and constant.

For years, Isabel had prided herself on her independence, on her ability to handle things alone. She had believed that solitude was a strength, a shield against the pain of opening herself up to others. But tonight, sitting by the fire with Gabe, she had felt something she hadn't allowed herself to feel in a long time—comfort. Not just the physical comfort of his presence, but the emotional safety of being with someone who seemed to understand her without needing explanations.

It was unsettling, that realization. Unsettling because it made her question everything she had believed about herself and her choices. Had she been wrong all this time? Had she been running from something she should have faced long ago?

Isabel sighed, running a hand through her hair as she tried to sort through the conflicting thoughts swirling in her mind. The truth was, she didn't have answers—not for herself, and certainly not for Gabe. All she knew was that something had shifted between them tonight, something subtle but undeniable. It was as if the storm outside had mirrored the storm within her, and now that it had passed, she was left with the quiet aftermath, unsure of what came next.

She stood up and walked over to the window, her reflection ghostly in the glass as she gazed out at the night. The rain had slowed to a fine mist, and the wind had calmed, leaving the island wrapped in a soft, damp stillness. It was the kind of night that invited introspection, that made the world feel both vast and small at the same time.

Isabel's thoughts drifted back to the island itself, to the reason she had returned after all these years. The memories were as tangled as her emotions, filled with both love and loss, joy and pain. This place had been her home once, a place where she had felt safe and rooted. But it had also been the place where everything had fallen apart, where she had lost not only her mother but also a piece of herself.

And now, here she was again, standing on the same ground, facing the same ghosts. Only this time, the ghosts weren't just memories—they were the unfinished conversations, the unresolved emotions she had been too afraid to confront.

As she stood there, lost in thought, her mind returned to the studio, to the painting she had found. It had felt like a doorway into her mother's world, a glimpse of something Isabel hadn't known existed. The image of the lighthouse, with its strange, obscured symbol, lingered in her mind, pulling at the edges of her consciousness. What had her mother been trying to say with that painting? What secrets had she hidden in her art?

The questions gnawed at Isabel, their weight growing heavier the more she thought about them. Her mother had always been a mystery, even when she was alive—a woman of few words, but deep, unspoken thoughts. Now, all these years later, it seemed that the mysteries hadn't faded with time; they had only deepened.

Isabel moved away from the window and began pacing the small living room, her mind racing with possibilities. She couldn't shake the feeling that the painting was a clue, a message left for her to discover. But what did it mean? And why had her mother been so secretive?

The words her mother had written on the sketches came back to her: "The light will reveal what's hidden." It had sounded cryptic at the time, but now Isabel wondered if there was more to it—if her mother had been trying to guide her toward something, some truth that had been obscured all these years.

She glanced toward the door, the urge to return to the studio bubbling up inside her. It was late, and the rain was still falling, but the pull of the painting was stronger than her need for sleep. She needed to see it again, needed to try to make sense of what her mother had left behind.

Without giving herself time to second-guess the decision, Isabel grabbed her raincoat and slipped it on, pulling the hood up over her head as she stepped outside. The mist clung to her skin as she made her way through the wet grass, her footsteps soft against the damp earth. The air smelled of rain and salt, the familiar scent of the island wrapping around her as she walked.

The studio loomed ahead, dark and silent, but the moment Isabel stepped inside, she felt the same sense of anticipation she had felt earlier, as if the room itself held its breath, waiting for her to uncover its secrets. She flicked on the light, the soft glow illuminating the unfinished canvases and scattered sketches that filled the space.

The painting was still there, propped against the easel where she had left it. Isabel approached it slowly, her eyes tracing the familiar lines of the lighthouse, the stormy sky, the waves crashing against the shore. But it was the symbol—the one partially obscured by the light—that drew her attention.

She crouched down in front of the canvas, studying it more closely than she had before. The symbol was strange, abstract, almost like a collection of lines and shapes that didn't quite form a coherent picture. But the more she looked at it, the more it felt like there was something just out of reach, something hidden beneath the surface, waiting to be uncovered.

"The light will reveal what's hidden," she whispered to herself, the words echoing in the quiet studio.

Isabel grabbed a nearby rag and began carefully wiping away the layer of dust and grime that had gathered on the surface of the painting. As she worked, the symbol began to take on more definition, the lines becoming clearer, though still strange and unfamiliar.

She leaned in closer, her breath catching in her throat as she realized what she was seeing. The symbol wasn't just random shapes—it was something much more deliberate, much more meaningful.

A wave of emotion washed over her, a mixture of awe and confusion, as the symbol slowly revealed itself to her. It was a lighthouse, but not just any lighthouse—it was the one on the island, the one she had visited so many times as a child. And surrounding it were symbols that seemed to hint at something deeper, something she couldn't quite grasp yet.

Her heart pounded in her chest as she stared at the painting, the weight of her mother's secrets pressing down on her. There was more to this than she had realized, more than just a painting or a cryptic note. This was a key, a map to something hidden in plain sight.

But what was it? And why had her mother kept it a secret?

Isabel sat back on her heels, the enormity of the discovery settling over her. She had come back to the island searching for answers, but now it seemed that she had only found more questions—questions that led back to the lighthouse, to her mother, to the part of herself she had never fully understood.

And now, standing in the quiet of the studio, Isabel knew that she couldn't ignore the pull any longer. She had to follow the clues, had to uncover the truth, no matter where it led her.

Her mother had left her a trail, and it was up to her to find the light that would reveal what had been hidden all these years.

As the storm outside began to wane, Isabel found herself still lost in thought, the traces of the tempest lingering in the chilled air of Gabe's cabin. The fire had dwindled to a gentle glow, casting long shadows on the walls that seemed to sway with the last gusts of wind. Gabe had quietly made his way to the small kitchenette, and Isabel could hear the faint clinking of dishes as he prepared something warm for them both.

Despite the storm's departure, the storm within Isabel remained. The night had stripped away her defenses, leaving her raw and exposed. The simple act of sitting so close to Gabe, sharing the space in such an intimate way, had stirred something deep within her—something she hadn't fully acknowledged until now. The silence between them was thick, laden with the weight of unsaid words and unspoken feelings.

Gabe returned with two mugs of steaming herbal tea, their scent mingling with the lingering aroma of rain and wood smoke. He handed one to Isabel, their fingers brushing lightly. The touch sent a shiver up her spine, and she looked up to meet his gaze. Gabe's eyes were soft, full of a quiet concern that she couldn't quite place.

"Thanks," she said, her voice barely more than a whisper. She took the mug from him, feeling the warmth seep through the ceramic into her cold hands. The heat was soothing, but it did little to dispel the turmoil inside her.

Gabe settled down on the other side of the small table, his movements deliberate and unhurried. He sipped his tea, his gaze not quite meeting hers but never straying too far. The silence was comfortable, yet charged, each of them wrapped in their own thoughts.

Isabel finally broke the silence, her voice trembling slightly. "I didn't expect the storm to be so... intense. It's been a while since I felt so vulnerable."

Gabe looked up, his expression thoughtful. "The island has a way of bringing out those feelings. It's like it's always been a part of us, even when we try to leave it behind."

Isabel nodded, the truth of his words resonating deeply within her. "I've been trying to figure out why I came back here, why I felt this pull to return after all these years. It's like the island is holding onto something, and I can't let go until I understand it."

Gabe leaned back in his chair, the flickering firelight playing across his face. "Sometimes, we have to confront the things we've left behind to move forward. It's not always easy, but it's necessary."

His words were both reassuring and unsettling. Isabel felt a pang of vulnerability, a desire to share her fears and regrets. But she hesitated, unsure of how much to reveal. She had always kept her emotions tightly controlled, preferring to deal with her struggles alone. But tonight had been different—Gabe's presence had made her feel exposed in a way she wasn't used to.

Taking a deep breath, she decided to test the waters. "There's something I've been hiding from myself. Something I've been afraid to face."

Gabe's eyes softened, and he set his mug down, giving her his full attention. "What is it?"

Isabel took another sip of her tea, trying to steady her nerves. "I've been running from my past for a long time. The engagement, my mother's death—everything just feels so overwhelming. I thought coming back here would help me find some clarity, but instead, it's made everything more complicated."

Gabe's gaze was steady, and for a moment, Isabel felt a flicker of hope. Maybe it was possible to open up, to let someone in after all these years of isolation. "I thought if I came back, I could figure things out. But instead, I'm finding more questions than answers. And the more I uncover, the more I realize how much I've been avoiding."

Gabe nodded, a trace of understanding in his eyes. "Facing our past is never easy. It's like we have to unravel the threads of our own lives to understand what they mean. And sometimes, we don't even know where to start."

Isabel looked down at her tea, the steam rising in delicate curls. "I found something in my mother's studio—a painting with a lighthouse and an obscure symbol. It feels like it's connected to something deeper, something I'm not fully grasping yet."

Gabe's interest was piqued, and he leaned forward slightly. "The lighthouse?"

Isabel nodded. "Yes. My mother had this way of hiding her emotions in her art. The painting seems to be a clue, but I don't know what it's pointing to. All I know is that it feels important, like it's part of a bigger picture I'm meant to uncover."

Gabe's expression was thoughtful. "Sometimes, art can be a way of communicating what words cannot. Maybe your mother left you these clues because she knew you'd need them."

Isabel's heart skipped a beat at the thought. "Do you really think so?"

Gabe nodded. "I do. And maybe the lighthouse is more than just a painting. Maybe it's a symbol of guidance, a way to lead you through your own storm."

Isabel looked at Gabe, her eyes searching his face for any hint of insincerity. But all she saw was genuine concern and a depth of understanding that she hadn't expected. For the first time in a long while, she felt like she wasn't alone in her struggle.

The silence between them was no longer uncomfortable but filled with a quiet camaraderie. Gabe's presence was a balm to her troubled soul, a reminder that she didn't have to face everything on her own. And in that moment, Isabel felt a glimmer of hope, a small but significant shift in her perception.

As the night wore on and the fire slowly burned down, Isabel and Gabe continued to talk, their conversation flowing easily despite the earlier tension. They shared stories from their past, their hopes and fears, their regrets and dreams. Gabe spoke of his life on the island, of the connections he had made with the land and its people. Isabel spoke of her travels, her career, and the emptiness she had felt despite her successes.

The more they talked, the more Isabel realized how much she had missed this kind of connection—this open, honest exchange of thoughts and feelings. It was something she had pushed away for so long, convinced that solitude was her only refuge. But now, in Gabe's presence, she saw a different path—one where vulnerability and connection could lead to healing and growth.

As the fire finally began to fade, Gabe rose from his chair and stretched, his movements slow and deliberate. "It's getting late. You should probably get some rest."

Isabel nodded, her heart feeling lighter than it had in a long time. "Thank you, Gabe. For everything. I didn't realize how much I needed this."

Gabe gave her a gentle smile. "Anytime. You don't have to face things alone, Isabel. Sometimes, sharing our burdens can make them easier to bear."

Isabel smiled back, feeling a warmth that went beyond the fire. "I'll remember that."

Gabe gave her a nod and made his way to the door, pausing for a moment before leaving. "Goodnight, Isabel."

"Goodnight, Gabe."

As Gabe stepped out into the misty night, Isabel watched him go, her heart full of a new sense of hope and connection. She turned back to the fire, the room now dim and quiet. The storm had passed, and though the night was still young, she felt a renewed sense of calm.

With a final glance at the flickering embers, Isabel turned and made her way to the small bedroom at the back of the cabin. The bed was simple but comfortable, and as she settled beneath the covers, she felt the weariness of the day begin to take its toll.

But even as she closed her eyes, she couldn't shake the feeling that something had shifted within her. The storm had not only changed the weather but had also opened a new chapter in her life—one filled with possibilities and discoveries. And with Gabe by her side, she felt ready to face whatever lay ahead.

As dawn broke, the island awoke with a renewed sense of calm, the storm's fury now a distant memory. Isabel stirred beneath the covers, the events of the previous night lingering in her mind. Gabe's quiet presence, their shared vulnerability, and the gentle warmth of the cabin all seemed to blend into a comforting haze.

She got out of bed, stretching with a sigh as she walked over to the window. The view was stunning: the storm had washed the island clean, leaving behind a serene landscape bathed in the soft light of morning. The air was crisp, and the sky was a clear, bril-

liant blue—a perfect day for reflection and perhaps, a new beginning.

Isabel took a moment to gather herself before heading to the
small kitchen, where the aroma of fresh coffee greeted her. Gabe
was already up, his movements easy and unhurried as he prepared
breakfast. He glanced up as she entered, a warm smile playing on
his lips.

"Good morning," he said, his voice carrying a soft, reassuring
tone.

"Morning," Isabel replied, her smile genuine. "You didn't have
to make breakfast."

Gabe shrugged, his eyes twinkling with a hint of amusement.
"Just thought I'd return the favor. You've had quite the night."

Isabel laughed softly. "I guess I have. Thank you."

They sat down at the small table, the conversation flowing easily as they shared a simple breakfast of eggs and toast. The storm
had left behind a quiet intimacy between them, and their conversation was filled with a newfound openness.

"So," Gabe said as he buttered his toast, "what are your plans
for today? More exploring, or are you going to tackle that studio?"

Isabel hesitated, her thoughts drifting back to the painting and
the clues it might hold. "I think I'll go back to the studio. There's
something about that painting—it feels like it's leading me somewhere."

Gabe nodded, his expression thoughtful. "If you need any help,
let me know. I know the island pretty well and might be able to
offer some insight."

Isabel's heart warmed at his offer. "I appreciate that. I might
just take you up on it."

After breakfast, they cleared the table together, their movements in sync as they worked side by side. The simple act of

sharing a meal had deepened their connection, and Isabel felt a growing sense of comfort with Gabe—a feeling she hadn't expected to find so quickly.

When they finished, Gabe gave her a nod toward the door. "I'll walk you to the studio if you're ready."

Isabel smiled, grateful for the company. "That would be great."

They stepped outside into the cool morning air, the remnants of the storm still visible in the scattered puddles and the occasional drifts of fog. The island felt peaceful, almost like it was holding its breath, waiting for Isabel to uncover its secrets.

As they walked along the winding path to the studio, Gabe fell into step beside her, their conversation shifting to lighter topics. They spoke about their favorite parts of the island, local events, and even a bit about their own lives. The easy rapport between them made the walk pleasant, and Isabel found herself opening up more than she had intended.

When they reached the studio, the sight of it brought back the intensity of the previous night. Isabel's heart raced as she approached the door, the sense of anticipation almost overwhelming.

Gabe watched her with a mixture of curiosity and support. "Do you want me to come in with you?"

Isabel glanced back at him, her eyes reflecting a mix of emotions. "I think I need to do this alone. But thank you for offering."

Gabe nodded, a look of understanding on his face. "Alright. I'll be here if you need anything."

Isabel took a deep breath and opened the door, stepping into the studio. The room was just as she had left it—filled with the musty scent of old paint and wood. The painting of the lighthouse still stood prominently on the easel, its enigmatic symbol calling to her.

She approached the painting with a mixture of trepidation and resolve. The lighthouse seemed to cast a shadow of mystery, its light and the obscure symbol on it whispering secrets she was eager to uncover. Isabel reached out, her fingers gently tracing the edges of the canvas.

The painting was even more intricate up close. The lighthouse was depicted with a sense of grandeur and solitude, its beacon a swirl of luminous hues that seemed to dance on the canvas. The symbol, an abstract intertwining of lines and shapes, was both alluring and perplexing. Isabel felt a shiver as she traced the symbol with her eyes, trying to decipher its meaning.

She took out her notebook, jotting down her observations and feelings. As she wrote, she couldn't help but reflect on the conversations she'd had with Gabe. His insights about the island and the painting had given her a new perspective, one that made her wonder about the connections between her mother's art and her own life.

Isabel continued to explore the studio, moving from one corner to another. She discovered a small drawer in an old wooden desk, which she had overlooked the night before. Inside were more sketches and notes—some of them seemed to be preliminary studies for the lighthouse painting, while others were abstract and filled with cryptic symbols.

One note in particular caught her attention. It read: "The light will reveal what's hidden." Isabel's heart skipped a beat. The phrase echoed Gabe's earlier words and seemed to hint at something significant. What could the light reveal? And what was it hiding?

She carefully folded the note and slipped it into her pocket, her mind racing with possibilities. The studio had become a place of revelation, but also a place of deepening mystery. Each discovery led her to more questions, and the more she delved into her mother's world, the more she realized how much she had yet to understand.

The sound of the door opening behind her broke her reverie. Isabel turned to see Gabe standing in the doorway, his expression one of gentle curiosity.

"Find anything interesting?" he asked, his voice soft.

Isabel nodded, her eyes bright with a mix of excitement and confusion. "Yes. There's a lot more here than I expected. And I found a note that might be important."

Gabe stepped inside, his gaze settling on the painting and then on the sketches spread out on the desk. "Do you want to talk about it? Sometimes discussing things can help make sense of them."

Isabel hesitated, her thoughts swirling. She glanced at the painting, then back at Gabe. The idea of sharing her discoveries, of unraveling the mystery together, felt comforting. "I'd like that."

Gabe walked over to the desk, and they sat together, Isabel showing him the sketches and notes. As they discussed the painting and the note, Gabe's insights and observations added new layers to Isabel's understanding. His presence was reassuring, and his perspectives helped her see connections she might have missed on her own.

As the morning turned into afternoon, Isabel and Gabe continued their exploration of the studio. The bond between them grew stronger with each shared insight and discovery. Isabel felt a deep sense of gratitude for Gabe's support, and the warmth between them was a stark contrast to the cold isolation she had felt before.

By the time they decided to leave the studio, Isabel felt a renewed sense of purpose. The mysteries of the painting and the note were just beginning to unravel, and the journey of discovery was far from over. But with Gabe by her side, she felt ready to face whatever lay ahead.

As they walked back to the cabin, the island seemed to embrace them, its beauty and tranquility a testament to the new chapter unfolding in Isabel's life. The storm had passed, but the calm it left behind was filled with promise and possibility. And as Isabel and Gabe continued their journey, they both knew that the path ahead was one they would navigate together.

The afternoon sun cast a golden glow over Rosemere Isle, the storm's remnants creating a breathtaking backdrop. As Isabel and Gabe walked back to the cabin, the air was filled with a gentle, reassuring warmth. The shared experience of the storm and the intimacy of the morning had forged a bond between them, an unspoken understanding that deepened with each step.

Gabe glanced at Isabel, noting the contemplative look on her face. "You seemed really focused in the studio today. Anything in particular that stood out to you?"

Isabel's eyes met his, her expression a mixture of curiosity and vulnerability. "The painting and the note have me thinking a lot. The lighthouse symbolizes something important, but I'm not entirely sure what. It feels like it's pointing me towards something I need to understand."

Gabe nodded, his gaze thoughtful. "Sometimes, symbols like that are more about personal interpretation than universal meaning. Maybe it's about what you need to find in your own life."

Isabel smiled faintly, appreciating his perspective. "I guess that makes sense. I'm still trying to piece together how all of this connects to my mom and to me."

As they approached the cabin, Isabel's heart felt lighter, buoyed by Gabe's presence. The comfort of the cabin seemed to welcome them, a sanctuary from the world outside. They entered together, and the warm, cozy atmosphere of the space contrasted with the stormy weather they had experienced.

Gabe gestured toward the small sitting area. "Why don't we sit down and relax for a bit? We've had quite the day."

Isabel nodded, settling onto the sofa as Gabe went to make them both some tea. She looked around the room, her thoughts drifting back to the studio and the sense of discovery it had brought. The room was filled with the gentle hum of the kettle and the soft clinking of cups, a soothing backdrop to her reflections.

Gabe returned with two steaming mugs, handing one to Isabel before sitting down beside her. "Here you go. I thought you might like something warm after all that time in the studio."

Isabel took the mug gratefully, savoring the comforting warmth of the tea. "Thank you. This is exactly what I needed."

They sipped their tea in a companionable silence, each lost in their own thoughts. The storm had left a sense of tranquility in its wake, and the quiet of the cabin was a welcome change from the chaos of the previous night.

After a while, Gabe broke the silence, his tone gentle. "You know, I've been thinking about what you said earlier, about the lighthouse and the symbols. Sometimes, the past can be like a storm—disruptive and overwhelming. But it can also clear the way for something new, something we might not have seen before."

Isabel looked at him, her eyes reflecting a mixture of gratitude and contemplation. "That's a really insightful way to put it. I hadn't thought of it like that. It feels like the storm is helping me see things more clearly."

Gabe's gaze softened. "I think that's true for a lot of people. Sometimes, it takes something dramatic to make us realize what we truly need or want."

Isabel nodded, her mind turning over his words. "I've been running from my past for a long time. Coming back here, seeing the studio and my mom's artwork—it's forcing me to confront things I'd rather avoid. But maybe that's exactly what I need."

Gabe reached out, gently placing his hand over hers. The touch was warm and reassuring, and Isabel felt a shiver of connection run through her. "Facing the past isn't easy, but you don't have to do it alone. I'm here to help, if you want."

The sincerity in Gabe's voice touched Isabel deeply. She looked at him, her eyes shining with a mix of gratitude and vulnerability. "Thank you, Gabe. That means a lot to me. I didn't expect to find such support here."

Gabe gave her hand a gentle squeeze. "I'm glad to be here for you. Sometimes, the support we need is closer than we think."

Their fingers lingered together for a moment, the contact a silent promise of solidarity and understanding. Isabel felt a surge of warmth and comfort, the tension of the past few days melting away in the quiet space they shared.

As the evening wore on, they continued to talk, their conversation weaving between light-hearted anecdotes and deeper reflections. Gabe's presence was a balm to Isabel's soul, and she found herself opening up in ways she hadn't anticipated.

At one point, Isabel shared a story about her mother, a memory from her childhood that had always stayed with her. "My mom used to take me to the lighthouse every summer. She'd tell me stories about the light guiding ships safely to shore, and she'd always say that the light was like a beacon of hope, even in the darkest times."

Gabe listened intently, his expression one of deep empathy. "That sounds like a special memory. It's no wonder the lighthouse is so significant to you."

Isabel nodded, a wistful smile on her lips. "Yes, it is. I've been thinking a lot about what she meant by those stories. It's like she was trying to teach me something important, something I'm only starting to understand now."

Gabe reached out, tucking a loose strand of hair behind her ear. The gesture was tender and intimate, and Isabel felt a flush of emotion. "Sometimes, the people we love leave us with clues about who we're meant to be. It sounds like your mom was trying to guide you, even from afar."

Isabel's eyes glistened with unshed tears, and she blinked rapidly to keep them at bay. "I think you're right. I just wish I knew how to make sense of it all."

Gabe's gaze was steady and reassuring. "You don't have to have all the answers right now. Sometimes, the journey is about exploring and discovering what resonates with you."

As the evening drew to a close, Gabe and Isabel continued to enjoy each other's company, the sense of intimacy growing stronger with each passing moment. The cabin, once a place of refuge, now felt like a space where new beginnings were possible.

When it was time for bed, Isabel felt a mixture of contentment and anticipation. The storm had passed, but its impact had left a lasting impression. The connection she felt with Gabe was something she hadn't expected, and it was becoming clear that the journey ahead was one she would not face alone.

As she lay in bed, the warmth of the cabin and the comfort of Gabe's presence lingered in her mind. She knew that the path to understanding her mother's secrets and her own past would be challenging, but she also felt a sense of hope. The storm had revealed not just the beauty of the island, but also the potential for healing and growth.

Isabel drifted off to sleep with a sense of peace, knowing that the journey ahead, though uncertain, was one she was ready to embrace. The storm had cleared the way, and the lighthouse, both a symbol and a guiding light, seemed to shine brighter than ever.

As dawn broke over Rosemere Isle, the morning light filtered through the cabin's windows, casting a soft glow over the room. The storm of the previous night had left the landscape refreshed, the world outside shimmering with renewed clarity. Isabel stirred slowly, feeling the gentle warmth beside her from where she lay on the sofa. Gabe's presence was a comforting anchor, his deep, rhythmic breathing a soothing background to her thoughts.

Isabel quietly slipped out from under the blanket, careful not to disturb Gabe, who had fallen asleep beside her after their shared tea and conversation. The cabin was still and peaceful, a stark contrast to the chaotic storm they had weathered together. She moved to the window and looked out at the island, its beauty now heightened by the aftermath of the storm.

She had spent the night reflecting on their conversation and the connection she felt with Gabe. The storm had revealed more than just the island's landscape; it had brought to light feelings and memories that Isabel had been avoiding. The shared intimacy of the night, combined with the physical closeness they had experienced, had created a bond that was both unexpected and profound.

As she gazed outside, her thoughts drifted to her mother's studio and the painting of the lighthouse. The symbolism of the lighthouse seemed to resonate more deeply now, its beam cutting through the darkness to reveal hidden truths. Isabel wondered if her mother's art was meant to guide her in the same way, offering insights into her past and her future.

The morning air was crisp as Isabel stepped outside, taking in the fresh scent of rain-soaked earth and the vibrant colors of the island. The world seemed to have been washed clean, each detail more vivid and alive. She walked along the path to the beach, her steps light and purposeful. The shoreline stretched out before her, the gentle waves lapping at the sand in a calming rhythm.

Isabel sat down on a smooth rock near the water's edge, her mind racing with thoughts about Gabe and the storm. The previous night had brought them closer, but it also left her with a sense of uncertainty. She was still grappling with her feelings and the implications of her growing connection with him.

As she sat there, she noticed a small, weathered boat anchored a short distance away. It was the same boat she had seen in Gabe's workshop, a reminder of their earlier interaction. She felt a pang of curiosity and a desire to understand more about Gabe's life and the world he had built on the island.

Lost in her thoughts, Isabel almost didn't notice when Gabe appeared beside her, his presence a quiet reassurance. He had dressed casually in jeans and a shirt, his hair still slightly tousled from sleep. He sat down next to her, his expression thoughtful.

"Morning," he said softly, his voice carrying the warmth of their shared night. "I hope I didn't wake you."

Isabel smiled, shaking her head. "No, not at all. I was just thinking about last night and everything we talked about. It feels like a lot has changed in a short time."

Gabe nodded, his gaze following the waves. "It has been a whirlwind. But sometimes, those moments of connection and clarity come when we least expect them."

Isabel looked at him, her eyes reflecting a mix of appreciation and uncertainty. "I feel like I'm starting to understand more about my mom and myself, but it's also overwhelming. I'm not sure where to go from here."

Gabe turned to face her, his expression gentle. "You don't have to have all the answers right now. Sometimes, it's about taking things one step at a time and letting the process unfold naturally."

Isabel's eyes met his, searching for reassurance. "I've been avoiding facing the past for so long. Now that I'm here, it feels like everything is catching up with me."

Gabe reached out, placing a comforting hand on her shoulder. "Facing the past is never easy, but you're not alone in this. I'm here to support you, and we can figure things out together."

The sincerity in his voice and the warmth of his touch gave Isabel a sense of comfort. She appreciated his presence and the way he seemed to understand her struggles without needing her to explain everything.

As they sat together, the sun continued to rise, casting a golden light over the island. The tranquility of the beach and the gentle sound of the waves created a serene atmosphere, and Isabel felt a renewed sense of hope. The storm had cleared the way, revealing not just the beauty of the island but also the potential for personal growth and healing.

After a while, Gabe stood up and extended his hand to Isabel. "How about we go for a walk and explore the island a bit? I can show you some of the places that are special to me."

Isabel took his hand, feeling a rush of warmth at the simple gesture. "I'd like that. I think it would be good to get out and see more of the island."

They walked along the shoreline, the sand warm beneath their feet. Gabe pointed out various landmarks, sharing stories about the island's history and his own experiences growing up there. Isabel listened intently, her curiosity about Gabe's life growing with each story he told.

As they ventured further, Gabe led her to a secluded cove, its beauty hidden from the main paths. The water here was a striking shade of turquoise, and the surrounding cliffs provided a dramatic backdrop. Isabel stood in awe, taking in the view.

"This is one of my favorite spots," Gabe said, his voice carrying a sense of pride. "It's quiet and peaceful, a place where I come to think and reflect."

Isabel looked at him, her eyes filled with admiration. "It's absolutely beautiful. Thank you for sharing it with me."

Gabe smiled, his expression warm. "I'm glad you like it. It feels special to share these places with someone who appreciates them."

As they continued to explore, Isabel felt a growing sense of connection with Gabe. The more she learned about him and the island, the more she felt that their paths were intertwined. The storm had not only brought them closer but had also opened up new possibilities for their relationship.

By the time they returned to the cabin, the sun was high in the sky, casting a golden light over the island. Isabel felt a renewed sense of clarity and hope. The storm had been a catalyst for change, and the journey she was on with Gabe was beginning to take shape.

As they reached the cabin, Gabe turned to her, his expression thoughtful. "How about we make some lunch and then head back to the studio? I'd like to help you with whatever you're working on."

Isabel's heart swelled with gratitude. "That sounds perfect. I'd appreciate your help."

They spent the afternoon working together in the studio, their conversation flowing easily as they tackled various tasks. Gabe's presence was a source of comfort and support, and Isabel found herself opening up more about her thoughts and feelings.

The connection they had forged during the storm continued to grow, and Isabel felt a deepening sense of intimacy with Gabe. The shared experiences and moments of vulnerability had created a strong foundation for their relationship, and she was beginning to see a future filled with possibilities.

As the day drew to a close, Isabel reflected on the journey she had been on since returning to the island. The storm had been a turning point, and the connection she felt with Gabe was a beacon of hope in her life. She knew that there were still challenges ahead, but with Gabe by her side, she felt ready to face them.

The evening arrived with a sense of calm, the island bathed in the soft glow of twilight. Isabel and Gabe sat together on the porch, watching as the sun dipped below the horizon. The world seemed to be settling into a peaceful rhythm, and Isabel felt a deep sense of contentment.

As they sat in comfortable silence, Isabel turned to Gabe, her expression filled with warmth. "Thank you for everything today. It's been a really meaningful day for me."

Gabe looked at her, his eyes reflecting his own gratitude. "I'm glad I could be here for you. It feels like we've made a lot of progress."

Isabel nodded, feeling a renewed sense of hope and possibility. The storm had cleared the way for a new chapter in her life, and with Gabe's support, she was ready to embrace whatever came next.

As the night settled in, Isabel and Gabe shared a quiet moment of connection, the stars shining brightly above them. The journey ahead was uncertain, but with each passing day, Isabel felt more confident in her ability to face the challenges and embrace the opportunities that awaited her. The storm had brought them closer, and the future seemed filled with promise.

As the evening wore on, Isabel and Gabe continued to sit on the porch, the last light of day slowly fading. The stars began to emerge, dotting the sky with their twinkling brilliance. The storm's aftermath had left the air crisp and clear, and a gentle breeze rustled the leaves, adding a soothing soundtrack to their shared silence.

Isabel leaned back in her chair, her thoughts drifting to the events of the past few days. The storm had not only transformed the landscape but also brought a new depth to her relationship with Gabe. She felt an unspoken bond growing between them, one that went beyond words and gestures. It was a connection forged in vulnerability and shared experiences, a bond that was beginning to shape her perception of her past and her future.

Gabe, sensing her contemplative mood, broke the silence gently. "You've been quiet tonight. Is there something on your mind?"

Isabel turned to him, her eyes meeting his with a mixture of hesitation and openness. "It's just... I've been thinking a lot about everything that's happened since I came back to the island. It feels like so much has changed, and I'm not sure where to go from here."

Gabe nodded, his expression one of understanding. "Change can be overwhelming, especially when it comes so quickly. Sometimes, it helps to talk about it, to sort through your thoughts with someone who's willing to listen."

Isabel took a deep breath, feeling a rush of gratitude for Gabe's presence. "I appreciate that. There's a lot I've been keeping to myself, and it's been hard to know what to share and what to keep hidden."

Gabe's gaze was steady, offering a sense of stability. "You don't have to share everything all at once. Take your time. What matters is that you're not alone in this. I'm here for you, and I want to understand what you're going through."

Isabel's heart swelled with a mixture of relief and affection. The support Gabe offered was genuine, and it gave her the courage to delve into her feelings more deeply. "I've been thinking about my mother a lot lately. The painting in the studio—it's been on my mind. It feels like there's something important about it, something I need to understand."

Gabe leaned forward slightly, his interest evident. "What about the painting? What do you think it's trying to tell you?"

Isabel hesitated for a moment, trying to articulate her thoughts. "It's not just the painting itself, but what it represents. My mother's art always had this way of capturing emotions and hidden meanings. I feel like the painting is a symbol of something I'm missing in my own life. Like it's trying to guide me, but I don't fully understand its message."

Gabe's expression softened, and he reached out to place a comforting hand on hers. "Sometimes, the answers we seek aren't immediately clear. It's about trusting the process and being open to the insights that come along the way."

Isabel looked at Gabe's hand on hers, feeling a deep sense of connection. The simple gesture was filled with empathy and support, and it made her realize how much she had come to rely on Gabe's presence. "You're right. It's just hard to be patient when you're eager for answers."

Gabe gave her hand a reassuring squeeze. "I understand. But remember, it's okay to take your time. You don't have to rush the process. It's about finding your own path and discovering what feels right for you."

They sat in companionable silence for a few moments, the stars above them shining with a quiet brilliance. The tranquility of the evening provided a peaceful backdrop for their conversation, and Isabel felt a sense of calm settling over her.

As the night wore on, Gabe stood up and stretched, his movements relaxed and easy. "How about we head inside and make some dinner? I've got a few recipes I've been wanting to try, and it could be a nice way to spend the evening."

Isabel smiled, feeling a renewed sense of warmth. "That sounds great. I'd love to help."

They moved inside the cabin, the cozy interior a welcome contrast to the cool night air. Gabe set about preparing a meal, his movements efficient and practiced. Isabel found herself enjoying the simple act of cooking together, the shared task providing a sense of normalcy and comfort.

As they worked side by side, the conversation flowed naturally. They talked about their favorite foods, shared anecdotes from their pasts, and laughed at each other's cooking mishaps. The atmosphere was light and easy, a testament to the growing ease in their relationship.

Dinner was soon ready, and they sat down at the small dining table, the meal a delicious blend of flavors and textures. As they ate, Isabel felt a deep sense of contentment. The earlier conversation had opened up new avenues of understanding, and the connection with Gabe felt more profound than ever.

After dinner, they cleaned up together, their movements synchronized in a way that spoke to their growing familiarity with each other. Gabe wiped down the counters while Isabel washed the dishes, their interactions filled with an unspoken understanding.

As they finished up, Gabe glanced at Isabel with a thoughtful expression. "I've been thinking about our conversation earlier. If you ever want to talk more about your mother or the painting, I'm here to listen. We can figure things out together."

Isabel's heart warmed at his offer. "Thank you, Gabe. That means a lot to me. I feel like I'm starting to make sense of things, but it helps to know that you're here to support me."

Gabe smiled, his eyes reflecting his sincerity. "I'm glad to be here for you. We're in this together, and I'm looking forward to seeing where this journey takes us."

They finished their evening with a quiet moment on the porch, the stars shining brightly above them. The night air was cool and refreshing, and the serenity of the island created a perfect backdrop for their growing connection.

As they sat together, Isabel felt a deep sense of peace. The storm had brought them closer, and the journey she was on with Gabe was beginning to take shape. The future was still uncertain, but with Gabe by her side, she felt ready to face whatever came next.

The stars continued to twinkle above, their light a reminder of the possibilities that lay ahead. Isabel and Gabe sat in comfortable silence, their presence together a testament to the bond they were building. The night was a promise of new beginnings and shared experiences, and Isabel felt a renewed sense of hope for the future.

As the evening came to a close, Isabel and Gabe shared a final, meaningful glance before heading inside. The night had been a turning point, and the journey ahead was filled with promise. With each passing day, Isabel felt more confident in her ability to face the challenges and embrace the opportunities that awaited her. The storm had cleared the way for a new chapter in her life, and with Gabe's support, she was ready to embrace it fully.

7

Chapter 7: The Lighthouse Clue

Isabel stood at the edge of the lighthouse, the old structure towering over her like a sentinel from another time. The soft glow of the lanterns scattered across the horizon provided a gentle illumination against the encroaching darkness, making the scene around her both serene and haunting. She had carefully followed the clues from the painting, the lighthouse now symbolizing the culmination of her search.

The storm had left the island damp and quiet, with the fresh scent of rain lingering in the air. The lighthouse was weathered but sturdy, its whitewashed walls marred by time and salt. Isabel's heart raced with a mixture of anticipation and trepidation as she approached the entrance, the iron door creaking open with a groan as she pushed it.

Inside, the lighthouse was a stark contrast to its exterior. The space was cramped, illuminated only by the dim light filtering through the narrow windows. Dust motes danced in the weak beams of light, adding an ethereal quality to the room. Isabel's eyes scanned the interior, searching for something that would connect her mother's secrets to her own life.

Her gaze fell upon an old wooden desk tucked into a corner, its surface cluttered with yellowed papers and aged ink pots. Isabel approached the desk, her fingers trembling slightly as she brushed aside the dust to reveal the papers. Among them, she found a journal, its leather cover worn and scuffed. The journal's presence felt like a silent promise, its contents holding the key to the mysteries she sought.

She opened the journal with careful hands, her eyes scanning the pages filled with neat, flowing script. The first few entries spoke of mundane daily activities, but as Isabel delved deeper, the tone shifted. Her mother's writing grew more emotional, revealing glimpses of a life Isabel had never known.

One entry caught Isabel's eye, dated several decades earlier. The handwriting was delicate, tinged with an almost palpable longing. It spoke of a man named Thomas, someone Isabel had never heard of before. Her mother described Thomas with a blend of affection and melancholy, her words painting a portrait of a romance that had been both beautiful and tragic.

As Isabel read on, she discovered that her mother had fallen deeply in love with Thomas during her youth. Their relationship was intense and passionate, but circumstances had forced them apart. Isabel's mother had never married Thomas, choosing instead to remain on the island and build a life that seemed safe and stable. The journal revealed that her mother had hidden this part of her life, not out of shame but out of a desire to protect Isabel from the pain and complexities of her own choices.

A lump formed in Isabel's throat as she read about her mother's internal struggle. Her mother had kept this secret as a way of shielding Isabel from the heartache of a love that had never fully blossomed. Isabel's heart ached with the realization that her mother had chosen to carry the burden of this lost love alone, all in an effort to provide Isabel with a sense of stability and normalcy.

Isabel's fingers traced the faded ink on the pages, her emotions a swirl of sadness and understanding. Her mother's choice to protect her had left Isabel with a void, one that she was only beginning to comprehend. The painting, the lighthouse, and now the journal—all these elements were coming together to reveal not just her mother's hidden past but also her own journey of self-discovery.

As she continued reading, Isabel encountered passages that spoke of her mother's hopes for Isabel's future. Her mother had always hoped that Isabel would find happiness and love, even if it meant facing the complexities and uncertainties that had once plagued her own life. Isabel realized that her mother's decision to keep these secrets was an act of love, meant to allow Isabel the freedom to forge her own path without the weight of unresolved pasts.

Tears welled in Isabel's eyes as she closed the journal. She felt a profound sense of connection to her mother, a connection that transcended the years and the silence that had often existed between them. Her mother's love and sacrifice were evident in every word, and Isabel now understood the depth of her mother's choices and the reasons behind them.

The discovery in the lighthouse had opened a new chapter in Isabel's journey. It was no longer just about uncovering the past but about understanding the intricacies of her own emotions and the legacy left behind by her mother. The lighthouse, once a symbol of mystery and distance, had become a beacon of revelation and healing.

Isabel took a deep breath, the cool night air filling her lungs and clearing her mind. The weight of the journal and her mother's secrets had been heavy, but it was also liberating. She felt a renewed sense of purpose and clarity, a realization that her own journey was intertwined with her mother's in ways she had never fully appreciated before.

As she made her way back to the cabin, the lighthouse standing tall and resolute behind her, Isabel felt a sense of calm and determination. She was ready to face the challenges and uncertainties that lay ahead, armed with the understanding of her mother's love and the strength it had given her. The journey of self-discovery was far from over, but Isabel now felt equipped to navigate its twists and turns with a newfound sense of resolve and insight.

Isabel's journey to the lighthouse had brought her more than just the answers she sought; it had given her a new perspective on her own life. As she made her way back to the cabin, the journal's revelations echoed in her mind, connecting her mother's past to her present in ways she had not anticipated. The raw emotions she had encountered in the journal seemed to deepen with each step she took, melding with the quiet solitude of the island night.

Back at the cabin, the warmth of the fire was a comforting contrast to the cold, damp air outside. Isabel poured herself a cup of tea, her hands still trembling slightly from the emotional revelations. She sat by the fire, the journal lying open beside her, and tried to piece together the fragments of her mother's story with her own scattered thoughts and feelings.

The storm had passed, leaving the night clear and calm. The moonlight streamed through the windows, casting a gentle glow on the room. Isabel's mind was restless, swirling with reflections on her mother's hidden love and the weight of those secrets. She knew that her journey was far from over and that the path forward would require more than just understanding her mother's past. It meant confronting her own fears and uncertainties.

As she sipped her tea, Isabel heard a soft knock on the door. The sound was unexpected, and a moment of hesitation passed before she rose to answer it. She opened the door to find Gabe standing on the threshold, his expression a mixture of concern and curiosity.

"Hey," Gabe said, his voice low. "I saw the lights on and thought I'd check in. I hope I'm not intruding."

Isabel shook her head, stepping aside to let him in. "No, not at all. I was just going through some things."

Gabe entered the cabin, his gaze sweeping over the cozy interior before resting on Isabel. There was a quiet intensity in his eyes, and Isabel could sense the unspoken questions and emotions he carried. The atmosphere between them was charged, the air thick with a blend of vulnerability and unvoiced feelings.

Gabe took a seat across from Isabel by the fire. For a moment, they sat in silence, the crackling of the fire filling the space between them. Isabel's mind was still reeling from the journal's revelations, and she found herself grappling with the urge to share her newfound insights with Gabe, even as she struggled to find the right words.

"I went to the lighthouse today," Isabel began, her voice hesitant but steady. "I found something... something that shed light on my mother's past."

Gabe's eyes widened slightly, his interest piqued. "What did you find?"

Isabel took a deep breath, gathering her thoughts. "I found my mother's journal. It turns out she had a relationship with someone before she married my father. Someone she never told me about."

Gabe's expression softened, his gaze attentive as he listened. "That sounds like a lot to process."

"It is," Isabel admitted, her voice trembling slightly. "She kept it a secret to protect me, but now that I know, it feels like there's so much more to understand. It's not just about her past—it's about how it's shaping my present and my future."

Gabe leaned forward slightly, his tone gentle. "You're not alone in this, you know. Sometimes, sharing what you're going through can help make sense of it all."

Isabel looked at Gabe, her emotions raw and exposed. "It's hard to know who to talk to. I've been so focused on protecting myself and avoiding the past that I've been shutting people out."

Gabe's eyes met hers with a depth of understanding. "I get that. I think we all have moments where we build walls around ourselves. But sometimes, letting someone in can help us see things more clearly."

A moment of silence fell between them, the firelight casting warm shadows on their faces. Isabel could feel the weight of Gabe's words, and she sensed that he was offering her not just his company, but his empathy and support. It was a rare and genuine connection, one that was beginning to break through the barriers Isabel had carefully constructed around her heart.

"I'm sorry for pushing you away," Isabel said softly, her voice tinged with regret. "I've been so focused on handling things on my own that I didn't realize how much I needed someone to be there for me."

Gabe's expression softened further, a faint smile playing at the corners of his lips. "You don't need to apologize. We all have our own ways of dealing with things. What matters is that you're here now, and I'm here for you."

Isabel felt a surge of gratitude and relief. It was a rare and precious moment of vulnerability, one that allowed her to let down her guard and begin to open up to Gabe. She realized that their shared experiences and the emotional connection they had forged were becoming a source of strength for her.

As the evening wore on, Isabel and Gabe continued to talk, their conversation flowing more freely as they shared their thoughts and feelings. The room was filled with a sense of warmth and intimacy, the firelight creating a cocoon of comfort around them. Gabe's presence was a balm to Isabel's weary soul, and she found solace in his quiet support and understanding.

Their conversation drifted from the journal and her mother's secrets to lighter topics, including their shared memories of the island and their hopes for the future. The ease with which they spoke to each other was a testament to the growing bond between them, a bond that was beginning to bridge the gap between their past and present.

As the night deepened, Isabel and Gabe found themselves sitting closer together, their shoulders brushing lightly as they spoke. The physical proximity was a reflection of the emotional closeness they were beginning to share. Isabel could feel the warmth of Gabe's presence, a comforting reminder that she was not alone in her journey.

When it was time for Gabe to leave, he stood by the door, his expression serious but kind. "If you need anything—if you want to talk or just need some company—please don't hesitate to reach out."

Isabel nodded, her heart swelling with appreciation. "Thank you, Gabe. I'll remember that."

Gabe gave her a reassuring smile before stepping out into the night, leaving Isabel alone in the cabin with her thoughts. The warmth of the fire and the gentle afterglow of their conversation created a sense of calm, allowing Isabel to reflect on the evening's events.

As she settled into bed, Isabel's mind was a whirlwind of emotions and revelations. The conversation with Gabe had been a turning point, a moment of connection that had begun to dismantle the walls she had built around herself. The journey ahead was still uncertain, but Isabel felt a renewed sense of hope and possibility.

The lighthouse, the journal, and Gabe's presence had all contributed to a profound shift in Isabel's perspective. She was beginning to see her mother's past not as a burden, but as a part of the tapestry of her own life. The secrets she had uncovered were no longer just shadows of the past but guiding lights leading her toward a deeper understanding of herself and her future.

As she drifted off to sleep, Isabel held onto the feeling of hope and connection that had emerged from her conversation with Gabe. The road ahead would undoubtedly be challenging, but she felt more prepared to face it with the support of those who cared for her and the strength she had found within herself.

As Isabel returned to the cabin, the journal clutched in her hand felt heavier than ever. The revelation of her mother's past had opened up a well of emotions she wasn't sure she was ready to handle. The secrets buried in the pages of that journal were not just relics of a bygone era but seemed to pulse with a life of their own, intertwining with Isabel's own narrative.

She lit a few candles to chase away the shadows that had gathered in the corners of the room. The soft glow cast flickering patterns on the walls, adding an almost ethereal quality to the space. Isabel settled into her favorite armchair, the journal resting on her lap, its leather cover worn and soft from years of use.

Flipping through the pages, she sought solace in the familiar script of her mother's handwriting. Each entry was a glimpse into a world Isabel had never known, a world where her mother had loved and lost in ways that seemed both distant and intimately close.

The lighthouse painting had struck a deep chord within Isabel. It was more than just a piece of art; it was a symbol of her mother's concealed heartache and unspoken dreams. As she examined the journal, Isabel was drawn to an entry that referenced the lighthouse again, a passage that hinted at more than just a location. Her mother had written about it with a sense of longing and melancholy that Isabel now understood on a personal level.

With the journal open to that particular entry, Isabel read aloud, her voice a soft murmur against the crackle of the fire:

"The lighthouse stands as a beacon in my life, guiding me through the fog of uncertainty. Its light reminds me of the promise I once made—to always seek the truth, even when it is shrouded in darkness. My love for him was like the lighthouse's light: unwavering yet hidden from those who could never understand."

Isabel's fingers traced the lines of the page as if she could somehow bridge the gap between her and her mother's emotions. The entry revealed a depth of feeling that was both profound and painfully personal. Her mother had obviously cherished her secret, but Isabel couldn't shake the feeling that there was something more to uncover.

Her thoughts were interrupted by a gentle knock at the door. Isabel hesitated before standing up, the journal still in hand. She wasn't expecting visitors, and the timing felt almost too coincidental.

Opening the door, she found Gabe standing there, his expression a mix of concern and curiosity. The evening was cool, and his breath formed little clouds in the air.

"I didn't mean to intrude," Gabe said, his voice gentle. "I thought you might want some company. It's a beautiful night, and I thought we could take a walk by the shore, if you're up for it."

Isabel considered his offer for a moment. The idea of sharing her thoughts with Gabe, of letting him in on the whirlwind of emotions she was experiencing, felt both comforting and daunting. She nodded, a small smile forming on her lips. "I'd like that."

They stepped outside into the crisp night air, the sky overhead a tapestry of stars. The moonlight shimmered on the water, casting a silvery glow that illuminated their path. Gabe walked beside her in silence, his presence a steady anchor amidst the storm of Isabel's thoughts.

As they reached the shoreline, Isabel took a deep breath, the salty sea air filling her lungs. The rhythmic sound of the waves crashing against the shore was soothing, a natural counterpoint to the turmoil within her. Gabe waited patiently as Isabel gathered her thoughts, the gentle touch of his hand against hers a subtle reminder of his support.

"I found something today," Isabel began, her voice trembling slightly. "Something that I wasn't expecting. My mother's journal, and... and the painting of the lighthouse."

Gabe turned to look at her, his gaze intent and encouraging. "What did you find in the journal?"

Isabel took a deep breath, trying to steady herself. "It's like she had this whole other life, this secret love that she never told anyone about. It's all wrapped up in this lighthouse painting, like it was a symbol for everything she couldn't say out loud."

Gabe's expression softened, his eyes reflecting the moonlight. "It sounds like a powerful discovery. How does it make you feel?"

"It's overwhelming," Isabel admitted. "It's like I'm trying to piece together a puzzle, but every piece reveals something new and confusing. I'm starting to see that her secrets weren't just about her past—they're part of who I am now, too."

Gabe took a step closer, his hand brushing against hers. "Sometimes, the things we uncover about our loved ones help us understand ourselves better. It's not always easy, but it can lead to a deeper connection with our own stories."

Isabel looked at Gabe, his words resonating deeply. She felt a surge of gratitude for his presence, for his willingness to listen and support her. The walk along the shore, the peaceful night, and Gabe's understanding gaze combined to create a moment of clarity amidst the chaos.

They continued to walk, their conversation flowing more freely as they discussed their reflections on the journal, the painting, and their own lives. Gabe shared his own experiences, revealing moments of vulnerability and self-discovery that paralleled Isabel's journey.

The lighthouse loomed in the distance, its silhouette a constant reminder of the secrets that had been uncovered. As they walked closer, Isabel felt a sense of inevitability, as if the lighthouse was drawing her to it, urging her to confront its significance in her mother's story and her own life.

When they reached the base of the lighthouse, Isabel paused, looking up at its towering structure. The beams of light that once guided sailors were now a metaphor for her own journey, illuminating paths she had previously kept in the dark.

"I need to go back inside," Isabel said softly, her voice carrying a mixture of resolve and uncertainty. "There's more I need to understand, more I need to explore."

Gabe nodded, his expression supportive. "If you ever need someone to talk to or just be there with you, I'm here. You don't have to go through this alone."

Isabel offered him a grateful smile, her heart swelling with warmth. "Thank you, Gabe. I really appreciate that."

As they walked back to the cabin, the night's serenity enveloped them. The conversation had opened new avenues of understanding, and Isabel felt a sense of hope and determination. The lighthouse, once a symbol of hidden secrets, now represented the light that was guiding her through her own personal journey.

Back at the cabin, Isabel sat by the fire, the journal spread out before her. The revelations of the day had brought her closer to understanding her mother's hidden world and, in turn, her own path. She knew there was still much to uncover, but the support of those around her, especially Gabe, was a source of strength.

With renewed focus, Isabel began to read through the journal again, her mind and heart open to the lessons it had to offer. The lighthouse stood as a beacon, not just for her mother's past but for Isabel's own future, a future she was beginning to embrace with a sense of clarity and purpose.

As Isabel left the lighthouse, the wind whispered secrets through the trees, and the sea roared its approval of her newfound resolve. Her footsteps were lighter, though her mind was still heavy with the weight of her discoveries. The journal had opened up a new world, one where her mother's secrets intertwined with her own journey, but Isabel knew there was still much more to unravel.

She made her way back to the cabin, the path illuminated by the moonlight that now felt like a guide rather than a mere light source. Her thoughts were a jumble of emotions, but one thing stood out clearly: her mother's past was far more intricate and deeply connected to Isabel's present than she had initially realized.

Upon returning to the cabin, Isabel took a deep breath and decided to revisit the journal. The fire in the hearth had died down to a soft glow, casting a warm and intimate light across the room.

She settled back into the armchair, the journal open on her lap. The lighthouse painting was propped up against the nearby wall, its mysterious symbol now a focal point in her mind.

Isabel's fingers lightly traced the edges of the pages as she flipped through them, searching for more clues. She found another entry that struck her as particularly poignant. It described a secret meeting her mother had had with the man she had once loved—a clandestine encounter that took place at a hidden cove on the island.

With a sense of urgency, Isabel read the passage aloud, her voice barely above a whisper.

"The cove is our sanctuary, a place where time stands still and the world fades away. It is where we shared our dreams and fears, where the light of the lighthouse was our silent witness. I have kept these moments hidden, not out of shame, but out of a desire to protect what was pure and sacred. It was not just about love; it was about a future that never came to be, a promise left unfulfilled."

As Isabel read, she felt a pang of empathy for her mother, realizing that these hidden memories were not just about a past love but about dreams and hopes that had been suppressed. Her mother's attempt to shield Isabel from this pain now felt like a double-edged sword—protective yet isolating.

Determined to uncover the full story, Isabel decided to visit the cove mentioned in the journal. It was a place she had never explored, a secluded spot that promised both discovery and reflection. She prepared herself for the journey, packing a small bag with essentials and taking a flashlight, knowing that the cove might be just as mysterious and dark as the emotions she was grappling with.

The next morning, Isabel set out toward the cove. The path was rugged and overgrown, and it required careful navigation. The journey was physically demanding, but the challenge only seemed to add to the anticipation of what she might find.

As she approached the cove, she could hear the faint sound of the waves crashing against the rocks, a rhythmic and calming presence. The cove was surrounded by high cliffs, and the entrance was partially hidden, making it a perfect secret haven. Isabel made her way carefully down the rocky incline until she reached the sheltered area.

The cove was more beautiful than she had imagined. The sand was fine and pristine, and the water was clear, with the sunlight creating shimmering patterns on the surface. She walked along the shore, taking in the serene beauty of the place, but her thoughts remained focused on her mother's hidden past.

Isabel explored the cove, looking for any physical remnants of the past. She found a small, weathered bench partially obscured by vines and foliage. It seemed like the perfect spot for quiet reflection, and she imagined her mother and her lover sitting there, sharing their dreams and fears as described in the journal.

Sitting on the bench, Isabel closed her eyes and allowed herself to be enveloped by the tranquility of the cove. The waves lapped gently at the shore, and the breeze rustled the leaves, creating a soothing soundtrack to her thoughts. The cove felt like a sacred space, a place where the past and present converged.

As she sat there, Isabel's thoughts turned to her own life and the decisions she faced. She was beginning to see how her mother's experiences mirrored her own struggles with love, loss, and the search for identity. The lighthouse, the journal, and now this cove—all were symbols of paths she needed to explore to understand herself better.

After some time, Isabel stood up and walked along the shore, her mind buzzing with new insights. She collected a few small stones as keepsakes, symbols of her journey and the connections she was beginning to forge with her mother's past. The stones would serve as tangible reminders of her exploration and the emotional growth that was occurring.

Before leaving the cove, Isabel took one last look around, feeling a deep sense of closure. She knew that this place, along with the lighthouse and the journal, would always be a part of her journey. The cove had offered her a glimpse into a world that was both haunting and beautiful, and it had helped her connect with her mother in a way she hadn't thought possible.

As she made her way back to the cabin, Isabel felt a renewed sense of purpose. She was no longer just uncovering her mother's secrets; she was also uncovering parts of herself. The path ahead was still uncertain, but she was beginning to see it with greater clarity.

Back at the cabin, she carefully placed the stones on the mantel, where they would serve as a reminder of her journey. The journal was still open, and Isabel took a moment to reflect on the words she had read. Each entry was a piece of the puzzle, and she was slowly putting together a picture of her mother's life and her own.

The evening was quiet, and the cabin felt more like a home than it had before. The discoveries of the day had deepened Isabel's connection to her mother's past and had given her a greater understanding of her own path. She knew that there was still more to learn and explore, but for now, she felt a sense of peace and acceptance.

Isabel picked up a pen and began to write in her own journal, documenting her thoughts and reflections from the day. She wrote about the cove, the lighthouse, and the revelations from her mother's journal. It was a way for her to process her experiences and to keep track of her emotional journey.

As she wrote, she felt a sense of gratitude for the support she had received from Gabe and the strength she had found within herself. The journey was far from over, but Isabel was beginning to embrace it with a newfound sense of purpose and clarity. The lighthouse, the cove, and her mother's secrets were all part of a greater story—a story that was leading her toward a deeper understanding of herself and her place in the world.

Isabel's return from the cove was marked by a profound sense of introspection. The journal she had found held more than just details of her mother's past; it was a mirror reflecting her own journey. Each page she had read had added layers to her understanding of her mother's life, and now, she was left grappling with the realization of how closely their experiences were intertwined.

That evening, Isabel sat by the window in her cabin, the moonlight casting a gentle glow over the room. She had laid out the stones she had collected from the cove on the small table beside her. Their smooth, rounded surfaces seemed to hold the essence of the place they came from—calm and enduring.

Her thoughts drifted back to the entries in her mother's journal, particularly the mention of the secret meeting at the cove. Isabel couldn't shake the feeling that there was something more to uncover, something that connected her mother's past with her own current dilemmas. She was eager to delve deeper, but she also needed to process the emotional weight of her discoveries.

The next day, Isabel decided to visit the lighthouse again. It had become a symbol of illumination in her journey, not just of her mother's secrets but of her own path forward. As she walked the familiar path towards the lighthouse, the cool breeze and the rhythmic sound of the waves provided a calming backdrop to her thoughts.

The lighthouse stood tall and resolute, a beacon of guidance amidst the shifting tides of Isabel's emotions. She entered the lighthouse, climbing the spiral staircase that led to the top. Each step seemed to echo her internal journey—a climb toward understanding and acceptance.

At the top, Isabel looked out over the vast expanse of the sea. The view was breathtaking, but it was the lighthouse's lantern that captivated her attention. It was an emblem of clarity and guidance, much like the path she was trying to navigate in her own life.

Isabel pulled out the journal and the painting she had found in the studio. The lighthouse painting, with its mysterious symbol, seemed to resonate with the view before her. She compared the symbol to the lighthouse's structure, trying to see if there were any connections. Her fingers traced the symbol on the painting, feeling the smooth texture of the paint under her touch.

As she examined the painting, Isabel remembered the entry in the journal that described how her mother had felt about this place. The writing spoke of the lighthouse as a metaphor for their unspoken love—how it had stood as a witness to their hidden relationship and dreams.

Isabel's thoughts were interrupted by a soft knock at the door. She turned to see Gabe standing there, a concerned look on his face. "I thought I might find you here," he said, his voice gentle.

Isabel smiled, though her eyes were clouded with the weight of her revelations. "I needed to come back. This place—it feels like it holds the answers I'm searching for."

Gabe stepped inside and looked around the lighthouse's top room, taking in the view and the items Isabel had brought with her. He approached her and asked, "What have you discovered?"

Isabel hesitated, then decided to share more of what she had found. "I found a journal in the cove," she began. "It belonged to my mother. There are entries about a secret relationship she had, and there's a painting of this lighthouse with a symbol that I can't quite understand."

Gabe's expression softened with understanding. He glanced at the painting and then back at Isabel. "It sounds like you've uncovered something deeply personal. How are you holding up?"

Isabel looked at him, her eyes reflecting a mix of gratitude and vulnerability. "It's a lot to take in. I feel like I'm getting to know my mother in a way I never expected, and it's making me question so much about my own life."

Gabe nodded, sensing the weight of her words. "Sometimes, understanding the past can help us make sense of the present. If you need someone to talk to or just to be here with you, I'm here."

Isabel felt a surge of warmth at his words. The comfort of his presence was reassuring, especially as she navigated this complex emotional landscape. "Thank you, Gabe. I appreciate that more than you know."

They stood together, side by side, looking out over the sea. The silence between them was filled with a quiet understanding, a moment of shared connection that spoke volumes. Gabe's presence was a calming anchor in the midst of Isabel's storm of emotions.

After a while, Isabel broke the silence. "I'm thinking of returning to the cove tomorrow. There's something about it that feels like it holds more answers."

Gabe nodded in agreement. "If you'd like, I could join you. Sometimes having someone else there can make a difference."

Isabel considered his offer, feeling a sense of relief at the thought of not facing her journey alone. "I'd like that. Thank you, Gabe."

As they left the lighthouse, the atmosphere between them was different—less charged with the intensity of unspoken feelings and more grounded in a mutual understanding. The lighthouse, with its symbol and its significance, had become a backdrop to their evolving relationship.

That evening, as Isabel prepared for the next day's journey, she reflected on the new layer of connection she had with Gabe. His presence had offered her comfort and clarity, and she was beginning to see how their shared experiences were drawing them closer.

In her cabin, Isabel carefully placed the journal and the painting on the desk, feeling a sense of reverence for the discoveries she had made. The cove, the lighthouse, and the symbols of her mother's past were all pieces of a larger puzzle she was determined to solve.

As she drifted off to sleep, Isabel felt a sense of anticipation for the journey ahead. The past was still full of mysteries, but she was more equipped to face them with Gabe by her side. The lighthouse had become a beacon of hope, guiding her through the emotional complexities of her life and offering a path toward healing and understanding.

The following morning, Isabel and Gabe set out for the cove. The air was crisp, and the sun was shining brightly, casting a warm glow over the landscape. The journey was a pleasant one, with the promise of new discoveries and the comfort of shared companionship.

As they arrived at the cove, Isabel felt a renewed sense of purpose. She and Gabe explored the area together, retracing her steps from the previous day. The cove, with its serene beauty and hidden secrets, felt like a sacred space where the past and present converged.

Isabel and Gabe spent the day in quiet exploration, their conversations punctuated by moments of reflective silence. They examined the rocks and the shoreline, searching for any additional clues that might shed light on Isabel's mother's past.

In the late afternoon, as the sun began to dip toward the horizon, Isabel found herself feeling a deep sense of connection to both her mother's legacy and Gabe's supportive presence. The cove had offered her solace and insight, and she was starting to see how her journey of self-discovery was intertwined with her mother's hidden story.

As they made their way back to the cabin, Isabel felt a renewed sense of hope and clarity. With Gabe by her side, she was more prepared to face the emotional challenges ahead. The lighthouse, the cove, and the journal had all become symbols of her journey, guiding her toward a deeper understanding of herself and her past.

The cove had become Isabel's sanctuary, a place where the secrets of her mother's past and her own quest for self-discovery intersected. As she walked back from the lighthouse, the journal clutched tightly in her hands, she felt a burgeoning sense of clarity and resolve. Gabe's presence had been a grounding force, a steady hand guiding her through the emotional labyrinth she was navigating.

That evening, as the sky turned to shades of deep blue and violet, Isabel sat on the porch of her cabin, the journal open before her. She reread the entries she had discovered, each one peeling back another layer of her mother's life. The intricate details of her mother's secret love affair had been heart-wrenching but also revealing, painting a picture of a woman caught between duty and desire, tradition and passion.

The faint glow of a lantern inside the cabin cast warm shadows on the wooden walls. Gabe had left earlier to give Isabel some space, respecting her need to process the day's revelations alone. The quiet of the evening was a stark contrast to the stormy night they had shared. Now, the calm was both soothing and unsettling, a peaceful veneer over the turbulence of Isabel's emotions.

As Isabel read through the journal, she came across a passage that seemed particularly poignant. It was an entry about a clandestine meeting at the lighthouse, a place her mother had described as a refuge from the constraints of their world. Her mother had written about the solace she found in the lighthouse, how it was a symbol of their love and a beacon of hope amidst their secrecy.

Isabel's thoughts were interrupted by a soft knock on the cabin door. She opened it to find Gabe standing there, holding a small, wrapped package. "I thought you might like this," he said, his eyes reflecting the soft light from inside the cabin.

Curious, Isabel took the package and unwrapped it to find a delicate, handcrafted journal. "I thought you might want a new journal," Gabe explained. "For your thoughts, your discoveries... whatever you need it for."

Isabel's eyes welled up with gratitude. "Thank you, Gabe. This means more to me than you know."

Gabe nodded, his expression gentle. "I'm glad. I know it's been a lot to process. If you need anything, or if you want to talk more, just let me know."

Isabel felt a deep sense of comfort in his presence. The gift of the journal was symbolic of his support and understanding, and she felt a growing sense of connection between them. "I'd like that," she said, her voice steady. "Let's sit for a while."

They settled into the cozy chairs on the porch, the lantern casting a soft glow over their faces. The stars above twinkled in the clear night sky, and the gentle rustling of the leaves created a soothing backdrop to their conversation.

Isabel hesitated for a moment, then spoke up. "Gabe, I've been thinking a lot about my mother's past, about the secrets she kept.

It's like I'm discovering pieces of her life that were hidden, and it's making me question so much about my own."

Gabe listened attentively, his gaze never leaving Isabel's face. "It's understandable to feel that way. Sometimes, uncovering the past can make us rethink our own choices and the paths we've taken."

Isabel nodded, her gaze drifting to the horizon. "It's not just about the secrets themselves, but about why she kept them. I'm starting to see that she might have been trying to protect me from something, but it also feels like there's a part of her that I never really knew."

Gabe reached out and took her hand, his touch warm and re-assuring. "It's natural to feel that way. We often try to shield those we love from the complexities of our own lives. But finding out the truth can also be a way to honor their memory and understand them more fully."

Isabel squeezed his hand, feeling a surge of emotion. "I'm start-ing to realize that understanding her is a way of understanding myself. It's like I'm piecing together parts of my own identity through her story."

Gabe's eyes were filled with empathy. "And you're not alone in this journey. I'm here with you, and I'm willing to help however I can. Sometimes, sharing these moments can make them a little easier to bear."

Their hands remained intertwined, a silent testament to their growing bond. The night continued to unfold around them, the stars shining brightly as if bearing witness to their shared vulnera-bility.

As the conversation deepened, Isabel began to feel a sense of re-lief and connection. Gabe's presence provided a safe space for her to explore her feelings, and his willingness to listen and support her was a source of comfort. The secrets of her mother's past were no longer just a burden to bear; they were becoming a part of her own journey, a path toward self-discovery and healing.

The hours passed unnoticed as they talked about their pasts, their hopes, and their fears. The warmth of the lantern and the soothing sounds of the night created an atmosphere of intimacy and trust. Isabel realized that Gabe's presence was not just a comfort but a meaningful part of her journey—a companion who was helping her navigate the complexities of her emotions and the revelations she had uncovered.

As the night wore on, the conversation gradually faded into a comfortable silence. Isabel leaned back in her chair, feeling a sense of peace and contentment she hadn't experienced in a long time. The stars above seemed to shine a little brighter, and the gentle breeze carried the promise of new beginnings.

Gabe's hand still rested gently in hers, a silent affirmation of their connection. Isabel closed her eyes for a moment, letting the tranquility of the night wash over her. The secrets of her mother's past were no longer just echoes from the past; they were intertwined with her own story, shaping her journey toward understanding and acceptance.

Eventually, they stood up, and Gabe helped Isabel inside the cabin. The lantern's glow cast a warm light over the room, and Isabel placed the new journal on her desk, feeling a renewed sense of purpose. The journey ahead was still filled with uncertainties, but with Gabe by her side, she felt ready to face whatever lay ahead.

As they said their goodbyes for the night, Isabel looked at Gabe with a heartfelt smile. "Thank you for being here, for listening, and for understanding. It means more to me than I can express."

Gabe returned her smile, his eyes reflecting a deep sense of connection. "I'm glad I could be here for you. Let's continue to face this journey together."

With that, they parted ways for the night, each carrying the warmth of their shared moments and the promise of what was to come. Isabel settled into bed, her mind still buzzing with thoughts and emotions, but her heart felt lighter and more at ease. The secrets of the past were becoming a part of her present, guiding her toward a deeper understanding of herself and her mother.

As she drifted off to sleep, Isabel felt a renewed sense of hope and clarity. The journey was far from over, but she was no longer walking it alone. The lighthouse, the cove, and the journal had all become symbols of her quest for truth and healing, and with Gabe by her side, she felt ready to continue exploring the mysteries of her past and the possibilities of her future.

The lighthouse stood as a sentinel against the encroaching night, its solitary beam slicing through the darkness. Isabel returned there after her poignant conversation with Gabe, the weight of the day's revelations settling heavily on her shoulders. The lighthouse, once a symbol of her mother's hidden love, now beckoned with the promise of further discovery.

Inside the lighthouse, Isabel approached the study where her mother's secretive past had begun to unfold. The room, dimly lit by the remnants of daylight filtering through the small, round windows, was filled with the scent of aged paper and the faintest hint of sea salt. Isabel moved methodically, her eyes scanning the familiar surroundings with renewed purpose.

The journal had revealed much, but Isabel sensed there were more layers to uncover. The detailed entries about her mother's love affair and the references to the lighthouse hinted at deeper truths, perhaps hidden in the very walls of the structure. She needed to understand more fully the nature of her mother's relationship and its impact on her own life.

As she started examining the studio again, Isabel noticed something she had missed before: an old wooden chest, partially concealed behind a stack of canvas-covered frames. With some effort, she dragged it into the center of the room. The chest was dusty, its surface marked by years of neglect, but Isabel's heart quickened with anticipation.

She knelt beside the chest and fumbled with the rusty latch. It creaked open, revealing a jumble of old letters and photographs, their edges yellowed with age. Isabel's fingers trembled slightly as she picked up the first letter, its envelope bearing a familiar, elegant handwriting.

She carefully opened the letter, her eyes scanning the carefully penned words. The letter was from a man named Adrian, someone her mother had mentioned only briefly in the journal. The writing was filled with longing and affection, each word betraying a deep emotional connection that went beyond mere romance.

In one particular passage, Adrian wrote about a place where they could meet in secret, a place of refuge that echoed the descriptions of the lighthouse. Isabel's heart pounded as she read the lines that spoke of their dreams and promises, their hopes for a future that was never realized.

The letters were filled with a kind of raw honesty that Isabel had never seen before. Her mother's words, both in the letters and the journal, painted a picture of a woman torn between the love she felt and the life she was expected to lead. Isabel began to understand the depth of her mother's internal struggle and the sacrifices she made to protect those she loved.

Next to the letters, Isabel found a bundle of photographs. She picked up one showing her mother and Adrian, both young and vibrant. They were standing close together, their faces lit up with a happiness that Isabel had never seen in her mother's later years. It was a stark contrast to the reserved and cautious woman Isabel had known.

The photographs were a poignant reminder of the joy her mother had once experienced and the profound impact that Adrian had on her life. Isabel felt a pang of sadness mixed with a sense of gratitude for the glimpse into her mother's past. These artifacts were helping her piece together a story that had been shrouded in secrecy for so long.

As Isabel continued to sift through the contents of the chest, she found an old sketchbook, its cover worn and edges frayed. The sketches inside were of various landscapes and scenes, many of them resembling the coastline and the lighthouse. Some sketches were accompanied by notes, and one caught Isabel's eye: a sketch of a lighthouse with an inscription that read, "The light will reveal what's hidden."

The phrase resonated deeply with Isabel. It was as if her mother had left a message for her, a clue to understanding the hidden parts of her life. Isabel's mind raced with possibilities, her heart filled with a mix of excitement and trepidation. The lighthouse had been a place of refuge and secrecy for her mother, and now it was calling Isabel to uncover more.

As she examined the final item in the chest, a small, ornate box, Isabel's hands were steady despite the whirlwind of emotions inside her. She opened the box to find a collection of trinkets and keepsakes: a locket, a faded ticket stub, and a small, intricately carved wooden figure. Each item seemed to tell its own story, a fragment of her mother's hidden life.

Isabel picked up the locket and opened it, revealing a tiny portrait of her mother and Adrian. The image was delicate and heartfelt, capturing a moment of profound intimacy. It was clear that these items were precious to her mother, symbols of a love that had been both cherished and concealed.

The discoveries in the lighthouse had shifted Isabel's understanding of her mother and her own place in the world. It was becoming evident that her mother's decisions were not solely driven by her own desires but were deeply intertwined with her love for Isabel and the need to protect her from the complexities of adult life.

With the new understanding, Isabel felt a renewed sense of connection to her mother. The secrets of the past were not just remnants of an old story but were integral to Isabel's journey of self-discovery. The lighthouse, once a symbol of hidden truths, had become a beacon guiding Isabel toward a deeper understanding of herself and her family's history.

As the night deepened, Isabel left the lighthouse, carrying with her the weight of her mother's secrets and the knowledge they brought. She walked back to her cabin with a sense of purpose, ready to face the next steps in her journey. The past was no longer just a collection of old memories; it was a living, breathing part of her present, shaping her understanding of her identity and her place in the world.

The lighthouse stood silent and steadfast in the background, its light continuing to sweep across the darkened sea. It was a symbol of clarity and revelation, a reminder that even in the midst of darkness, there was always the potential for illumination and understanding.

Isabel knew that the journey was far from over, but she felt more prepared to navigate the complexities ahead. The secrets she had uncovered were not just about her mother's past but were deeply intertwined with her own path to healing and self-acceptance. As she settled into bed, the newly discovered journal by her side, Isabel felt a sense of peace and determination.

The lighthouse had revealed its secrets, but the true illumination came from within Isabel herself. The journey of uncovering the past had become a profound exploration of her own heart and soul, and with each revelation, she felt more connected to the legacy her mother had left behind.

As Isabel left the lighthouse, the cool night air seemed to offer a reprieve from the weight of her discoveries. The beam of the lighthouse's lantern swept over the landscape, a rhythmic reminder of the secrets hidden in its walls. Her steps were heavy, laden with the revelations she had unearthed. Each item she had found—the letters, the photographs, the sketchbook—was a piece of her mother's life she had never known, and it was reshaping her understanding of both her mother and herself.

Isabel walked slowly back to her cabin, the quiet of the island night punctuated only by the distant sound of the waves crashing against the rocky shore. The events of the day swirled in her mind, each revelation interweaving with her thoughts about her mother's hidden past. Her mother's love affair, once a mere fragment of a distant memory, had now become a vivid narrative, revealing layers of her mother's personality and choices that Isabel had never fully appreciated.

When she arrived at her cabin, Isabel hesitated before going inside. The weight of her discoveries felt almost tangible, like a heavy cloak draped over her shoulders. She needed to process what she had found, to make sense of it all before she could share it with anyone—or even fully comprehend it herself. The night seemed to offer a necessary solitude, a chance to reflect and gather her thoughts.

Inside, the cabin was dimly lit by the soft glow of a single lamp. Isabel placed the items from the chest carefully on the table, her hands trembling slightly as she did so. The locket, the letters, and the sketches were all a testament to a side of her mother's life that had been kept hidden, even from her own daughter. The intricacy of her mother's emotions, the depth of her past relationships, were all laid bare before Isabel, and she was left to piece together the fragments of a story that had been carefully concealed.

She picked up the sketchbook once more, flipping through the pages as she tried to find meaning in the drawings and notes. The lighthouse sketches were particularly striking. The way her mother had portrayed the lighthouse, not just as a building but as a symbol of light and revelation, seemed to resonate deeply with Isabel. The inscription, "The light will reveal what's hidden," felt almost like a personal message from her mother, urging Isabel to uncover the truths that had been kept in the shadows.

Isabel thought about her mother's choices, about why she had kept this part of her life secret. The more she reflected, the more she began to see a pattern—a narrative of protection and sacrifice. Her mother had made choices that she believed were in Isabel's best interest, even if those choices had been made at the cost of her own happiness. It was a realization that both saddened and enlightened Isabel, and it underscored the complexity of her mother's life and the love she had tried to shield her from.

As the night wore on, Isabel found herself unable to sleep. She lay in bed, staring at the ceiling, her mind racing with thoughts and emotions. The lighthouse and its secrets had become a metaphor for her own internal journey. Just as the lighthouse revealed hidden truths, so too was Isabel uncovering the deeper layers of her own heart and her relationship with her mother.

In the early hours of the morning, Isabel decided to revisit the lighthouse. She felt a strong pull, a need to see it again and to find a deeper connection with the place that had become a symbol of her mother's hidden life. The idea of returning to the lighthouse felt both comforting and necessary. It was as if the lighthouse held the final pieces of the puzzle that she needed to understand.

Wrapped in a warm coat against the chill of the dawn, Isabel made her way back to the lighthouse. The sky was still dark, the first light of morning just beginning to pierce the horizon. The lighthouse stood as a solitary sentinel, its beam still sweeping the coastline, guiding ships safely through the night.

As she approached, Isabel felt a sense of calm wash over her. The lighthouse, bathed in the soft glow of the early morning light, seemed less intimidating and more like a trusted guide. She entered the building, moving with a quiet reverence as she ascended the spiral staircase to the top. The climb was familiar now, each step a part of her journey of discovery.

At the top of the lighthouse, Isabel looked out over the sea. The view was breathtaking, the water shimmering in the early morning light, the horizon stretching endlessly. It was a moment of clarity, a chance for Isabel to take in the beauty of the world and to reflect on the path she was walking.

The lighthouse's beam had become a metaphor for her own journey—its light cutting through the darkness, revealing what had been hidden. Isabel felt a sense of peace and determination. She knew that understanding her mother's past was only part of her journey. The real challenge lay in reconciling those revelations with her own life and decisions.

As Isabel stood there, taking in the view, she thought about Gabe and their growing connection. His presence had been a steadying force in her life, offering support and understanding as she navigated her mother's secrets. The quiet moments they had shared, the conversations that had revealed their vulnerabilities, had helped her see him in a new light. His support was invaluable, and she knew that their relationship was becoming more significant with each passing day.

She also thought about Dylan and the unresolved feelings that had resurfaced with his return. The old memories, the lingering connections, were complex and emotionally charged. Isabel was beginning to understand that her feelings for Dylan were intertwined with her past, with the person she had been before returning to the island. The challenge would be to distinguish between past attachments and present realities, to make choices that were true to who she had become.

With a deep breath, Isabel turned away from the view and descended the staircase, ready to face the day. The lighthouse had offered her a new perspective, a chance to see her mother's legacy and her own journey in a clearer light. As she left the lighthouse and walked back to her cabin, Isabel felt a renewed sense of purpose.

The discoveries she had made were shaping her understanding of her mother's life and her own path forward. The journey was far from over, but Isabel felt more equipped to face the challenges ahead. The lighthouse, with its secrets and its light, had become a symbol of hope and clarity—a reminder that even in the midst of uncertainty, there was always a path to understanding and resolution.

Isabel knew that her journey of self-discovery and healing was just beginning. The lighthouse had illuminated the past, but it was up to her to chart her course for the future. With each step, she was finding her way, guided by the light of the past and the promise of what lay ahead.

8

Chapter 8: Festival of Lights

As the Festival of Lights unfolded across Rosemere Isle, the island seemed to glow with a warmth and vibrancy that belied the crisp autumn air. Lanterns of every shape and color floated in the gentle breeze, their soft light dancing across the cobblestone streets and reflecting off the waves of the bay. The festival, a time-honored tradition on the island, was in full swing, bringing the community together in a shared celebration of light and life.

Isabel walked through the festival, feeling a mix of emotions. The island's beauty was undeniable, and the festival's magic was palpable. The air was filled with the sounds of laughter, the hum of music, and the scent of freshly baked pastries. People milled about, enjoying the festivities, while the flickering lanterns created a fairy-tale ambiance that seemed to invite a sense of wonder and possibility.

Gabe found Isabel among the crowd, his presence as steady and reassuring as ever. His eyes searched for hers through the sea of festival-goers, and when they finally met, a smile spread across his face. The sight of him standing amidst the lanterns, bathed in their warm glow, seemed to embody the spirit of the festival itself—a symbol of hope and renewal.

As they approached each other, Gabe extended his hand to Isabel, his touch gentle but firm. "Would you care to dance?" he asked, his voice soft and inviting. There was a vulnerability in his eyes, a hopefulness that matched the night's ambiance.

Isabel hesitated for a moment, her heart fluttering with a mix of excitement and apprehension. The dance was more than just a simple gesture; it was a significant step in their growing connection. The festival's magical atmosphere seemed to amplify the emotions she had been grappling with, making the moment feel even more profound.

With a nod, she placed her hand in his, and together they made their way to the open space where a small band played a gentle waltz. The music was soothing, a perfect accompaniment to the intimate setting of the festival. As they moved onto the dance floor, Isabel felt a shiver of anticipation, a sensation of stepping into a new chapter of her life.

Gabe led her gracefully, his movements smooth and assured. The world around them seemed to fade as they focused on each other, their steps in sync with the rhythm of the music. The lanterns above created a canopy of light, casting a soft glow on their faces and making the dance feel like a moment suspended in time.

Isabel could feel the warmth of Gabe's hand against her back, the strength of his arm supporting her as they swayed to the music. There was something deeply comforting about his presence, a reassurance that she hadn't realized she needed until now. The closeness of their bodies, the gentle pressure of his hand on hers, all conveyed a sense of connection that words alone could not express.

As they danced, Isabel couldn't help but reflect on the festival's symbolism. The lanterns, representing hopes and dreams, seemed to mirror the possibilities that were unfolding in her own life. The festival was a celebration of light overcoming darkness, of renewal and new beginnings—concepts that resonated deeply with her as she navigated her own journey of self-discovery and healing.

In the midst of the dance, Gabe leaned in slightly, his breath warm against her ear. "You look beautiful tonight," he murmured, his voice low and sincere. The compliment, simple yet heartfelt, sent a rush of warmth through Isabel. It was as if Gabe's words were a confirmation of the connection they were building, a reflection of the feelings that had been growing between them.

Isabel turned her head to meet his gaze, her eyes meeting his with a mixture of vulnerability and trust. "Thank you," she said softly, her voice almost lost in the gentle hum of the festival. The moment felt significant, a turning point in their relationship where unspoken emotions were finally being acknowledged and shared.

As the dance continued, the music took on a more intimate tone, its melody weaving through the night air like a tender whisper. The festival's lights seemed to shimmer even more brightly, casting an ethereal glow on the couple as they moved together. Each step, each glance, became a testament to their growing affection and the possibilities that lay ahead.

The surrounding crowd, though present, seemed distant, as if the world had narrowed to just the two of them. Isabel felt a sense of peace and contentment that she hadn't experienced in a long time. The worries and uncertainties that had plagued her seemed to dissolve in the warmth of Gabe's embrace, leaving her with a renewed sense of hope.

The dance came to an end, and as the final notes of the music faded, Gabe and Isabel lingered in each other's arms for a moment longer. The world around them seemed to hold its breath, as if acknowledging the significance of the connection they had just shared. Gabe's hands rested gently on Isabel's waist, and she could feel the steady rhythm of his heartbeat, a reassuring reminder of the bond they were forming.

As they stepped away from the dance floor, Gabe's hand remained in hers, a silent promise of support and understanding. The festival continued around them, but the experience had transformed their evening into something deeply personal and meaningful.

Isabel looked up at Gabe, her eyes reflecting the glow of the lanterns. "Thank you for this," she said softly, her voice filled with sincerity. "It means more to me than I can say."

Gabe's smile was warm and tender. "I'm glad," he replied. "I've been wanting to share this moment with you for a long time."

The words hung in the air, a testament to the depth of Gabe's feelings and the significance of their connection. Isabel could see the sincerity in his eyes, and it reassured her that their growing relationship was rooted in something real and profound.

As they walked hand in hand through the festival, the lanterns casting their soft light around them, Isabel felt a sense of renewal and possibility. The dance had been a pivotal moment, a symbol of the love and connection that were slowly unfolding in her life. The festival had provided a beautiful backdrop for their shared experience, a celebration of light and hope that mirrored the journey Isabel was on.

The night continued, the festival's lights flickering like a promise of new beginnings. Isabel and Gabe moved through the crowd, their connection deepened by the dance and the shared moments of vulnerability and trust. The island, with its festive atmosphere and the beauty of the lanterns, had become a symbol of the love and renewal that were blossoming in Isabel's life.

As the evening drew to a close and the festival's lights began to dim, Isabel felt a sense of contentment and anticipation for the future. The dance had marked a turning point, a moment of emotional intimacy that would shape the path ahead. With Gabe by her side, she was ready to face whatever challenges lay ahead, knowing that the light of the festival—and the connection they had shared—would guide them through the darkness.

The Festival of Lights continued to illuminate Rosemere Isle, its vibrant hues painting the night sky with a tapestry of hope and joy. The lanterns, now casting a warm glow over the gathered crowd, seemed to breathe life into the evening, creating a mesmerizing scene that felt almost magical. Isabel and Gabe wandered through the festival, their hands intertwined, their connection palpable.

As they strolled among the stalls and booths, Isabel took in the festive atmosphere, her heart still buzzing from the dance. She couldn't shake the feeling that this night was a turning point—a moment of clarity and renewal. Gabe's presence beside her was comforting, and the way he looked at her, with a mixture of admiration and affection, made her heart flutter with a new sense of possibility.

They paused near a stall adorned with twinkling lights, where local artisans sold handcrafted trinkets and ornaments. Gabe picked up a small lantern, its delicate design catching the light of the nearby lanterns. "What do you think of this?" he asked, holding it up for Isabel to see.

Isabel studied the lantern, its intricate patterns reflecting the festival's spirit. "It's beautiful," she said, her voice tinged with a hint of wonder. "It's like a tiny piece of the festival itself."

Gabe smiled, his eyes reflecting the same warmth as the lanterns. "I thought it might be a nice keepsake," he said, his tone light and hopeful. "Something to remember tonight by."

Isabel's heart skipped a beat. The gesture was simple yet profoundly meaningful. It was as if Gabe was offering a tangible symbol of their connection, a reminder of the evening they had shared. She accepted the lantern with a grateful smile, feeling a deep sense of appreciation for his thoughtfulness.

As they continued their walk, they came to a quieter part of the festival, where the noise of the crowd faded into a soft murmur. The lanterns here were more sparse, casting a gentle glow that created an intimate atmosphere. Gabe led Isabel to a secluded spot, where a small bench overlooked the bay, the water shimmering with the reflections of the festival lights.

They sat down together, the silence between them comfortable and filled with unspoken understanding. The view was breathtaking—the bay, the lanterns floating on the water, and the soft glow of the festival lights merging into a scene of serene beauty. The world seemed to slow down around them, allowing the significance of their shared moment to settle in.

Gabe turned to Isabel, his expression serious but gentle. "Isabel, I know we haven't known each other for very long, but tonight has felt... special," he began, his voice filled with sincerity. "I feel like we've connected on a deeper level, and I want to be honest with you about how I feel."

Isabel looked at him, her heart racing. The vulnerability in Gabe's voice resonated with her own feelings, and she felt a surge of emotion. "I feel it too," she admitted softly. "Tonight has been more than just a festival for me. It's been a chance to reconnect with something I thought I'd lost—hope, and a sense of belonging."

Gabe reached out, taking her hand in his. "I'm glad to hear that," he said. "I've been thinking a lot about us and what we've shared. I know it's only been a short time, but I can't help but feel like we've been brought together for a reason. There's something real here, something worth exploring."

Isabel squeezed his hand, feeling a wave of emotion wash over her. Gabe's words echoed her own thoughts and fears, and the honesty between them created a space of deep connection. "I agree," she said, her voice trembling slightly. "There's a lot I'm still figuring out about myself and my past, but being with you tonight has made me realize that I'm ready to embrace what's ahead. I want to see where this connection can take us."

They sat in silence for a moment, the sounds of the festival continuing in the background. The gentle rhythm of the bay's waves and the soft rustling of leaves created a soothing backdrop to their conversation. The quiet was filled with a sense of anticipation, as if the night itself was holding its breath in recognition of their shared understanding.

Gabe's eyes met Isabel's with a look of deep affection. "I'm here for you, Isabel," he said. "Whatever you need, whatever you're going through, I want to be a part of it. I care about you, and I'm willing to be patient and supportive as you navigate this journey."

Isabel felt a lump form in her throat, her emotions overwhelming her. Gabe's commitment and kindness were exactly what she had been yearning for, and the trust she felt in him was both comforting and exhilarating. "Thank you, Gabe," she said, her voice choked with emotion. "Your support means more to me than I can put into words. I'm grateful for you and for this moment."

They leaned in, their foreheads gently touching as they shared a tender kiss. The kiss was slow and sweet, a reflection of the deep feelings that had been building between them. It was a moment of intimacy and connection, a culmination of the evening's shared experiences and emotions.

As they pulled away, Gabe smiled, his eyes shining with warmth. "Let's enjoy the rest of the festival," he suggested. "We've got a lot more to explore, and I want to make the most of this night with you."

Isabel nodded, her heart full of hope and contentment. "I'd like that," she said, her smile mirroring his. "Let's make it a night to remember."

They stood up, their hands still intertwined, and rejoined the festival's festivities. The night was still young, and the lanterns continued to float above them, casting their gentle light over the celebration. The community's joy and the beauty of the festival seemed to symbolize the possibilities that lay ahead for Isabel and Gabe.

As they walked through the crowd, their connection felt stronger than ever. The shared experiences of the evening—the dance, the quiet conversation, and the kiss—had brought them closer together, and the promise of what was to come filled Isabel with a sense of excitement and anticipation.

The Festival of Lights continued around them, a celebration of hope, renewal, and love. For Isabel and Gabe, it was a night that marked the beginning of something beautiful and meaningful, a chance to explore their connection and embrace the future together. The lanterns, with their warm glow and gentle light, would serve as a lasting reminder of their shared journey and the possibilities that lay ahead.

The Festival of Lights carried on around Isabel and Gabe, but in their shared space, the world seemed to quieten, leaving only the soft murmur of the crowd and the occasional laughter drifting through the air. The lanterns, now casting long, dancing shadows across the grass, created a dreamlike setting that felt almost ethereal.

As they wandered further, Isabel noticed how Gabe's presence was both grounding and liberating. The festival's exuberant colors and the festival-goers' joyous energy provided a stark contrast to the quieter, more intimate moments they had shared earlier. This juxtaposition heightened the significance of their connection. Gabe's hand in hers felt like an anchor in a sea of uncertainty, offering a sense of stability and warmth that she hadn't expected but now cherished deeply.

They stopped by a booth that offered hot cider, and Gabe handed Isabel a steaming cup. The warmth of the drink seeped through the paper cup and into her fingers, a pleasant counterpoint to the cool evening breeze. She took a sip, the sweet and spicy flavor filling her senses and evoking a sense of comfort that she hadn't felt in a long time.

"Do you remember the first festival we went to together?" Gabe asked, his eyes twinkling with nostalgia. "It was a few years ago, and we were both so awkward trying to figure out how to dance."

Isabel laughed softly, the sound light and genuine. "Yes, I remember. I think we both stumbled over our feet a lot. But it was fun, wasn't it?"

Gabe's smile widened. "Definitely. It was one of those moments where you realize how much more enjoyable something can be when you're with the right person. And tonight, it feels even more special, doesn't it?"

Isabel looked at Gabe, her heart swelling with emotion. His words resonated with her, reflecting her own feelings about their connection. "It does," she agreed, her voice soft. "Tonight has felt like a turning point for me. It's like I'm rediscovering parts of myself that I had buried away."

Gabe's expression grew serious, his gaze steady. "I'm glad to hear that," he said. "I've been thinking a lot about us and what this means. I want you to know that I'm here for you, no matter what."

The sincerity in Gabe's voice struck Isabel deeply. She took a deep breath, feeling a wave of vulnerability wash over her. "There's something I've been meaning to share with you," she said, her tone hesitant. "It's not easy for me to talk about, but I think it's important for us to be honest with each other."

Gabe's concern deepened, and he gently squeezed her hand, encouraging her to continue. "You can tell me anything, Isabel," he said. "I'm listening."

Isabel looked down at her cup of cider, her mind racing as she searched for the right words. "When I was growing up, I had this idealized image of what life was supposed to be like," she began, her voice trembling slightly. "I wanted to be successful, to have everything figured out. But over the years, I've realized that I've been chasing this version of myself that I thought was expected of me. And now, I'm facing the reality that I've lost touch with who I really am."

Gabe listened intently, his gaze never wavering. "That sounds incredibly tough," he said softly. "But the fact that you're acknowledging it and trying to reconnect with yourself is a powerful step. It takes a lot of courage to face those feelings."

Isabel met his gaze, feeling a rush of gratitude for his understanding. "Thank you," she said. "It means a lot to me that you're here and that you're willing to listen. I've been so afraid of being judged or misunderstood, but with you, I feel like I can be honest about what I'm going through."

Gabe's expression softened, and he reached out to gently brush a stray lock of hair from Isabel's face. "I'm glad you feel that way," he said. "I care about you, Isabel. And I want to support you as you navigate this journey. We're in this together."

The warmth of Gabe's words and the tenderness of his touch made Isabel's heart swell with emotion. She felt a deep sense of relief and connection, as if the walls she had built around herself were slowly crumbling away.

As they continued to walk through the festival, the atmosphere felt charged with a new kind of intimacy. The lanterns above them seemed to glow even brighter, casting a soft, golden light that symbolized the hope and possibility that lay ahead.

Gabe led Isabel to a quieter corner of the festival where a small stage had been set up for local performers. A band was playing a mellow tune, their music weaving through the night air and adding to the evening's magical ambiance. Gabe pulled Isabel closer, their bodies pressed together as they swayed to the music.

The closeness between them was electric, a testament to the deepening connection they had forged. Isabel could feel Gabe's heartbeat against her own, and the rhythm of the music seemed to mirror the beat of their hearts. In that moment, it felt as though the world outside the festival ceased to exist, leaving only the two of them in their shared space of intimacy and understanding.

As the song reached its crescendo, Gabe leaned in, his lips brushing against Isabel's ear. "Tonight has been incredible," he murmured, his breath warm against her skin. "I'm really happy to be here with you."

Isabel's pulse quickened, her emotions a swirling mix of joy and vulnerability. "Me too," she whispered back, her voice tinged with emotion. "This is exactly what I needed. To feel this connected and supported."

The song ended, and the crowd erupted in applause, but Isabel and Gabe remained wrapped in their own bubble of contentment.

The music and the festival's vibrant energy seemed to fade into the background, leaving them in their private world of shared moments and heartfelt connection.

As they walked back toward the festival's main area, the atmosphere was filled with a sense of newfound possibility. Isabel's earlier apprehensions had been replaced by a growing sense of hope and optimism, fueled by Gabe's unwavering support and the promise of what lay ahead.

The Festival of Lights continued to shine around them, its glow a reminder of the beauty and potential that existed in their lives. For Isabel and Gabe, the night had become a celebration of their connection and the beginning of a new chapter in their journey together. The lanterns, the music, and the shared moments would forever symbolize their evolving relationship and the possibilities that awaited them in the future.

The Festival of Lights continued around them, the energy of the crowd mingling with the soft, enchanting glow of the lanterns. Gabe and Isabel walked hand in hand, their previous conversation adding a new layer to their shared experience. The festival's magic seemed to enhance the closeness they were beginning to feel, making the night feel like a turning point in their relationship.

As they made their way through the throng of people, Isabel found herself lost in thought, reflecting on the evening's events. The blend of festive cheer and Gabe's quiet support had created a cocoon of warmth and hope. The festival, with its lively colors and joyful sounds, felt like a backdrop to their own unfolding story—a story that was beginning to feel more promising and real.

Gabe led Isabel to a small hill on the edge of the festival grounds, where they could see the entire event laid out before them. The view was breathtaking. Lanterns floated like stars against the dark sky, and the laughter and music of the festival seemed to hum softly in the background.

"This is my favorite spot," Gabe said, his voice filled with a mix of pride and nostalgia. "It's where I come when I need to think or just enjoy the view. It feels like you're in a different world up here, doesn't it?"

Isabel nodded, her gaze sweeping over the scene below. "It's beautiful," she agreed. "It's like seeing everything from a new perspective."

Gabe's hand tightened around hers, and he turned to face her, his expression serious. "I wanted to talk to you about something," he began, his tone earnest. "Earlier, when we were dancing and talking, I realized how important it is for us to be open with each other. I know we've only just started reconnecting, but I feel like there's something real here, something worth exploring."

Isabel's heart skipped a beat. She had sensed the deepening of their connection throughout the evening, but hearing Gabe articulate it made the feeling even more tangible. "I feel the same way," she said, her voice steady despite the flutter of nerves. "Tonight has made me realize how much I've missed this kind of connection. It feels like I'm starting to find pieces of myself that I'd forgotten."

Gabe's eyes softened, and he stepped closer, closing the space between them. "I'm glad to hear that," he said softly. "I've been thinking about how to tell you what's been on my mind. I want to be honest with you about where I stand. I've been hesitant to make any assumptions or rush things, but I can't deny how much I care about you."

Isabel looked up at him, her emotions swirling in a mix of excitement and apprehension. "Gabe," she began, "I'm grateful for your honesty. This evening has been one of the most genuine experiences I've had in a long time. I've been carrying so much uncertainty, but being with you has helped me see things more clearly."

Gabe's gaze never wavered, and he took a deep breath before continuing. "I know this is all new and we're still figuring things out, but I want to be there for you, in whatever way you need. Whether it's exploring what's between us or just being a friend, I'm here."

The sincerity in Gabe's voice and the depth of his feelings touched Isabel profoundly. She reached up and placed a hand gently on his cheek, feeling the warmth of his skin under her fingertips. "Thank you," she said softly. "Your support means more to me than I can express. I'm still processing a lot of things, but having you here, being open and understanding, makes a huge difference."

Gabe smiled, his expression reflecting a mix of relief and affection. "I'm glad," he said. "We're in this together, and we'll take it one step at a time. I'm just happy to be a part of your journey."

They stood together, watching the festival below, the weight of their conversation giving way to a sense of peace and anticipation. The lanterns continued to glow, their light a symbol of the new beginnings and possibilities that lay ahead for both of them.

As the evening wore on, the festival began to wind down, and the crowd slowly dispersed. Gabe and Isabel remained on the hill, wrapped in their own world of shared understanding and growing affection. The sounds of the festival faded into the distance, leaving them in a quiet, intimate space where they could focus solely on each other.

Isabel leaned her head against Gabe's shoulder, feeling a deep sense of comfort and connection. The cool night air, the distant hum of the festival, and the warmth of Gabe's presence created a cocoon of tranquility that felt both soothing and exhilarating.

For the first time in a long while, Isabel allowed herself to fully embrace the moment, letting go of her doubts and fears. The festival had not only brought them together but had also given her a renewed sense of hope and possibility. Gabe's presence and their shared experience had illuminated a path forward, one filled with promise and potential.

As they prepared to leave, Gabe took Isabel's hand once more, their fingers interlaced. "Thank you for spending the evening with me," he said softly. "It's been an incredible night."

Isabel smiled, her heart full. "Thank you for being here," she replied. "Tonight has been a turning point for me, and I'm grateful to have shared it with you."

They walked back toward the festival grounds, their steps light and their hearts full. The lanterns continued to cast their gentle glow, a reminder of the beauty and possibilities that awaited them. For Isabel and Gabe, the Festival of Lights had become a symbol of their growing connection and the bright future they were beginning to build together.

As they walked back toward the festival grounds, the lanterns' gentle glow reflected in Gabe's eyes, adding a soft brilliance to his expression. Isabel felt a deep sense of contentment, but also a fluttering uncertainty about what lay ahead. The evening had stirred emotions she hadn't fully confronted, leaving her both exhilarated and introspective.

The festival's vibrant atmosphere began to wind down, the laughter and music gradually fading as the night grew quieter. The lanterns, which had been so bright and abundant, now seemed to dim, their light casting long shadows that danced around them.

Gabe squeezed Isabel's hand gently, breaking the silence. "It's amazing how something as simple as lights and music can bring out such strong emotions," he said, his voice reflective.

Isabel glanced up at him, her thoughts still swirling from their earlier conversation. "It really is," she agreed. "I guess it's moments like these that make me realize how much I've missed being part of something like this. The island feels different tonight, like it's offering me a chance to reconnect with everything I've lost."

Gabe's gaze softened, and he stopped walking, pulling Isabel to a quieter spot away from the remaining festivalgoers. They stood under a canopy of trees, their surroundings now bathed in the muted glow of lanterns still hanging from the branches.

"Isabel," Gabe began, his tone gentle but earnest. "Tonight has been special for me, too. I've been trying to figure out the right way to express what I'm feeling. This evening has shown me that there's something real between us. Something I want to explore further."

Isabel's heart raced, and she took a deep breath, feeling the weight of Gabe's words. "I've been feeling the same way," she confessed. "It's like everything tonight has aligned in a way that makes me see things more clearly. I've been holding back for so long, but being here with you, experiencing this, it's making me reconsider what I truly want."

Gabe's eyes searched hers, seeking clarity. "What do you want, Isabel?" he asked softly.

Isabel hesitated, the question stirring up a mix of emotions. She looked down at their intertwined hands, then back up at Gabe. "I want to take a chance," she said, her voice steadying. "I want to allow myself to be open to what's happening between us. But I also need to understand what that means for me, for us."

Gabe nodded, his expression thoughtful. "I'm here for whatever that means," he said. "I want to support you as you figure things out. I don't want to rush you, but I also want you to know that I'm serious about what I feel for you."

They stood in comfortable silence for a moment, each lost in their thoughts. The night air was cool, and the occasional rustle of leaves added a soothing backdrop to their conversation. Gabe reached out and tucked a strand of hair behind Isabel's ear, a tender gesture that spoke volumes.

Isabel looked up at him, her eyes reflecting a mixture of vulnerability and resolve. "Thank you for being patient with me," she said. "It means a lot to have someone who understands the complexities of what I'm going through."

Gabe's smile was warm and reassuring. "I'm glad you feel that way. I care about you, Isabel, and I want to be here for you. We don't have to have all the answers right now. We just need to take things one step at a time."

They stood close, the world around them seeming to pause as they shared this intimate moment. The lanterns swayed gently in the breeze, their soft light casting a romantic glow over the scene. Gabe and Isabel were wrapped in a cocoon of warmth and understanding, their connection deepening with each passing second.

As the final lanterns were packed away and the festival grounds grew quieter, Gabe and Isabel decided to take a slow walk back to her mother's estate. The path was illuminated by the occasional streetlight, and the stars above added a touch of magic to the night sky.

During the walk, they talked about their favorite festival memories and shared more about their personal lives. Gabe spoke about his love for the island and his work with the boat-building business, while Isabel revealed more about her photography and the challenges she faced in her career. The conversation flowed easily, and their laughter and shared stories created a bond that felt both natural and profound.

When they reached the estate, the house looked serene and welcoming under the starlit sky. Isabel felt a pang of nostalgia as she gazed at the familiar, yet distant, home. Gabe noticed the change in her expression and gently squeezed her hand.

"Do you want to talk more, or would you prefer to get some rest?" he asked.

Isabel considered the options for a moment, then smiled softly. "I think I'd like to stay outside for a bit longer," she said. "It's been a meaningful evening, and I want to savor it."

Gabe nodded in agreement. "I'm happy to stay with you," he said. "We can sit on the porch and talk or just enjoy the quiet."

They settled onto the porch, sitting side by side in the comfortable chairs that had been there for as long as Isabel could remember. The sounds of the night—crickets chirping, the rustle of leaves—added a peaceful soundtrack to their conversation. Gabe's presence was soothing, and Isabel felt a deep sense of calm and contentment as they talked about their hopes and dreams.

As the hours passed, Isabel felt her earlier tensions and uncertainties melt away. The evening had been a turning point for her, and she was beginning to embrace the possibility of what lay ahead. Gabe's support and understanding had opened a door to new possibilities, and she felt ready to explore them with an open heart.

Eventually, the conversation tapered off, and they sat in comfortable silence, watching the stars and listening to the night. Gabe's hand remained in Isabel's, their fingers intertwined in a gesture of connection and promise.

The night had been a revelation for both of them. The Festival of Lights had illuminated more than just the island; it had shed light on their growing feelings and the potential for a future together. Isabel was beginning to see that her journey of rediscovery and healing was intertwined with her relationship with Gabe, and she was ready to embrace the adventure that lay ahead.

As the first light of dawn began to break over the horizon, Isabel and Gabe reluctantly prepared to say their goodbyes. The night had been a beautiful blend of celebration and introspection, and they had both taken important steps toward understanding their feelings and their future.

"Thank you for a wonderful evening," Isabel said softly as they stood up to leave. "Tonight has been incredibly special, and I'm grateful to have shared it with you."

Gabe's smile was gentle and full of affection. "Thank you for being open and honest with me," he replied. "I'm looking forward to what's next for us."

They shared a final, lingering embrace before parting ways for the night. As Isabel watched Gabe walk away, she felt a renewed sense of hope and possibility. The Festival of Lights had indeed been a turning point, and she was ready to face whatever came next with an open heart and a sense of anticipation.

The night had illuminated not only the island but also the path forward for Isabel and Gabe, and as the dawn broke, it marked the beginning of a new chapter in their lives.

As the first light of dawn began to break over the horizon, Isabel found herself lying awake in her bed, the remnants of the festival still vivid in her mind. The night's events had been transformative, not only rekindling old emotions but also opening her heart to new possibilities with Gabe. She felt a delicate balance between hope and apprehension, the excitement of what might come next mingling with the natural trepidation of stepping into the unknown.

The morning sun filtered through the thin curtains, casting a gentle, golden hue across the room. Isabel stretched and sat up, her thoughts still swirling from the intimate moments shared with Gabe. She felt a profound sense of peace, yet an underlying current of nervous anticipation. Today, she knew, would bring new challenges and decisions.

She decided to take a walk along the beach to clear her mind. The island's early morning calm, with its serene waves and soft, salty breeze, offered a perfect backdrop for reflection. Pulling on a cozy sweater and slipping into her shoes, she stepped out into the fresh morning air, savoring the tranquility that the early hour provided.

As Isabel walked along the shoreline, she couldn't help but replay the previous night's events in her mind. The festival had been more than a celebration; it had been a canvas for her emotions, a place where she could confront her feelings and her past. Gabe's presence had been a reassuring constant, his sincerity and support providing a safe haven amidst her internal chaos.

Reaching a secluded spot on the beach, Isabel sat on a large, weathered rock, watching the waves gently lap against the shore. The rhythmic sound of the ocean was soothing, and she took a deep breath, letting the cool air fill her lungs. The calm of the beach contrasted sharply with the storm of emotions she had felt the night before, and she appreciated the moment of solitude.

Her thoughts drifted to her mother's painting and the lighthouse clue that had become a central part of her journey. Isabel realized that her mother's secrets were not just about hidden love affairs but also about a deeper layer of vulnerability and sacrifice. Her mother had kept these secrets to protect Isabel, to shield her from the pain and complexity of her own life. This realization made Isabel feel a stronger connection to her mother, as if she were uncovering not only her mother's past but also a part of herself that had been obscured by years of distance and unresolved emotions.

The gentle tapping of footsteps on the sand interrupted her reverie. Isabel looked up to see Gabe approaching, his expression thoughtful and serene. He had evidently decided to join her for a morning walk, perhaps sensing her need for company.

"Good morning," Gabe said softly as he reached her side. "I hope you don't mind me intruding. I thought a morning walk might be nice, especially after last night."

Isabel smiled, appreciating his presence. "I was just thinking about how much last night meant to me," she said. "It's been a long time since I felt such clarity and connection."

Gabe sat down beside her on the rock, his gaze following the horizon. "I feel the same way. There's something about being here, in this place, with you, that feels incredibly right."

They sat in comfortable silence for a few moments, watching the sun climb higher in the sky. The warmth of the morning sun began to chase away the last remnants of the night's chill, and Isabel felt a renewed sense of hope. The festival had indeed been a pivotal moment, but the quiet morning was providing a space for deeper reflection and connection.

"So," Gabe said eventually, breaking the silence, "what's next for you? I know you've been on this journey of rediscovery, but what are you hoping to find or achieve?"

Isabel took a deep breath, her mind still processing the myriad of emotions from the previous night. "I think I'm starting to understand what I really want," she said slowly. "It's not just about uncovering my mother's past or figuring out where I fit in on the island. It's about finding a balance between my past and my future, between who I was and who I want to become."

Gabe nodded, his expression attentive and supportive. "That sounds like an important journey. And I want you to know that I'm here to support you through it. Whether it's exploring your mother's history or figuring out what comes next for us, I want to be a part of that journey."

Isabel felt a surge of warmth at Gabe's words. His support was invaluable, and it made her feel more secure about the uncertainties she faced. "Thank you, Gabe," she said, her voice filled with gratitude. "Your presence and understanding mean a lot to me."

They continued their walk along the beach, the conversation flowing naturally as they discussed their dreams and aspirations. Gabe talked about his plans for the future, his desire to continue contributing to the island community and to explore new opportunities in his personal and professional life. Isabel shared her hopes for her photography career and her desire to delve deeper into her mother's legacy, seeking to understand not only her past but also the impact it had on her present.

As they walked, the landscape around them seemed to mirror their evolving relationship. The sun continued its ascent, casting a warm glow over the ocean and highlighting the beauty of their surroundings. The beach, with its gentle waves and expansive views, became a metaphor for the journey Isabel and Gabe were embarking on together.

Eventually, they reached a small café by the beach that had recently reopened for the season. The aroma of freshly brewed coffee and baked goods wafted through the air, inviting them inside. They decided to stop for a quick breakfast, and as they settled at a cozy table by the window, the conversation turned to lighter topics, punctuated by easy laughter and shared smiles.

Over coffee and pastries, Isabel felt a deep sense of connection with Gabe. The morning had been a perfect complement to the previous night's festival, providing a space for reflection and growth. Their conversation, filled with mutual support and understanding, solidified the bond between them and offered a glimpse of what their future might hold.

As they finished their breakfast, Gabe reached across the table and took Isabel's hand in his. "I'm really glad we had this time together," he said. "It's given me a lot to think about, and I hope it has for you too."

Isabel squeezed his hand, her heart full of gratitude and hope. "It has," she replied. "This morning has been a perfect continuation of last night, and I feel more certain about what I want and where I'm headed."

With a renewed sense of purpose and a strengthened connection, Isabel and Gabe left the café and continued their walk along the beach. The day was just beginning, and with it, the promise of new experiences and deeper understanding awaited them. The Festival of Lights had illuminated more than just the island; it had shed light on their journey together and the possibilities that lay ahead.

As the last of the festival's vibrant lights began to flicker and fade into the early hours of the morning, Isabel found herself caught between the lingering magic of the night and the sober light of dawn. She and Gabe had retreated to a quieter corner of the beach, where the sounds of the festival had softened to a distant hum, replaced by the soothing, rhythmic crash of waves against the shore.

They sat close together, the night air crisp and cool after the warmth of the festival. Gabe had draped his jacket over Isabel's shoulders, a thoughtful gesture that made her heart flutter with a mixture of gratitude and burgeoning affection. The proximity between them felt comfortable and natural, their silent closeness speaking volumes more than words ever could.

The festival had been a whirlwind of colors and emotions, a spectacle that seemed to mirror Isabel's internal transformation. Gabe had been a constant presence throughout, his supportive gaze and gentle touches reassuring her in ways that words could not. The dance they had shared had been more than just a physical expression; it was as if their souls had briefly intertwined, revealing glimpses of something deeper and more profound.

Isabel looked out at the ocean, the moonlight casting a silvery sheen over the water, and felt a wave of reflection wash over her. The festival's enchantment had illuminated not just the island but her own journey of self-discovery. She realized that her time on the island was not merely about uncovering her mother's past but also about finding a place for herself in a world that had once seemed so distant.

Gabe's presence beside her was a grounding force. She could sense that he was deep in thought as well, his occasional glances at her betraying a mix of curiosity and contemplation. It was as though he was trying to understand the depth of her feelings, to grasp the significance of the night and the path it might carve for them both.

After a few moments of silence, Gabe spoke softly, his voice carrying the weight of unspoken thoughts. "Last night was... incredible," he said, his tone reflective. "It felt like more than just a celebration. It was like a new beginning for both of us."

Isabel turned to him, her eyes meeting his in the dim light. "Yes, it did feel that way. The festival was beautiful, but it was also a reminder of how much I've been missing in my life. It's like I've been walking around with a veil over my eyes, and last night lifted it just a little."

Gabe's expression softened, and he took a deep breath before continuing. "I know we haven't talked about it much, but I've been thinking about us and what this connection might mean. I feel like we're on the brink of something significant, something that goes beyond just the moments we've shared."

Isabel's heart skipped a beat at his words. The sincerity in Gabe's voice and the earnest look in his eyes made her feel vulnerable but also deeply understood. "I've felt that too," she admitted, her voice barely above a whisper. "It's like there's something between us that's been building for a long time, even if we didn't realize it until recently."

Gabe reached out and gently tucked a strand of hair behind her ear, his touch tender and reassuring. "I want to be honest with you, Isabel. I care about you deeply, and I'm not sure where this journey will lead us, but I want to explore it with you. I want to be here for you, to support you as you navigate your past and your future."

Isabel's heart swelled at his words. She could feel the depth of his commitment, and it made her feel both hopeful and apprehensive. The intensity of their connection was undeniable, but it also carried with it the weight of uncertainty and the fear of what might come next.

"I care about you too, Gabe," she said, her voice trembling slightly. "Last night, I realized how much I've been holding back, how much I've been afraid to let anyone in. But with you, it feels different. It feels like I can be open and honest, and that's something I haven't felt in a long time."

Gabe's smile was warm and reassuring. "I'm glad you feel that way. We don't have to have all the answers right now. What matters is that we're here, together, and we're willing to take this journey one step at a time."

The sense of relief that washed over Isabel was palpable. The weight of her fears and uncertainties seemed to lift, replaced by a sense of shared purpose and connection. The night had been a turning point, and now, with the first light of dawn beginning to break through the darkness, she felt ready to face whatever came next.

They remained on the beach for a while longer, the silence between them comfortable and filled with unspoken understanding. The waves continued their gentle dance against the shore, the rhythmic sound providing a soothing backdrop to their intimate conversation.

Eventually, the sky began to lighten, the first hints of sunrise casting a soft, golden glow over the horizon. The beauty of the morning was a stark contrast to the festival's vibrant chaos, yet it felt like a fitting continuation of the night's revelations.

Gabe stood up and extended his hand to Isabel. "Shall we head back?" he asked, his eyes sparkling with a mix of affection and anticipation.

Isabel took his hand, feeling a sense of completeness as their fingers intertwined. "Yes, let's go," she said, her voice filled with renewed determination. "I'm ready to face whatever comes next, and I'm glad I'll be doing it with you by my side."

As they walked back toward the town, the morning light casting a warm glow over their path, Isabel felt a renewed sense of purpose and hope. The festival had been a celebration of their connection, and the quiet morning was a reminder of the journey they were about to embark on together.

The path ahead was still uncertain, filled with the promise of discovery and the challenge of navigating their emotions. But with Gabe by her side and the island's beauty surrounding them, Isabel felt more prepared than ever to embrace the future. The dawn of a new day marked the beginning of a new chapter in their lives, one filled with potential and the possibility of love and renewal.

As the morning sun began to paint the horizon with its warm, golden hues, Isabel and Gabe walked back to town, their fingers still entwined. The Festival of Lights had left an indelible mark on Isabel, not just through its visual splendor but also through the intimate moments shared with Gabe. Each step they took seemed to carry the weight of unspoken promises and the lightness of newfound hope.

The town, now bathed in the soft light of dawn, appeared serene and unhurried, a stark contrast to the vibrant festival atmosphere. The streets were slowly coming to life as the townsfolk began their morning routines, the festival's remnants being cleared away. Isabel couldn't help but feel a sense of peaceful transition, as if the night had transformed both her and the town in subtle, significant ways.

Gabe led her toward the edge of town, where the beach met the rocky coastline. The path was familiar to Isabel, a place she had often wandered alone, but today it felt different, imbued with the warmth of their shared experience. The tranquility of the morning was punctuated by the distant calls of seabirds and the gentle lapping of the waves against the shore.

Isabel and Gabe settled onto a grassy knoll overlooking the beach. They sat in comfortable silence for a while, the calm of the morning providing a serene backdrop to their thoughts. Gabe's hand rested on Isabel's shoulder, a gesture of quiet support that spoke volumes.

Isabel took a deep breath, letting the fresh sea air fill her lungs. The previous night's revelations and the tenderness of their dance had stirred something deep within her, a blend of exhilaration and vulnerability. She turned to Gabe, her eyes reflecting a mix of gratitude and contemplation.

"I've been thinking a lot about what last night meant," Isabel began, her voice soft but steady. "The festival was beautiful, but it was more than just the lights and the music. It felt like a turning point for me, a chance to see things in a new light."

Gabe's gaze was attentive, his expression open and encouraging. "I felt that too," he said. "It was like we were both stepping into something new, something that had been waiting for us. And not just in terms of our relationship, but in how we view our lives and our pasts."

Isabel nodded, her thoughts drifting back to the previous night's dance. "When we danced together, it felt like a moment of pure connection. It was as if everything else faded away, and there was just us, sharing something that went beyond words."

Gabe's eyes met hers with a depth of understanding. "I felt that too. It was like we were creating our own space, a bubble where nothing else mattered. And in that moment, I felt like I could truly be myself with you."

Isabel took Gabe's hand in hers, feeling the warmth of his touch. "I've been holding back for so long," she admitted. "There's been so much I've kept to myself, fears and regrets that I haven't shared with anyone. But with you, it feels like I can let go of some of that weight."

Gabe squeezed her hand gently, his voice earnest. "You don't have to carry those burdens alone. I'm here for you, and I want to understand what's been weighing on you. Whatever it is, we can face it together."

Isabel looked out at the vast expanse of the ocean, the waves shimmering in the morning light. "There's something I haven't told you," she said slowly. "It's about my mother and the secrets she kept. I've been trying to piece together her past, and it's been both enlightening and painful."

Gabe's expression softened with empathy. "I can only imagine how difficult that must be. If you're comfortable sharing, I'd like to hear more about it. It might help to talk through what you've discovered."

Isabel took a deep breath, gathering her thoughts. "I found a painting in my mother's studio. It was hidden away, and when I finally uncovered it, I saw something that left me stunned. It was a portrait of a man, and it was signed with a name I didn't recognize. There were notes and letters that seemed to hint at a secret relationship she had."

Gabe listened intently, his gaze fixed on Isabel with unwavering support. "That must have been a shock," he said. "It's understandable that you would feel unsettled by finding out such personal details about your mother's life."

Isabel nodded, her voice trembling slightly. "Yes, it was. And it made me question so much about her, about how much I really knew her. But it also made me realize that there's a part of her life that she kept hidden, not just from me, but from everyone."

Gabe's hand gently brushed Isabel's cheek, his touch tender and reassuring. "It sounds like you're uncovering pieces of your mother's life that were deliberately kept out of view. It's natural to feel a mix of emotions about that, especially when it connects to your own sense of identity and understanding."

Isabel met Gabe's gaze, her eyes reflecting a blend of vulnerability and determination. "I want to understand more, to know why she kept these secrets and what it means for me. It's like I'm on this journey to uncover not just her past but also my own sense of self."

Gabe's smile was warm and supportive. "I believe that understanding your mother's past will help you gain clarity about your own path. And I want to be here to support you in that journey, every step of the way."

The sun continued to rise, casting a golden glow over the beach and the surrounding landscape. The warmth of the morning light seemed to mirror the growing warmth between Isabel and Gabe, a sign of their deepening connection and the promise of a shared future.

As the day unfolded, Isabel felt a renewed sense of purpose and hope. The Festival of Lights had been a celebration of their connection, but the quiet moments that followed had solidified the bond between them. With Gabe by her side, she felt more prepared to face the challenges ahead and to explore the depths of her own journey.

The beach, with its tranquil beauty and the gentle rhythm of the waves, became a symbol of the new chapter in their lives. As Isabel and Gabe walked hand in hand along the shore, they embraced the possibility of love and renewal, ready to face whatever came next with a sense of shared commitment and understanding.

The dawn of the new day marked not just the end of a magical festival but the beginning of a new chapter in Isabel's life. With Gabe's support and the island's serene beauty, she felt ready to continue her journey of self-discovery and to embrace the possibilities of love and connection.

9

Chapter 9: Eliza's Struggle

Isabel hadn't spoken much to Eliza since the night of the Festival of Lights. They had shared a brief, warm conversation in passing, but something in Eliza's eyes had seemed distant, a bit off. Isabel noticed it, but she wasn't sure if it was her place to dig into it. That night, Gabe had been her focus—their dance, the electricity in the air, the unspoken understanding between them. But now, the air had shifted, and Isabel couldn't ignore the tension in Eliza's behavior any longer.

Eliza had always been a symbol of quiet strength. While the islanders saw her as a woman who had weathered life's storms with grace, Isabel knew there were deeper currents beneath her friend's composed exterior. They had been close once, but time and distance had frayed that connection. Yet, even with the years between them, Isabel recognized when something was wrong. And right now, Eliza was struggling, even if she wouldn't admit it.

Isabel found Eliza at the dock, sitting on a weathered bench overlooking the water, her shoulders slightly hunched. She was holding something—a small, crumpled piece of paper that she kept turning over in her hands as though it held the answers to questions she couldn't ask. Isabel approached quietly, her footsteps light on the worn wood of the pier.

"Eliza?" she called gently, her voice tentative but caring.

Eliza didn't turn immediately, but after a moment, she folded the paper and tucked it into her coat pocket. She looked out over the water for a long beat before finally glancing at Isabel. "I thought you'd be with Gabe."

Isabel smiled softly, but there was a sadness in Eliza's tone that made her pause. "I wanted to check on you."

Eliza let out a breath that wasn't quite a sigh but carried the weight of one. "I'm fine, really."

But Isabel knew better. She sat down beside her, close enough to offer comfort but far enough to give Eliza the space to decide how much she wanted to reveal. They sat in silence for a while, the rhythmic lapping of the waves filling the space between them. It was a silence Isabel had learned to appreciate on the island—a space for thoughts to form, for emotions to settle.

Eliza was the first to break the silence. "I don't know why I thought it would get easier," she said, her voice so low Isabel had to lean in to catch the words. "I thought... coming back here, maybe I'd find some peace. Maybe the island could heal me the way it heals everyone else. But it's not working."

Isabel frowned, her heart aching for her friend. "What's not working?"

Eliza hesitated, glancing away as if the admission was too much to bear. But then she spoke, her words raw and unfiltered. "Living with the past. It doesn't go away just because you run from it."

Isabel felt a pang of understanding. She knew that struggle all too well. "Running only makes it follow you more closely," she said quietly, her eyes on the horizon where the sky met the sea.

Eliza's hands tightened in her lap, her knuckles pale against the dark fabric of her coat. "I thought I could fix things. I thought... if I came back, if I pretended everything was fine, maybe it would be. But now, all I have is this mess of regrets. It's suffocating."

Isabel's gaze softened. She recognized the weight of what Eliza was saying because it mirrored her own struggles in a way she hadn't fully faced yet. She had come back to the island thinking she could find answers, too, but she was beginning to realize that the answers weren't simply waiting to be uncovered. They were tangled in the unresolved knots of her own heart.

"Tell me what's going on," Isabel pressed gently, leaning a little closer now.

Eliza swallowed hard, her throat bobbing as she tried to find the words. "It's too late," she whispered. "For everything. For him. For me."

Isabel reached out, placing a hand on Eliza's arm, a silent offering of solidarity. "It's never too late," she said firmly, hoping Eliza would believe her.

But Eliza just shook her head. "For you, maybe. For me... I lost my chance a long time ago."

The air felt thick with the weight of unspoken words, and Isabel's thoughts flickered to her own situation with Gabe. She hadn't lost her chance yet, but if she wasn't careful, if she kept her guard up, she might. She could see that now. Eliza's pain was a mirror reflecting her own fears, and Isabel couldn't ignore it.

Eliza sighed, her hand reaching back into her pocket to pull out the crumpled piece of paper. She handed it to Isabel without a word, her eyes fixed on the water. Isabel unfolded it slowly, the paper soft from being handled too many times. It was a letter, worn and tear-stained. The words on the page were simple but filled with emotion.

It was from him—Eliza's lost love. The one she had never spoken about, the one she had buried beneath years of silence.

"I never sent it," Eliza whispered, her voice breaking. "I wrote it, over and over, but I never sent it. And now... it's too late."

Isabel read the letter, her heart aching as the words filled in the gaps of Eliza's sorrow. She understood now. This wasn't just about lost love. It was about the fear of vulnerability, the same fear that had kept Isabel from fully opening up to Gabe. Eliza had run away from her emotions, and in doing so, she had lost something irreplaceable.

Isabel folded the letter carefully and handed it back to Eliza. "It's never too late to say what you need to say," she murmured. "Even if it feels like it."

Eliza's eyes filled with tears, and for the first time in a long while, she let them fall. Isabel didn't try to stop them. Sometimes, tears were the only way to wash away the pain that words couldn't express.

After a long pause, Eliza wiped her face and gave Isabel a weak smile. "I'm scared, Isabel. I'm scared that I'll never be able to fix it. That I'll never be able to fix me."

Isabel took a deep breath, her own chest tightening with emotions she hadn't fully acknowledged. "I think... the hardest part isn't fixing things. It's allowing ourselves to be broken and trusting that we'll come back together again. Maybe not the way we were, but better. Stronger."

Eliza looked at her for a long time, her gaze searching, as if she were seeing Isabel in a new light. "When did you get so wise?"

Isabel smiled, a soft, almost bittersweet smile. "I'm still learning."

Eliza gave a soft laugh, though it was tinged with sadness. "Aren't we all?"

They sat in silence again, but this time, it felt lighter, less suffocating. Isabel felt something shift in her, a deep recognition of her own fears and regrets. Eliza's struggle wasn't just hers—it was a reflection of what Isabel had been avoiding. Gabe had opened a door for her, but she had been too afraid to step through. Watching Eliza wrestle with her own regrets made Isabel realize how much she had to lose if she kept holding back.

Isabel squeezed Eliza's hand gently before standing. "You're not alone in this," she said quietly. "None of us are."

Eliza nodded, a tearful but hopeful glint in her eyes. "Thank you."

Isabel turned toward the path that led back to the village, her thoughts swirling. She needed to see Gabe. She needed to face whatever it was between them before it became too late—before she lost the chance to say the things Eliza had never been able to.

The wind picked up as Isabel walked, the cool breeze tugging at her hair. The island, with all its beauty and mystery, had become a place of both comfort and challenge. It was a place where secrets were uncovered, not just about her mother, but about herself. And now, as she approached the familiar bend in the path, she felt ready to face them.

Isabel walked slowly back toward the village, her thoughts tangled in the emotions that had surfaced during her conversation with Eliza. The winds stirred, pulling strands of her hair across her face, but she didn't bother to brush them away. Eliza's words had struck a chord deep within her, unsettling her in a way she hadn't expected.

The weight of unspoken feelings lingered on her chest. She couldn't help but wonder if she, too, had been running from something. From the past? From her feelings for Gabe? Or maybe from the woman she thought she had to be. She had come back to the island searching for answers about her mother's life, but it was becoming clear that the journey was just as much about her own unresolved emotions.

As she neared the small row of cottages on the edge of the village, Isabel hesitated. She could see Gabe's house from here, the light in his front room glowing softly through the windows. A part of her wanted to keep walking, to delay the conversation she knew they needed to have. But Eliza's struggle had opened her eyes. She couldn't let fear dictate her choices any longer.

She took a deep breath, her hand tightening around the strap of her bag. She needed to talk to Gabe, to tell him what she had been holding back—about her mother, about her own fears, and about the growing connection between them that scared her more than she wanted to admit.

The path to his house seemed longer than usual as she made her way across the damp grass, her footsteps heavy with anticipation. She had shared so much with Gabe already, but this was different. This conversation felt pivotal, a turning point she couldn't avoid.

When she finally reached the front porch, Isabel paused, her hand hovering over the door for a moment before she knocked. The sound echoed in the quiet night, and she waited, her heart beating a little faster than it should have.

A few moments later, Gabe opened the door, his face softening when he saw her standing there. "Isabel," he said, a warmth in his voice that she found both comforting and disarming. "I wasn't expecting you tonight."

"I wasn't sure I was coming," she admitted, stepping inside as he held the door open for her. The house smelled of wood and something earthy, like pine needles after rain. It was cozy, much like Gabe himself—steady and familiar, a refuge she wasn't sure she deserved.

He closed the door behind her, watching her carefully. "Everything alright?"

Isabel smiled faintly, but it didn't reach her eyes. "I don't know." She turned toward him, taking in the way he stood so easily in his space, the way he made everything seem a little less complicated. "Can we talk?"

Gabe nodded, gesturing for her to follow him into the living room. He sat down on the couch, and she took a seat beside him, though she left some distance between them. The space felt deliberate, as if it mirrored the emotional distance she had been maintaining for too long.

For a moment, neither of them spoke, the silence stretching between them like a thin thread that could snap at any moment. Gabe, sensing her hesitation, leaned forward, resting his elbows on his knees. "Isabel, what's going on?"

She let out a shaky breath, looking down at her hands. "I've been thinking a lot about my mother... and about myself. And you."

Gabe's brows furrowed, his concern deepening. "What about your mother?"

Isabel closed her eyes for a brief second, trying to gather the courage to say what she had been holding inside for so long. "I found something. In her studio. A painting... but more than that. It was like I was seeing a part of her I never knew existed."

She paused, feeling the words catch in her throat. Gabe didn't rush her. He waited, his gaze steady, giving her the space to open up in her own time.

"She had secrets," Isabel continued, her voice quieter now. "Things she never told me—about her past, about a love affair. I think she hid them to protect me, but now I'm starting to realize she wasn't just hiding her life. She was hiding pieces of me, too. And I think... I've been doing the same thing."

Gabe's expression softened as he reached out, gently placing a hand over hers. His touch was warm, grounding her in the moment. "What do you mean?"

Isabel met his gaze, the vulnerability in her chest swelling. "I've been running from things, Gabe. From my past, from my feelings. From the part of me that's scared to let people in. I thought coming back here would give me clarity, but it's just shown me how much I've been hiding."

Gabe's thumb brushed over her knuckles, a small but comforting gesture. "Isabel, you don't have to hide anything from me."

She smiled sadly, her heart aching with the weight of her confession. "But I have been. Even with you. Especially with you."

Gabe frowned slightly, his hand still holding hers. "Why?"

Isabel swallowed, feeling the vulnerability of the moment settle over her. She had never been good at talking about her emotions, about the things that scared her. But she owed Gabe the truth. She owed herself the truth.

"Because you make me feel things I'm not sure I'm ready for. Things I thought I could avoid if I just kept my distance. But every time I'm with you..." Her voice faltered, and she looked away, blinking back the sudden sting of tears. "Every time I'm with you, I feel like I'm coming back to life. And that scares me."

Gabe was quiet for a moment, his expression softening into something she hadn't seen before. It was a mixture of understanding and something deeper, something she wasn't sure she could name.

"You don't have to be afraid with me, Isabel," he said, his voice low but steady. "I'm not going anywhere."

Isabel looked at him, her heart pounding in her chest. She wanted to believe him, wanted to believe that she could let go of the fear that had been holding her back for so long. But the scars of her past still lingered, the pain of losing her mother, of never fully understanding her. And now, the possibility of opening herself up to love, to Gabe, felt both terrifying and inevitable.

She let out a shaky breath, her voice barely above a whisper. "I don't know how to do this."

Gabe's hand tightened around hers, a gentle reassurance. "You don't have to know how. We'll figure it out together."

Isabel blinked, her vision blurring with unshed tears. The sincerity in Gabe's voice, the quiet strength in his words, made something inside her crack open. She had spent so long building walls around her heart, trying to protect herself from the possibility of pain, but in doing so, she had also shut herself off from the possibility of love.

For the first time in what felt like forever, Isabel allowed herself to hope. To believe that maybe, just maybe, she didn't have to carry the weight of her past alone. That maybe, she could find healing, not just in the memories of her mother, but in the possibility of a future with Gabe.

"I'm scared," she admitted, her voice barely audible.

Gabe's gaze softened, his thumb still brushing gently over her hand. "So am I."

The vulnerability in his eyes mirrored her own, and in that moment, Isabel realized that she wasn't alone in her fear. Gabe wasn't asking her to be perfect, to have all the answers. He was just asking her to be honest, to be real.

Isabel leaned in slightly, her eyes searching his. "I don't want to lose you."

Gabe smiled, a small, almost bittersweet smile. "You won't."

In the quiet space between them, something shifted. The walls Isabel had built around her heart began to crumble, piece by piece, as she let herself feel the weight of her emotions. It wasn't easy, and it wasn't comfortable, but it was real. And for the first time in a long time, Isabel felt like she was exactly where she was supposed to be.

With Gabe.

The storm inside her finally began to calm.

The fire crackled softly in the hearth, casting flickering shadows on the walls of Gabe's living room. Outside, the wind had picked up, a reminder of the island's ever-changing moods, but inside, the space felt warm, intimate—almost suspended in time. Isabel sat beside Gabe, the weight of their conversation settling in, though the silence between them now felt different. It wasn't the heavy, unspoken tension that had lingered for so long; it was a comfortable quiet, as if both of them were simply letting the vulnerability of the moment sink in.

Gabe hadn't moved his hand from hers. His thumb still brushed absently across her knuckles, a grounding gesture that kept Isabel tethered to the present. She glanced at him, her heart still heavy with everything she had shared, but there was a lightness too, a release she hadn't expected. For so long, she had carried her pain and fear alone, but sitting here with Gabe, she realized she didn't have to anymore.

He hadn't pushed her for more than she was ready to give. Instead, he had just been there—steady, quiet, offering her a space to be honest without judgment. And for the first time, she allowed herself to appreciate just how much that meant.

"I've been thinking about something Eliza said earlier," Isabel finally spoke, her voice soft but sure.

Gabe's gaze shifted to her, his brows knitting slightly in concern. "What did she say?"

Isabel took a deep breath, her fingers curling slightly around his. "She was talking about how we run from things. From the parts of ourselves we're afraid to face. I think... I think that's what I've been doing. With you. With everything."

Gabe's expression softened, but he didn't speak. He just listened, the way he always did, his presence a quiet reassurance that made it easier for her to continue.

"I've been so focused on trying to understand my mother, on uncovering her secrets, that I didn't realize how much of myself I've been hiding in the process. I thought if I could figure out why she kept things from me, I'd somehow feel more complete. But maybe I was just using her story to avoid my own." Isabel looked down at their intertwined hands, her thumb brushing against his. "I've been so scared of what it means to open myself up to this—this life, this place, and to you."

Gabe's thumb stilled on her hand, and for a moment, he just looked at her, as if weighing his next words. "I get it," he finally said, his voice low. "I do. But Isabel, you don't have to figure everything out all at once. You don't have to have all the answers."

His words were a balm to her restless thoughts, and she felt her shoulders relax, the tension she hadn't even realized she was carrying easing away.

"I know," she whispered. "But I want to try."

Gabe's hand tightened around hers, a silent affirmation that they were in this together. "That's all that matters."

They sat in silence for a while, the crackle of the fire filling the room as they both processed the conversation. It wasn't the end of Isabel's struggle—far from it—but for the first time, she felt like she wasn't walking through it alone. And that made all the difference.

After a while, Gabe leaned back on the couch, pulling her with him until they were both sitting comfortably, the space between them having disappeared entirely. Isabel rested her head on his shoulder, and Gabe's arm draped around her, his fingers lightly tracing patterns on her back.

The intimacy of the moment wasn't just physical; it was emotional. It was the kind of closeness that came from shared vulnerability, from allowing the other person to see the parts of yourself you usually kept hidden. Isabel had never let anyone see those parts of her before—not since her mother's death, not since she had left the island. But Gabe had seen them, and he hadn't turned away. He had stayed.

Isabel felt something inside her shift, the deep ache of loneliness she had carried for so long beginning to ease. The island, Gabe, her mother's secrets—none of it felt as overwhelming anymore. She still didn't have all the answers, but maybe she didn't need them right now. Maybe, for the first time, it was okay to just be here, in this moment, with him.

As the firelight flickered and the wind howled softly outside, Isabel let herself sink into the comfort of Gabe's presence. She closed her eyes, her breathing steadying as she allowed the warmth of the room—and of Gabe's embrace—to soothe the lingering edges of her fear.

"I never thought I'd feel this again," she murmured, the words slipping out before she could stop them.

Gabe's hand stilled on her back, and he looked down at her, his brow furrowed. "Feel what?"

Isabel hesitated, her heart pounding. She had already shared so much tonight—more than she had planned—but this felt different. More personal. More real.

"Safe," she whispered.

Gabe's expression softened, and he pressed a kiss to the top of her head, his lips lingering for a moment longer than necessary. "You are safe, Isabel. You always will be."

The sincerity in his voice wrapped around her like a blanket, and for the first time in a long time, Isabel believed him.

As they sat there, the night deepening around them, Isabel thought of her mother—of the secrets she had kept, the choices she had made. Maybe, like her, her mother had been scared. Scared of love, of loss, of opening herself up to the possibility of getting hurt. But in the end, her mother's secrets hadn't protected her from pain. They had only made the ache of what she had lost more profound.

Isabel didn't want that for herself. She didn't want to live in the shadows of her own fear, always wondering what might have been if she had just allowed herself to be vulnerable. She didn't want to run anymore.

For the first time, Isabel realized that her mother's story didn't have to define her. It could guide her, yes, but it didn't have to be the map by which she charted her own life. She could make her own choices, her own mistakes. She could write her own story.

And as she lay there, wrapped in the warmth of Gabe's arms, Isabel made a silent promise to herself: she would stop running. She would face whatever came next—whether it was more secrets, more revelations, or even more pain—with an open heart. Because for the first time, she understood that it wasn't the secrets themselves that had held her back. It was the fear of what they meant, the fear of what they could reveal about her.

234 - EMMA DREAMWEAVER

But now, sitting here with Gabe, Isabel knew that she didn't have to be afraid anymore. She wasn't alone.

As the fire burned low, casting the room in soft, fading light, Isabel felt herself drifting into sleep, her head resting against Gabe's chest, his heartbeat a steady, comforting rhythm beneath her ear. The storm outside raged on, but inside, everything was quiet. Peaceful. Whole.

And for the first time in a long time, Isabel felt like she had found her way home.

The morning sun streamed through the windows, casting long shadows across the floor of the small room where Isabel sat. She rubbed her eyes, feeling the weight of the previous night still lingering. Her conversation with Gabe had opened a door she wasn't entirely prepared to walk through. It had been comforting, yes, but also overwhelming. She had shared more of herself than she had in years, but the vulnerability it had required still left her feeling exposed.

Isabel hadn't slept much after Gabe left, his words about safety and not needing all the answers replaying in her mind. She had appreciated his patience, his ability to stay calm even when she was clearly battling her own inner turmoil. But now, as daylight filled the room, the calm of the night seemed like a distant memory.

She had to keep moving forward. The lighthouse was still waiting, and the secrets she had uncovered about her mother were only the beginning. Isabel knew that if she stopped now—if she retreated into the safety of Gabe's assurances—she might never find the courage to face what she needed to.

It was in this contemplative state that Eliza's voice broke the silence, calling from the front door. "Isabel, are you awake?"

Isabel stood, glancing at the reflection in the nearby mirror. She barely recognized herself—there was a newfound softness in her features, an openness she hadn't seen in years. Perhaps Gabe had been right; maybe she didn't have to figure it all out just yet. But that didn't mean she could ignore the pull of her past, either.

"Come in, Eliza," Isabel called out, smoothing her hair back as she prepared herself for whatever new conversation awaited. She hadn't seen much of Eliza since their last talk, and she could sense that today would be significant.

Eliza entered, her expression concerned but resolute. "I wanted to check on you," she said softly, her eyes scanning Isabel's face. "After everything that happened yesterday, I figured you might need someone to talk to."

Isabel offered her a tired smile. "You're not wrong. It's been... a lot."

Eliza took a seat across from Isabel, folding her hands in her lap. "Do you want to tell me what's going on in that head of yours? It's not easy carrying everything alone, Isabel."

Isabel hesitated, her thoughts still swirling from her conversation with Gabe. But Eliza's presence felt different, gentler somehow, and the need to unburden herself outweighed her instinct to hold back.

"I've been learning things about my mother," Isabel began. "Things I never knew. It feels like everything I thought I understood about her—about our family—was only half the story."

Eliza nodded slowly, her expression thoughtful. "Sometimes our parents hide things from us, not because they don't trust us, but because they're trying to protect us."

The words struck a chord, and Isabel looked away, the tension in her chest tightening. "That's what I'm afraid of. I think she was trying to protect me, but in doing that, she kept me in the dark. I don't know how to reconcile the mother I knew with the one I'm discovering."

Eliza reached out and gently placed her hand on Isabel's. "We all have parts of ourselves that we keep hidden, even from the people we love the most. Sometimes it's because we're afraid of being seen fully, flaws and all."

Isabel's eyes flickered to Eliza's face, and she suddenly understood why her friend's words carried such weight. "You're talking about yourself, aren't you?"

Eliza gave a small, sad smile. "I suppose I am. I've made my own share of mistakes, Isabel. I've kept my own secrets. And I've lost people because of them."

Isabel sat back, her heart sinking. "Eliza, I—"

But Eliza shook her head. "Don't apologize. I didn't tell you that to make you feel bad. I'm telling you because I don't want you to make the same mistakes. Don't shut people out because you're afraid they won't understand. Don't let your fear of the truth stop you from living your life."

Isabel felt tears sting her eyes, and she blinked them away quickly. Eliza's words were too close, too raw. They spoke to the very heart of what she had been struggling with. She had spent so long building walls around herself—walls that had kept her isolated from everyone, even the people who mattered most.

"But how do I do that?" Isabel asked, her voice shaky. "How do I let go of the fear when it feels like it's all I've ever known?"

Eliza's expression softened, and she leaned forward, her voice low and gentle. "You take it one step at a time. You let people in, even when it scares you. You let yourself feel the fear, but you don't let it control you."

Isabel closed her eyes, taking in a deep breath. Eliza's advice resonated, but it also felt daunting. Could she really allow herself to be vulnerable like that? Could she face the truths about her mother—and herself—without letting them define her?

As if sensing her hesitation, Eliza continued. "I know it's not easy. But you don't have to do it alone, Isabel. You've got Gabe, and you've got me. We'll be here for you, no matter what you find."

Isabel opened her eyes, her gaze meeting Eliza's. There was something so reassuring in her friend's eyes, something that made Isabel feel like maybe, just maybe, she could do this.

"Thank you," Isabel whispered, her voice barely audible. "I don't know what I would do without you."

Eliza smiled, the warmth in her expression brightening the room. "You'd be just fine, Isabel. But I'm glad you don't have to find out."

They sat in silence for a moment, the weight of their conversation hanging in the air. Isabel felt lighter, though, as if the walls she had built were finally beginning to crumble. It would take time—she knew that—but the cracks were there.

Eliza rose to leave, but before she walked out the door, she turned back to Isabel, her expression serious. "You're stronger than you think, Isabel. Don't forget that."

Isabel nodded, her throat tight with emotion. "I won't."

After Eliza left, Isabel sat in the quiet of the room, her thoughts drifting back to her mother. She had spent so much time searching for answers, for explanations that might make sense of the choices her mother had made. But maybe what Eliza had said was true—maybe her mother had been trying to protect her all along. Maybe, in keeping her secrets, she had been trying to spare Isabel from pain.

But the pain had come anyway, hadn't it?

Isabel stood, her eyes falling on the stack of sketches she had found in the studio. Her mother's art had always been her refuge, her way of communicating when words had failed. And now, those drawings were all Isabel had left of her—clues, breadcrumbs leading her deeper into the past.

She picked up one of the sketches, her fingers tracing the lines of a lighthouse—her mother's recurring symbol. The lighthouse had always represented guidance, safety, but now it felt like something more. There was a message hidden here, Isabel was sure of it. A message meant for her.

"The light will reveal what's hidden," she whispered to herself, recalling the note scrawled in the margins of one of the sketches. It was a clue, a puzzle she hadn't yet solved.

Isabel's heart raced as the realization hit her. She needed to go back to the lighthouse. There was something there, something her mother had left for her to find. And this time, Isabel wouldn't be afraid to face it.

With renewed determination, Isabel grabbed her coat and headed for the door. She didn't know what she would find at the lighthouse, but for the first time in a long time, she wasn't afraid of the truth. She was ready to face whatever secrets her mother had left behind.

Isabel stood at the edge of the cliffs, the wind whipping her hair around her face as she gazed out at the lighthouse in the distance. The path ahead was steep, rugged, but she knew she had to take it. The lighthouse had been calling her ever since she'd discovered those sketches—each one a puzzle piece, fragments of her mother's hidden life.

This time, though, it felt different. The lighthouse wasn't just a symbol of her mother's secrets; it was also a mirror reflecting back Isabel's own uncertainties, her own need to reconcile the past with the person she was becoming.

As she began the walk toward it, her feet crunching on the rocky ground, her mind kept returning to the conversation with

Eliza. The depth of what her friend had revealed had stirred something inside her. Eliza's words about vulnerability and fear had struck a chord. And although Eliza had shared her own story of mistakes, the lesson for Isabel was clear—she couldn't keep hiding behind the barriers she'd built to protect herself. There was no safety in silence, in keeping things buried.

By the time she reached the lighthouse, Isabel's chest was heaving from the climb, but she didn't pause. Instead, she pushed open the door with trembling hands. The old wooden structure creaked as she stepped inside, the same eerie silence surrounding her as before. The air smelled of salt and mildew, and a faint light from the cloudy sky seeped in through the cracks in the walls.

The lighthouse had always been mysterious to her, even as a child. Her mother had spent countless hours here, painting and sketching in solitude. Isabel used to think it was just her mother's retreat, but now she saw it for what it really was—her mother's sanctuary for the truths she couldn't speak.

With each step Isabel took, her heartbeat quickened, as though the lighthouse held the answers she'd been seeking all along.

When she reached the small room at the top, she saw it. The painting. The one that had lingered in her dreams ever since she first discovered it in her mother's studio. But this time, there was something new—a sketch resting against the easel, tucked partially behind the canvas. Isabel pulled it out, her fingers brushing over the familiar charcoal strokes.

The sketch was of the lighthouse, like so many before it, but this one had something else. A figure standing at the base, barely visible, cloaked in shadow. Isabel felt a cold shiver down her spine. Her mother had drawn herself there, watching the light above, but something about the figure felt... lonely. Desolate. It was a side of her mother she had never seen, a vulnerability that she had always kept hidden beneath her calm, artistic exterior.

Her throat tightened, and as she lowered the sketch, her eyes fell on the painting itself. The colors seemed more vivid today, more alive, as though the stormy sky and turbulent waves in the artwork were moving with the same energy as the storm within her. She looked closer at the horizon in the painting—the lighthouse standing strong against the storm, and there, just below the waves, was another hidden detail: a keyhole.

Isabel blinked. It had been there all along, but she hadn't seen it until now.

Her pulse raced as she realized what this meant. Her mother hadn't just painted her pain; she'd hidden something, a physical object connected to the painting. Isabel felt her breath catch as she looked around the small room, scanning for anything that might be connected to the keyhole. She searched the walls, the floorboards, the old furniture that had been left behind. But there was nothing out of the ordinary—at least, nothing that stood out.

Frustration began to build inside her. Her mother had left her all these clues, but why? Why had she kept these secrets? And what was she trying to protect Isabel from?

The wind howled outside, rattling the windows as Isabel crouched near the base of the wall, inspecting the floor for any sign of disturbance. And that's when she saw it. A loose board.

Her heart skipped a beat. She pried the board up with her fingertips, her hands shaking slightly as she pulled it free. Beneath the wood was a small metal box, weathered and tarnished from years of exposure. Isabel stared at it for a long moment before carefully lifting it from its hiding place.

The box was locked, the keyhole in front matching the one in the painting. She swallowed hard, her mind racing. The key. Where was the key?

She stood up, her legs shaky as she scanned the room again. This time, her eyes landed on a small brass key hanging from the window ledge, tucked into the corner as though waiting for her. Isabel approached it slowly, her fingers trembling as she took it in her hand. Her mother had hidden it in plain sight.

With the key in hand, she returned to the metal box, kneeling beside it as she carefully turned the lock. The click echoed in the quiet room, and with a deep breath, Isabel lifted the lid.

Inside, there were letters. Dozens of them, neatly tied together with a faded ribbon. Her mother's handwriting scrawled across the envelopes in the same flowing script Isabel remembered from her childhood. She recognized the name on the front of the letters—Isabel's father. These were letters her mother had written to him over the years, letters she had never sent.

Isabel's hands shook as she untied the ribbon and opened the first letter. Her mother's voice came alive in the words on the page, and as Isabel read, tears filled her eyes.

"My dearest Isabel, you are the light in my life, and I have always been proud of you. But there are things I could never say out loud, things I hope you will forgive me for..."

Her mother's words were filled with regret, love, and an overwhelming desire to protect Isabel from the truth. The letters spoke of a love affair, a man her mother had loved deeply but could never be with. It was a love that had shaped her mother's life, a love that had led her to keep secrets from Isabel, all in an effort to shield her from the pain of knowing.

Isabel's tears flowed freely as she read each letter, the weight of her mother's hidden life crashing down on her. Her mother had carried so much alone—her love, her fears, her regrets—and in do-ing so, she had built walls that had separated them in ways Isabel was only now beginning to understand.

But as she read on, something else became clear. Her mother's love for her had been the guiding force behind every decision, every secret. Her mother hadn't kept things hidden out of shame or guilt; she had done it out of love. She had wanted to spare Isabel from the heartache she had lived through, even if it meant keeping parts of herself locked away.

Isabel wiped her tears, her heart aching with the weight of this revelation. She had spent so long trying to understand her mother's actions, trying to piece together the fragments of a life that had felt so distant. And now, in the quiet of the lighthouse, with the letters spread out before her, she finally understood. Her mother had loved her fiercely, and in her own way, she had been trying to protect her.

The realization settled over Isabel like a warm blanket, and for the first time in years, she felt a sense of peace. The answers she had been searching for were finally within reach, and though there was still more to uncover, she no longer felt afraid. She was ready to face whatever else her mother had left behind.

As Isabel stood up, her gaze drifted out the window, where the ocean stretched endlessly toward the horizon. The lighthouse stood tall, its light cutting through the mist, guiding her home.

Isabel smiled through her tears, knowing that her journey wasn't over. There were still more secrets to uncover, more truths to face. But for now, she had found something far more impor-tant—she had found a way to reconnect with her mother, and in doing so, she had begun to find herself.

Isabel returned to the studio, her mother's letters still on her mind. The weight of what she had uncovered felt overwhelming, but it also brought with it a strange sense of relief. As she walked through the door, the familiar scent of paint and wood filled the air, grounding her in the present moment.

She had always thought of this space as belonging solely to her mother, a place where secrets were hidden beneath layers of paint. But now, it felt different. It wasn't just her mother's sanctuary anymore—it was her own. She was uncovering not only the truth about her mother's life but also the truths about herself, ones she had buried deep beneath the surface.

The sound of footsteps interrupted her thoughts. Isabel turned to see Eliza standing in the doorway, her face etched with concern.

"I've been looking for you," Eliza said softly, stepping into the room.

Isabel forced a small smile. "Sorry, I just needed some time."

Eliza nodded, crossing the room to stand beside her. "I understand. It's a lot to process."

Isabel glanced at her, feeling the heaviness of the letters in her pocket. "It's more than I expected," she admitted. "I found some letters... from my mom. Things she never told me, things she kept hidden."

Eliza's expression softened, and she placed a comforting hand on Isabel's shoulder. "Sometimes people think they're protecting us by keeping things hidden. But in the end, the truth always finds its way out."

Isabel sighed, her gaze drifting to the painting on the easel. "I just wish she could have told me. Maybe things would have been different."

Eliza stayed silent for a moment, her eyes tracing the contours of the artwork before her. Then, after a long pause, she spoke. "You know... I've been there. Holding on to things that I thought would keep the people I care about safe. But it didn't work. In the end, all it did was hurt me and everyone around me."

Isabel looked at her, surprised by the vulnerability in her voice. Eliza had always been the strong one, the one who seemed to have everything figured out. To hear her speak this way felt like seeing her in a new light.

Eliza continued, her voice steady but laced with a hint of sadness. "After my father passed, I kept so much bottled up. I didn't want to face the things I'd done, the choices I made that I regretted. I thought if I didn't talk about it, it would just... go away. But it doesn't. It festers."

Isabel's heart ached for her friend. She had never known the depth of Eliza's struggles, the pain she had carried alone. "Why didn't you tell me?" Isabel asked gently.

Eliza smiled, though it didn't quite reach her eyes. "Because I didn't want you to see me as weak. I thought if I kept it together, if I didn't let anyone in, I could pretend everything was fine." She shook her head, a bitter laugh escaping her lips. "But I was wrong. And I don't want you to make the same mistake, Isabel."

The room fell into a quiet stillness, the weight of Eliza's words hanging in the air. Isabel felt a lump form in her throat, the familiar feeling of wanting to hide, to protect herself from the vulnerability that was rising inside her.

But Eliza's presence was a reminder that she wasn't alone in this. For the first time in a long time, Isabel felt safe enough to let her guard down.

"There's something I haven't told you either," Isabel said quietly, her voice barely above a whisper. "It's about Gabe."

Eliza's brow furrowed slightly, but she remained silent, waiting for Isabel to continue.

Isabel took a deep breath, the words feeling heavy as they spilled from her lips. "When I left the island all those years ago... it wasn't just because of my mom. It was because of him. I loved him, Eliza. But I didn't know how to stay. I was afraid of what that would mean, of how it would change everything. So I ran."

The confession felt like a weight lifted from her chest, though it left her feeling exposed, raw.

Eliza watched her carefully, her eyes filled with understanding. "You were protecting yourself," she said softly. "But running doesn't make the feelings go away, does it?"

Isabel shook her head, tears prickling at the corners of her eyes. "No, it doesn't. And now... being back here, seeing him again, it's all coming back. But I don't know if I can face it. What if I run again?"

Eliza's hand squeezed her shoulder, firm but reassuring. "You won't run this time. Because you're stronger now, Isabel. You've faced things you never thought you could. And you're still here."

Isabel blinked away the tears, her heart pounding with the truth of Eliza's words. She had faced her mother's secrets, uncovered the layers of her own past, and now, she was standing at the edge of something new.

"I don't want to keep running," Isabel said, her voice steady, though still tinged with uncertainty. "But I don't know if I'm ready to let him in again."

Eliza smiled softly, her eyes shining with empathy. "You don't have to know right now. Just take it one step at a time. And when you're ready, you'll know."

Isabel nodded, grateful for her friend's presence, for the wisdom she hadn't realized she needed.

The silence that followed wasn't uncomfortable. Instead, it felt like a shared moment of understanding, a connection between them that went deeper than words. Isabel realized, in that moment, that vulnerability wasn't a weakness—it was a strength. And by letting Eliza in, by sharing her fears, she had taken the first real step toward healing.

The quiet of the studio was interrupted by the soft sound of the door opening. Isabel looked up to see Gabe standing in the doorway, his expression unreadable. For a moment, their eyes met, and Isabel's heart skipped a beat. She knew this was another turning point, another moment where she had to decide whether to stay or to run.

But this time, as Gabe's gaze softened, and a small smile tugged at the corner of his lips, Isabel felt something shift inside her.

She didn't want to run anymore.

"Hey," Gabe said, his voice low but filled with a warmth that sent a wave of comfort through her.

"Hey," Isabel replied, a small smile of her own forming as she stepped toward him, feeling the weight of the past begin to lift.

Eliza gave her a gentle pat on the back before slipping quietly out of the room, leaving Isabel and Gabe alone. The silence between them was filled with the unspoken words, the shared history they had never quite resolved.

But now, standing here with him, Isabel felt something she hadn't felt in a long time—hope.

For the first time, she was ready to let go of the fear that had kept her from facing the truth. And for the first time, she felt like she was ready to open herself up to the possibility of love again.

"Do you want to take a walk?" Gabe asked, his voice soft, almost tentative.

Isabel nodded, feeling the beginning of something new stir inside her. As they walked out of the studio together, the weight of her mother's secrets and her own began to fade, replaced by the lightness of a future she was finally ready to embrace.

As Isabel and Gabe walked out of the studio, the salty breeze from the ocean wrapped around them, making the silence between them more intimate. Isabel felt a strange mixture of comfort and uncertainty. It was as if the weight of their shared history lingered in the air, but neither of them knew quite how to address it.

The path they walked was familiar, winding through the dunes toward the shore. It reminded Isabel of the countless nights they had spent together as teenagers, talking about dreams and futures they hadn't fully understood. Now, the past felt more like a shadow, something that connected them but also kept them apart.

Gabe was the first to break the silence. "It's been strange, hasn't it? Being back."

Isabel nodded, her gaze fixed on the horizon. "Yeah, it has. I never thought I'd be back here. Not like this."

Gabe glanced at her, his expression unreadable, though there was something in his eyes—a softness that pulled at her. "And yet, here you are."

Isabel couldn't help but smile at the truth in his words. Here she was, back in the place she'd spent years avoiding, with the one person who had once been her closest confidant. "I didn't expect this, though," she admitted, her voice quieter. "I didn't expect to see you again."

Gabe's lips twitched into a faint smile, but there was something wistful in his expression. "You say that like it's a bad thing."

"No," she replied quickly, shaking her head. "It's not bad. Just... unexpected."

The waves crashed against the shore, their rhythmic pulse soothing the tension that had been building in her chest. Isabel wrapped her arms around herself, more out of habit than cold.

Being next to Gabe again brought back so many memories—both good and painful ones.

They walked in silence for a few more minutes, letting the sounds of the sea fill the space between them. Isabel felt like she was on the edge of saying something important, something she hadn't allowed herself to express for years.

"Gabe..." she began hesitantly.

He looked at her, his expression open and patient.

"I never really explained why I left, did I?" Her voice wavered as the words tumbled out, exposing the vulnerability she had kept hidden for so long. "It wasn't just because of my mom."

Gabe stopped walking, turning to face her fully. "I always wondered. But I never wanted to push you."

Isabel inhaled deeply, her chest tightening. This was it—the moment she had spent years avoiding, the truth she had buried beneath layers of excuses and fear. "I was scared," she admitted, her eyes meeting his. "Of staying. Of what it would mean to be with you. It felt too big, too permanent."

Gabe's gaze didn't falter, but she saw the flicker of hurt in his eyes, quickly masked by understanding. "You didn't have to stay for me, Isabel. I never wanted you to feel trapped."

"I know," she said quickly. "It wasn't you. It was me. I wasn't ready. I wasn't brave enough to face what staying meant. I thought if I left, I could figure it out on my own."

"And did you?" His question was gentle, not accusatory, but it cut through her defenses all the same.

Isabel shook her head, her throat tight with emotion. "No. I didn't. I just kept running, from everything."

Gabe's expression softened, and he took a step closer to her. "You don't have to run anymore, Isabel. Not from me, and not from yourself."

His words hit her harder than she expected. For so long, she had convinced herself that distance was safety, that running meant freedom. But standing here, in front of Gabe, she realized that running had only kept her trapped in the past.

"I don't want to run," she whispered, her voice breaking slightly. "But I'm still scared."

Gabe reached out, gently placing a hand on her arm, his touch grounding her in the present moment. "It's okay to be scared. But you don't have to do this alone."

For the first time in a long time, Isabel felt the weight of her fears start to lift. Gabe's presence wasn't just a reminder of the past—it was a promise of something more, something new. And though she didn't have all the answers, she knew she didn't want to keep pushing him away.

They continued walking, the silence between them now comfortable, almost healing. The beach stretched out before them, a symbol of the open future they both faced.

Eventually, they reached a small cove, where the rocks formed a natural barrier against the waves. Gabe sat down on one of the larger stones, and Isabel followed, the two of them side by side, gazing out at the sea.

"I've been thinking a lot about your mom," Gabe said after a while. "And about how much she meant to you."

Isabel nodded, her mind flashing to the letters she had found, the secrets her mother had kept. "She was everything to me. But there was so much I didn't know about her."

Gabe's brow furrowed slightly. "Like what?"

Isabel hesitated for a moment, then decided to tell him. "I found some letters in her studio. Letters about someone she loved—someone I never knew about. She kept it all hidden from me, like she was trying to protect me from something."

Gabe was quiet for a moment, processing her words. "Maybe she thought she was protecting you by keeping it to herself. But that doesn't mean she didn't want you to know her fully."

"I guess," Isabel said, her voice tinged with sadness. "But it feels like I'm uncovering pieces of her that I wasn't ready for."

Gabe's hand rested gently on hers, a small but comforting gesture. "You're allowed to feel that way. But you're also allowed to take your time with it. She left those things for you to find, and maybe now is the right time for you to discover them."

Isabel let his words sink in, feeling a strange mix of sadness and acceptance. Maybe Gabe was right—maybe her mother had left those secrets behind, trusting Isabel would find them when she was ready.

As the sun began to set, casting an orange glow across the water, Isabel felt something shift inside her. The fear and uncertainty she had carried for so long were still there, but they didn't feel as overwhelming.

For the first time, she allowed herself to consider the possibility of staying. Not just on the island, but in this moment—with Gabe, with the memories of her mother, with everything she had been running from.

And for the first time, staying didn't feel like a trap. It felt like coming home.

"Thank you," Isabel said softly, her voice almost lost in the sound of the waves.

Gabe smiled, his eyes reflecting the warmth of the setting sun. "For what?"

"For being here. For not giving up on me."

He didn't say anything in return, but the look in his eyes said it all. There was no need for words between them anymore. The unspoken understanding, the shared history, and the promise of what could be was enough.

They sat in silence, watching the sun disappear below the horizon, the last rays of light casting a golden glow over the water. And for the first time in a long time, Isabel felt at peace.

Maybe the answers wouldn't come all at once. Maybe she would still be afraid of what the future held. But as long as she had this—this moment, this connection—she knew she was strong enough to face whatever came next.

The night was settling over the island, casting long shadows that stretched across the shoreline. Isabel and Gabe remained seated on the rocks, the rhythmic sound of the waves filling the space between them. The earlier conversation had peeled back layers she had kept tightly wound for years, and now, with Gabe by her side, a sense of quietness had settled over her heart.

Isabel exhaled slowly, her eyes tracing the distant horizon where the sea met the sky. The colors had faded to deep indigos and purples, but the memory of the sunset lingered, much like the feelings she couldn't yet name. She felt Gabe shift beside her, his presence grounding her in the moment, reminding her she wasn't alone.

After what felt like hours, Isabel broke the silence again, her voice soft but sure. "You remember Eliza, don't you?"

Gabe glanced at her, his brow lifting slightly in curiosity. "Of course. She's been through a lot lately, hasn't she?"

Isabel nodded, thinking of her friend. Eliza had always been the strong one, the one who never faltered under pressure, but lately, there had been cracks in her armor. They had grown closer since Isabel's return, and though Eliza rarely talked about her own struggles, Isabel could see them in the way she moved, in the tiredness behind her eyes.

"She's going through something," Isabel admitted. "But I don't think she's ready to talk about it."

Gabe sighed, running a hand through his hair. "Eliza's always been like that. She keeps everything close to her chest, never wanting to burden anyone."

Isabel smiled faintly. "Kind of like someone else I know."

Gabe gave her a look that was part amusement, part understanding. "Takes one to know one, I guess."

They both fell silent again, the weight of their shared acknowledgment settling between them. But the thought of Eliza lingered in Isabel's mind. She had been trying to help her friend, offering support in quiet ways—sharing meals, spending time together—but she knew there was something deeper at play. Something Eliza hadn't yet revealed.

"I think she's afraid," Isabel said quietly, her fingers tracing the rough surface of the rock beneath her. "She's afraid of admitting that she can't handle everything on her own."

Gabe nodded thoughtfully. "I've seen that look in her eyes. She's always been so independent, but sometimes, the strongest people are the ones who need the most support."

Isabel glanced at him, his words echoing something she had felt herself. She thought about how she had spent so many years believing that running was the same as being strong, that avoiding her emotions was a sign of resilience. But now, sitting beside Gabe, she realized that true strength wasn't about running—it was about facing what scared you most, even if that meant asking for help.

"Eliza's always been there for me," Isabel said softly, the truth of it settling in her chest. "I think it's time I return the favor."

Gabe turned to face her, his expression serious but warm. "And how do you plan to do that?"

Isabel thought for a moment, her mind drifting back to their recent conversations, to the moments when Eliza had let her guard down, even if only for a brief second. "I'm not sure yet," she admitted. "But I know she needs someone to see her, to really see her. And I think I'm the only one who can."

Gabe reached out, placing a reassuring hand on her arm. "You're right. Eliza trusts you in a way she doesn't trust many people. If anyone can help her, it's you."

Isabel looked down at Gabe's hand on her arm, the warmth of his touch steadying her. She nodded, feeling a quiet sense of determination settle in. Eliza had been there for her, through every heartbreak, every difficult moment. Now it was Isabel's turn to return that support.

They stayed by the water for a while longer, until the night had fully claimed the sky. The stars twinkled above them, a reminder of the vastness of the world and the smallness of their own troubles. When they finally stood to leave, Isabel felt lighter, as though the conversation with Gabe had lifted a weight she hadn't realized she was carrying.

Walking back toward the village, they didn't say much more, but the silence was comfortable, filled with the quiet understanding that something had shifted between them. The connection they had once shared wasn't just a relic of the past; it was something living, something they were rebuilding, moment by moment.

When they reached Isabel's cottage, Gabe hesitated at the door. "You're going to be okay," he said, his voice low but steady.

Isabel looked up at him, searching his face for any trace of doubt. But all she saw was the same warmth and support that had always been there. She nodded, a small smile tugging at the corners of her lips. "I know."

Gabe smiled in return, and without another word, he turned and walked back toward his own house, leaving Isabel standing at the threshold of her cottage.

Inside, the air was cool and still, the remnants of the evening's breeze filtering through the open window. Isabel sat down at the small table by the window, her thoughts drifting back to Eliza. She had always admired her friend's strength, but now she saw the vulnerability beneath it, the cracks in her carefully constructed façade.

Eliza's struggle was her own, but it was one Isabel recognized all too well. The fear of letting others in, of showing weakness, was something they had both carried for years. But perhaps, in helping Eliza, Isabel could help herself too.

The next morning, Isabel found Eliza at the small café in the village, sipping coffee and staring out at the harbor. The tension in her friend's shoulders was unmistakable, and Isabel knew that whatever Eliza was going through, it was weighing heavily on her.

"Hey," Isabel said as she slid into the seat across from her.

Eliza looked up, her usual smile not quite reaching her eyes. "Hey."

Isabel hesitated for a moment, unsure of how to start, but then the words came. "I've been thinking about you. I know you've been dealing with a lot lately, and I just want you to know I'm here if you want to talk."

Eliza's expression flickered, something close to vulnerability flashing across her face before she quickly masked it. "I'm fine, really. Just... tired."

Isabel reached across the table, placing her hand over Eliza's. "You don't have to be fine all the time, you know. It's okay to lean on someone else."

Eliza's eyes widened slightly, as if the suggestion surprised her. For a moment, she seemed unsure of how to respond, her guard slipping just a little.

"I don't know how to do that," Eliza admitted quietly, her voice barely above a whisper.

Isabel squeezed her hand gently. "You don't have to know how. You just have to trust that I'm here for you, no matter what."

Eliza looked down at their hands, her walls beginning to crumble. "It's hard," she said after a moment, her voice thick with emotion. "I've always been the strong one. I don't know how to let anyone in."

Isabel's heart ached for her friend, but she also understood. "You don't have to be strong all the time. Sometimes, strength is letting someone else carry the weight with you."

Eliza blinked, a tear slipping down her cheek before she quickly wiped it away. "I've been trying to hold everything together, but I don't think I can anymore."

"You don't have to," Isabel whispered. "Let me help."

For a long moment, Eliza didn't say anything, but then she nodded, her defenses finally giving way. "Thank you," she whispered, her voice cracking with emotion.

Isabel smiled softly, her heart full. "Always."

In that moment, Isabel realized that helping Eliza was helping her too. By allowing herself to be there for her friend, she was learning to face her own fears, to confront the parts of herself she had kept hidden for so long.

And as they sat there, hand in hand, Isabel knew that this was only the beginning—for both of them.

Chapter 10: Gabe's Confession

The air was thick with anticipation, the kind that settles in when words have yet to be spoken. Isabel stood on the cottage porch, looking out at the gathering clouds in the distance. The storm from days ago had left its mark on the island, but the village had moved on, resilient as ever. Still, there was something unsettled within her, something she couldn't shake since her conversation with Eliza and the growing closeness with Gabe.

The lighthouse stood tall in the distance, a beacon of constancy, but even that didn't soothe the turmoil inside her. And now, Gabe was coming. She hadn't expected him to stop by tonight, not after the silence that had lingered between them the past few days.

A knock sounded on the doorframe, and she turned to find Gabe standing there, his usual confident demeanor tempered by something else tonight. His hands were stuffed in his pockets, his gaze steady but softer than usual. He didn't need to speak for her to know something was weighing on him.

"Hey," she said, her voice catching in her throat.

He gave her a slight smile. "Hey."

For a moment, neither of them moved. The air between them felt charged, as though both were waiting for the other to break the silence.

Finally, Gabe stepped forward. "I've been meaning to talk to you."

Isabel's heart gave a small, nervous flutter. She wasn't sure what she expected him to say, but something about the way he looked at her made her think that this conversation was different. She could feel it in the way he held himself—tentative, as if measuring his words carefully.

She gestured toward the small bench on the porch. "Let's sit."

They both settled into the familiar space, but instead of the comfort she usually found with him, there was tension, unspoken and yet so present it nearly crackled in the air.

Gabe stared out at the horizon, his jaw clenched slightly. It was rare for him to hesitate, and it made Isabel uneasy. She had never seen him this way, and the realization that something was deeply troubling him made her stomach twist.

"I've been thinking about a lot of things lately," he started, his voice low. "About the past, the decisions I've made... the people I've hurt."

His words hung between them, and Isabel felt her breath catch. There was a weight to what he wasn't saying, something just beneath the surface, like a current threatening to pull them under.

She waited, not wanting to push, but the silence between them was unbearable.

"What are you saying, Gabe?" she finally asked, her voice barely above a whisper.

He turned toward her, his gaze meeting hers with an intensity that made her chest tighten. "You and I," he said, his words careful, deliberate, "we've been through a lot, haven't we?"

Isabel swallowed hard. "Yeah, we have."

There was something raw in his expression now, something that made her feel like he was standing on the edge of a precipice, and if he spoke the next words, there would be no going back.

"I've been thinking about why I came back here," he continued. "Why I stayed."

Isabel's heart raced, her mind scrambling to keep up. She could feel the ground shifting beneath her, the unspoken truth pressing against the walls they had both built.

Gabe exhaled slowly, running a hand through his hair. "I didn't just come back because this is home," he admitted, his voice quiet but steady. "I came back because of you."

Her breath caught in her throat, but he didn't stop.

"There's always been something between us, Isabel," he said, his words heavy with meaning. "Even when we were younger, even when we tried to pretend there wasn't."

The intensity in his voice sent a shiver down her spine. She knew what he was saying—she had felt it too, the pull between them, the unspoken connection that had always lingered beneath the surface. But hearing him say it, admitting it out loud, made it real in a way it hadn't been before.

"I tried to fight it," Gabe continued, his gaze unwavering. "I thought I could move on, that maybe we both could. But when you came back, it all came rushing back too."

Isabel felt her chest tighten. His words were so close to what she had felt herself, the same unresolved feelings she had tried to bury when she left the island. But now, sitting here, with Gabe looking at her like that, she couldn't ignore it anymore.

"Gabe, I—" she started, but he shook his head, cutting her off.

"I'm not asking for anything," he said, his voice softer now. "I just needed you to know. Needed you to understand why it's been so hard for me to be around you, why I've been holding back."

She could hear the vulnerability in his voice, the fear that had been lurking behind his usual calm exterior. He was laying himself bare, exposing the feelings he had kept hidden for so long, and it left her feeling both overwhelmed and deeply moved.

"I've tried to bury it, Isabel, believe me," he continued. "But being with you, seeing you... it's different now. I don't think I can keep pretending."

His words hung in the air, a confession without directly saying the words she knew were in his heart. And yet, he didn't say he loved her. Not in the way people usually did. Instead, it was the weight of the years between them, the shared history, the way he had stayed on this island when he could have gone anywhere else. That, more than anything, was his confession.

Isabel stared at him, her heart pounding in her chest. She felt the familiar pull, the way his presence had always grounded her, made her feel things she hadn't wanted to feel. And yet, she couldn't ignore the conflict inside her, the part of her that was terrified to open herself up again, to let herself believe in something that could so easily slip away.

Gabe watched her, his eyes searching her face for any sign of what she was feeling. But Isabel couldn't give him that—not yet. She was still trying to process everything, still trying to understand how to reconcile the past with the present.

"I don't know what to say," she admitted, her voice barely audible.

Gabe's expression softened, and he reached for her hand, his fingers brushing against hers in a way that sent a jolt through her.

"You don't have to say anything," he murmured. "I just wanted you to know."

For a moment, they sat in silence, their hands resting together between them. The quiet was thick with unspoken emotions, the kind that didn't need words to be understood. Isabel felt the warmth of his hand, the strength in his grip, and something in her softened, just a little.

She didn't pull away. Instead, she let the silence linger, let herself feel the weight of everything he had said. There was no rush, no need to force an answer or a decision. For now, it was enough just to be here, with him.

The storm clouds in the distance rumbled, a low growl that matched the tension in the air. Isabel glanced toward the horizon, feeling the first drops of rain begin to fall.

Gabe stood, still holding her hand. "We should get inside," he said, his voice gentle.

Isabel nodded, following him into the cottage as the rain began to fall in earnest. But even as they sought shelter from the storm, Isabel knew that the real storm was still brewing inside her—one that wouldn't pass so easily.

As they stood in the warmth of the small cottage, the storm raging outside, Isabel looked at Gabe and knew that this was only the beginning. His confession—subtle as it was—had opened a door she wasn't sure she was ready to walk through. But now, with the rain pouring down and Gabe standing by her side, she couldn't help but wonder if, just maybe, it was a door she needed to open after all.

The storm outside was relentless, pounding against the windows of the cottage like a physical manifestation of the turmoil inside Isabel. She could hear the wind howl, feel the walls tremble slightly under the force of the rain, but all she could focus on was

Gabe—standing so close, his presence both comforting and over-whelming at the same time.

The warmth of his hand had lingered even after he'd let go, leaving a ghostly imprint on her skin. She wrapped her arms around herself, as if to shield herself from the thoughts and feelings swirling around her mind.

Gabe stood by the window, his back to her, watching the storm with a quiet intensity. He hadn't said anything since they'd stepped inside, but his silence spoke volumes. He had laid his feelings bare, opened himself up in a way Isabel hadn't expected, and now the ball was in her court.

But what could she say? The truth was, she didn't know. She had spent so long running from her past, from her feelings, from the island itself. Now, everything she had tried to keep at bay was crashing back in all at once, and she wasn't sure she was strong enough to face it.

She walked over to the small fireplace, crouching down to add another log to the smoldering embers. The flickering light bathed the room in a soft, golden glow, casting shadows on the walls. It was a comforting sight, but Isabel felt anything but comforted.

"What do you want me to say, Gabe?" she asked, her voice barely above a whisper. She didn't look at him, afraid of what she might see in his eyes if she did.

He didn't answer right away, and the silence between them stretched, long and taut.

"I don't want you to say anything you're not ready to," he finally said, his voice steady, but with an underlying tension. "But I had to be honest with you. I couldn't keep pretending."

Isabel nodded, staring into the flames. "I don't know if I'm ready for this," she admitted. "I don't know if I'll ever be ready."

Gabe moved toward her, stopping just behind her. She could feel his presence, the warmth of his body radiating toward her, but he didn't touch her. He was giving her space, even as the distance between them felt like it was closing in.

"I understand," he said quietly. "But I need you to know... I'm not going anywhere. I'm here, Isabel. Whether you want me to be or not."

His words, so simple and yet so full of meaning, hit her harder than she expected. She stood, turning to face him, her arms still wrapped around herself as if to keep everything from spilling out.

"Why?" she asked, her voice trembling. "Why stay? Why risk it?"

Gabe's eyes softened, and for the first time that night, she saw a flicker of something she couldn't quite place. Fear? Hope? It was hard to tell.

"Because you're worth the risk," he said, and there was no hesitation in his voice, no doubt. "You've always been worth it."

Isabel's heart twisted painfully in her chest. She wanted to believe him—wanted to believe that she was worth something, that she deserved the kind of love he was offering. But a part of her, the part that had been hurt so many times before, couldn't help but push back.

"And what if I'm not?" she whispered, her voice breaking. "What if I hurt you? What if I can't give you what you want?"

Gabe stepped closer, his hand reaching up to gently brush a strand of hair away from her face. His touch was light, almost hesitant, as if he was afraid of breaking the fragile moment between them.

"You don't have to give me anything," he said softly. "I'm not asking for promises or guarantees. I just want you to be honest—with me, and with yourself."

Isabel's throat tightened, and for a moment, she couldn't speak. Gabe's words were cutting through all her defenses, all the walls she had built to protect herself. It scared her how easily he could see through her, how much he understood the things she had tried to hide.

"I don't know how to be that person," she said, her voice barely audible. "The one who can let someone in. The one who can trust."

Gabe's hand cupped her cheek, his thumb brushing gently over her skin. "Then don't be that person," he said, his voice low and steady. "Just be you. That's all I'm asking."

Isabel felt tears prick at the corners of her eyes, and she blinked them away, refusing to let them fall. She wasn't used to this—being vulnerable, being seen for who she really was. It felt too raw, too dangerous.

"I'm scared, Gabe," she admitted, her voice breaking. "I'm scared of letting you in, of getting hurt again. I don't know if I can handle it."

Gabe's expression softened, and he lowered his hand, giving her space. "I'm scared too," he confessed quietly. "But I'm willing to take that risk. For you."

Isabel looked up at him, her heart pounding in her chest. She could see the truth in his eyes, the sincerity in his words. He wasn't trying to push her, wasn't trying to force her into anything. He was just... there. Waiting. Ready to meet her wherever she was.

And for the first time in a long time, Isabel felt the smallest flicker of hope. Maybe, just maybe, she didn't have to do this alone.

"I don't know what happens next," she said, her voice shaky. "I don't know if I can give you the answers you're looking for."

Gabe smiled, a soft, understanding smile that made her heart ache. "I'm not looking for answers," he said gently. "I'm just looking for you."

Isabel felt her breath catch in her throat, and for a moment, all the fear, all the doubts, seemed to melt away. There was something so simple, so pure in what he was offering. Not demands, not expectations—just him, just them.

She stepped forward, closing the small distance between them. Gabe watched her carefully, his eyes never leaving hers, as if he was waiting for her to make the first move.

And then, slowly, tentatively, Isabel reached up and placed her hand on his chest. She could feel the steady thrum of his heartbeat beneath her palm, and it grounded her, anchoring her in the moment.

"I don't know where this is going," she whispered, her voice trembling. "But I'm willing to try."

Gabe's hand came up to cover hers, his fingers warm and steady against her skin. "That's all I need," he said softly.

For a long moment, they stood there, the storm raging outside but the world between them still and quiet. Isabel could feel the weight of everything unsaid, everything unresolved, but for the first time, it didn't feel impossible to face.

Maybe, just maybe, they could figure it out together.

Gabe leaned down, his forehead resting gently against hers, and Isabel closed her eyes, letting herself breathe him in. The scent of rain clung to his skin, and she could feel the warmth of his breath on her cheek. It was intimate, but not in a way that demanded anything more. It was simply... them.

"I'm here," Gabe whispered, his voice so soft it was barely audible. "I'm not going anywhere."

Isabel didn't have the words to respond, but she didn't need them. Instead, she let herself lean into him, let herself be held by him, just for a moment.

And in that moment, it was enough.

The storm outside had calmed to a steady, rhythmic drizzle, the intensity of the wind dying down to a gentle sigh. The soft patter of rain against the windows created a soothing background to the quiet room, casting a tranquil ambiance over the tension that still hung between Isabel and Gabe.

Isabel's hand remained on Gabe's chest, her fingers lightly tracing the contours of his shirt. She could feel the steady, reassuring beat of his heart beneath her palm, a rhythm that seemed to sync with her own troubled pulse. It was grounding and comforting, a stark contrast to the chaos of her thoughts.

Gabe's hand was still over hers, a gentle but firm pressure that communicated more than words ever could. He was giving her space, but also a clear sign of his presence and commitment. The silence between them was filled with an unspoken understanding, a mutual acknowledgment of the vulnerability they had both laid bare.

After a long, silent moment, Gabe pulled back slightly, his eyes searching Isabel's face with a mixture of hope and concern. "Isabel," he began, his voice softer now, almost reverent. "I need you to know something."

Isabel looked up at him, her eyes meeting his with a blend of apprehension and curiosity. "What is it?"

Gabe took a deep breath, collecting his thoughts. "I've always admired how strong you are," he said, his gaze steady. "But I also see the struggle behind that strength. I know you've been through a lot, and I respect your need to protect yourself. But I want you to know that you don't have to go through this alone."

Isabel's heart ached at his words, a lump forming in her throat. She wanted to respond, to tell him how much his words meant to her, but she struggled to find the right words. Instead, she simply nodded, trying to convey her gratitude through her eyes.

Gabe's gaze softened, and he reached up to gently cup her face with both hands. "I'm here," he said again, his voice filled with quiet conviction. "And I'm not asking you to change anything about yourself. I just want to be a part of your life, in whatever way you're comfortable with."

Isabel felt tears well up in her eyes, and she blinked them away, trying to maintain her composure. The raw honesty in Gabe's voice, the genuine care he was showing, was overwhelming. It was a stark contrast to the guarded isolation she had become accustomed to.

"I don't know how to let go of my fears," she admitted, her voice trembling. "I don't know how to trust that things won't fall apart."

Gabe's thumb gently wiped away a tear that had escaped, his touch tender and reassuring. "Trust takes time," he said softly. "And it's okay to be scared. I'm not asking you to have all the answers. I'm just asking you to take a chance on us."

Isabel closed her eyes, letting his words wash over her. The promise of taking a chance, of opening herself up to the possibility of something real and meaningful, was both terrifying and exhilarating. She had spent so long guarding her heart, building walls to protect herself from potential hurt. And now, Gabe was asking her to tear those walls down, to take a leap of faith.

She took a deep breath, letting the warmth of the moment seep into her. "Okay," she finally said, her voice barely above a whisper. "I'll try. I'll try to let go of my fears and see where this goes."

Gabe's eyes lit up with relief and happiness, and he pulled her into a gentle embrace. Isabel melted into his arms, feeling the solid, reassuring strength of him around her. It was a simple gesture, but it conveyed more than words ever could.

For a few moments, they stood there, wrapped in each other's embrace, the storm outside a distant memory. The warmth of the fire and the soft patter of rain created a cocoon of comfort and safety around them.

When they finally pulled away, Gabe's eyes were filled with a tender, hopeful light. "Thank you," he said quietly. "For giving us a chance."

Isabel smiled, a small but genuine smile that reflected the tentative hope she was beginning to feel. "Thank you for being patient with me," she replied. "For understanding where I'm coming from."

Gabe nodded, his expression full of understanding and appreciation. "I don't want to rush you," he said. "We'll take things one step at a time. Whatever pace you need."

Isabel nodded, feeling a sense of relief and gratitude. The path ahead was still uncertain, but for the first time in a long time, she felt like she was moving in the right direction. With Gabe by her side, she felt a glimmer of hope that perhaps she could learn to trust again, to open her heart to the possibility of something real.

As the storm continued to softly rain outside, Isabel and Gabe sat together by the fire, the warmth of the flames a stark contrast to the chill of the storm. Their conversation flowed easily, the earlier tension giving way to a more relaxed and intimate connection. They talked about their pasts, their dreams, and their hopes for the future, finding common ground and deepening their bond.

The night wore on, and the storm outside began to wane, the rain tapering off into a gentle drizzle. The room was filled with a sense of calm and contentment, a peacefulness that seemed to reflect the quiet but profound changes taking place within Isabel.

As they sat together, their hands occasionally brushing against each other, Isabel felt a sense of acceptance and belonging that she hadn't felt in a long time. Gabe's presence was a reassuring anchor, a steady support that gave her the courage to face her fears and uncertainties.

When the time came for them to say goodnight, Gabe's parting words were gentle and heartfelt. "Rest well," he said, his voice warm and soothing. "We'll talk more tomorrow. Just know that I'm here, no matter what."

Isabel watched as he left, the door closing softly behind him. She stood there for a moment, her mind and heart still reeling from the depth of their conversation. But amidst the confusion and emotion, she felt a growing sense of hope and possibility.

The storm had passed, and with it, a new chapter of her life was beginning to unfold. It was a chapter filled with uncertainty and potential, but also with the promise of something real and meaningful. And as Isabel prepared for bed, she carried with her the comforting knowledge that she didn't have to face it alone.

The journey ahead would be challenging, but with Gabe's support and understanding, she felt more ready than ever to take that leap of faith and see where it led.

The morning sun peeked through the curtains, casting a warm, golden glow across the room. Isabel stirred from her sleep, her dreams a tangled mix of emotions and the echoes of the previous night's conversation. The storm had left the air crisp and fresh, a stark contrast to the turmoil she had felt just hours before. As she sat up and rubbed the sleep from her eyes, her thoughts were filled with the lingering weight of Gabe's words and the new sense of hope they had brought.

In the kitchen, the scent of coffee brewing filled the air, mingling with the faint aroma of rain and pine. Isabel moved through her morning routine with a quiet sense of anticipation. She wasn't sure what the day would bring, but she felt an undercurrent of excitement—a feeling she hadn't allowed herself to fully embrace in a long time.

As she poured herself a cup of coffee, she glanced out the window, watching as the town slowly came to life. The streets were still wet from the storm, the puddles shimmering in the early light. Isabel wondered about Gabe's plans for the day and whether he would reach out to her. The thought of seeing him again, of continuing their conversation, filled her with a mix of nervousness and eager expectation.

Her phone buzzed on the counter, and she quickly grabbed it, her heart skipping a beat when she saw Gabe's name on the screen. The message was simple, yet it carried a warmth that made her smile.

Good morning, Isabel. I hope you slept well. I was thinking we could meet at the café later this morning if you're free. We could talk more about yesterday or just enjoy a relaxed morning. Let me know what you think.

Isabel typed a quick reply, her fingers moving with a newfound confidence.

Good morning, Gabe. I'd love to meet at the café. What time works for you?

She hit send and finished her coffee, her mind racing with thoughts of their upcoming meeting. The café had always been a favorite spot of hers, a place where she could lose herself in a good book or the comforting buzz of conversation. The idea of sharing that space with Gabe, of continuing their dialogue, felt both exciting and reassuring.

At the café, the atmosphere was warm and inviting, the chatter of patrons creating a cozy background hum. Gabe was already there when Isabel arrived, sitting at a corner table with a steaming cup of coffee in front of him. He looked up as she approached, a smile spreading across his face that made her heart flutter.

"Morning," he greeted, standing up to pull out a chair for her. "I'm glad you could make it."

"Morning," Isabel replied, returning his smile as she took her seat. "Thank you for inviting me."

Gabe gestured to the menu on the table. "I've already ordered coffee for us. Anything else you'd like? Breakfast, maybe?"

Isabel shook her head, feeling a sense of ease in his presence. "No, I'm good with just coffee for now. Thank you."

They settled into a comfortable rhythm, their conversation flowing naturally as they talked about their plans for the day and their reflections on the previous night. Gabe's presence was calming, and Isabel found herself opening up more than she had anticipated.

"So, what did you think of last night?" Gabe asked, his tone casual but his eyes holding a deeper curiosity.

Isabel took a sip of her coffee, considering her response. "It was... overwhelming, but in a good way. I've been so caught up in my own head lately, it felt really nice to have someone understand and be there for me."

Gabe nodded, his gaze steady. "I'm glad to hear that. I know it's not always easy to let your guard down, especially after everything you've been through."

She nodded, feeling a mix of gratitude and vulnerability. "It's been a long time since I've allowed myself to be so open with someone. I think I've been afraid of getting hurt or disappointed, so I've kept everyone at a distance."

Gabe reached across the table, his hand brushing against hers in a gesture of comfort. "I understand. And I want you to know that I'm not going anywhere. I'm here for you, and I want to be part of your life, however that works for you."

Isabel felt a warmth spread through her at his words, a sense of relief and hope that she hadn't felt in a long time. "Thank you, Gabe. That means a lot to me. I'm still figuring things out, but having your support is really helping."

Their conversation continued, covering a range of topics from their childhood memories to their future aspirations. The more they talked, the more Isabel felt a sense of connection and understanding growing between them. Gabe's openness and willingness to listen were deeply reassuring, and she found herself wanting to share more about her past and her dreams.

As they finished their coffee and Gabe signaled for the check, he leaned in slightly, his expression earnest. "Isabel, I know it might be too soon to talk about this, but I want you to know that I'm serious about us. I'm not trying to rush anything, but I care about you, and I want to build something meaningful together."

Isabel's heart skipped a beat at his words, the weight of his confession settling over her. She hadn't expected such a direct admission, but the sincerity in his voice made her heart swell with emotion.

"I care about you too, Gabe," she said softly. "And I'm open to seeing where this goes. I just need to take it one step at a time."

Gabe's eyes softened with relief and affection. "Of course. We'll take it at your pace. I just want you to know that I'm here for you, and I'm excited to see where this journey takes us."

Isabel smiled, feeling a renewed sense of hope and excitement. The future was still uncertain, but with Gabe's support and understanding, she felt more prepared to face the challenges ahead.

As they left the café and walked out into the crisp morning air, Isabel felt a sense of clarity and purpose. The conversation with Gabe had been a turning point, a moment of emotional openness that had deepened their connection. And as they strolled through the town together, the promise of a new beginning seemed more tangible than ever.

The day was filled with a mix of reflection and anticipation, and Isabel found herself looking forward to the future with a renewed sense of optimism. With Gabe by her side, she felt more ready than ever to embrace the possibilities of love and connection that lay ahead.

As Isabel and Gabe walked side by side through the charming streets of the island town, the morning sun bathed everything in a soft, golden light. The lingering chill from the storm had left the air crisp and invigorating, adding a freshness to the day that seemed to mirror Isabel's mood. She glanced at Gabe, his profile illuminated by the sunlight, and felt a flutter of excitement mixed with nervous anticipation.

Their earlier conversation had left Isabel feeling both exhilarated and uncertain. Gabe's confession, though not overt, had hinted at deep feelings, and Isabel was left to decipher the nuances of his affection. The subtlety of his admission had created a tension that was both thrilling and daunting. She could sense that Gabe was serious about their connection, but she was still grappling with her own emotions and the implications of his words.

As they approached the harbor, the vibrant colors of the boats and the gentle lapping of the water created a picturesque scene. Gabe led the way to a quiet spot overlooking the bay, where they could sit and enjoy the view without interruption.

"This is one of my favorite places," Gabe said, gesturing to a wooden bench that provided a perfect vantage point of the water. "It's peaceful here, and I find it's a good place to clear my head."

Isabel took a seat, her heart still racing from their earlier conversation. She glanced at Gabe, who was standing beside her, his expression thoughtful. She could see the sincerity in his eyes, and it made her own feelings feel even more complex.

"I can see why," Isabel said, her voice soft. "It's beautiful here. And calming."

Gabe sat down next to her, his body close but not touching. The proximity was comforting, and Isabel felt a surge of warmth at his presence. They sat in silence for a few moments, both lost in their thoughts. The sound of seagulls and the gentle breeze added to the tranquility of the moment.

Finally, Gabe broke the silence, his voice tentative. "Isabel, I know we've been talking about taking things slow, and I respect that. But I also want to be honest with you about how I feel."

Isabel turned to face him, her heart pounding in her chest. "What do you mean?"

Gabe looked out at the water, his gaze distant but focused. "I care about you more than I thought I would. When we first reconnected, I wasn't sure what to expect. But the more time we've spent together, the more I realize how much I want to be a part of your life."

Isabel's breath caught in her throat. She had been hoping for clarity, but Gabe's words were both reassuring and overwhelming. She had grown to care deeply for him, but the weight of his admission made her question how ready she was for a serious relationship.

"I'm not saying this to pressure you," Gabe continued, his voice gentle. "I just wanted you to know that I'm here for you, and I'm willing to wait for you to figure things out. I want to build something real with you, but I understand if you need more time."

Isabel took a deep breath, trying to steady her racing thoughts. Gabe's honesty and patience were both comforting and challenging. She wanted to be open with him, but she also needed to confront her own fears and uncertainties.

"I appreciate that," Isabel said, her voice trembling slightly. "And I care about you too. I'm just... not sure how to navigate all of this yet. I've been so focused on my own struggles and trying to find my way that it's hard to know what I'm ready for."

Gabe reached out and took her hand in his, his touch warm and reassuring. "I understand. And I'm here to support you, no matter what. We don't have to rush anything. I just wanted you to know where I stand."

The gesture was simple, but it conveyed a depth of emotion that words alone could not express. Isabel felt a mixture of relief and vulnerability, grateful for Gabe's understanding and patience. She squeezed his hand gently, her heart swelling with affection.

"Thank you, Gabe," Isabel said softly. "Your support means more to me than I can say. I'm still figuring things out, but having you by my side makes it a lot easier."

Gabe smiled, his eyes filled with warmth. "I'm glad to hear that. And I'm looking forward to seeing where this journey takes us."

They sat together for a while longer, enjoying the serene beauty of the harbor and the growing sense of connection between them. The gentle sway of the boats and the rhythmic sound of the waves created a peaceful backdrop, and Isabel felt a sense of calm she hadn't experienced in a long time.

As they walked back to town, the sun climbing higher in the sky, Isabel felt a renewed sense of hope and possibility. Gabe's confession had opened up new possibilities, and while she was still uncertain about the future, she felt more prepared to face it with him by her side.

The day unfolded with a sense of possibility and promise. Isabel and Gabe continued to explore the island together, their conversations flowing easily and their moments of silence filled with unspoken understanding. The connection between them deepened, and Isabel began to feel more at ease with her own emotions.

As evening approached, they found themselves back at the café, where they had first shared their feelings. The café's cozy ambiance and the warm glow of the lamps created a comforting atmosphere, and Isabel felt a sense of familiarity and contentment.

Gabe looked at her with a gentle smile. "I'm really glad we had this time together today. It's been nice to talk and just be with you."

Isabel nodded, her heart full. "I'm glad too. It's been a meaningful day, and I feel like we've made some real progress."

Gabe's expression softened, and he reached across the table to take her hand once more. "I'm looking forward to what comes next. I know we're both still figuring things out, but I'm excited about the possibilities."

Isabel's heart swelled with emotion as she looked into Gabe's eyes. The sincerity and affection in his gaze made her feel hopeful about the future. She knew there were still challenges to face and uncertainties to navigate, but with Gabe by her side, she felt more ready than ever to embrace the journey ahead.

As they left the café and walked into the cool evening air, Isabel felt a sense of contentment and anticipation. The day had been a turning point, a moment of emotional clarity that had deepened her connection with Gabe and opened up new possibilities for their future.

The road ahead was still uncertain, but with Gabe's support and their growing bond, Isabel felt more hopeful about the path she was embarking on. The promise of a new beginning and the excitement of exploring their relationship together made her feel optimistic about the future.

And as they walked hand in hand, their steps in sync and their hearts aligned, Isabel knew that whatever lay ahead, they would face it together, with hope, courage, and a deepening sense of love.

As Isabel and Gabe strolled hand in hand through the twilight streets of the island, the earlier tension between them seemed to have softened, replaced by a deep sense of companionship. Yet, beneath the surface, Isabel could feel the quiet, unspoken emotion that lingered between them. Gabe hadn't said the words outright, but his subtle confession had left a mark on her heart. It felt fragile, this budding connection between them, and Isabel was afraid of ruining it by pushing too hard or not pushing enough.

The path ahead was illuminated by the soft glow of streetlights, their light casting a warm halo over everything. The island had a way of making even the most complicated moments feel like they belonged to something timeless. The air was crisp, cool with the promise of autumn, and the distant sound of the ocean waves brushing against the shore was a constant, soothing backdrop.

They stopped at the foot of a small hill overlooking the water, where the lighthouse stood. It was the same place where Isabel had made her earlier discoveries, the same place that had begun to reveal the layers of her mother's secrets. Now, standing here again, with Gabe beside her, the lighthouse held new meaning.

Gabe let go of her hand, moving to lean against the fence that overlooked the water. His silence wasn't heavy; it felt as though he was waiting, giving Isabel space to gather her thoughts.

"You brought me here," Isabel said softly, stepping up beside him. "Is there something you want me to see?"

Gabe turned his head to look at her, the faint smile on his lips shadowed by the low light. "I thought you might want to come back. Sometimes, seeing the same place from a different perspective helps." His gaze drifted to the lighthouse. "It seems like this place is important to you."

Isabel's throat tightened as memories of her mother's sketches and the cryptic notes surfaced in her mind. Gabe was right. The lighthouse had become a place of significance—both for the secrets it had kept and the ones it was slowly revealing. She glanced at Gabe, wondering if this moment was the right one to tell him everything.

But instead of diving into that, she found herself speaking about something else, something she hadn't yet admitted to anyone—not even herself. "I think... I've been hiding, Gabe," she said, her voice barely above a whisper. "Not just from my mother's secrets, but from my own."

Gabe didn't say anything. He simply stood there, his presence steady, his eyes searching hers in the dim light. He was giving her the space to speak, and Isabel felt the weight of her confession pressing down on her.

"I came back here thinking I could uncover the truth about my mother and understand why she kept things from me," Isabel continued. "But now, I realize that I've been running away from my own life. I've been afraid of facing the things I don't want to admit—like how lost I've felt, even before I came back."

The words hung in the air, heavy and raw, and Isabel felt an overwhelming vulnerability settle over her. This was the part of her that she hadn't shown to anyone—the part that felt like a failure for leaving her old life behind, for not knowing what came next.

Gabe's voice, when he spoke, was soft but steady. "I know what it's like to run away. I think we all do, in our own way. But you're not running anymore, Isabel. You're here. You're facing things, even if they're hard."

She turned to look at him, her heart swelling with both gratitude and the fear of being truly seen. His words were gentle, but they struck deeply. For so long, she had been terrified of this very moment—of being exposed, of having her fears laid bare. But with Gabe, it didn't feel like judgment. It felt like understanding.

"I don't know if I'm ready to face all of it," Isabel admitted. "Sometimes it feels like there's so much that's still unresolved. My mother's secrets, my life before the island... and now, with you."

Gabe's eyes softened, and he took a step closer to her. "We don't have to have all the answers right now. But whatever you're going through, you don't have to do it alone. I'm here. We'll figure it out, together."

The sincerity in his voice broke something open inside Isabel. For so long, she had been carrying the weight of her past alone. And here was Gabe, offering her a lifeline—a chance to share the burden, to lean on someone else for once.

Isabel felt the distance between them shrink, not just physically but emotionally. Gabe's presence, his words, were offering her a sense of comfort and safety that she hadn't realized she needed. It was as if the walls she had built around herself were slowly coming down, brick by brick.

"I've been scared," Isabel said, her voice trembling slightly. "Scared of what it means to let someone in. Scared of what comes next."

Gabe's expression was gentle, his gaze unwavering. "I'm scared too, Isabel. But sometimes, the things we're most afraid of are the things that matter the most."

They stood there in the quiet, their breaths mingling in the cool night air. The lighthouse beam swept across the water, its light illuminating the vast expanse of ocean before them. The symbolism wasn't lost on Isabel—the light cutting through the darkness, revealing what had been hidden. Just like her journey with Gabe, just like her journey with herself.

Gabe reached for her hand, his fingers curling around hers with a tenderness that made Isabel's heart ache. His touch was both grounding and electric, and she felt the unspoken emotion between them growing, taking root in the silence.

"I don't want to lose you," Gabe said softly, his voice barely audible over the sound of the waves. "But I also don't want to rush you. I just want you to know that I'm here, and I'm not going anywhere."

Isabel's breath caught in her throat at his words. It was the closest thing to a confession she had heard from him, and yet, it wasn't a declaration of love—it was something deeper. It was a promise. A promise that he would stand by her, no matter what.

The vulnerability in his voice, the quiet strength behind his words, made Isabel realize how much Gabe meant to her. She had been so focused on her own fears and uncertainties that she hadn't fully acknowledged what she stood to lose. And now, standing here with him, she knew that she didn't want to let go.

Isabel turned to face him, her hand still clasped in his. "I don't want to lose you either, Gabe," she whispered, her voice trembling with emotion. "I don't know what the future holds, but I know that I want you to be a part of it."

The weight of her confession hung in the air, and for a moment, they simply stood there, looking at each other. Then, slowly, Gabe pulled her into his arms, holding her close against his chest. Isabel melted into his embrace, her heart pounding in her chest, and for the first time in a long time, she felt truly at peace.

They stood there for what felt like an eternity, the lighthouse beam sweeping over them, the sound of the ocean a constant reminder of the world around them. But in that moment, it felt like it was just the two of them—two souls finding their way toward each other in the darkness.

When Gabe finally pulled back, his hand still resting on her back, his eyes searched hers. "We'll take it one step at a time," he said, his voice steady. "No rush. Just... us."

Isabel nodded, a tear slipping down her cheek as she smiled. "Just us."

And in that moment, Isabel knew that no matter what happened next—no matter what secrets were uncovered or what challenges lay ahead—she wouldn't face them alone.

The night air was crisp as Isabel and Gabe stood together at the base of the lighthouse. The lighthouse beam continued its slow, methodical sweep across the water, and the soft, rhythmic sound of waves against the shore seemed to synchronize with the quiet beating of Isabel's heart. The emotional weight of their earlier conversation hung between them like a fragile thread, binding their hearts in a shared understanding.

Gabe's hand was still gently resting on Isabel's back, his touch a comforting presence. She could feel the warmth of his body against hers, a stark contrast to the cool night air. It was a reassuring warmth, like the first hint of dawn after a long night.

After a few moments of silence, Gabe spoke again, his voice low and thoughtful. "You know, this place—the lighthouse—it's always been a symbol of something steady, something reliable. Even when everything around it changes, it stays the same. Maybe that's why it's important to you."

Isabel nodded, appreciating the metaphor Gabe had drawn. "It's strange," she said, her voice soft. "I always thought it was just a structure. But now it feels like it's been a part of my journey, a part of discovering who I am and what I've been hiding from."

Gabe's gaze remained steady, his eyes reflecting the light of the lighthouse. "Sometimes, we need something constant in our lives, something that helps us navigate through our own storms. For you, maybe that's this place, or maybe it's something else."

Isabel turned her head slightly to look at him, her eyes searching his face for any hint of hesitation or judgment. Instead, she found only sincerity. "I've spent so much time trying to make sense of things," she admitted, "trying to figure out what my mother's secrets mean for me. But I think what I've been avoiding is the idea that I might have my own secrets too—things I've buried because I didn't want to face them."

Gabe's hand moved slightly, brushing against Isabel's shoulder as he spoke. "It's not always easy to confront those things. But you don't have to do it alone. Sometimes, talking about it, sharing it with someone you trust, can make a difference."

Isabel felt a lump form in her throat as Gabe's words resonated deeply with her. She had always been so careful to keep her fears and regrets hidden, fearing that showing them would make her vulnerable, make her weak. But here was Gabe, offering her a safe space to open up, to let go of the burden she had carried for so long.

"You know," Gabe said, his voice gentle, "there's something I've been wanting to tell you. It's not something I've been holding back intentionally, but it's just something that's hard to put into words."

Isabel looked at him, a mix of curiosity and apprehension in her eyes. "What is it?"

Gabe hesitated for a moment, his gaze dropping to the ground as he gathered his thoughts. "I've been in this place for a long time. I've seen people come and go, and I've had my own share of ups and downs. But ever since you came back, there's been something different. It's like... you've brought a new light into this place, a light that I didn't know I needed."

Isabel's heart skipped a beat at his words. She could sense the depth of his emotion, the sincerity behind his confession. "I didn't realize I had that kind of impact," she said, her voice barely above a whisper.

Gabe met her gaze, his eyes filled with an intensity that made Isabel's breath catch. "You do. And it's more than just your presence. It's the way you're willing to face your fears, the way you're trying to make sense of everything. It's inspiring."

The compliment took Isabel by surprise, and she felt a rush of warmth spread through her chest. For so long, she had felt like she was stumbling through her life, unsure of her path, unsure of her place. But Gabe's words made her realize that maybe she was on the right track after all.

"I'm trying," Isabel said, her voice trembling slightly. "I'm trying to understand what all of this means. But it's hard. Sometimes, I feel like I'm just making things worse."

Gabe took a step closer, his hand reaching out to gently cup Isabel's cheek. His touch was tender, and the warmth of his hand against her skin was a soothing contrast to the chill of the night. "You're not making things worse," he said softly. "You're just navigating through your own journey. And you're not alone in it."

Isabel felt a tear slip down her cheek, and she didn't bother to wipe it away. Instead, she leaned into Gabe's touch, finding solace in his presence. "Thank you," she said quietly. "For being here. For understanding."

Gabe's eyes softened, and he pulled her into a gentle embrace. Isabel rested her head against his chest, feeling the steady rhythm of his heartbeat. In that moment, everything felt right. The confusion, the fear, the uncertainty—it all seemed to melt away, replaced by a sense of calm and reassurance.

They stood there for a while, simply holding each other, the lighthouse beam sweeping over them like a guardian of their new-found closeness. Isabel could feel the weight of her worries beginning to lift, replaced by a sense of hope and possibility.

Finally, Gabe broke the silence, his voice barely above a whisper. "I know things are still complicated. I know there's a lot you're dealing with. But I want you to know that I'm here for you, no matter what."

Isabel looked up at him, her eyes filled with gratitude and something else—something that felt like a blossoming affection. "I appreciate that more than you know," she said, her voice trembling with emotion.

Gabe leaned in, his lips brushing against her forehead in a tender kiss. "We'll take it one day at a time," he said softly. "Together."

As the lighthouse beam continued its steady sweep across the water, Isabel felt a sense of clarity begin to settle over her. The path ahead was still uncertain, but with Gabe by her side, she felt a renewed sense of strength and hope. The journey of self-discovery was far from over, but for the first time, she felt like she wasn't walking it alone.

They lingered there for a few more moments, savoring the quiet connection between them. The night was still and peaceful, the lighthouse a constant symbol of guidance and support. And as they eventually began to walk back down the hill, hand in hand, Isabel knew that no matter what challenges lay ahead, she had found something truly valuable—someone who believed in her, someone who was willing to stand by her side through the storm.

And for Isabel, that was a comforting thought.

As they descended the hill together, the light from the lighthouse receded behind them, leaving only the glow of distant street lamps to guide their way. The night seemed to wrap around them like a protective shroud, concealing the uncertainties of the future while amplifying the warmth they felt in each other's presence.

The path was illuminated by the faint glow of lanterns strung along the way, casting a gentle light that flickered like fireflies in the darkness. Gabe's hand, still clasping Isabel's, seemed to pulse with an energy that bridged the space between their hearts. Each step they took felt deliberate, measured, as if they were navigating not just the physical terrain but also the delicate terrain of their burgeoning connection.

Isabel glanced at Gabe, his profile etched in the soft light. She could see the subtle lines of stress around his eyes, the way his jaw tightened slightly when he was deep in thought. It was a new side of him she had begun to notice—one that spoke of unspoken burdens and silent hopes. She had sensed that there was more to Gabe than the easygoing exterior he often presented, and tonight, she felt like she had caught a glimpse of his true self.

Gabe's voice broke the silence, soft and reflective. "I've been thinking a lot about what you said earlier—about how you're struggling to make sense of everything. It made me realize something."

Isabel turned to him, her curiosity piqued. "What's that?"

He hesitated for a moment, choosing his words carefully. "Sometimes, when we're faced with our own struggles, we try to make sense of them in a way that feels logical or safe. But often, it's the emotional journey—the raw, messy feelings—that lead us to the real answers."

Isabel nodded, her thoughts swirling. "I've always tried to be rational about things, to analyze them until they make sense. But lately, I've been finding that emotions are harder to control, harder to make sense of."

Gabe's gaze softened as he looked at her. "Emotions aren't always meant to be controlled. Sometimes, they're meant to be felt, to be understood in their own way. It's not always easy, but it's part of the journey."

Isabel appreciated the depth of Gabe's insight. It was one of those moments where his wisdom seemed to align perfectly with her own thoughts, and she felt a profound sense of connection. "It's comforting to hear that," she said, her voice barely above a whisper. "I've been so focused on trying to understand everything logically that I've ignored what my heart is trying to tell me."

They continued walking in comfortable silence for a while, their hands still intertwined. Isabel's thoughts drifted back to the lighthouse and the revelations of the evening. She felt a renewed sense of purpose, as though the pieces of her life were slowly beginning to fall into place. The metaphorical light from the lighthouse seemed to symbolize more than just guidance; it was a beacon of hope and possibility.

As they reached the edge of town, where the streetlights cast longer shadows and the buildings seemed to grow quieter, Gabe stopped and turned to face Isabel. The quiet intensity in his eyes made Isabel's heart race, and she wondered what he was thinking.

"There's something I've been meaning to tell you," Gabe said, his voice earnest. "It's not just about what I said tonight. It's more about how I feel."

Isabel looked at him, her pulse quickening. "What do you mean?"

Gabe took a deep breath, his expression thoughtful. "Since you've been back, there's been something different for me. I didn't realize it at first, but as we've spent more time together, I've felt something growing—something I didn't expect."

Isabel's heart skipped a beat as she processed his words. "Something growing? What do you mean?"

Gabe's gaze remained steady, his eyes locked on hers. "I've felt this connection with you, something that's more than just friendship. It's been there for a while, but I didn't want to rush anything or make you uncomfortable. I just wanted to be honest with you about how I feel."

The vulnerability in Gabe's voice touched something deep within Isabel. She could see the sincerity in his eyes, the way his emotions seemed to lay bare before her. It was a moment of profound honesty, and it made her reflect on her own feelings.

"I feel it too," Isabel admitted, her voice trembling slightly. "This connection, this sense of something deeper—it's been growing for me as well. But I've been so caught up in my own fears and uncertainties that I haven't fully let myself acknowledge it."

Gabe's eyes softened, a look of relief and understanding crossing his face. "I'm glad to hear that. It's been hard for me to gauge where we stand, especially with everything going on in your life. But I wanted you to know that I care about you, more than I thought possible."

Isabel felt a rush of emotion, a blend of relief, joy, and apprehension. She had been grappling with her own internal conflicts, trying to make sense of her feelings amidst the chaos of her life. Gabe's confession was like a lighthouse beam cutting through the fog, offering clarity and direction.

"I care about you too, Gabe," Isabel said, her voice steady now. "This connection we have—it's something I don't want to ignore or take for granted. But I need to be honest with you—I'm still figuring things out. I'm still processing everything that's happened and what it means for me."

Gabe nodded, his expression thoughtful. "I understand. And I'm here for you, no matter what. We don't have to rush anything or force anything. We can take it one step at a time, at a pace that feels right for both of us."

Isabel felt a surge of gratitude for Gabe's understanding and patience. His willingness to support her as she navigated her own journey made her feel more confident in her own path. She knew that their connection was real and meaningful, but it was also a journey that required time and patience.

As they stood there, their hands still clasped together, Isabel felt a renewed sense of hope. The path ahead was still uncertain, but with Gabe by her side, she felt a sense of companionship and support that she had longed for. The night was calm and peaceful, the gentle breeze carrying the promise of new beginnings.

"Thank you," Isabel said softly, her eyes meeting Gabe's. "For being here, for being honest with me. It means more than I can express."

Gabe's smile was warm and reassuring. "You're welcome. And thank you for being open and honest with me. It's a journey we're on together, and I'm grateful for every step of it."

They stood there for a few more moments, savoring the quiet connection between them. The night air was still and peaceful, the distant sounds of the town barely reaching their ears. Isabel felt a sense of calm wash over her, knowing that she had found something truly special in Gabe—a partner who understood her, who was willing to stand by her side through the ups and downs of life.

As they eventually began walking back toward town, the night seemed to embrace them in its gentle arms, a symbol of the new possibilities that lay ahead. The journey of self-discovery and connection was far from over, but Isabel felt more prepared to face it with Gabe by her side.

Together, they walked down the quiet streets, their steps in sync, their hearts intertwined. The future was still uncertain, but with each other's support, they felt ready to face whatever challenges and opportunities lay ahead. And as they continued their journey, they knew that their bond would only grow stronger, guiding them through the storm and into the light of a new dawn.

11

Chapter 11: Confronting the Past

The morning sun had barely crested the horizon when Isabel woke, the dawning light filtering through her window like a herald of the challenges she faced. The house was silent, save for the distant calls of seabirds and the gentle rustle of leaves outside. The calm of the morning belied the turmoil simmering within her, a stark contrast to the emotional storm she was about to confront.

Isabel had spent the night turning over her mother's journal in her mind, replaying the revelations she had uncovered and the poignant note that lingered in her thoughts: "The light will reveal what's hidden." It was a cryptic message that seemed to echo both her mother's regrets and her own quest for understanding.

Determined to uncover the full extent of her mother's secrets, Isabel had resolved to confront her past head-on. The journal had hinted at hidden truths, and she needed to face them before she could truly move forward. She made her way to the study, where the journal was safely tucked away. Her heart raced with a mix of dread and anticipation as she retrieved it from its resting place, the leather cover worn but still resilient.

She settled into the comfortable armchair by the window, where sunlight streamed in and cast gentle patterns across the room. Opening the journal, Isabel's fingers trembled slightly as she turned the pages, each one revealing more about her mother's life and the inner turmoil that had been hidden from view.

The journal's entries were written in her mother's delicate script, each one brimming with raw emotion and confessions that painted a picture of a woman grappling with her own demons. The earlier entries had been filled with the everyday concerns of raising a child and managing household responsibilities. But as Isabel continued reading, the tone shifted dramatically, revealing the deeper layers of her mother's struggles.

One entry caught Isabel's eye, dated several months before her mother's death. It began with a sense of urgency, the words flowing with a desperate need to be heard. Isabel read it with a growing sense of unease:

October 12, 2000

I feel like a burden, an anchor dragging everyone around me into a sea of sorrow. I've made so many mistakes, and the weight of them is unbearable. I've hidden my pain behind a mask of normalcy, but the cracks are beginning to show. I've tried to protect Isabel from the truth, from the shadows of my past, but I wonder if my silence is more damaging than the truth itself.

I made choices that I regret, choices that I've kept hidden for years. There's a secret, one that involves more than just me—it involves our family, our history. I've kept it buried, hoping that it would disappear, but it lingers like a ghost, haunting me.

I wish I could undo the past, but I can't. I can only hope that Isabel will find a way to understand, to see past the facade I've maintained. I hope she will find forgiveness, not just for me but for herself as well. The light will reveal what's hidden, but will it be enough to heal the wounds I've inflicted?

Isabel's eyes brimmed with tears as she read the passage. The pain and regret in her mother's words were palpable, a reflection of the struggles Isabel had been grappling with her entire life. It was clear that her mother had been carrying a burden far greater than Isabel had ever realized.

The mention of a hidden family secret sent a chill down Isabel's spine. She needed to understand more about this secret, to piece together the fragments of her mother's life that had been shrouded in darkness. She turned the pages with renewed urgency, searching for any clues that could provide answers.

Another entry, dated a few weeks later, offered more insight:

November 5, 2000

The secret I've kept is more than just my own burden—it's a part of our family's history, a shadow that stretches back generations. I've always believed that if I kept it hidden, it would protect Isabel from the pain it might bring. But I see now that this secrecy has only caused more harm. The truth has a way of seeping through the cracks, and I fear that it will be too late for forgiveness.

I've found old letters and documents that hint at the truth, but I've never had the courage to confront them. I've hidden them away, hoping that they would remain forgotten. But now, I realize that the truth must be faced. If Isabel is to find healing, she must uncover the full story, however painful it may be.

The revelation that there were old letters and documents filled Isabel with a sense of urgency. She needed to find these hidden items, to uncover the full extent of her mother's secrets. Her heart ached for the pain her mother had endured, but she also felt a deep sense of determination to face the truth.

Isabel carefully closed the journal, her mind racing with thoughts and emotions. She knew that confronting the past was a necessary step in her journey, but it was also an overwhelming task. The weight of her mother's regrets and the hidden family secrets were now in her hands, and she needed to find a way to reconcile them with her own understanding of her past.

With a renewed sense of purpose, Isabel set out to search the house for the old letters and documents her mother had mentioned. She began in the study, examining the drawers and cabinets where her mother might have kept her most cherished possessions. The room was filled with the scent of old books and the faint trace of her mother's perfume, a reminder of the woman who had been both a loving parent and a figure of mystery.

After a thorough search, Isabel discovered a hidden compartment behind a bookshelf. Inside, she found a stack of aged envelopes and faded documents, each one marked with her mother's handwriting. Her heart raced as she carefully opened the first envelope, revealing a collection of letters that had been written decades earlier.

The letters were addressed to a man named Richard, a name Isabel had never heard before. As she read through the correspondence, she uncovered a story of a love affair that had taken place before her mother's marriage to Isabel's father. The letters were filled with expressions of love and longing, but they also revealed a painful decision that had been made in the name of protecting her family.

Isabel's hands shook as she read the final letter in the stack. It was a heartfelt confession from her mother, explaining the reasons behind her decision to end the relationship and marry Isabel's father. The letter spoke of regret and the burden of carrying a secret that had shaped her life in ways Isabel had never imagined.

As Isabel finished reading, she felt a profound sense of empathy for her mother. The secrets and regrets that had been hidden away for so long were now laid bare, and Isabel realized that her mother's struggles were a reflection of her own. The emotional weight of the past had been passed down, and now it was up to Isabel to find a way to heal the wounds and move forward.

Sitting in the quiet of the study, Isabel allowed herself to process the revelations. The pain and regret in her mother's letters were a reminder of the complexities of human emotions and relationships. But they were also a testament to the strength it took to confront the truth and seek forgiveness.

As the sun continued its ascent, casting a warm glow over the room, Isabel felt a sense of clarity beginning to emerge. The journey of confronting the past had been arduous, but it was a necessary step in her quest for self-discovery and healing. The secrets she had uncovered were a part of her heritage, and understanding them was crucial to understanding herself.

With a deep breath, Isabel gathered the letters and documents, carefully placing them back in their hiding place. She knew that the process of healing and forgiveness would take time, but she also felt a renewed sense of hope. The past was no longer a shadow hanging over her; it was a part of her story that she could now face with courage and compassion.

As Isabel left the study, she felt a newfound sense of resolve. The journey ahead was still uncertain, but with the weight of the past acknowledged and understood, she was ready to embrace the future with an open heart. The secrets of the past had been revealed, and now it was up to Isabel to navigate the path of healing and growth that lay ahead.

As Isabel placed the final letter back into its envelope, a wave of exhaustion washed over her. The emotional intensity of her morning's discoveries had taken a toll, but she also felt a strange sense of relief. The weight of her mother's secrets was no longer solely hers to bear. Instead, they were now part of a larger narrative she was beginning to understand.

The sun had climbed higher in the sky, casting a brighter, more hopeful light across the room. Isabel took a deep breath, her resolve solidifying with each passing moment. She knew that understanding her mother's past was just one part of her journey; she needed to reconcile these revelations with her own path forward.

She took a moment to collect herself, the quiet of the house offering a brief sanctuary from the emotional whirlwind. With renewed focus, she decided it was time to have a conversation with Gabe, someone who had become an important part of her life. The growing connection between them had provided her with a sense of stability, and she needed his support more than ever.

Isabel left the study and walked through the sunlit corridors of the house, her mind racing with thoughts. She found Gabe in the kitchen, where he was preparing a pot of coffee. His presence was a calming influence, and she felt a surge of gratitude for his constant support.

"Good morning," Isabel greeted him softly, trying to mask the depth of her emotions. "I was hoping we could talk."

Gabe looked up from his task, his brow furrowing with concern. "Of course. Everything okay?"

Isabel hesitated, the weight of her recent discoveries heavy on her shoulders. "I've been going through my mother's old letters and journal entries. There's a lot more to her past than I ever knew. I found out she kept secrets, and it's affecting me in ways I didn't expect."

Gabe's expression softened as he gestured to a nearby table. "Why don't we sit down? It sounds like you've been through a lot."

They settled at the table, and Isabel took a seat, feeling the warmth of Gabe's supportive gaze. She took a deep breath, gathering her thoughts before speaking.

"My mother had a love affair before she married my father. She never told anyone about it, not even me. I found letters she wrote to this man, and they were full of love and regret. She ended the relationship to protect our family, but she carried the burden of that decision with her."

Gabe listened intently, his eyes reflecting the empathy he felt. "That must have been incredibly difficult for you to discover. It's clear that your mother's past had a significant impact on her, and now on you."

Isabel nodded, her voice trembling slightly. "It's hard to reconcile what I thought I knew with what I've learned. I feel like I'm carrying this emotional weight, trying to understand her choices and their impact on me. It's like I'm stuck between what was hidden and what's now revealed."

Gabe reached across the table, taking her hand in his. The gesture was simple but profound, conveying a depth of support that words alone could not capture. "Isabel, you're not alone in this. I can't pretend to fully understand what you're going through, but I'm here for you. Whatever you need, whether it's to talk or just to have someone by your side, I'm here."

The sincerity in Gabe's voice was comforting, and Isabel felt a tear escape her eye. She squeezed his hand gently, grateful for his presence. "Thank you. It means a lot to me. I feel like I'm at a crossroads, trying to make sense of the past while figuring out what it means for my future."

Gabe's gaze was steady and reassuring. "It's okay to feel lost right now. Sometimes, understanding the past is the first step toward finding clarity. You've already made so much progress by facing these difficult truths. You don't have to have all the answers right away."

Isabel appreciated Gabe's wisdom. His words provided a sense of perspective that she needed at that moment. She realized that her journey was ongoing and that healing was a process that couldn't be rushed.

"Can I ask for your help?" Isabel said, her voice steadying. "I'm planning to visit the lighthouse again. There's something about it that I feel drawn to, something that might help me piece together the remaining fragments of my mother's story. I'd like for you to come with me."

Gabe's eyes lit up with understanding. "Absolutely. I'd be honored to join you. If there's anything I can do to support you, just let me know."

Isabel smiled, feeling a sense of relief at Gabe's willingness to stand by her. "Thank you. I really appreciate it. I think having you there will make a big difference."

With their plans set, Isabel and Gabe finished their coffee and prepared for their visit to the lighthouse. The anticipation of returning to the place that had already played a significant role in her journey added a new layer of hope to Isabel's heart.

As they drove towards the lighthouse, Isabel reflected on the revelations from the journal and the letters. The lighthouse, once a symbol of mystery, now felt like a beacon guiding her toward resolution. She hoped that the visit would provide further insights into her mother's past and, perhaps, offer answers to the questions that lingered in her mind.

Gabe's presence was a comforting anchor throughout the drive. They talked about their plans and the potential discoveries awaiting them, but there were also moments of silence that allowed Isabel to gather her thoughts. The peaceful surroundings of the island and the steady rhythm of the car provided a serene backdrop for her reflections.

When they finally arrived at the lighthouse, Isabel was struck by its grandeur. The tall, white structure stood proudly against the backdrop of the sea, its light flickering in the distance like a guiding star. Isabel's heart raced with anticipation as she and Gabe made their way toward the entrance.

The lighthouse, with its historic charm and evocative presence, seemed to hold the promise of further revelations. Isabel felt a sense of determination as she approached, ready to confront the past and seek the answers she needed.

As they climbed the stairs to the top of the lighthouse, Isabel and Gabe shared a quiet camaraderie. The climb was a symbolic ascent, representing Isabel's journey towards understanding and acceptance. Each step brought her closer to the heart of her mother's secrets and the possibility of finding closure.

Reaching the top, Isabel gazed out over the expanse of the sea, the view stretching out before her like a canvas of endless possibilities. The sight was breathtaking, but it was the connection to her mother's past that truly captivated her.

Gabe stood beside her, his presence a reassuring constant. "This place is incredible," he said softly. "It's easy to see why it might hold significance for you."

Isabel nodded, her gaze fixed on the horizon. "It's more than just a beautiful view. It's a place where I feel connected to my mother's past and the secrets she carried. I'm hoping that being here will help me make sense of everything."

They spent time exploring the lighthouse and its surroundings, the tranquility of the setting offering Isabel a space to reflect and gather her thoughts. The discoveries she had made about her mother's life and the hidden truths were starting to settle within her, but she knew that the journey was far from over.

As the sun began to set, casting a golden glow over the lighthouse and the sea, Isabel felt a renewed sense of clarity. The past had been revealed in fragments, and the journey to understanding it was a process that required patience and compassion.

With Gabe by her side, Isabel felt a sense of hope and resilience. The lighthouse, once a symbol of uncertainty, had become a place of potential resolution. As they prepared to leave, Isabel took one last look at the view, feeling a profound sense of gratitude for the journey she was on and the support she had received.

The drive back was filled with a quiet sense of accomplishment and anticipation for the future. Isabel knew that the path ahead would continue to present challenges, but with each step, she was moving closer to understanding and healing.

As they arrived back at the house, Isabel felt a renewed sense of purpose. The secrets of the past were no longer an insurmountable barrier; they were a part of her story that she was learning to embrace. With Gabe's support and the clarity she had gained, Isabel was ready to face whatever came next with an open heart and a determined spirit.

The journey was far from over, but Isabel was no longer alone in her quest for understanding. The past had been confronted, and the future awaited with a sense of hope and possibility. As she looked ahead, Isabel felt a deep sense of peace, knowing that she was on the path to healing and self-discovery.

Isabel returned to the house after the lighthouse visit, her thoughts still racing with everything she had uncovered. Her mother's letters had stirred up emotions she didn't know she had buried so deeply. It wasn't just about her mother's hidden love affair—it was about what it all meant for her own life, her own choices. For years, Isabel had struggled with the same fear of opening up, the same instinct to guard herself, never fully understanding where it came from. But now, standing in the same house where her mother had kept her secrets, she realized the truth: her mother hadn't just hidden her past out of shame, but out of a desire to protect her.

Isabel sat on the porch, the sea breeze gentle against her skin, and unfolded the last letter she had found in her mother's journal. She read it slowly, her eyes tracing the familiar handwriting.

"My dearest Isabel,

If you are reading this, it means you've found the truth. I never wanted to hide it from you, but sometimes we do things to protect those we love. I didn't want my mistakes, my regrets, to become yours. I didn't want you to carry the burden of my choices. But now, I see that you are stronger than I ever was. You have always been stronger. You deserve to know the truth, because only then can you make peace with your own path."

Isabel's eyes burned with unshed tears as she read the words over and over. Her mother's regrets—her fears—had seeped into Isabel's life without her even realizing it. She had become so much like her mother, keeping herself closed off from love, pushing away the very things that could heal her. It wasn't just about understanding her mother's past anymore—it was about seeing how deeply that past had shaped her own life.

The revelation felt like both a burden and a gift. It hurt, knowing how much her mother had struggled, but it also freed Isabel in a way she hadn't expected. For the first time, she could see her own choices more clearly. She didn't have to repeat her mother's mistakes.

She folded the letter carefully and placed it in her lap, letting the silence of the evening settle around her. The waves crashing softly against the shore seemed to echo her own inner turmoil, as if the sea itself was urging her to let go of the weight she had carried for so long.

Gabe's voice broke the stillness. He had been watching her from the doorway, his face filled with concern. "Isabel? You've been out here a while. Everything okay?"

Isabel looked up, her eyes meeting his. She wanted to tell him everything—the letters, the affair, her mother's regrets—but the words felt too heavy. Instead, she motioned for him to sit beside her.

He joined her on the porch, sitting close enough that their shoulders brushed. "You don't have to say anything if you're not ready," he said quietly. "But I'm here."

Isabel smiled weakly, grateful for his presence. She reached for his hand, holding it tightly. "I've learned so much about my mother... more than I ever expected. She hid so much of herself, but not because she was ashamed. She wanted to protect me, and in doing that, she passed her fears onto me. I've been living with those same fears for so long, without even realizing it."

Gabe squeezed her hand gently, his gaze steady. "It's a lot to take in. But just because your mother made certain choices doesn't mean you have to follow the same path."

"I know," Isabel whispered, her voice trembling. "I just... I don't want to be afraid anymore. I don't want to keep pushing people away. I've already done that with so many people in my life."

Gabe's eyes softened. "You're not pushing me away."

Isabel looked at him, the weight of his words settling into her chest. "I'm trying not to. But sometimes, it feels easier to protect myself by keeping people at a distance. I didn't even realize how much of that came from my mother."

Gabe nodded, understanding dawning in his expression. "It's hard to let go of those patterns, especially when they've been a part of you for so long. But you're already breaking the cycle, Isabel. You're facing the truth head-on, and that takes courage."

Isabel swallowed the lump in her throat, her heart pounding. "I don't know if I'm ready to face everything yet."

"You don't have to do it all at once," Gabe said softly. "Take your time. I'll be here, no matter how long it takes."

For a moment, they sat in silence, the unspoken understanding between them deeper than any words could convey. Isabel felt the warmth of Gabe's hand in hers, an anchor in the storm of emotions swirling inside her. She didn't have all the answers yet, but she was starting to realize that she didn't need to figure everything out alone.

As the sun dipped lower in the sky, painting the horizon with soft hues of pink and orange, Isabel leaned her head on Gabe's shoulder. For the first time in what felt like forever, she allowed herself to rest in the comfort of someone else's presence. She didn't have to carry the weight of her past—or her mother's—alone.

The journal, the letters, her mother's hidden life... they were pieces of a puzzle that had shaped who she was. But now, Isabel was determined to forge her own path. To love without fear, to embrace the uncertainty of the future, and to let herself heal from the wounds she had unknowingly carried.

The secrets of the past had been uncovered, but they no longer defined her. She had the power to choose what came next.

And with Gabe by her side, she knew she wouldn't have to face it alone.

Isabel remained curled against Gabe's shoulder, the rhythmic sound of the waves lapping against the shore blending with the distant hum of the wind. The weight of her mother's secrets, the letters, and the hidden truths seemed to lift in the quiet moments they shared, even if just for a little while. She felt like she was standing on the edge of something immense, something life-changing. But it wasn't fear that gripped her—it was a strange mixture of relief and uncertainty.

"I used to think that if I ignored it all, it would stay buried," Isabel said, her voice barely above a whisper. "That if I just kept moving forward, the past wouldn't matter. But now... I feel like it's all unraveling. The things I thought I knew about my mother, and even about myself, they were all... half-truths."

Gabe shifted slightly, turning to face her, his gaze soft and steady. "Sometimes we have to confront the past to really move forward. Maybe it's painful, but I think it's also freeing, don't you?"

Isabel let his words settle in, trying to make sense of the whirlwind of emotions inside her. She wanted to agree with him, but the complexity of it all made it hard to untangle her thoughts.

"I'm afraid that by uncovering all of this, I'll just end up feeling lost. Like I won't know who I am anymore, or worse, I'll become just like her—living with regrets."

Gabe's hand gently traced her fingers, grounding her in the present. "You're not her, Isabel. And you're already making different choices. You came back here, didn't you? You're facing things most people would run from. That's not a sign of weakness, or of becoming like someone else. It's a sign that you're ready to take control of your own story."

His words struck a chord in her, deepening her awareness of the choices she was making—not out of fear, but out of necessity. She wasn't destined to repeat her mother's mistakes, but it would take time and patience to figure out how to move forward.

"I found a journal," Isabel said suddenly, her voice wavering. "One of my mother's. It had letters she wrote, but never sent. I think she was trying to explain things to me—about her affair, about why she kept so much hidden. But there was something else too."

Gabe listened quietly, his expression attentive but not pressing her to continue. Isabel took a deep breath, her words spilling out faster now, needing to be said.

"There was a letter where she wrote about a man... not just the one she had an affair with. Someone else. I don't know who he was, but she mentioned something about him being part of our family's past, and that's why she felt she had to protect me."

"Do you think this man was connected to her regrets? Or maybe to her reasons for keeping you in the dark?"

Isabel nodded, the pieces beginning to fall into place as she spoke. "I don't know exactly. But the way she wrote about him... it was like he was tied to something bigger. Something that affected not just her, but all of us. I can't explain it, but I have this feeling like there's more to the story than just her relationship."

A chill ran through Isabel as she realized the weight of her own words. The hidden family secret she had glimpsed in the letters was more than just an affair—it was a thread connecting her past and her present in ways she hadn't fully grasped until now.

"I don't want to be afraid of what I'll find," she murmured, her voice filled with both determination and hesitation. "But I don't know if I'm ready for the answers either."

Gabe leaned closer, his voice low and steady. "You don't have to be ready all at once. But I think you already know that whatever the truth is, it's not going to change who you are. The past might shape us, but it doesn't have to define us."

Isabel absorbed his words, letting them sink into her. She had been living in fear of becoming her mother—of repeating the same patterns, making the same mistakes. But Gabe was right. She wasn't the same person, and she had the power to choose a different path.

The sound of the waves, constant and rhythmic, mirrored the ebb and flow of her thoughts. The pull of the past, the fear of facing the unknown, and the desire to reclaim her life all mingled together. But at the center of it all was a glimmer of hope—hope that she could untangle the threads of her mother's life without losing herself in the process.

"I need to know what happened," Isabel whispered, almost to herself. "But I don't want to do it alone."

"You don't have to," Gabe said, his hand still warm in hers. "Whatever you find, whatever you decide, I'll be here."

For the first time in a long time, Isabel believed him. There was a sense of safety in Gabe's presence, a feeling that she didn't have to carry the weight of the world on her shoulders anymore. It wasn't just about the secrets of her mother's life—it was about healing the fractures in her own.

Isabel stood, feeling the cool night air on her skin as she gazed out at the ocean. The waves seemed to stretch out endlessly, like the unknown future before her, and she realized that she was no longer as afraid of it as she had once been.

She would uncover the truth—about her mother, her family, and herself. But for now, in this moment, she allowed herself the peace of simply being.

With Gabe at her side, Isabel took a deep breath and turned her back on the ocean, ready to face whatever came next.

The journal lay on the small table next to the porch chair, its pages still waiting to be fully explored. But Isabel wasn't in a rush. The answers would come in time, and when they did, she would be ready.

For now, she let the warmth of the night and the closeness of Gabe be enough.

There was a future waiting for her, and for the first time in a long while, Isabel felt like she was ready to embrace it.

Isabel stood on the porch, her fingers brushing over the weathered cover of her mother's journal. The crickets in the distance seemed louder tonight, or maybe it was just the absence of her usual internal noise, the endless replay of memories and half-formed fears that had plagued her for so long. Now, there was something else—a quiet resolve that hadn't been there before. She felt it in the way her body no longer tensed at the mere thought of what she might uncover, in the way she no longer shied away from the emotions that surfaced when she thought about her mother.

She could still feel Gabe's presence, lingering beside her even though he had gone back inside the house a few moments ago. There was something comforting in his steadiness. For so long, she had believed she had to carry all of this alone—the secrets, the guilt, the confusion—but Gabe was teaching her that maybe it didn't have to be that way. Maybe sharing her burden, piece by piece, wouldn't diminish her but allow her to find strength in her vulnerability.

Isabel exhaled, opening the journal to where she had last left off. Her mother's neat, careful handwriting filled the pages, an echo of the woman who had raised her, a woman Isabel now realized she had never truly known.

July 4th, 1998. I can't stop thinking about him. Even after all these years, the way he looks at me makes me feel like I'm the only person in the world. But I can't let Isabel know. She deserves better than this confusion, better than the tangled mess of my heart. I've made so many mistakes... so many.

The words felt like an intrusion, as though Isabel were reading something she was never meant to see. But she kept going, flipping through the pages until she reached a letter, dated a year before her mother's death. It was addressed to Isabel, but never sent.

Isabel,

I don't know how to explain this in a way that will make sense. I've hidden so much from you because I thought it would protect you. But now, as I look back, I realize I've only made things harder. There's something you need to know, something I should have told you long ago. You weren't just a part of my life—you were my anchor. But you were also the reason I stayed, even when I wanted to leave. The truth is, I loved two men. Your father and someone else. I thought I could keep that part of my life separate, but it seeped into everything. It's the reason I kept so many things from you. I was trying to shield you from my mistakes. But now I wonder if I was wrong. If keeping you in the dark was more harmful than anything else...

Isabel's breath caught in her throat. The words confirmed her suspicions, but hearing them—or rather, seeing them—on the page, in her mother's own hand, made it real in a way she wasn't prepared for.

She closed the journal, unable to read more just yet. The weight of the truth pressed down on her chest, constricting her breath. Her mother had loved two men. That part, she had come to terms with. But the idea that her mother had kept this hidden for years, out of a misguided attempt to protect her—it felt like a betrayal.

Isabel stood, pacing the length of the porch as she tried to shake the feelings that were threatening to overwhelm her. She had known her mother wasn't perfect, that she had secrets, but this—this was different. It wasn't just a secret. It was a fundamental part of who her mother had been, and by extension, a part of Isabel's life that she had never even known existed.

A part of her wanted to tear the journal apart, to throw it into the ocean and let the waves carry away the painful revelations. But another part of her—the stronger part—knew that she needed to keep reading, needed to confront whatever else her mother had hidden from her. There were answers here, answers to questions Isabel had been carrying for years. And if she didn't face them now, they would continue to haunt her.

She sat back down, pulling the journal into her lap and turning the pages again. Her mother's words blurred slightly as tears filled her eyes, but she forced herself to keep reading.

There's something else I need to tell you, something I never could have explained while I was alive. It's about him—the man I loved, the one I never told you about. He was connected to our family, to a part of our history that I thought I could outrun. But it's not something you can escape. It's in your blood, just like it's in mine.

Isabel's heart raced as she read the words. Her mother had always been so composed, so careful with her emotions. To see her writing like this, so raw and unfiltered, was both shocking and heartbreaking. But it was the last sentence that sent a chill down Isabel's spine.

It's in your blood, just like it's in mine.

What did that mean? Was her mother referring to the man she had loved? Or was it something deeper, something darker? Isabel's mind raced with possibilities, each one more unsettling than the last.

She flipped through the rest of the journal, searching for more clues, but there was nothing—just more letters, more unsent words filled with regret and longing. Whatever her mother had been hinting at, she hadn't left enough behind to fully explain it.

Frustration bubbled up inside Isabel, mingling with the grief and confusion that had been building for days. She wanted answers—needed them—but it seemed like the more she uncovered, the more questions she was left with.

The porch door creaked open, and Gabe stepped outside, his gaze immediately finding hers. He didn't say anything, but the concern in his eyes was unmistakable. Isabel wiped at her face, suddenly feeling exposed.

"I thought I was ready for this," she said, her voice shaky. "But I don't think I am."

Gabe crossed the porch and sat down beside her, close enough that their shoulders touched. He didn't ask any questions, didn't push her to explain. He just sat there, offering his presence as a steadying force in the midst of her emotional storm.

"You don't have to do this all at once," Gabe said quietly. "There's no timeline, Isabel. Take it one step at a time."

She nodded, grateful for his understanding. For a moment, they sat in silence, the journal heavy in her lap, the weight of her mother's words still lingering in the air.

"I just... I keep thinking that if I can figure this out, if I can understand why she kept all of this from me, maybe it'll make sense. Maybe I'll be able to forgive her."

Gabe's hand found hers, his fingers intertwining with her own. "Maybe it's not about understanding why she did it. Maybe it's about accepting that she did, and figuring out how to move forward from there."

Isabel squeezed his hand, letting the comfort of his words wash over her. He was right, of course. There were some things she might never fully understand about her mother. But that didn't mean she had to stay stuck in the past, trying to unravel every mystery.

Maybe the answers she needed weren't in the journal, or in the letters her mother had left behind. Maybe they were inside her, waiting to be uncovered in their own time.

As the night deepened and the stars began to peek through the sky, Isabel leaned into Gabe, her heart still heavy but just a little lighter than before. She didn't have all the answers, and maybe she never would. But she was no longer afraid of the truth.

Whatever came next, she knew she wasn't facing it alone.

Isabel sat there, nestled beside Gabe, the warmth of his presence grounding her as the gravity of her mother's secrets weighed heavily on her chest. Her mind replayed her mother's words over and over—*"It's in your blood, just like it's in mine."* She had always known her mother had layers, but now it felt like she was peeling away a lifetime of walls, exposing not just her mother's pain but also something much deeper—something that might connect directly to her own struggles.

She slowly closed the journal, the old leather cover cool beneath her fingers, and stared out at the ocean. The waves lapped gently against the shore, a rhythm so steady it felt like a heartbeat. Isabel's heart, however, was anything but steady. It was racing—caught between the past and the present, between what she had discovered and what she still didn't understand.

"You ever wonder if some things are better left buried?" she asked Gabe, her voice barely above a whisper. Her fingers brushed the worn edges of the journal as though seeking comfort from the object that had unearthed so much.

Gabe remained silent for a moment, thoughtful, before responding. "I think... sometimes, we dig things up because we're ready to face them, whether we realize it or not."

Isabel turned to him, her eyes searching his. "But what if facing it only leads to more pain?"

"That's possible," Gabe said softly, "but maybe facing it is also the only way to heal." His words were simple, but they carried a weight of understanding. He wasn't just speaking about her; he was speaking about them both, their connection deepened by the weight of unspoken truths.

She closed her eyes for a moment, leaning into his warmth. Gabe's presence had become a quiet refuge—a place where she could confront her deepest fears without judgment. His calm reassured her, even as the storm of emotions churned inside her.

"Do you think she was trying to protect me?" Isabel finally asked, her voice catching.

Gabe exhaled softly, his arm sliding around her, pulling her closer. "It sounds like she was. Maybe she thought keeping you away from her mistakes would protect you, but..." He hesitated, choosing his words carefully. "Sometimes parents forget that hiding things doesn't always shield us. Sometimes it creates wounds of its own."

Isabel nodded, the knot in her chest tightening. The very act of shielding her had created the mystery she was now forced to unravel, alone. Her mother's attempts to protect her had only delayed the inevitable—this reckoning with the past. The thought stirred a new kind of grief in Isabel, one that she couldn't quite name.

But it wasn't just grief. It was anger too. Anger at her mother for not trusting her, for not believing that Isabel could have handled the truth. And anger at herself—for not seeing the cracks sooner, for blindly accepting the version of her mother that had been presented to her.

Isabel leaned forward, burying her face in her hands, the weight of it all pressing down on her. She had never felt so lost.

Gabe, sensing her inner turmoil, didn't pull away. Instead, he let his hand rest on her back, a steady, grounding presence in the storm of emotions that threatened to overwhelm her. His silence was more powerful than words—a silent promise that he wasn't going anywhere, that he was with her, no matter how messy or painful the journey became.

"I feel like I don't know her at all," Isabel whispered, her voice trembling. "How could she keep this from me? How could she live her entire life hiding something like this?"

Gabe's voice was soft, soothing. "Maybe she was afraid. Afraid of how you'd see her. Afraid of what it might change between you."

Isabel lifted her head, staring out at the dark horizon. "But it changes everything, Gabe. How can I reconcile the mother I knew with this... this woman who lived an entirely different life behind closed doors?"

"I don't think you have to," he said gently. "Your mother was complicated, just like all of us. And I think, in her own way, she loved you more than anything. Maybe she thought keeping you away from that part of her life was the only way to make sure you were happy."

Isabel's eyes filled with tears, and she shook her head. "But it wasn't fair. I needed to know her—really know her."

Gabe let out a soft sigh. "I know. But she's gone now, and the only thing you can do is figure out how to move forward with what you've learned."

Isabel wiped at her eyes, the tears falling freely now. She hated how much this hurt. She had thought coming back to the island would give her closure, but instead, it had only uncovered more wounds, more questions without answers. And yet, there was also a strange comfort in the revelations, a sense that maybe, just maybe, she was closer to the truth than she had ever been before.

Her mother's secrets no longer felt like walls between them. Instead, they felt like pieces of a puzzle that Isabel was slowly putting together, piece by painful piece.

As the night stretched on, Isabel felt something begin to shift inside her. It wasn't a resolution—far from it—but it was the beginning of something. A new chapter, perhaps. A chance to redefine her relationship with her mother, even if it was too late to speak the truth aloud.

She looked at Gabe, her heart aching with the weight of everything she had learned, but also with the strange hope that had begun to blossom inside her. Gabe had been right—it wasn't about understanding everything. It was about accepting what was, and moving forward.

Isabel leaned into Gabe once more, letting herself rest in the safety of his arms. Maybe she didn't have all the answers yet, but for the first time, she felt like she might be able to find peace. Not by unraveling every mystery, but by learning to live with the ones that remained.

And maybe, just maybe, that would be enough.

"I think I'm ready," she whispered, her voice steady now.

Gabe pressed a kiss to the top of her head, his hand stroking her back in gentle circles. "Ready for what?"

"To let go," Isabel said softly. "To stop trying to figure out every little thing and just... let it be."

For the first time in what felt like years, Isabel felt something in her chest loosen, like a knot that had been tied too tight for too long finally beginning to unravel. And as she sat there, her mother's journal resting on her lap, the ocean stretching out before them, she realized that she wasn't as alone as she had once believed.

In the darkness of the night, with Gabe by her side, Isabel began to heal.

Isabel stood, pacing the small living room. The journal felt heavier in her hands than it had before, like it was dragging her down. It wasn't just the secrets inside. It was the weight of time—the years spent not knowing. The years her mother had spent hiding.

Gabe's eyes followed her, his calm demeanor a stark contrast to the storm that was building within her. He knew not to speak, not yet. She needed space to sort through this on her own. But his presence, steady and unyielding, kept her grounded.

Isabel let out a breath she hadn't realized she'd been holding. "It just doesn't make sense," she muttered, more to herself than to Gabe. "She loved me, I know she did. But why—why would she keep something so important from me?"

"Maybe she thought it was for the best," Gabe offered quietly, not pushing, just gently presenting the possibility.

She stopped pacing, her eyes darting to him. "For the best? How could she possibly think hiding an entire piece of her life from me was for the best?"

Gabe leaned forward, his elbows resting on his knees, hands clasped in front of him. "Isabel, sometimes people believe that shielding others from their pain will protect them. Maybe your mother didn't want you to see her mistakes, or feel the weight of the choices she had made. Maybe she thought keeping those parts of herself locked away would make your life easier."

"Easier," Isabel echoed, shaking her head. "It doesn't feel easier. It feels like I've been living a lie. How can you love someone your whole life and not really know them?"

Gabe's gaze softened. "You did know her. The parts of her that she shared with you, those were real. But no one can ever know all of another person, not even their child. We all have pieces of ourselves we keep hidden, even from the people we love most."

Isabel sank down onto the couch, her legs suddenly feeling weak. She placed the journal beside her, staring at the worn cover.

"I just keep wondering if... if she didn't trust me enough to tell me. Or worse, if she didn't think I'd love her if I knew the truth."

Gabe's face was full of compassion as he reached out, taking her hand in his. "I don't think it was about trust, Isabel. I think it was fear. Fear of what you'd think, fear of how it might change things between you. Sometimes fear can make people do things that don't make sense."

The silence stretched between them, but it wasn't uncomfortable. Gabe's fingers tightened around hers, anchoring her in the midst of the turmoil swirling in her mind. She looked down at their joined hands, the warmth of his touch seeping into her skin, slowly dissolving the coldness that had settled in her chest.

"I guess," Isabel whispered, her voice barely audible, "I'm afraid too. Afraid of what it means now that I know."

Gabe's thumb brushed across the back of her hand, his voice low and reassuring. "It doesn't have to change how you feel about her. You can still love her, Isabel. Even with the mistakes, even with the secrets."

Isabel swallowed hard, her throat tight with emotion. She wanted to believe that. She wanted to believe she could hold on to the mother she had known, even as the truth unfolded in front of her, reshaping everything she thought she understood.

But could she? Could she love the woman who had lived a double life, who had hidden so much from her? Could she forgive her for the lies, for the half-truths that had shaped their relationship?

"I want to," she finally admitted. "But it feels... complicated."

"Love always is," Gabe said softly, his gaze never leaving hers. "But it's worth it."

She met his eyes, searching for something—an answer, maybe, or just a sense of clarity that felt so elusive right now. But all she saw in his expression was understanding, patience. And in that moment, she realized something else: Gabe wasn't just talking about her relationship with her mother. He was talking about them too.

The weight of that realization settled in her chest, different from the heaviness she had felt earlier. This was something else. Something warmer. Softer. Isabel had spent so long keeping her heart at arm's length, afraid of letting anyone too close. But with Gabe, it had always been different. She had let him in without even realizing it, and now, she didn't know how to close herself off again.

"Gabe..." she began, her voice hesitant.

But he shook his head, offering her a small, reassuring smile. "You don't have to say anything. I'm here, Isabel. I'm not going anywhere."

And just like that, the tension inside her unraveled a little more. Gabe's presence, his quiet strength, gave her the courage to face the truth she had been running from—both about her mother and about herself.

Isabel reached for the journal again, her fingers tracing the leather binding. She flipped it open, her eyes scanning the familiar handwriting, the words that had once brought her comfort now tainted with new meaning. Her mother's secrets were painful, yes, but they were also human. And as much as it hurt, Isabel couldn't deny that there was a strange kind of relief in finally knowing.

"I think I'm ready to keep reading," she whispered, glancing up at Gabe.

He gave her a nod of encouragement, his hand still holding hers. "Take your time. I'm right here."

With a deep breath, Isabel turned the page, letting the words unfold before her. Her mother's voice came alive once more, but this time, it was different. There was no longer a veil between them. It was raw, vulnerable—just like Isabel herself was beginning to feel.

She read about her mother's regrets, the choices she had made that had led her down a path of secrecy. And then, there it was—a confession. A hidden family secret, buried deep within the pages of the journal, one that mirrored Isabel's own internal struggles in a way that made her heart ache.

Her mother had been in love. Not just with Isabel's father, but with someone else—a man Isabel had never known existed. The affair had been brief, but intense, and it had left scars on her mother's heart that had never truly healed. She had kept it hidden, not just from Isabel, but from everyone, afraid of the consequences, afraid of what it might do to her family.

Isabel's breath caught in her throat as she read the final lines of the entry, her mother's words etched in a shaky hand. *"I never wanted you to know this part of me, Isabel. I never wanted you to carry the weight of my mistakes. But I see now that I can't protect you from everything. I can only hope you'll forgive me."*

Tears welled in Isabel's eyes, blurring the words on the page. Her mother had carried so much pain, so much guilt, all on her own. And now, it was Isabel's turn to bear the weight of that knowledge.

She closed the journal, her chest tight with emotion. But this time, the heaviness felt different. It wasn't just pain. It was understanding. And maybe, just maybe, it was the beginning of forgiveness.

Isabel looked up at Gabe, her voice thick with unshed tears. "She was trying to protect me. But in the end, she was just trying to protect herself."

Gabe nodded, his eyes full of empathy. "It sounds like she loved you enough to try. Even if she didn't always get it right."

Isabel wiped at her eyes, the tears falling freely now. She wasn't sure what the future held, or how she would move forward from this. But for the first time in a long time, she felt like she was on the right path. The path toward healing, toward understanding. Toward finally letting go.

And with Gabe by her side, she knew she wouldn't have to face it alone.

Isabel sat in silence, the journal lying on her lap, its pages fluttering slightly in the breeze from the open window. The words on those pages had shattered the image of her mother she had carried for so long—an image of perfection, love, and unwavering strength. But now, with the truth laid bare, Isabel saw her mother not as an untouchable figure but as a flawed, vulnerable woman who had made painful choices.

Her fingers ran over the last lines of the journal entry. The revelation of her mother's affair echoed Isabel's own fears—fears of making mistakes, of carrying secrets that could devastate the people she loved. There was a haunting similarity between her mother's desire to protect herself and Isabel's own reluctance to fully open up to the world, especially to Gabe.

Isabel's eyes drifted over to the lighthouse, visible through the window, standing tall and resolute on the cliffside. The light it cast was unwavering, illuminating the dark waters below, but it was the shadows it left behind that now called to her. Her mother's words—"The light will reveal what's hidden"—played on a loop in her mind. For years, Isabel had avoided her own shadows, keeping parts of herself locked away, just as her mother had.

Gabe remained beside her, his quiet presence grounding her. He hadn't said anything for a while, content to give her the space she needed, but his hand still held hers—a lifeline she clung to as she tried to process everything.

"I feel like I've been living in two worlds," Isabel said finally, her voice soft but edged with a raw vulnerability. "There's the person I show everyone else—who's strong, independent, and capable. And then there's the part of me I keep hidden. The part that's scared. The part that's afraid of getting hurt."

Gabe squeezed her hand gently. "We all have those parts, Isabel. No one is just one thing."

Isabel shook her head. "But I've spent so long pretending I don't. Pretending that I'm fine, that I don't need anyone. My mother did the same thing. And look where it got her—carrying a secret so heavy it broke her."

She glanced down at the journal again, her heart aching for the woman she now understood so much better. "She was trying to protect me from her mistakes, from the parts of herself she didn't want me to see. But by hiding them, she pushed me away. I didn't really know her."

Gabe's voice was soft but steady. "Maybe it's not about knowing every part of someone, but about accepting the parts they choose to share—and the parts they don't. Your mother made mistakes, but it doesn't erase the love she had for you. It doesn't change what you meant to her."

Isabel looked at him, her gaze searching. "Do you really believe that?"

"I do," he said simply. "And I believe the same is true for you."

"What do you mean?" Isabel asked, feeling a shift in the conversation.

Gabe's eyes held hers, a deep intensity in his gaze. "I mean that you don't have to show me every part of yourself for me to care about you. I know you've been holding back, Isabel. I know you've been scared to let me in. But I'm here. I'm not going anywhere."

Isabel's heart quickened. The tenderness in his voice, the way he looked at her—it was almost too much. She had been so careful, so determined to keep her distance, even as they had grown closer. But Gabe saw through her walls, through the facade she put up to protect herself.

"I don't know if I can do that," she admitted, her voice trembling. "I don't know if I can be as open as you want me to be. It's... terrifying."

Gabe smiled, his thumb brushing lightly over her knuckles. "It's terrifying for me too. But that doesn't mean it's not worth it."

The vulnerability in his words caught her off guard. Gabe had always seemed so sure of himself, so steady. But now, he was admitting that he was just as scared as she was. And yet, he was still willing to take the risk—to open his heart to her, despite the uncertainty.

Isabel's eyes filled with tears again, but this time, they weren't just from the pain of her mother's revelations. They were from the realization that she wasn't alone in her fear. Gabe was right there with her, ready to face the unknown together.

She turned toward him, her voice quiet but firm. "I don't want to make the same mistake my mother did. I don't want to keep hiding from the people I care about."

Gabe's smile widened, relief and affection shining in his eyes. "Then don't. Let me in, Isabel. Whatever you're afraid of, we'll face it together."

Isabel took a deep breath, feeling the weight of her fear start to lift, piece by piece. She had spent so long running from her emotions, from the parts of herself that she didn't want to face. But now, with Gabe beside her, she realized that maybe she didn't have to carry it all alone.

"I'm scared," she admitted, her voice barely above a whisper. "But I don't want to keep pushing you away."

"You don't have to," Gabe said softly. "I'm not going anywhere."

Isabel closed the journal, setting it aside. For the first time in what felt like years, she felt a flicker of hope. Hope that she could move forward, that she could confront the past without letting it define her future. And with Gabe by her side, maybe—just maybe—she could start to believe in love again.

The lighthouse's beam swept across the room, casting long shadows on the walls. But this time, the darkness didn't feel so overwhelming. Isabel could see the light too—the promise of something brighter, something new.

She looked at Gabe, her heart swelling with gratitude and affection. "Thank you. For being here. For everything."

Gabe leaned closer, his forehead resting gently against hers. "Always."

And in that moment, Isabel knew she was no longer alone in her journey. She had found her way back to the island, back to her past, and now, she was ready to face whatever came next—one step at a time.

Isabel sat with Gabe's words echoing in her mind. She could feel the weight of the journal beside her, its revelations still fresh, still cutting. The truth about her mother, about the affair, and the burden of secrets, had left Isabel grappling with emotions she hadn't expected.

For years, she had idolized her mother, placing her on a pedestal, believing that her strength and grace were unmatched. Yet, the journal revealed her mother's struggles, weaknesses, and vulnerabilities—the parts of her that Isabel had never seen. Now, with the journal in her lap, Isabel was forced to confront not only her mother's past but her own fears as well. They were similar in ways she never realized before.

"I feel like I never really knew her," Isabel whispered, her voice trembling with emotion.

Gabe shifted beside her, his hand still clasped gently in hers. "Maybe that's true," he said softly, "but it doesn't mean she didn't love you with everything she had."

Isabel swallowed hard, nodding. "She kept so much from me, Gabe. She was protecting me, I know that now, but it feels like she built this wall between us. And I'm realizing I've done the same thing to everyone around me, especially you."

Gabe's grip tightened slightly, his thumb brushing over the back of her hand in silent reassurance. "Walls don't just keep people out," he said quietly. "They trap you inside too. Maybe it's time to start breaking them down."

The thought was daunting. Letting Gabe in, fully, meant opening herself up to pain, to vulnerability, to the possibility of losing something precious. But it also meant the possibility of finding something real—something lasting.

Isabel drew a shaky breath and leaned back in her chair, her eyes once again drawn to the lighthouse standing sentinel on the cliffs. Its steady beam cut through the darkness like a promise, a reminder that even in the shadows, there was light to guide her forward.

"My mother's choices... her secrets... I think she was trying to protect me, but I wonder if she was also trying to protect herself," Isabel said, her voice barely above a whisper. "Maybe she was afraid—afraid of losing me, afraid of showing me who she really was."

Gabe nodded, his gaze never leaving her face. "Maybe. But that doesn't mean you have to do the same."

"I know," Isabel whispered, closing her eyes for a moment. "But I don't know how to do it, Gabe. I don't know how to let go of all these fears."

"You start by trusting yourself," he said gently. "And then you trust me. One step at a time."

The vulnerability in Gabe's words touched her deeply. For all the walls she had built around her heart, she could see that Gabe had patiently stayed by her side, never demanding more than she was willing to give, but always waiting, always offering his support. His presence was unwavering, steady—just like the lighthouse.

"I'm trying," she said, her voice thick with emotion. "I'm trying to trust. It's just... I'm scared of what it means to be open. What if I get hurt?"

Gabe shifted in his seat, moving closer to her, his eyes filled with an unspoken understanding. "You will get hurt, Isabel. That's part of life. But you'll also feel things you've never felt before—joy, love, connection. It's worth it."

His words hung in the air between them, weighty with truth. Isabel could feel the barriers she had built around her heart trembling, threatening to come down piece by piece. But there was still something holding her back—something deeper, something that had to do with more than just Gabe, more than just the past.

"I've always been afraid of losing people," she admitted, the confession raw and unfiltered. "After my mom died, it felt like everyone I loved would eventually leave me. So I kept people at a distance, thinking it would hurt less that way. But it hasn't."

Gabe leaned forward, his forehead almost touching hers. "I'm not going anywhere, Isabel. I'm here, and I'm not leaving."

Isabel's breath caught in her throat. The sincerity in Gabe's eyes was undeniable. It wasn't just words. It was a promise. And for the first time in a long time, she felt the smallest flicker of hope.

Maybe she didn't have to face everything alone. Maybe there was room for love, for vulnerability, for connection.

"I want to believe that," she whispered. "I really do."

"Then start by believing in us," Gabe said, his voice steady and sure.

Isabel closed her eyes, feeling the warmth of his presence beside her, the strength of his hand in hers. The storm that had been raging inside her for so long began to quiet, replaced by something gentler, something more powerful. She wasn't ready to tear down all the walls just yet, but for the first time, she was ready to start taking them apart, one brick at a time.

The journal lay beside them, its secrets revealed, its weight heavy. But it no longer felt like a burden Isabel had to carry alone. Her mother's past was her past, but it didn't have to define her future.

"I think I'm ready to start letting go," she said softly, her eyes opening to meet Gabe's. "Of the fear. Of the pain. Of all the things I've been holding on to for so long."

Gabe smiled, a small, hopeful smile that made Isabel's heart ache with something she couldn't quite name. "I'll be here, every step of the way."

For the first time in years, Isabel felt a sense of peace wash over her. The past, with all its secrets and pain, was still there, but it no longer had the power to hold her captive. She had the power to shape her own future, to open herself to love, to connection, to the possibility of happiness.

And with Gabe beside her, maybe—just maybe—she could finally start to believe in a future that was full of light.

Isabel sat quietly, absorbing Gabe's words, the weight of everything sinking in. The journal still lay open beside her, but it no longer held the power to undo her. She felt lighter somehow, as if sharing her fears, her vulnerabilities with Gabe had eased the burden she had carried alone for so long. But there was still a nagging thought in the back of her mind—something she hadn't yet fully confronted. Something that lingered beneath the surface of her mother's words.

"I wonder if she ever found peace," Isabel said, her voice soft as she stared at the journal's weathered pages.

Gabe looked at her, his brow furrowed. "Your mother?"

She nodded. "She was always so strong, so composed. But now, reading this, I realize she must have been struggling for a long time. And I never knew. I don't know if she ever found what she was looking for."

Gabe was silent for a moment, his gaze thoughtful as he followed the direction of her thoughts. "Sometimes we don't get to see that in the people we love. But that doesn't mean they didn't try. Maybe your mother did find peace, in her own way, even if you didn't get to witness it."

Isabel bit her lip, unsure of how to respond. The journal had revealed so much about her mother's hidden life, about the affair that had shaped her mother's decisions and ultimately left her distant from her daughter. But there was something more, something Isabel hadn't been able to put into words until now. It wasn't just about her mother's secrets. It was about her own.

"There's something I've been avoiding," Isabel confessed, her voice barely above a whisper. "I keep thinking about all the things my mother kept from me, but the truth is, I've been doing the same thing. I've been hiding from the truth."

Gabe looked at her, his expression unreadable. "What do you mean?"

Isabel felt her chest tighten, the words she had avoided for so long rising to the surface. "I've been running from my own guilt.

From the choices I made... the things I left behind. And I don't know if I can ever make peace with them."

Gabe's hand found hers again, his touch warm and grounding. "What guilt, Isabel? What are you talking about?"

She swallowed hard, her eyes dropping to the floor. "It's about my father. When he left... I never tried to understand. I was so angry with him for abandoning us that I just shut him out. I never asked why. And then, when he reached out to me years later, I didn't respond. I thought I was protecting myself, but maybe I was just protecting my pride."

Gabe's eyes softened as he listened, his thumb tracing small circles on the back of her hand. "You were hurting, Isabel. You were allowed to feel that way."

"But what if I was wrong?" she said, her voice trembling. "What if I missed my chance to know him? What if I was so caught up in my own pain that I never gave him a chance to explain?"

The silence that followed was thick, heavy with the weight of her confession. For the first time, Isabel felt the full impact of her choices, the years of resentment and anger that had shaped her relationship with her father—and with herself.

Gabe leaned forward, his voice low and gentle. "Isabel, we all have regrets. We all make mistakes. But that doesn't mean you're beyond forgiveness. It doesn't mean you can't find peace."

She shook her head, tears brimming in her eyes. "I don't know if I deserve it. I don't know if I deserve to feel peace after everything I've done."

Gabe reached up, his hand cupping her cheek, his touch warm and reassuring. "You do, Isabel. You deserve every bit of peace you can find. And you're allowed to forgive yourself. You don't have to carry this guilt forever."

The words hit her like a wave, crashing through the defenses she had built around herself. For so long, she had held on to her guilt, her anger, her pain—believing that it was the only way to protect herself from the hurt of losing people she loved. But now, with Gabe's words echoing in her mind, she realized that holding on to the past had only kept her trapped.

Isabel closed her eyes, letting the tears fall freely. "I'm so tired of carrying it, Gabe. I'm so tired of feeling like I have to keep everything inside."

"Then let it go," he whispered, his voice steady. "Let me carry it with you."

Isabel opened her eyes, meeting Gabe's steady gaze. The vulnerability in his expression mirrored her own, and for the first time, she felt like she didn't have to face everything alone. Gabe wasn't just offering her comfort—he was offering her a way forward, a path to healing that she hadn't thought possible.

"I don't know how to do that," she admitted, her voice small.

Gabe smiled gently. "You don't have to know right now. You just have to be willing to try."

Isabel took a deep breath, nodding slowly. It wasn't going to be easy, but for the first time, she felt like she had the strength to start. Maybe Gabe was right—maybe she didn't have to carry everything on her own. Maybe she could find a way to forgive herself, to let go of the past, and to finally allow herself to feel the peace she so desperately craved.

"I want to try," she whispered, her voice steadying. "I want to try to forgive myself. And I want to try to let you in."

Gabe's smile widened, his hand still resting against her cheek. "I'll be here, Isabel. Every step of the way."

The weight on Isabel's chest seemed to lift, just a little, as she allowed herself to lean into his touch. For the first time in years, she felt like she wasn't alone in her struggle. Gabe was there—steady, unwavering, and willing to face the storm with her. And that, more than anything, gave her hope.

As the evening light faded into twilight, Isabel felt a quiet sense of resolution settle over her. The journal, with all its secrets and pain, was no longer something to fear. It was a piece of her past, but it didn't have to define her future. And with Gabe by her side, maybe—just maybe—she could find the strength to move forward.

They sat in silence for a long while, the waves crashing against the shore in the distance, the lighthouse's beam sweeping over the cliffs. Isabel felt the weight of everything she had carried for so long—the guilt, the anger, the pain—slowly begin to dissolve.

She wasn't healed, not yet. But for the first time, she felt like she could be.

12

Chapter 12: Dylan's True Intentions

Isabel stood at the edge of the cliff, the wind pulling at her hair as she stared out at the waves crashing against the rocks below. The lighthouse's beam swept across the darkening sky, casting fleeting shadows over the coastline. She had always found solace here, in the isolation, in the vastness of the sea. But tonight, the sound of footsteps behind her broke the fragile peace.

"Isabel."

She knew that voice without turning. Dylan. His presence, once a comfort, now filled her with a mix of unease and uncertainty. She had thought of him often during her time on the island—his un-wavering presence in her past, the steady, reliable force that had once kept her grounded. But now, standing here, she realized that Dylan had always been a part of the life she had run away from. A life where she had hidden behind her own fear, never daring to confront the truth of who she was or what she truly wanted.

She turned to face him, her heart heavy. He stood a few feet away, his expression unreadable, though his eyes carried the weight of unspoken words.

"I didn't think you'd come," she said quietly, her voice lost in the wind.

Dylan took a step closer, his jaw tight. "I couldn't stay away, Isabel. Not after everything that's happened."

Her chest tightened at his words. There was something so familiar in the way he looked at her, in the way his voice carried that same gentle reassurance. But it wasn't enough anymore. Not after everything she had discovered about herself—about her mother, about the island, about Gabe.

"I'm glad you came," Isabel said, though the words felt hollow. She wasn't sure if she meant them. Part of her was glad for the closure, but another part of her felt like she was standing on the precipice of something she couldn't quite articulate. "But I think we need to talk."

Dylan's eyes flickered with something—disappointment, maybe, or resignation. He nodded slowly. "Yeah, I think we do."

They stood in silence for a moment, the wind howling between them. Isabel wanted to find the right words, to explain everything she was feeling, but the more she tried to organize her thoughts, the more tangled they became. She had always been able to rely on Dylan to be the rational one, to provide clarity when her emotions clouded her judgment. But now, she wasn't sure she wanted clarity. She wanted the truth.

"Why did you come, Dylan?" she asked finally, her voice soft but steady.

He seemed taken aback by the question. "I came because I care about you, Isabel. I thought you needed me."

Isabel swallowed hard, her gaze dropping to the ground. "I did need you. I always needed you. But now... I don't know if that's enough."

Dylan frowned, taking another step closer. "What are you saying?"

She lifted her eyes to meet his, feeling the weight of everything between them. "I think I was clinging to the idea of you because it felt safe. Familiar. You were always there for me, Dylan, and I'm grateful for that. But I don't think it was ever about you. It was about me. I was scared of being alone, of facing my past, and I used you as a way to avoid that."

His face tightened, his eyes searching hers for an explanation. "Isabel, we've been through so much together. I've always been there for you—when no one else was. How can you say it wasn't real?"

Isabel felt a pang of guilt, a deep sense of responsibility for the pain in his voice. She had always valued his loyalty, the way he had stood by her side no matter what. But that loyalty had also kept her tethered to a version of herself she no longer recognized.

"I'm not saying it wasn't real," she said softly. "I'm saying that I wasn't real. I wasn't being honest with myself, and because of that, I wasn't honest with you either. I let myself believe that being with you was the right thing because it was easy. But now, after everything that's happened here, I see things differently. I see myself differently."

Dylan's expression shifted, a flicker of frustration crossing his features. "So this is about Gabe, isn't it? You've been spending time with him, and now you're questioning everything between us."

Isabel shook her head, though the mention of Gabe sent a ripple through her. "This isn't about Gabe. It's about me. I've been avoiding the truth for so long, and I can't do that anymore. I need to figure out who I am—without you, without anyone telling me what I should want."

Dylan's hands clenched at his sides, the hurt in his eyes undeniable. "So what are you saying, Isabel? That I was just a crutch? That everything we had meant nothing?"

Isabel felt her throat tighten with emotion. "No, that's not what I'm saying. You meant a lot to me. You still do. But I think I've been holding on to you because I was too afraid to face my own fears. And that's not fair to either of us."

The silence between them was deafening. For a moment, Dylan just stared at her, his chest rising and falling with shallow breaths. Isabel could feel the weight of his disappointment, the sting of betrayal that lingered in the air.

"I thought we had a future," Dylan said, his voice low. "I thought we were building something."

Isabel's heart ached at his words, but she knew the truth now, even if it was painful to admit. "I thought so too," she whispered. "But I think we were building something based on what we thought we should be, not who we really are."

Dylan ran a hand through his hair, frustration radiating off him. "So what now? You're just going to walk away?"

Isabel took a deep breath, her hands trembling slightly. "I don't know, Dylan. I don't have all the answers. But I know that I can't keep pretending that everything's okay between us when it's not. I need time to figure things out."

He looked at her, his eyes searching hers one last time, as if trying to find something that would change her mind. But Isabel knew that this conversation had been a long time coming. They had been drifting apart for longer than either of them had realized.

Finally, Dylan nodded, his shoulders sagging with the weight of acceptance. "I just wish you'd told me sooner," he said quietly, the hurt clear in his voice.

"I'm sorry," Isabel whispered, her heart heavy with guilt. "I never meant to hurt you."

Dylan gave her a sad smile, the distance between them suddenly feeling much larger than it had ever been. "I know. But sometimes, that's just how things turn out."

With that, he turned and walked away, leaving Isabel standing alone on the cliff, the wind whipping around her like the echoes of everything left unsaid.

As she watched Dylan's figure disappear into the twilight, Isabel felt a strange mix of relief and sadness wash over her. She had lost something familiar, something safe. But in its place, she had gained something far more important: the truth.

And for the first time, she wasn't afraid to face it.

The echo of Dylan's footsteps faded, leaving Isabel alone with the rush of the wind and the crash of the waves below. She stood frozen, her mind swirling with the weight of the conversation they'd just had. The air felt colder now, the vastness of the sea pressing against her like an unwelcome guest.

Isabel had expected to feel some sense of closure after finally confronting Dylan, but all she felt was a hollow ache deep in her chest. She had let go of something that had been her anchor for so long, and now the emptiness felt as vast as the ocean before her.

The truth was, Isabel wasn't just mourning the end of her relationship with Dylan. She was mourning the end of the person she had been with him—the person who had found comfort in his stability and security, even when it no longer served her. And now, with him gone, she was left to face the uncertainty of who she was becoming.

Isabel took a shaky breath, her thoughts turning to Gabe. The connection between them had been undeniable, a slow burn that had built over the weeks since her return to the island. But as much as she had felt drawn to him, part of her was terrified of what that connection meant. Dylan had been safe, familiar. Gabe was something else entirely—something unpredictable, something that made her heart race in a way that scared her.

She wrapped her arms around herself, trying to steady the trembling that had taken hold of her. As the sun dipped lower on the horizon, the lighthouse's beam cut through the twilight, its steady rhythm a reminder of the path she was on. The path of self-discovery, of understanding her mother's choices, and ultimately, her own.

Isabel turned away from the sea, her feet carrying her back toward the village. The Festival of Lights would soon be in full swing, and she wasn't ready to face the crowd just yet, but there was something else she needed to do. Something that had been gnawing at the edges of her consciousness ever since she had uncovered her mother's hidden journal.

The journal held secrets—regrets, confessions, and whispers of a life Isabel had never truly known. But there was something else, something Isabel hadn't been able to shake. The mention of a hidden family secret, something her mother had carried for years, weighing her down in ways that had mirrored Isabel's own struggles.

As she made her way toward the old studio, where she had found the journal and the painting, a sense of dread began to creep over her. What had her mother been hiding? And why had she kept it buried for so long?

The door to the studio creaked open, the familiar scent of paint and dust hitting her like a wave of nostalgia. The room was dim, but Isabel knew exactly where to go. She crossed to the work-bench where she had left the journal, her fingers brushing over its worn cover as she picked it up. She hadn't read every entry yet—there had been too many emotions, too many unanswered questions swirling in her mind.

Isabel sat down on the small stool, opening the journal to where she had last left off. Her mother's handwriting was neat but shaky, the words becoming more erratic the further she went.

I did what I thought was right. I kept this from you to protect you, Isabel, but I fear it has done more harm than good.

The words hit her like a punch to the gut. Protect her? From what?

Her eyes scanned the next few entries, her heart pounding in her chest.

I was wrong to think I could carry this burden alone. I should have told you about your father.

Isabel froze, her fingers tightening around the edges of the journal. She had always known her mother and father's relationship had been complicated, but there had been so much left unspoken between them. Was this it? The secret that had haunted her mother for years?

He wasn't the man you thought he was. There are things you don't know about him—things I should have told you. I'm sorry, Isabel. I kept it from you because I wanted to shield you from the truth, but now I see that only hurt you more.

Isabel's breath caught in her throat. Her father? What could her mother have been hiding about him? Her mind raced with possibilities, but none of them made sense. He had always been distant, yes, but he had loved her, hadn't he?

She flipped through the next few pages, searching for answers. And then she found it—a single line that changed everything.

Your father wasn't the man I married. He had another life, another family. And I... I was a part of his secret.

Isabel's heart stopped. Another life? Another family? She stared at the words, her mind struggling to comprehend what she was reading. Her father had kept an entire life hidden from her—and from her mother. The weight of the revelation hit her like a tidal wave, pulling her under.

Her mother's journal continued, detailing the years of deception, the lies her father had told to keep both families in the dark. He had lived a double life, and her mother had been complicit in the lie, too afraid to confront the truth.

Tears blurred Isabel's vision as she read on, her heart breaking with each word. Her mother had stayed with him, not out of love, but out of fear—fear of what would happen if the truth came out, fear of what it would do to Isabel if she found out. And so, she had kept the secret, sacrificing her own happiness to protect Isabel from the pain.

But now, the pain was all-consuming, and Isabel wasn't sure how to handle it. She felt betrayed, not just by her father, but by her mother as well. The woman who had raised her, who had been her guiding light, had kept her in the dark for so long.

The journal slipped from her hands, landing on the floor with a soft thud. Isabel pressed her palms to her face, trying to breathe through the sobs that were threatening to break free. How could her mother have done this? How could she have kept such a monumental secret?

But as the initial shock began to fade, a new emotion crept in—understanding. Her mother hadn't been perfect. She had made mistakes, just like Isabel had. She had been trying to protect her, even if it had been misguided. And in some strange way, that made

Isabel feel closer to her. She understood now, more than ever, the weight of carrying secrets. The cost of living in fear.

Isabel wiped her tears, her mind spinning with this new reality. The lighthouse's beam swept through the room, illuminating the scattered pages of the journal on the floor. Her past had been shattered, but maybe, just maybe, this was the beginning of something new. A chance to rebuild—on her own terms.

And as much as it hurt, Isabel knew that facing the truth, no matter how painful, was the only way forward.

Isabel stood outside the studio, the journal's revelations still a raw wound, as if they had stripped away the last remnants of the life she thought she knew. Her feet felt heavy as she made her way back toward the center of the village. The Festival of Lights flickered in the distance, but she could barely see it through the haze of thoughts clouding her mind.

Dylan had been part of that past—safe, familiar, like an anchor in the stormy seas of her memories. His presence had offered her comfort when everything else felt like it was slipping away. But now, after their confrontation, the truth had settled in her chest like a stone. She hadn't held on to him out of love, but because of the stability he represented.

The journal's revelations had peeled away the layers of illusion she had wrapped herself in. It wasn't just her father's secret life or her mother's silent suffering that had shaken her; it was the realization that she, too, had been hiding—from herself, from her feelings, and from the possibility of real love.

Dylan had said all the right things in their final conversation. He had spoken of the future, of the life they could build together, but Isabel had felt none of it. Not in the way she had wanted to. She had clung to him because it was easier than confronting her own fear of moving forward.

Her footsteps slowed as she approached the lantern-lit square. The sounds of laughter, of joy, filled the air, but Isabel couldn't bring herself to join in. She spotted Dylan standing near the edge of the square, talking to someone she didn't recognize. For a moment, their eyes met, and in that fleeting second, she saw it—the finality in his expression. He knew. They both did.

It was over.

Isabel tore her gaze away, her heart racing as she continued walking. She passed through the crowd, the warmth of the festival brushing against her skin but unable to reach the cold knot in her chest. She needed to breathe, to think, to make sense of the storm that had erupted inside her.

But as she neared the edge of the village, her eyes landed on a familiar figure standing alone beneath the glowing lanterns. Gabe. He was facing the sea, his back to the festivities, but the way he stood—still, contemplative—made her pulse quicken. She had always felt the pull between them, but tonight it was different. The weight of her discoveries, of her past unraveling, had opened a new door inside her, one she wasn't sure she was ready to walk through.

Isabel hesitated, her feet rooted to the ground. She wasn't sure what to say or how to approach him after everything that had happened, after Dylan. The guilt gnawed at her, but something deeper urged her forward—something that whispered of possibility, of healing.

She took a step, then another, until she was standing beside him. Gabe turned his head slightly, acknowledging her presence with a soft, almost imperceptible smile. They stood like that for a moment, side by side, neither of them speaking. The silence between them was thick with unspoken words, with emotions Isabel wasn't ready to confront.

But Gabe, in his quiet way, seemed to understand. He didn't press her, didn't ask any questions. He simply existed beside her, his presence a calm in the storm she hadn't realized she needed.

Isabel glanced at him from the corner of her eye. His face was illuminated by the soft glow of the lanterns, his expression serene but thoughtful. The way he carried himself, the way he looked out at the sea as if it held all the answers, made her chest tighten with something she couldn't quite name.

"I found my mother's journal," Isabel said softly, her voice barely audible above the sound of the waves. She wasn't sure why she said it, why she chose this moment to open up, but the words tumbled out before she could stop them.

Gabe turned to face her fully now, his brows furrowing in concern. "What did it say?"

She swallowed, the lump in her throat making it hard to speak. "It's... complicated. My father—he had another life, another family. My mother knew. She kept it from me. To protect me, she said."

Gabe's eyes softened, his gaze steady and unflinching. He didn't say anything, didn't try to fill the silence with empty reassurances. Instead, he reached out, his hand brushing against hers, a simple, grounding touch that sent warmth flooding through her.

Isabel exhaled, the tension in her shoulders easing slightly. She hadn't realized how much she needed that—just the comfort of another person, of not being alone in this moment.

"I don't know how to feel," she admitted, her voice trembling. "Everything I thought I knew... it's gone. My family, my past, even Dylan. I don't know who I am without all of it."

Gabe's hand closed gently around hers, his thumb brushing over her knuckles in a soothing rhythm. "You're still you, Isabel," he said softly. "And you don't have to have all the answers right now."

His words, simple and steady, broke something inside her. The walls she had built around herself, the need to be strong, to hold it all together, crumbled in that moment. Tears welled in her eyes, and before she could stop herself, she turned toward him, burying her face in his chest.

Gabe's arms came around her without hesitation, holding her close as she let the sobs come. The weight of the past, of her mother's secrets, of her own fears and doubts, spilled out in the safety of his embrace. And for the first time in what felt like forever, Isabel let herself be vulnerable, let herself be held.

They stood like that for what felt like hours, the festival's distant hum fading into the background. It was just the two of them, wrapped in the quiet of the night, the rhythm of the sea echoing their own hearts.

When Isabel finally pulled back, wiping at her tear-streaked face, she found Gabe watching her with an intensity that made her heart flutter. There was something in his gaze, something she hadn't been ready to see before.

"Isabel," he began, his voice low and hesitant, "I don't want to push you, but... I need you to know how I feel."

Her breath caught in her throat, the tension between them thickening.

"I'm not good with words, but... you mean more to me than I think you realize," Gabe said, his voice rough with emotion. "I've been waiting—for you to see it. For you to know that I'm here, no matter what."

Isabel's heart raced, her pulse thudding in her ears. He wasn't saying the words outright, but she could hear them in the spaces between. He was in love with her, and maybe—just maybe—she was ready to hear it.

And just like that, the weight of the past didn't feel quite so heavy anymore.

Isabel stood frozen, Gabe's words echoing in her mind, leaving her more conflicted than she'd ever imagined. His subtle confession, the way he had laid his heart bare without pressing for a response, struck something deep inside her. And yet, the guilt over Dylan lingered, clawing at her like an unresolved wound.

She turned away from Gabe, her gaze drifting toward the ocean, waves crashing rhythmically against the shore. Dylan had always been the constant—a part of her life that made sense when everything else didn't. He had been safe, predictable, a tether to a past that, in retrospect, felt like a false comfort. But now, in the light of everything she'd learned about her family and her own fears, Dylan's presence had begun to feel more like a reminder of the person she used to be, not the person she was becoming.

As the festival sounds grew distant, Isabel's mind raced back to their last conversation, just a few hours before. Dylan had confronted her, his words tinged with frustration but also with a kind of desperation she hadn't fully understood until now.

"You're pulling away from me," he'd said, his brow furrowed, his eyes searching hers for an answer she couldn't give. "I can feel it, Isabel. We used to be in sync, but now... it's like you're not even here."

She hadn't responded immediately then, unsure of how to explain the shift she'd felt. A part of her had clung to Dylan because it was easier than facing the uncertainty of what lay ahead. But now, standing here beside Gabe, she realized how deeply rooted that avoidance had been.

Isabel let out a shaky breath, her hands trembling as she folded them over her chest. "I should've been honest with him," she muttered under her breath, the weight of regret pressing down on her.

Gabe's hand touched her shoulder gently, grounding her in the present. "Honest about what?"

Isabel turned to face him, her heart heavy. "About why I was holding on to him. It wasn't love... not really. I think I was just afraid. Afraid of what it meant to let go of the familiar, to face the unknown. With Dylan, everything felt... safe."

Gabe's expression softened, his understanding clear without judgment. "Sometimes it's easier to stay where it's comfortable, even if it's not where you're meant to be."

Isabel nodded, her throat tightening. "But it wasn't fair to him. He deserves someone who loves him fully, and I..." She trailed off, unable to finish the thought aloud, but the truth lingered between them.

She didn't love Dylan—not the way he deserved to be loved, and not the way she was beginning to feel for Gabe.

The realization was both freeing and terrifying.

"I've been running from my feelings for so long," Isabel confessed, her voice barely above a whisper. "Running from what's real because I was afraid of getting hurt. My mother did the same thing... she ran from the truth, hid it from me, thinking it would protect me. But all it did was leave me more confused, more lost."

Gabe stepped closer, his eyes never leaving hers. "You're not your mother, Isabel. And you don't have to make the same choices she did. You can face this, whatever it is, head-on."

Isabel's breath hitched, her emotions swirling in a whirlwind of fear, guilt, and something else she wasn't quite ready to name. Gabe's presence was steady, unwavering, and the intensity in his gaze was enough to make her chest tighten with longing. But there was still so much she hadn't figured out yet, so much she wasn't sure about.

"I don't want to hurt him," she whispered, her voice breaking with emotion. "Dylan... he's been good to me. He's been there when no one else was. I owe him that much."

"You don't owe him your heart," Gabe said quietly. "Not if it's not what you want."

Isabel looked down at the ground, the guilt gnawing at her insides. She knew Gabe was right, but that didn't make the truth any easier to bear. Dylan had always been a part of her life, a constant in the storm, but now it was time to let go, to face the reality of who she had become.

She straightened, her resolve hardening, even as tears welled up in her eyes. "I need to talk to him," she said, her voice firm despite the tremble.

Gabe nodded, his expression full of quiet support. "Do what you need to do, Isabel. I'll be here when you're ready."

The weight of his words settled into her heart, and as she turned to walk away, she couldn't help but glance back at him one last time. Gabe stood under the lantern's glow, his silhouette framed by the soft light, his eyes following her as she disappeared into the night.

Isabel made her way through the village square, the sounds of the festival fading into the background. She found Dylan standing near the edge of the festivities, talking quietly with a few others, but as soon as he saw her approach, he excused himself and walked over to her.

"Isabel," he said softly, his voice full of something she hadn't quite been ready to hear earlier—hope.

She swallowed hard, her heart racing in her chest. "Dylan, we need to talk."

His face fell slightly, and for a brief moment, Isabel wished she could take it all back, wished she could spare him the pain she was about to cause. But she knew that doing so would only prolong the inevitable.

They walked to a quieter spot near the edge of the festival, the lanterns casting long shadows across the ground. The air between them felt thick with unspoken words, with the weight of everything that had gone unsaid for far too long.

"Dylan," Isabel began, her voice shaking slightly, "I've been holding on to us... to what we had... because it felt safe. You've always been there for me, and I've relied on that more than I realized. But it's not fair to you."

He looked at her, his eyes wide with confusion and hurt. "What are you saying?"

Isabel took a deep breath, her heart breaking as she forced the words out. "I don't love you the way you deserve to be loved. And I can't keep pretending that I do. You deserve someone who can give you their whole heart, and I... I'm not that person."

For a moment, Dylan said nothing, his expression unreadable. Then, slowly, he nodded, though the pain in his eyes was unmistakable. "I always knew," he said quietly, his voice strained. "I always knew you weren't really in love with me... but I thought maybe, with time..."

Isabel's throat tightened, and she reached out to touch his arm, a gesture of comfort she wasn't sure he would welcome. "I'm sorry, Dylan. I never meant to hurt you."

He shook his head, stepping back slightly. "It's not your fault. I think, deep down, I knew this was coming. But it still hurts."

They stood there for a moment, the silence between them heavy with the weight of goodbye. Dylan's expression was one of quiet resignation, but there was also a strange sort of relief in his eyes, as if he had been waiting for this moment just as much as she had.

"Take care of yourself, Isabel," he said softly, his voice thick with emotion. Then, without another word, he turned and walked away, leaving her standing there, alone with her thoughts.

The night stretched out before her, vast and endless, but for the first time in a long time, Isabel didn't feel lost. She had faced the truth, had let go of the past, and now... now she was ready to move forward, wherever that might take her.

As Dylan walked away, the weight of their final conversation settled in Isabel's chest. She stood there, the distant murmur of the festival a faint echo in the background. The lanterns swayed gently above her, casting shifting shadows across the ground, but she barely noticed. Everything felt strangely still, as if the world had paused just long enough for her to grasp what had truly happened.

She'd let go—of Dylan, of the idea of them, of the life she had thought she needed. And while the sharp pang of guilt lingered, it was accompanied by something else: a sense of freedom. The knot in her chest loosened ever so slightly, and for the first time in years, Isabel felt like she could finally breathe.

But with that freedom came fear. A deep, unsettling fear of what lay ahead—of the unknown, of her own heart. She had always chosen the safe path, the one that hurt the least. Now, she stood at a precipice, her feelings for Gabe swirling in her mind, unresolved and raw.

Isabel took a deep breath, willing herself to stay present. She watched Dylan's silhouette blend into the crowd until he was completely out of sight. The part of her that had held on to him for so long was aching, but now, the ache felt like something she could survive.

The festival lights flickered, pulling her attention back to the world around her. The village square was alive with laughter and music, the warmth of the community contrasting sharply with the coldness she felt inside. The festival was meant to be a celebration—a moment of renewal, of love and light. Yet here she was, standing on the edge of an emotional cliff, unsure of what would come next.

She took one last glance at the crowd, her eyes scanning the faces, but there was only one she was searching for.

Gabe.

Isabel turned and began walking toward the far end of the village, her steps quickening as she pushed through the clusters of people. Her heart raced, not from the cold or the festival energy, but from the thought of seeing him again. Of confronting what was truly happening between them.

She found him standing at the edge of the cliffside path that overlooked the ocean, away from the festival. His back was to her, hands in his pockets, his stance calm and contemplative. The sound of the waves crashing against the rocks below filled the air, a rhythmic pulse that matched the thudding in her chest.

For a moment, Isabel hesitated, unsure of what to say. Gabe had always been so sure of himself, so grounded in his feelings. But Isabel? She had been avoiding the truth for so long she wasn't sure she knew how to face it.

But now, after everything that had happened, after saying goodbye to Dylan, she had no choice but to confront it.

"Gabe," she called softly, her voice barely rising above the wind.

He turned slowly, his eyes meeting hers with that same intensity that had always unnerved her. There was something about Gabe—about the way he saw her, truly saw her—that made Isabel feel exposed, vulnerable. It scared her. But at the same time, it was the very thing that drew her to him.

"You okay?" he asked, his voice gentle, though his eyes searched hers for answers.

Isabel didn't respond right away. Instead, she stepped closer, joining him at the edge of the cliff. The ocean stretched out before them, vast and endless, a reflection of the uncertainty that now filled her heart.

"I ended things with Dylan," she said quietly, her gaze focused on the horizon. "I needed to... I needed to stop pretending that I could love him the way he deserved. It wasn't fair to either of us."

Gabe's expression softened, though he remained quiet, allowing her the space to continue.

"And now... now I don't know what to do," she admitted, her voice trembling slightly. "I feel like everything I thought I knew has changed. Like I've been running in circles, avoiding what's really going on inside me."

Gabe watched her closely, his presence steady as always. "You don't have to figure it all out right now, Isabel. It's okay to take things slow. To let yourself feel what you need to feel."

Isabel nodded, though the uncertainty still gnawed at her. She turned to face him fully, her heart pounding in her chest. "But what if I don't know what I feel? What if I don't know how to let myself trust... or love... or be vulnerable again?"

Gabe's gaze softened even more, and he took a step closer to her, his eyes holding hers. "Isabel, I'm not asking for answers. I'm not asking for anything you're not ready to give. I'm just... here."

He paused, his next words filled with a quiet intensity that made her pulse quicken. "But I need you to know something. Whatever happens... wherever this goes... you don't have to face it alone. I'm here, whether you're ready or not."

Isabel's breath caught in her throat. Gabe hadn't confessed his love outright, but the message was clear. He cared about her—deeply—and he was willing to wait. To give her the space she needed, while also being a constant presence in her life.

The vulnerability of the moment left Isabel feeling exposed, raw. But instead of pulling away, she took a step closer, her fingers brushing his. It was a small gesture, but it felt like the first step toward something new—something she wasn't entirely sure of, but something she was willing to explore.

"I don't know where this is going," Isabel whispered, her voice shaking slightly. "But I... I want to try. I want to figure it out."

Gabe's lips curled into a soft smile, his eyes bright with hope. "That's all I need to hear."

They stood there, side by side, the wind tousling their hair as the ocean roared beneath them. The festival lights twinkled in the distance, but here, in this quiet moment, it was just the two of them—two people on the edge of something new, something uncertain, but something real.

Isabel's heart was still tangled with doubts and fears, but as she looked at Gabe, she felt a spark of something she hadn't felt in a long time.

Possibility.

And for the first time, she was ready to take the leap.

Isabel let out a long breath as the weight of the moment settled between them. The winds whipped around the cliffside, but all she felt was the steady warmth radiating from Gabe's presence. It wasn't just what he had said, but how he had said it—without pressure, without expectation, just quiet understanding. She wasn't sure how to move forward, but with Gabe beside her, the uncertainty felt a little less overwhelming.

The night around them was alive with distant festival sounds—laughter, music, and the occasional burst of light from the fireworks—but here, at the edge of the world, it was just her and Gabe. There was something sacred about the stillness between them, as if the rest of the world had faded into the background.

"I've been running for so long," Isabel whispered, her gaze fixed on the endless ocean. "Running from the past, from everything I didn't want to face. And now, here I am... finally standing still, but I don't know how to stop the momentum."

Gabe turned slightly, watching her, his expression soft with understanding. "Maybe you don't need to stop it. Maybe you just need to learn how to move with it."

Isabel looked up at him, surprised by the simplicity of his words. He always had a way of cutting through her internal chaos with a kind of clarity she couldn't find on her own.

"Move with it," she repeated quietly, letting the idea settle. She hadn't thought of it that way—hadn't considered that maybe her journey didn't have to be about halting everything she was afraid of, but learning how to face it without being consumed.

Her mind drifted back to Dylan. Their final conversation had left her with a hollow ache, not because she regretted ending things, but because she had clung to him for reasons she was only now starting to understand. Dylan had represented safety—a tether to the life she had known. He was someone she could love without risking too much. But that wasn't real love, not the kind that could last.

"I think... I think I held on to Dylan because it felt safe," she admitted, the words coming out slowly as if she were still piecing them together. "But safety isn't what I want anymore."

Gabe's expression didn't change, but she saw the flicker of emotion in his eyes. He didn't push her to elaborate. He didn't need to. Instead, he took a step closer, his hand gently brushing hers, grounding her in the present moment.

"And what do you want, Isabel?" His voice was low, almost a whisper, but the question carried a weight that made her pulse quicken.

Isabel felt her throat tighten. What did she want? The answer was right in front of her, but saying it out loud felt terrifying. She had spent so long protecting herself, keeping her heart guarded, that admitting what she truly desired felt like stepping into the unknown.

"I want... I want something real," she finally said, her voice barely above a whisper. "I want to stop hiding. I want to stop running from what scares me."

She glanced up at Gabe, her heart pounding in her chest. His eyes never left hers, and in that moment, she knew he understood what she was saying without her having to spell it out.

"I don't know how to do this," she added, her voice trembling with vulnerability. "But I'm tired of pretending I don't feel anything."

Gabe's hand gently wrapped around hers, his touch steady and sure. "You don't have to do it alone, Isabel."

Her chest tightened with a rush of emotion, and for the first time in a long time, she allowed herself to believe that maybe she didn't have to. Maybe there was a way forward—one that didn't involve running or hiding, but instead, embracing the messiness of her feelings and the uncertainty of the future.

For a moment, they stood in silence, the wind whipping around them as the waves crashed against the rocks below. The space between them was charged with an unspoken understanding, and Isabel felt something shift inside her—a soft, tentative opening of her heart.

Without thinking, she stepped closer, her fingers tightening around his. The proximity was both comforting and electrifying, a reminder of how deeply she had come to care for him. Her eyes flicked to his lips, and for the briefest second, she considered closing the gap between them. But instead, she rested her forehead against his chest, letting out a breath she didn't realize she'd been holding.

Gabe's arms wrapped around her, pulling her into a warm embrace. It wasn't a moment of passion, but of quiet intimacy, a kind of connection that didn't need words. And in that silence, Isabel felt something she hadn't felt in years: safety. Not the kind of safety that came from familiarity, but the kind that came from being truly seen and accepted.

The sound of the festival in the distance grew softer as they stood there, wrapped in each other's arms, the world falling away. Isabel wasn't sure where things would go from here—she still had so much to figure out, so much to confront—but in this moment, with Gabe holding her, she felt like maybe, just maybe, she could stop running.

The following morning, as the village began to wake from the festivities of the night before, Isabel found herself back at the lighthouse, the place where her journey had begun. The journal lay open in her lap, her mother's handwriting dancing across the pages like a whisper from the past.

Her mother's regrets were laid bare in the words, the weight of the secrets she had kept pressing down on Isabel like an invisible force. There was pain here—raw and unfiltered—but there was also love. A deep, unyielding love that her mother had tried to protect her from. Isabel now understood that her mother's silence had been out of fear—fear of losing her, fear of her own mistakes spilling over into Isabel's life.

But there was something else too. A truth Isabel hadn't been prepared for. A secret that mirrored her own struggles in a way that was almost too painful to face.

Her mother had loved someone else, deeply, but she had chosen to stay with Isabel's father out of duty, out of a sense of obligation.

The echoes of that choice had reverberated through Isabel's own life, shaping her in ways she hadn't even realized. She had inherited her mother's fear of letting go, of choosing what her heart truly wanted.

Tears blurred her vision as she read the final entry, a confession of love and regret, and a hope that Isabel would one day find the courage to choose differently. To choose her own happiness, no matter the cost.

The words hit Isabel like a wave, pulling her under, and for a moment, all she could do was sit there, the pages trembling in her hands.

Her mother's voice, quiet but insistent, seemed to whisper through the lighthouse: *The light will reveal what's hidden.*

Isabel sat on the rocks by the shore, the journal still clutched in her hands. The weight of her mother's words echoed through her mind, layering with the turmoil of her own emotions. Everything felt sharper now—more painful, more real. The truth about her mother's secret love affair, and the way it mirrored her own fears, had shaken her in ways she hadn't expected.

Dylan's voice cut through her thoughts, pulling her back to the present.

"You've been distant ever since you came back, Isabel," he said, standing a few feet away, his arms crossed defensively. His tone was accusatory but softened by the hint of vulnerability in his eyes. "What happened between us... it doesn't just disappear."

Isabel exhaled, feeling the familiar pull of guilt and the comfort of what she had once known. Dylan had always been safe, dependable—everything she thought she had wanted. But that safety had come at a price. She had stayed with him because it was easy, because it fit the version of herself she had tried so hard to maintain.

But now, after everything she had uncovered about her mother, about herself, she couldn't continue pretending.

"No, it doesn't disappear," Isabel admitted, her voice quiet but resolute. "But that doesn't mean it's right for me anymore."

Dylan's brow furrowed, a flicker of hurt crossing his features. He took a step closer, his voice lowering as he asked, "Is it because of him? Because of Gabe?"

Isabel shook her head slowly. It wasn't just about Gabe. Gabe had shown her what she was truly capable of feeling—how deep her emotions could run when she allowed herself to be vulnerable. But this decision wasn't about choosing between two men. It was about choosing herself, her own happiness, for once.

"It's not just about Gabe," she said, standing up and facing Dylan directly. "It's about me. For so long, I've been afraid to step outside of what's comfortable. I thought being with you was the only way to protect myself from getting hurt. But I've realized I've been hurting myself all along by not being honest about what I really want."

Dylan's jaw tightened, and he looked away, clearly wrestling with her words. The tension between them crackled in the cool evening air, and for a moment, Isabel wondered if he would walk away, leaving their conversation unresolved.

But then he turned back to her, his eyes softer, his voice resigned. "I guess I always knew you weren't really happy, even if I didn't want to admit it. I just didn't think you'd leave."

Isabel's chest tightened with emotion. There had been love between them once, a deep connection that had made sense in her old life. But it was a different kind of love, one built on comfort and familiarity, not the passion and self-discovery she was starting to embrace.

"I wasn't really leaving," she whispered. "I was staying in one place, but I wasn't living. I think that's what my mother did too."

Dylan's eyes flickered with confusion. "Your mother?"

Isabel looked down at the journal in her hands, her fingers tracing the worn edges of the pages. "She stayed in a marriage because it felt like the right thing to do, but she was in love with someone else. She thought she was protecting me, but really, she was just afraid."

The wind rustled around them, carrying the weight of her words. Dylan's expression shifted from confusion to something softer—understanding, perhaps. He had always been a good person, even if their relationship had run its course.

"I never wanted to make you feel trapped," Dylan said quietly, his voice filled with regret.

"I know," Isabel replied gently. "And I didn't realize how trapped I felt until I came back here."

The silence stretched between them, but this time, it wasn't uncomfortable. It was the kind of silence that signaled the end of something, the closing of a chapter that had needed to be closed for a long time.

Isabel stepped closer, her gaze softening. "You'll always mean something to me, Dylan. But I need to figure out who I am without holding on to what feels safe."

Dylan looked at her for a long moment, then nodded, his shoulders slumping in quiet acceptance. "I hope you find what you're looking for, Isabel."

With that, he turned and walked away, his footsteps crunching against the gravel as he disappeared into the twilight. Isabel watched him go, a mixture of sadness and relief washing over her. The past had a way of holding on, but she had made the decision to let it go.

She stood there for a moment longer, feeling the crisp evening air against her skin, the journal heavy in her hands. Her mother's secrets had cast a long shadow over her life, but now, for the first time, Isabel felt like she was stepping into the light. The realization that her mother had been as scared and vulnerable as she was—trapped by the choices she thought she had to make—made Isabel's own journey more poignant.

With one last glance toward the path Dylan had taken, Isabel turned back to the lighthouse, her mind already beginning to piece together the final truths she needed to uncover. The journal wasn't just her mother's story. It was hers too.

As she made her way back to the studio, the sky darkening overhead, Isabel felt something shift inside her. She wasn't running anymore. She wasn't hiding. She was walking into the unknown with her eyes wide open.

Isabel walked along the familiar path back to the lighthouse, her heart heavier than she had anticipated. The confrontation with Dylan had been necessary, but that didn't mean it was easy. As the wind picked up around her, swirling the scent of the sea through the air, she held the journal tighter, her thoughts spiraling in rhythm with the waves crashing against the rocks below.

Dylan's parting words lingered in her mind—"I hope you find what you're looking for." But what was she looking for? Was it closure? Freedom? Love? Or maybe all of those things intertwined in ways she hadn't quite realized.

When she finally reached the lighthouse, its tall silhouette casting a familiar shadow in the moonlight, Isabel paused at the threshold. She glanced up at the structure towering over her, a symbol of both protection and isolation. Much like her mother's life, and now her own.

Opening the door, she stepped inside, greeted by the quiet hum of the space. The air was still, filled with the echoes of her mother's secrets and her own growing clarity. This was where she would piece together the final clues—where she'd uncover the truth her mother had hidden for so long.

The journal felt like a bridge between their two lives, connecting the woman her mother had been to the woman Isabel was becoming. As she settled into the small, rustic chair by the window, she flipped through the remaining pages with careful hands, the words unraveling the last of her mother's story.

There was one final entry that caught her attention—dated just days before her mother's passing. Isabel's breath hitched as her eyes scanned the page, her pulse quickening as the familiar handwriting took on a tone of desperation.

"I've made too many mistakes to count, but the one I regret most is not telling Isabel the truth. I thought I was protecting her, that keeping these parts of myself hidden would shield her from the pain I've carried all these years. But I was wrong. She deserves to know the real me, the woman who loved, who feared, who made choices she couldn't undo. Maybe it's too late now, but if she ever finds this, I hope she'll understand that my silence was out of love. I didn't want her to repeat my mistakes. I didn't want her to be afraid."

Isabel's throat tightened, tears burning the back of her eyes as she read those final, vulnerable words. Her mother's life had been one of quiet suffering, bound by choices she believed she couldn't escape. And in her own way, Isabel had been doing the same—avoiding risks, clinging to what was familiar, protecting herself from heartache but also from truly living.

She had been so afraid of making the wrong choices, just like her mother.

The realization hit her with a force she wasn't prepared for. All this time, she had been trying to escape the past, to distance herself from the mistakes and regrets she thought had defined her. But now, she saw the truth. It wasn't about avoiding mistakes. It was about facing them, acknowledging them, and choosing to move forward anyway.

Her mother hadn't given herself that chance. But Isabel still could.

With trembling hands, Isabel closed the journal, holding it close to her chest. She sat in silence for a long moment, the weight of her mother's story—and her own—pressing down on her. The wind howled outside, and the lighthouse stood firm against it, much like Isabel felt she needed to stand firm against the storm that had been raging inside her for so long.

Her mother had loved someone she wasn't supposed to, had lived with regrets that had haunted her. But through that love, through those regrets, she had also found moments of beauty, moments where she had been truly herself.

Maybe, Isabel thought, that was what life was about—finding those moments, even when they were fleeting. Living in them fully, even when fear threatened to take over.

The quiet creak of the door interrupted her thoughts, and she turned to see Gabe standing in the doorway, his face shadowed but unmistakably tender. His presence was like an anchor, grounding her in the present, even as her emotions swirled.

"I wasn't sure if I should come," he said softly, stepping into the room. "But I had a feeling you might need someone."

Isabel wiped the stray tear from her cheek and gave him a small, grateful smile. "I'm glad you're here."

Gabe walked over to her, his eyes searching hers with concern. "Are you okay?"

She nodded, though her emotions still felt raw. "I think I am. It's just... there's so much I didn't know about my mother. So much she kept hidden because she thought it was for the best."

Gabe sat beside her, the warmth of his presence comforting. "What did you find?"

Isabel took a deep breath, her eyes glancing at the journal. "She was in love with someone else. All those years, she stayed in a marriage that wasn't right for her because she thought it was the only way to protect me. She thought keeping it all a secret was the only way to shield me from the pain she went through."

Gabe's brow furrowed in empathy, and he reached for her hand, his fingers brushing against hers. "That must have been hard for her... and for you."

Isabel squeezed his hand, her chest tightening with emotion. "It was. But I think I understand now. She wasn't trying to hurt me. She was just scared. Scared of losing control, scared of making the wrong choices, scared of repeating the mistakes she thought she couldn't fix."

Gabe's eyes softened as he looked at her, his voice gentle. "And what about you, Isabel? What are you scared of?"

The question hung in the air between them, and for a moment, Isabel didn't know how to answer. But then she realized—she had been running from her fears for so long, it was time to face them.

"I'm scared of not living," she admitted quietly. "Of making the same mistakes my mother did, of holding back because it feels safer than risking my heart."

Gabe leaned closer, his gaze unwavering. "You're not her, Isabel. You don't have to make the same choices she did."

Isabel looked into his eyes, feeling the truth of his words settle deep within her. He was right. Her mother's story didn't have to be her own. She could choose differently. She could choose to embrace the uncertainty, the vulnerability, the love she had been so afraid of.

And maybe, just maybe, she could find happiness on the other side of that fear.

"Thank you," she whispered, her voice filled with gratitude and a newfound sense of peace.

Gabe smiled, the corners of his eyes crinkling in that way she had grown to love. "You don't have to thank me."

But she did. Because in that moment, with the storm outside howling and the lighthouse standing tall, Isabel realized that Gabe had given her more than comfort. He had given her the courage to face herself, to face her past, and to step into her future without fear.

They sat in silence for a long time, their hands intertwined, the weight of their unspoken connection growing stronger with each passing moment. It was a silence filled with understanding, with love, with the promise of what could be.

And as the storm outside raged on, Isabel knew—this was her moment to live. To choose love, not out of fear, but out of hope. To let go of the past and step into the light, just as her mother had once longed to do.

And this time, Isabel wouldn't be afraid to take that step.

13

Chapter 13: A Leap of Faith

The sun filtered through the large windows of the newly renovated space, casting long, warm rays across the floor. The photography studio was modest but full of potential, much like Isabel herself. She stood in the center of the room, hands on her hips, taking in every detail. The walls, painted a soft shade of cream, provided the perfect backdrop for the photos she planned to display. There was a certain serenity in the quiet of the room, yet Isabel's heart beat with a mixture of excitement and doubt.

She had done it—taken the leap.

It was strange, really, how the decision had felt both liberating and terrifying at the same time. Opening the studio was more than just a professional move; it was personal. It was her chance to root herself in the island, to create something of her own after so many years of uncertainty and wandering. But as the day of the grand opening neared, her insecurities crept in, whispering doubts into her mind.

Was this the right choice? Would she be able to make it work? What if she failed?

Isabel sighed, crossing her arms as she surveyed the empty space. The anticipation that had initially fueled her energy was starting to give way to a familiar sense of apprehension. Memories of past decisions—leaving the island, her strained relationship with her father, and the unresolved feelings for Gabe—hovered at the edges of her thoughts.

"Taking risks never felt easy, did it, Mom?" she murmured, glancing toward the framed photograph of her mother that rested on a shelf near the entrance. The photo had been one of the few things she had salvaged from her mother's collection after discovering the truth about her past.

Her mother's love for photography had once been an escape, a way to see the world through a different lens. Isabel had inherited that passion, yet she often wondered if she was capable of honoring it. Her mother had been afraid to fully embrace her desires, and Isabel was determined not to let fear hold her back in the same way.

The bell over the door chimed, interrupting her reverie, and she turned to see Eliza walk in, her face lighting up with a bright smile as she took in the space.

"Wow," Eliza exclaimed, walking slowly through the room, her eyes scanning the walls and the sunlight bouncing off the polished floor. "This place is amazing, Isabel. You've really outdone yourself."

"Thanks," Isabel said softly, trying to match Eliza's enthusiasm. "It's a work in progress."

Eliza stopped in front of her and gave her a knowing look. "What's wrong? I can practically feel the uncertainty radiating off you."

Isabel hesitated, biting her lip as she struggled to put her feelings into words. "I don't know... It's just a lot. I keep thinking, what if this doesn't work? What if I'm not cut out for this?"

Eliza raised an eyebrow, crossing her arms. "Is that the same Isabel who left the city to come back here and find herself? The one who's faced her past, reconnected with Gabe, and made some pretty big decisions along the way?"

Isabel shook her head, chuckling softly. "It's not the same."

"Of course it is," Eliza countered. "You've already done the hard part—taking that first step. You opened the studio because you believe in yourself, and that's huge. Sure, you'll have doubts, but you wouldn't be human if you didn't. The important thing is that you're here. You're doing this."

Isabel let Eliza's words sink in, feeling a sense of comfort wash over her. She had spent so much time worrying about whether or not she was capable, but she had already proven her strength in so many ways. The studio was a reflection of her growth, both personally and professionally. It wasn't just a business; it was a symbol of her courage to embrace change.

"Maybe you're right," Isabel admitted, a small smile tugging at her lips. "I guess I just didn't expect it to feel this scary."

Eliza gave her a playful nudge. "That's because it means something to you. If it didn't, you wouldn't care so much. And believe me, this is going to be amazing. Everyone on the island is talking about it."

Isabel felt a flutter of hope in her chest. The island had always been her home, even when she tried to distance herself from it. Now, with the studio opening, it felt like she was truly part of the community again. She wasn't just a visitor passing through; she was rooted here, building something meaningful.

"I guess it's a leap of faith," Isabel mused, glancing at the photographs she had already hung on the walls—images of the island, the lighthouse, and the vibrant festival lights that had ignited her heart.

Eliza smiled warmly. "And you've got a good net to catch you if you fall. You've got people who care about you. And you've got Gabe."

Isabel's heart skipped a beat at the mention of his name. Gabe had been her anchor, her steady presence through all the uncertainty. Their relationship had deepened since that night at the festival, but even now, there were moments where she wondered if she was ready to fully open herself to him.

"He's been incredible," Isabel admitted softly, her voice carrying a mix of affection and hesitation. "But I don't want to rely on him for everything. This studio, this decision—it has to be mine."

"And it is," Eliza assured her. "But letting someone support you doesn't make you weak. It just makes you human."

Isabel nodded, feeling the weight of her friend's words settle into her heart. She had spent so much of her life guarding herself, afraid of depending on anyone else. But maybe Eliza was right. Maybe part of growing meant allowing others to stand with you, to share in both your triumphs and your struggles.

As they stood together, the bell over the door chimed again, and this time it was Gabe who entered. He hesitated in the doorway, his eyes scanning the room until they landed on Isabel, a soft smile spreading across his face.

"Am I interrupting?" he asked, stepping inside with the kind of easy confidence that always seemed to calm her nerves.

"Not at all," Isabel replied, meeting his gaze with a warmth she couldn't hide.

Gabe approached slowly, his eyes flickering to the photographs on the walls. "The place looks great. You've done an amazing job."

"Thanks," Isabel said, her voice more confident than she felt. "It's starting to feel real."

He nodded, his expression thoughtful. "It's more than real, Isabel. It's you—putting your heart into something and making it happen."

His words struck a chord deep within her, and she realized how true they were. The studio was a manifestation of her journey—of the risks she had taken, the fears she had faced, and the growth she had experienced. It was her leap of faith, and standing there, surrounded by the photographs she had captured, Isabel felt a quiet sense of peace settle over her.

For the first time in a long while, she wasn't running from anything. She wasn't hiding from her past, or from her feelings, or from the future. She was here, fully present, ready to embrace whatever came next.

And as she looked at Gabe, standing there with that steady, patient love in his eyes, she knew—she was ready to embrace him too.

"Are you sure you're okay?" Gabe asked, stepping closer.

Isabel smiled, her doubts finally giving way to clarity. "I am. For the first time in a long time, I really am."

The afternoon sunlight cast a golden hue over the studio, filling the room with a tranquil warmth. Isabel stood by the large window, her gaze sweeping over the island that stretched out before her, its beauty a constant reminder of why she had returned. Gabe's presence was a comforting reassurance, and as he took in the studio's details, Isabel felt a renewed sense of purpose.

"You know," Gabe began, breaking the comfortable silence, "when I first heard you were opening this studio, I had this image in my mind of what it might look like. But seeing it now... it's even better than I imagined."

Isabel turned to face him, her heart swelling with a mixture of pride and vulnerability. "I'm glad you think so. It's been a lot of work. Sometimes I wonder if I've done enough."

Gabe shook his head, his expression sincere. "You've done more than enough. You've created a space that feels like you—warm, inviting, full of life. It's a reflection of your journey."

She could see the genuine admiration in his eyes, and it made her realize how much this venture meant to her. It wasn't just about the studio itself but what it represented: a new beginning, a chance to heal, and an opportunity to connect with others in a meaningful way.

"Thank you," Isabel said softly, her voice tinged with emotion. "It means a lot to hear that."

Gabe took a step closer, his gaze steady. "I mean it. And I'm proud of you for taking this leap. It's not easy to put yourself out there, especially when you've been through so much."

Isabel felt a surge of warmth at his words. She had been so focused on the practicalities and her own insecurities that she hadn't fully appreciated the support she had from Gabe. His belief in her was like a beacon, guiding her through the fog of doubt that had clouded her mind.

As they stood together in the studio, the space filled with the soft glow of the setting sun, Isabel felt a sense of calm wash over her. The decisions she had made, the challenges she had faced, and the support she had received were all leading her to this moment—a moment where she could finally embrace her own dreams.

"I've been thinking a lot about what's next," Isabel said, her voice reflective. "This studio is just the beginning. I want to do more—create a space where people can find beauty and connection, just like I've found here."

Gabe's eyes lit up with encouragement. "That sounds incredible. I know you'll make it happen. You've got the passion and the drive."

She smiled, feeling a surge of determination. "I hope so. It's a lot to take on, but I'm ready. For the first time, I feel like I'm in the right place, doing what I'm meant to do."

As if on cue, the bell over the door chimed again, signaling the arrival of a few early visitors for the studio's soft opening. The anticipation in the air was palpable, and Isabel could feel the excitement bubbling within her.

Gabe looked at her with a reassuring smile. "Are you ready?"

Isabel took a deep breath, her nerves mixing with exhilaration. "As ready as I'll ever be."

Gabe gave her a supportive nod. "Then let's do this."

Together, they welcomed the visitors, and Isabel's heart swelled with gratitude as she observed the reactions to her work. The studio was alive with conversations and laughter, the energy palpable as people admired the photographs and explored the space.

Throughout the evening, Isabel and Gabe moved among the guests, their interactions a blend of warmth and connection. Gabe's presence by her side was a steadying force, his support evident in the way he engaged with the visitors and encouraged Isabel.

As the night wore on and the last guests began to leave, Isabel found a moment of quiet with Gabe by the window. The studio, now empty of visitors, seemed to glow with a soft, serene light.

"I couldn't have done this without you," Isabel said, her voice filled with heartfelt gratitude.

Gabe looked at her, his expression tender. "You did it because you believed in yourself. I just got to be a part of it."

Isabel took his hand, feeling a deep connection that went beyond words. The studio, the photographs, and the shared moments had brought them closer together, and she realized how much he meant to her.

"I'm glad you were here," Isabel said, her eyes meeting his. "I'm glad we're doing this together."

Gabe squeezed her hand gently, a smile spreading across his face. "Me too."

As they stood together in the quiet of the studio, the weight of the day's events settled over them. Isabel felt a profound sense of accomplishment, not just for the success of the studio's opening, but for the personal growth she had achieved. She had faced her fears, embraced her dreams, and found a sense of belonging.

The studio was more than just a space; it was a testament to her journey, her resilience, and her willingness to take a leap of faith. And as she looked at Gabe, standing beside her with unwavering support, she knew that this was just the beginning of a new chapter in her life—one filled with promise, love, and endless possibilities.

The evening wrapped around the studio like a comforting blanket. Isabel felt a mix of exhaustion and elation, a deep-seated satisfaction that came from watching her dreams come to fruition. The soft murmur of guests and the faint echo of their laughter still lingered in the air as she and Gabe tidied up, their movements synchronized and unspoken.

"Looks like the opening was a success," Gabe remarked, his eyes scanning the studio. "You've created something truly special here."

Isabel nodded, her gaze lingering on the photographs that adorned the walls. Each frame was a piece of her journey, a snapshot of her life's most intimate moments. "It's surreal," she admitted. "I've wanted this for so long, and now that it's finally happening, it feels like a dream."

Gabe's gaze softened as he approached her, his expression thoughtful. "It's not a dream. It's reality. And you've earned every bit of it."

A comfortable silence settled between them, punctuated only by the soft clinking of glassware being returned to its place. Isabel's thoughts drifted back to earlier that day, to the moments of doubt and fear she had wrestled with. The decision to open the studio had been fraught with uncertainty, but now, standing here with Gabe by her side, she felt an overwhelming sense of rightness.

"I was so scared," Isabel confessed, her voice barely above a whisper. "Scared that it wouldn't be enough, that I'd be a failure. But seeing everyone's reactions today... it's like I finally took a step towards something real."

Gabe's eyes met hers, his expression a blend of understanding and warmth. "I don't think you ever had to worry about failing. You have a way of making people see the world differently, and that's something special."

Isabel felt a surge of gratitude at his words. "Thank you for believing in me," she said. "For being here, through all the uncertainty."

Gabe smiled, his gaze steady and reassuring. "It's easy to believe in someone like you. You're strong, talented, and incredibly brave. It's been amazing to watch you grow."

As they continued to clean up, the intimacy of their shared space felt more pronounced. The soft light from the studio's lamps cast gentle shadows on the walls, creating a serene atmosphere that seemed to wrap around them like a cocoon. Isabel found herself reflecting on how much had changed since her return to the island, and how much Gabe had come to mean to her.

"So, what's next?" Gabe asked, breaking the silence. "What are your plans for the studio?"

Isabel looked around, her mind racing with possibilities. "I want to create more community events, workshops for aspiring photographers, and maybe even collaborate with local artists. I want this place to be a hub for creativity and connection."

Gabe nodded, his enthusiasm evident. "That sounds incredible. I'm sure it will be a huge success. And I'd love to help out however I can."

Isabel's heart swelled with appreciation at his offer. "I'd really like that. Having your support means a lot to me."

They finished tidying up, the last traces of the opening fading into the night. As the studio grew quiet, Gabe and Isabel stood together by the window, looking out at the twinkling lights of the island. The world outside seemed to hold its breath, as if waiting for the next chapter to unfold.

"You know," Gabe said softly, "I've been thinking a lot about our conversation the other day, about taking risks and following your heart."

Isabel turned to him, curious. "And?"

Gabe's gaze was steady, his expression thoughtful. "I realized that taking risks isn't just about chasing dreams. It's also about being open to new possibilities and allowing yourself to embrace change. You've done that so well."

Isabel felt a flicker of realization at his words. She had been so focused on the practical aspects of her new venture that she hadn't fully acknowledged the emotional journey she had undertaken. The studio was more than just a place—it was a manifestation of her growth, her willingness to confront her fears, and her desire to build a life that was true to herself.

"I guess you're right," she said, her voice tinged with reflection. "It's not just about achieving a goal. It's about the journey and the people you meet along the way."

Gabe's eyes softened with warmth. "And the person you become in the process."

Isabel felt a deep sense of contentment, a realization that her journey had brought her to a place of clarity and purpose. The studio was a symbol of her growth, and Gabe's presence had been an integral part of that process.

As they stood together in the quiet of the studio, Isabel felt a profound connection with Gabe, a bond that had deepened through their shared experiences and conversations. The studio had become a backdrop for their evolving relationship, and she knew that whatever the future held, she was ready to face it with him by her side.

Gabe reached out, taking her hand in his. "You've done something amazing here, Isabel. And I'm excited to see where this journey takes you."

Isabel squeezed his hand gently, a smile of gratitude on her lips. "Thank you. For everything."

Gabe returned her smile, his eyes reflecting the same sense of hope and possibility that Isabel felt. As they stood together, their hands clasped and their hearts aligned, Isabel knew that she had made the right choice. The leap of faith she had taken was not just about opening a studio; it was about embracing her own potential, confronting her past, and finding a future that was filled with promise.

The studio, now bathed in the soft glow of the moonlight, felt like a sanctuary—a place where dreams were realized and connections were made. And as Isabel looked at Gabe, she felt a deep sense of peace, knowing that she was embarking on a new chapter, one that was rich with opportunity and brimming with the potential for love and growth.

The night continued to unfold peacefully, with the soft hum of the city outside the studio's windows. Isabel and Gabe had finished their cleanup, but neither seemed in a hurry to leave. The air between them was charged with an unspoken understanding, a quiet acknowledgment of the significance of the evening.

Isabel moved to the center of the studio, where the array of her photographs continued to tell their stories in the dim light. She traced her fingers lightly over one of her favorite pieces—a black-and-white portrait of an elderly couple holding hands, their love timeless and evident. It had been a labor of love, capturing the essence of a bond that spanned decades.

"Looking at this," Gabe said, his voice soft as he approached her, "it's clear how much your work means to you. You've captured something truly profound here."

Isabel glanced at him, her eyes reflecting a mix of pride and vulnerability. "I've always believed that photography is more than just taking pictures. It's about capturing moments that reveal something deeper about the people and the world around us."

Gabe nodded, his gaze lingering on the photograph. "And you've done that so beautifully. It's like you've given these moments a voice, a chance to be seen and appreciated."

Isabel's heart swelled with gratitude at his words. She had poured so much of herself into her work, and it was comforting to know that others saw its value. "Thank you," she said softly. "Your support means a lot to me. More than I can say."

Gabe took a step closer, his eyes searching hers. "Isabel, I've been thinking a lot about what you said the other day, about how taking risks can lead to unexpected places. I realized that this journey you're on—opening the studio, following your dreams—it's not just about achieving something tangible. It's about the person you're becoming along the way."

Isabel's breath caught in her throat as she processed his words. They resonated with her deeply, echoing the internal struggles and triumphs she had experienced. "I never really thought about it that way," she admitted. "I've been so focused on the end result that I didn't fully appreciate the journey itself."

Gabe's expression softened, his eyes filled with a mix of affection and encouragement. "Sometimes, the journey is the most important part. It's where we discover who we are and what we truly want."

As they stood together, the closeness between them felt almost tangible. Isabel could sense the depth of Gabe's understanding and the sincerity of his feelings. She realized that their connection had grown stronger through their shared experiences and conversations, and that their bond was becoming something more meaningful.

The studio, with its soft lighting and the remnants of the evening's festivities, felt like a sacred space—a place where vulnerabilities were shared and dreams were nurtured. Isabel found herself reflecting on her own transformation, the fears she had overcome, and the hopes she had embraced.

"I've been thinking a lot about what you said about taking risks," Isabel said, her voice steady but emotional. "It's not just about following a dream. It's about opening yourself up to possibilities and allowing yourself to grow."

Gabe's gaze was unwavering, his expression filled with warmth. "You've done that, Isabel. You've taken a leap of faith, and it's led you to something truly amazing. I'm proud of you."

The sincerity in Gabe's voice touched Isabel deeply. She had spent so long navigating her own uncertainties, and hearing his support was a balm to her soul. "I couldn't have done it without you," she said, her voice filled with genuine appreciation. "Your support and belief in me have been invaluable."

Gabe reached out, gently cupping her face with his hands. His touch was tender, his eyes searching hers for a deeper connection.

"I'm here for you, Isabel. Not just as a friend, but as someone who cares deeply about you. I want to be a part of your journey, whatever that may look like."

The intensity of the moment was palpable, and Isabel felt her heart open to the possibilities that lay ahead. She realized that her journey was not just about her personal growth, but also about the connections she had made along the way—connections that had the potential to become something even more profound.

As they stood together, their hands intertwined and their hearts aligned, Isabel felt a sense of clarity and peace. The studio, with its quiet ambiance and the lingering warmth of the evening, was a symbol of her journey and the new beginnings that awaited her.

Gabe's presence was a steadying force in her life, and she knew that whatever challenges lay ahead, she would face them with him by her side. The leap of faith she had taken had led her to a place of fulfillment and hope, and she was ready to embrace the future with an open heart.

As the night deepened and the city lights twinkled outside the studio, Isabel and Gabe stood together, their hearts brimming with anticipation for the journey ahead. The studio had become more than just a place of creative expression—it was a testament to their growth, their connection, and the possibilities that lay before them.

In the quiet of the studio, with the moon casting a gentle glow over their intertwined hands, Isabel felt a profound sense of peace. The leap of faith she had taken had brought her to a place of clarity and purpose, and she was ready to embrace the future with hope and excitement.

As the evening drew to a close and the last traces of the opening faded into memory, Isabel and Gabe shared a moment of quiet reflection, their hearts aligned and their dreams intertwined. The journey ahead was filled with promise, and together, they were ready to face whatever came their way.

The night deepened, casting long shadows over the studio's floor. The gentle hum of the city outside felt like a distant lullaby, and the soft light from the street lamps filtered through the windows, creating a tranquil ambiance.

Isabel and Gabe remained in the studio, their conversation gradually tapering off into a comfortable silence. Gabe's words about the journey resonated with Isabel, and she found herself reflecting on the weight of their meaning. The photographs on the walls seemed to echo her internal journey, each one a testament to her growth and the risks she had taken.

Isabel turned her attention back to the photographs, her fingers grazing the edges of the frames. She stopped at one of her favorites, a candid shot of a young couple dancing in the rain. The raw emotion in their expressions reminded her of the vulnerability and joy that came with embracing life's uncertainties.

Gabe approached her, his footsteps quiet against the wooden floor. "This one," he said softly, pointing to the photograph. "It's incredible. You've captured something really special here."

Isabel smiled, her gaze still fixed on the photograph. "I love this one too. It was one of those spontaneous moments where everything just felt right. I didn't plan it, didn't stage it—just let the moment unfold."

Gabe's eyes lingered on her with a hint of admiration. "Sometimes the best moments are the ones that happen naturally. I think that's what makes your work so powerful. You capture the essence of what it means to be alive."

The sincerity in his voice made Isabel's heart swell. It was clear that Gabe saw more than just the surface; he understood the depth and the effort that went into each photograph. His support and appreciation meant more to her than she could express.

"I've been thinking a lot about what you said earlier," Isabel admitted, turning to face him. "About the journey and the risk. It's strange, but this studio—this leap of faith—it's felt like a way to reconnect with who I am. I've been so focused on the end goal that I forgot to appreciate the steps it took to get here."

Gabe nodded, his expression thoughtful. "It's easy to get caught up in the destination and forget about the journey. But sometimes, the journey itself is where we find our true selves. It's where we grow, learn, and discover what really matters."

Isabel's gaze met Gabe's, and for a moment, the world outside the studio seemed to fade away. She felt a deep sense of connection with him, a shared understanding that transcended words. It was as if their conversations and experiences had created a bridge between them, leading to a place of mutual respect and affection.

"Gabe," Isabel began, her voice trembling slightly with emotion, "I've been through so much over the past few months. Returning to the island, confronting my past, and finally taking this step with the studio—it's been overwhelming. And through it all, your support has been a constant source of strength for me."

Gabe took her hand gently, his touch warm and reassuring. "I'm glad I could be here for you, Isabel. You've shown so much courage and resilience. It's inspiring to see how you've faced your fears and embraced this new chapter in your life."

Their fingers intertwined, and Isabel felt a surge of warmth and comfort. The connection between them was undeniable, and she realized that Gabe had become a crucial part of her journey. His presence had been a guiding light, helping her navigate the complexities of her emotions and decisions.

As the evening continued to unfold, Isabel and Gabe found themselves drawn closer together. The studio, with its soft lighting and the remnants of the celebration, felt like a sanctuary—a place where they could be their true selves without pretense.

Isabel's mind wandered back to the photograph she had been admiring earlier, and she realized that it wasn't just a representation of a fleeting moment; it was a reflection of the deeper emotions she had been experiencing. The raw vulnerability, the joy, and the spontaneity captured in the image were all part of her own journey.

Gabe's gaze followed her thoughts, his eyes filled with understanding. "It's amazing how art can capture such profound emotions. Your photographs are a testament to your journey, your growth, and your ability to see beauty in the world."

Isabel nodded, her heart full. "Thank you, Gabe. Your words mean so much to me. I think it's time for me to fully embrace this new chapter, to let go of the doubts and fears, and to move forward with an open heart."

Gabe's smile was warm and encouraging. "I believe in you, Isabel. You've already accomplished so much, and I have no doubt that you'll continue to find success and fulfillment in everything you do."

As the night drew to a close, the studio felt like a haven of possibility. Isabel and Gabe stood together, their hands still entwined, their hearts aligned. The leap of faith Isabel had taken had led her to a place of clarity and hope, and she was ready to embrace whatever came next with confidence and optimism.

In the quiet of the studio, with the soft glow of the city lights filtering through the windows, Isabel felt a profound sense of peace. The journey she had embarked upon was not just about achieving her dreams but about discovering her true self and connecting with the people who mattered most.

Gabe's presence was a constant source of support and encouragement, and Isabel knew that with him by her side, she could face any challenge that came her way. The future was filled with possibilities, and she was ready to embrace it with an open heart.

As they shared a final moment of quiet reflection, Isabel and Gabe knew that their connection had deepened in ways they hadn't anticipated. The studio, with its gentle ambiance and the memories of the evening, was a symbol of their shared journey—a journey filled with hope, growth, and the promise of new beginnings.

With the night drawing to a close and the city outside continuing to hum with life, Isabel felt a renewed sense of purpose and excitement. The leap of faith she had taken had brought her to a place of fulfillment and joy, and she was ready to embrace the future with confidence and grace.

As the last traces of the evening faded into memory, Isabel and Gabe stood together, their hearts aligned and their dreams intertwined. The journey ahead was filled with promise, and together, they were ready to face whatever came their way.

The city lights flickered through the windows, casting a soft glow across the studio. Isabel and Gabe stood in a comfortable silence, their shared moments of vulnerability and reflection hanging in the air like a fragile promise. The evening had brought them closer, and as Isabel looked around the studio, she realized that this place—this studio—had become a symbol of her journey and her leap of faith.

Isabel walked over to the window and looked out at the cityscape, her mind racing with thoughts and emotions. The familiar hustle of the city seemed distant now, replaced by a sense of calm and clarity she hadn't felt in a long time. Gabe joined her, standing close but not too close, respecting her space as she processed her thoughts.

"You know," Isabel began softly, her voice barely above a whisper, "I never imagined I'd feel this way about the studio. I thought it would just be a place where I could do what I love, but it's become so much more."

Gabe turned his gaze to her, his expression thoughtful. "It's amazing how places can take on such personal significance. Sometimes, what we think is just a step toward something bigger turns out to be a whole journey in itself."

Isabel nodded, her eyes fixed on the distant city lights. "It's true. I've been so focused on making this studio a success that I didn't realize it was also a way for me to reconnect with myself. It's like I'm rediscovering parts of me that I lost along the way."

Gabe's gaze was warm and understanding. "It's incredible to see how far you've come, Isabel. Your art reflects your inner journey, and it's clear that this studio is a reflection of who you are and what you've been through."

The silence that followed was filled with a deep sense of understanding. Gabe's support and encouragement had been a guiding force for Isabel, and she was grateful for his presence in her life. She turned to him, her eyes searching his for the reassurance she needed.

"Gabe, I've been thinking a lot about the future. About what's next. I feel like this studio is just the beginning of something new, but I'm still figuring out what that looks like."

Gabe took her hand in his, his touch gentle and reassuring. "It's okay to not have everything figured out. Sometimes, the best way to find your path is to take things one step at a time. You've already proven that you have the courage to take risks and embrace change. Trust yourself, and the path will reveal itself."

Isabel's heart swelled with emotion at his words. Gabe's faith in her was a powerful motivator, and she felt a renewed sense of purpose. She squeezed his hand, grateful for his support and the way he made her feel seen and understood.

"You're right," Isabel said, her voice steady and determined. "I've come this far by taking risks and embracing the unknown. I can't stop now. There's so much more I want to do, and I'm ready to face whatever comes next."

Gabe smiled, his eyes filled with admiration. "I have no doubt that you'll achieve everything you set your mind to. You're incredibly talented and resilient, and I'm honored to be a part of your journey."

As the night wore on, Isabel and Gabe continued to talk, their conversation flowing easily and naturally. They discussed their dreams, their fears, and their hopes for the future. The studio, with its warm ambiance and the glow of the city lights, felt like a safe haven where they could be their true selves.

Isabel felt a deep sense of contentment and peace as she talked with Gabe. The studio had become a symbol of her growth, and the support and encouragement she received from him were invaluable. It was clear that their connection had grown stronger, and she felt a profound sense of gratitude for his presence in her life.

Eventually, their conversation slowed, and a comfortable silence settled between them. Isabel looked around the studio, taking in the photographs and the memories they represented. She felt a sense of fulfillment and joy, knowing that she had taken a significant step toward realizing her dreams.

Gabe's presence was a constant source of support, and Isabel knew that with him by her side, she could face any challenge that came her way. The future was filled with possibilities, and she was ready to embrace it with an open heart.

As the evening drew to a close, Isabel and Gabe shared a final moment of quiet reflection. The studio, with its soft lighting and the memories of the night, was a symbol of their shared journey—a journey filled with hope, growth, and the promise of new beginnings.

Isabel felt a renewed sense of purpose as she stood with Gabe, their hands still intertwined. The leap of faith she had taken had brought her to a place of fulfillment and joy, and she was ready to embrace the future with confidence and grace.

The city outside continued to hum with life, but inside the studio, Isabel felt a profound sense of peace. The journey she had embarked upon was not just about achieving her dreams but about discovering her true self and connecting with the people who mattered most.

With the night growing darker and the city lights shimmering in the distance, Isabel and Gabe stood together, their hearts aligned and their dreams intertwined. The future was filled with promise, and together, they were ready to face whatever came their way.

As they prepared to leave the studio, Isabel felt a sense of excitement and anticipation. The path ahead was uncertain, but with Gabe by her side and her heart open to new possibilities, she was ready to embrace whatever the future held.

With one last look around the studio, Isabel took a deep breath and stepped into the night, ready to face the next chapter of her journey with confidence and hope.

The first light of dawn crept through the studio's windows, casting a soft glow over Isabel as she sat at her desk, the earlier night's conversations with Gabe replaying in her mind. The studio, now filled with early morning light, seemed even more alive, buzzing with the promise of new beginnings. Isabel felt a mix of excitement and trepidation as she considered the path she was about to embark on.

As she sipped her coffee, her gaze wandered to the corner where she had placed a series of photographs she had taken over the past few weeks. Each image represented a step in her journey, capturing moments of growth, pain, and joy. She picked up one photo, a portrait of an elderly woman with kind eyes and a serene smile, and traced the lines on the woman's face with her fingers. This photograph, in particular, seemed to encapsulate the essence of what Isabel was striving for in her work—authenticity, depth, and a connection to the stories people held within them.

A soft knock on the door startled her from her reverie. Gabe stood in the doorway, his expression a mix of curiosity and concern. "Morning, Isabel," he said, his voice gentle. "I didn't want to interrupt, but I brought some breakfast. Thought you might like some company."

Isabel's face lit up with a smile. "Thank you, Gabe. I could use a little company and a good breakfast. Come on in."

Gabe entered the studio, carrying a small bag from a local bakery. As he set the bag down on the table, Isabel noticed the familiar scent of freshly baked pastries filling the room. It was a comforting aroma, one that seemed to ground her in the present moment.

Gabe unwrapped the pastries and placed them on a plate. "I figured we could take a break from all the heavy thinking and just enjoy a simple breakfast together."

Isabel appreciated the gesture more than she could express. They sat down at the small table, the morning sun casting a warm glow over them. As they ate, their conversation shifted to lighter topics—favorite childhood memories, recent hobbies, and the quirks of the neighborhood. It was a welcome change from the intense emotions of the previous days.

As they talked, Isabel felt a sense of ease she hadn't experienced in a long time. Gabe's presence had a calming effect on her, and she realized how much she valued his companionship. It wasn't just about his support for her professional endeavors, but also about the way he made her feel seen and understood.

After breakfast, Gabe helped Isabel tidy up the studio, their movements in sync and their conversations flowing effortlessly. As they worked, Gabe's phone buzzed with a text message. He glanced at it and then looked up at Isabel with a thoughtful expression.

"I have to run an errand this morning," Gabe said, hesitating slightly. "I'll be back later. Do you need anything before I go?"

Isabel shook her head, her smile warm. "No, I'm all set. Thanks for breakfast and for being here, Gabe. I appreciate it more than you know."

Gabe's eyes softened, and he gave her a reassuring smile. "Anytime, Isabel. I'll see you later."

As Gabe left the studio, Isabel returned to her desk, her thoughts swirling with a mix of excitement and nervousness. The studio, with its warm, inviting light, seemed like a beacon of hope and possibility. Isabel knew that opening it to the public was a significant step, but it was also a chance to fully embrace her passion and connect with others in a meaningful way.

She glanced at the photograph of the elderly woman once more, feeling a renewed sense of purpose. The image captured a depth of character that Isabel aspired to bring out in her own work. She had always been drawn to the stories people carried with them, and she wanted her studio to be a place where those stories could be told and cherished.

With a deep breath, Isabel started to prepare for the studio's grand opening. She spent the morning organizing her portfolio, ensuring that each photograph was displayed in a way that highlighted its unique qualities. She also took the time to set up a small reception area where guests could feel welcomed and comfortable.

As the hours passed, Isabel's anticipation grew. The grand opening was just a few hours away, and she was eager to see how the community would respond to her new venture. She felt a mix of excitement and anxiety, but she reminded herself of the journey that had brought her to this point.

By midday, the studio was ready. Isabel stood at the entrance, looking around at the space she had worked so hard to create. The walls were adorned with her photographs, each one telling a different story. The reception area was set up with refreshments and information about her work. The studio was a reflection of her passion and dedication, and she felt proud of what she had accomplished.

As she waited for the first guests to arrive, Isabel took a moment to reflect on her journey. She thought about her decision to return to the island, her reconnection with Gabe, the revelations about her mother, and the growth she had experienced along the way. Each step had brought her closer to understanding herself and her purpose.

The sound of footsteps approaching the studio door snapped Isabel out of her reverie. She took a deep breath and smiled, ready to welcome the guests who would be the first to experience her new venture. The grand opening was a chance to share her work with others, to connect with the community, and to take another step forward in her journey of self-discovery.

As the door opened and the first guests walked in, Isabel felt a surge of excitement. She greeted each person warmly, eager to share her passion for photography and to learn about their own stories. The studio quickly filled with the hum of conversation and the clinking of glasses, and Isabel felt a sense of fulfillment as she watched her vision come to life.

The evening continued with a steady flow of guests, and Isabel found herself engaged in meaningful conversations about her work and the stories behind her photographs. Each interaction reinforced her belief in the importance of capturing and sharing the human experience, and she felt a deep sense of connection with those who visited the studio.

As the night drew to a close, Isabel stood by the door, watching as the last guests left with smiles and words of appreciation. The studio had been a success, and she felt a profound sense of accomplishment. Gabe had returned later in the evening, and they had shared a quiet moment together, reflecting on the day's events.

With the studio now closed for the night, Isabel and Gabe sat together, their earlier conversation about dreams and aspirations taking on a new meaning. Isabel felt a deep sense of gratitude for Gabe's support and for the opportunities that lay ahead. The leap of faith she had taken had brought her to this moment of fulfillment, and she was excited to see where her journey would lead next.

As they sat in the quiet of the studio, Isabel realized that the path she had chosen was not just about achieving her dreams but about embracing her true self and connecting with others in a meaningful way. The studio was a symbol of her growth and her commitment to her passion, and she felt a renewed sense of purpose and hope.

With the night growing darker, Isabel and Gabe shared a final moment of reflection. The studio, with its warm glow and the echoes of the day's conversations, felt like a safe and inspiring space. Isabel knew that with Gabe by her side and her heart open to new possibilities, she was ready to face whatever the future held.

As they prepared to leave, Isabel took one last look around the studio, her heart filled with a sense of accomplishment and anticipation. The journey had been challenging, but it had also been incredibly rewarding. With a deep breath and a smile, Isabel stepped into the night, ready to embrace the next chapter of her journey with confidence and hope.

The morning of the grand opening was a blend of anticipation and nerves. Isabel had spent the early hours fine-tuning every detail in the studio, ensuring everything was perfect. She had chosen a classic, elegant setup for the reception area, with soft music playing in the background to create a warm, inviting atmosphere. Her heart raced with excitement as she prepared to welcome the community into a space that had become a reflection of her inner journey.

By mid-afternoon, Isabel was ready. She stood by the entrance, taking one last look around the studio. The walls were adorned with her most cherished photographs—images that captured the essence of human emotions and stories. Each photograph was thoughtfully framed and arranged to create a narrative that wove through the room. The reception table was set with an array of refreshments, and a guestbook lay open for visitors to leave their thoughts and feedback.

As the first guests began to arrive, Isabel felt a surge of both pride and anxiety. She greeted each person with a warm smile, her eyes scanning the room as she tried to gauge their reactions. The initial trickle of visitors quickly turned into a steady stream, and Isabel found herself engaging in conversations about her work and the stories behind each photograph.

One of the first guests, Mrs. Harrington, a longtime resident of the island, took a moment to express her appreciation. "Isabel, this is truly remarkable. Your photographs capture something so profound. It's like you've managed to freeze a moment in time and give it new life."

Isabel felt a rush of gratitude. "Thank you, Mrs. Harrington. That means a lot to me. I've always believed in the power of photography to tell stories and connect people."

As the afternoon turned into evening, the studio buzzed with energy. Guests wandered through the space, stopping to admire individual pieces and share their own stories. Isabel found herself caught up in a whirl of conversations, each interaction reinforcing her belief in the power of human connection.

Among the guests was a young couple, Lily and Mark, who had recently moved to the island. They were captivated by a photograph of a sunset over the ocean, the colors blending into a breathtaking display of nature's beauty. "This one really speaks to us," Lily said, her eyes lingering on the image. "It reminds us of our own journey and the new beginnings we've found here."

Isabel smiled, touched by their response. "I'm glad it resonates with you. That was one of the first photographs I took after returning to the island. It symbolizes the fresh start I was hoping for."

As the evening progressed, Gabe reappeared, having completed his errands. He stood back for a moment, observing the scene with a look of satisfaction. Isabel noticed him and made her way over, her heart warming at the sight of his supportive presence.

"You made it back," Isabel said, her voice tinged with relief. "How was your errand?"

Gabe shrugged, a playful grin on his face. "It went well. I've been looking forward to this all day. I wanted to be here for the grand opening and to see how it all came together."

They spent some time together, moving through the studio and chatting with guests. Gabe's presence was a comforting constant, and Isabel found herself grateful for his unwavering support. As they stood together, watching the guests enjoy the space, Isabel felt a deep sense of accomplishment.

Later in the evening, the studio quieted down as the final guests departed. Isabel and Gabe were left alone, the room now a calm sanctuary illuminated by the soft glow of the studio lights. Isabel took a deep breath, letting the quietude wash over her.

"You know," Gabe said, breaking the silence, "I'm really proud of you. This place is more than just a studio. It's a testament to your journey and your passion."

Isabel looked at him, her eyes reflecting a mix of emotion and gratitude. "Thank you, Gabe. I couldn't have done this without your support. It means the world to me."

Gabe's gaze softened, and he reached out to gently touch her arm. "I'm glad to have been a part of it. You've created something truly special here."

As they stood together, Isabel felt a deep sense of contentment. The grand opening had been a success, and the studio had come alive with the energy and stories of the people who had visited. She knew that this was just the beginning, and she was excited to see where this new chapter would lead.

With the last of the guests gone and the studio now quiet, Isabel and Gabe began to clean up. The process felt almost ceremonial, a way to close the chapter on this significant day and prepare for the future. Isabel moved through the space with a sense of purpose, each action a reflection of her commitment to her craft and her vision.

As they worked, Gabe noticed Isabel's thoughtful expression. "What's on your mind?" he asked.

Isabel paused, her hands stilling as she considered her response. "I've been thinking about everything that led up to this moment. It's been a long journey, and there were times when I doubted myself. But now, seeing how everything has come together, I feel like I'm finally where I'm meant to be."

Gabe nodded, his expression thoughtful. "It's incredible to see how much you've grown and how far you've come. This studio is a reflection of your resilience and your passion."

Isabel smiled, feeling a surge of warmth at Gabe's words. "Thank you. I'm excited about what the future holds and the opportunities this studio will bring."

As they finished tidying up, the studio began to feel like an extension of Isabel's dreams and aspirations. The photographs on the walls, the carefully arranged reception area, and the warm, inviting atmosphere all spoke to the journey she had undertaken and the new beginnings she was embracing.

With the studio now ready for its next chapter, Isabel and Gabe shared a quiet moment of reflection. They stood together by the entrance, looking out at the serene night sky. The stars sparkled overhead, a reminder of the endless possibilities that lay ahead.

Isabel took a deep breath, feeling a sense of peace and fulfillment. "Thank you for being here with me tonight, Gabe. Your support has meant more to me than I can express."

Gabe smiled, his gaze tender. "I'm just glad to be part of your journey. I believe in you, Isabel, and I know you're going to do amazing things with this studio."

As they prepared to leave, Isabel felt a renewed sense of purpose and excitement for the future. The studio was a symbol of her growth, her passions, and her commitment to connecting with others through her work. With Gabe by her side and her heart open to new possibilities, she was ready to embrace whatever lay ahead.

The night air was crisp and refreshing as they stepped outside, and Isabel felt a surge of hope and anticipation. The grand opening was just the beginning, and she was excited to see where her journey would lead. With a final glance back at the studio, Isabel and Gabe walked into the night, ready to face the future with confidence and optimism.

As Isabel and Gabe walked down the quiet street, the festive lights from the studio reflected softly on the cobblestones. The night air was filled with a gentle breeze, carrying the crisp, cool scent of the ocean from beyond the island. The serene atmosphere was a stark contrast to the bustling energy of the evening's event.

Gabe broke the silence, his voice soft but earnest. "You know, I've been thinking a lot about the studio and everything it means for you."

Isabel looked over at him, sensing the gravity in his tone. "What do you mean?"

Gabe took a deep breath, choosing his words carefully. "It's not just a place where you showcase your photography. It's a place where you've allowed yourself to heal and grow. I've seen how much effort you've put into making it a reflection of who you are."

Isabel's heart swelled with gratitude at his words. She had always appreciated Gabe's ability to see beyond the surface, and his understanding of her journey meant a lot. "It hasn't always been easy," she admitted. "There were times when I was so unsure about everything—whether this was the right path or if I was doing the right thing."

Gabe nodded, his gaze steady and comforting. "It's natural to have doubts. But what's important is that you kept going, even when it was tough. And look where you are now."

They continued walking in companionable silence, the warmth of their conversation mingling with the chill of the night. Gabe's presence felt like a steadying force, grounding Isabel as she navigated her mixed emotions. The weight of her decisions and the journey that led to this moment had been immense, and having someone who understood and supported her made a significant difference.

As they reached a small, picturesque park overlooking the harbor, they stopped to take in the view. The water sparkled under the moonlight, and the distant sound of waves gently lapping against the shore created a calming backdrop.

Isabel took a seat on a nearby bench, and Gabe joined her. The quiet of the park was a soothing balm after the evening's excitement. Isabel's mind raced with thoughts of the future, her new responsibilities, and the changes she had embraced.

Gabe turned to her, his expression thoughtful. "Isabel, do you ever wonder about the paths not taken? The choices we didn't make and how they might have shaped our lives differently?"

Isabel considered his question, her gaze fixed on the shimmering water. "Sometimes," she replied slowly. "I think about the life I might have had if I hadn't returned to the island. But then I remind myself that I can't change the past. What matters is where I am now and what I choose to do with it."

Gabe's eyes were filled with understanding. "It's easy to get caught up in what-ifs, but the important thing is that you're here now. You're building something meaningful and creating a space where people can connect with your work."

Isabel felt a surge of appreciation for Gabe's perspective. His words echoed her own realizations, reinforcing her sense of purpose. "I think you're right," she said, her voice steady. "It's about making the most of the present and shaping the future based on what I've learned."

Gabe reached over, taking her hand in his. The simple gesture was filled with warmth and support. "And you're doing just that. I'm proud of you, Isabel."

The intimacy of the moment was profound. Isabel looked at Gabe, her emotions laid bare. She had come to rely on him as a source of strength and encouragement, and his unwavering belief in her was something she cherished deeply.

"Thank you, Gabe," Isabel said, her voice filled with emotion. "For everything. For being here tonight and for believing in me."

Gabe smiled, his expression tender. "It's been an honor to be part of your journey. I believe in you not just as an artist, but as a person who's capable of incredible things."

The night wore on, and the park's peaceful ambiance provided a perfect backdrop for their conversation. The distant lights of the island's town twinkled like stars, and the gentle rustling of leaves in the breeze created a serene atmosphere.

As they sat together, Isabel felt a sense of clarity and resolve. The grand opening had been a pivotal moment, but it was also a stepping stone to the future. With Gabe's support and the community's positive response, she felt ready to embrace the challenges and opportunities that lay ahead.

Eventually, the park began to empty as the night grew late. Isabel and Gabe rose from the bench, their hands still intertwined. The connection between them felt stronger than ever, a testament to the bond they had formed.

"Shall we head back?" Gabe asked, his voice gentle.

Isabel nodded, feeling a sense of peace. "Yes, let's go."

As they walked back toward the studio, Isabel felt a renewed sense of optimism. The path ahead was still uncertain, but she was ready to face it with courage and determination. The studio was more than just a place; it was a symbol of her journey, her growth, and her commitment to making a difference through her work.

With Gabe by her side and a heart full of hope, Isabel was prepared to step into the future with confidence. The night sky stretched above them, a canvas of possibilities waiting to be explored. And as they walked together, Isabel knew that she was ready to embrace whatever came next, fueled by her passion, her dreams, and the unwavering support of those she cherished.

14

Chapter 14: The Final Test

The days following Isabel's decision to open her photography studio were filled with a whirlwind of activity and emotion. The studio was finally ready, a testament to her dedication and passion. Yet, despite the excitement, Isabel felt a gnawing uncertainty that shadowed her every step.

Gabe had been a constant presence, his support unwavering. But lately, there had been a subtle shift in him. He seemed more distant, and Isabel could sense an emotional wall forming between them. It wasn't overt or obvious—Gabe's smile was still warm, his gestures still kind. Yet, something was different, and Isabel couldn't shake the feeling that he was pulling away.

One evening, as the sun dipped below the horizon, casting a golden glow over the island, Isabel and Gabe found themselves sitting on the porch of the studio. The new sign, "Isabel Marlowe Photography," hung proudly above the entrance, illuminated by soft, welcoming lights. The studio was a beacon of her dreams and hard work, but the tension between them cast a shadow over the joy.

Gabe was lost in thought, his gaze fixed on the distant horizon. Isabel watched him, her heart heavy with the weight of unspoken words. She knew something was troubling him but wasn't sure how to address it.

Breaking the silence, Isabel said softly, "Gabe, is everything okay?"

He turned to her, a fleeting smile crossing his lips. "Yeah, everything's fine. Just been a lot on my mind lately."

Isabel's worry deepened. "You've seemed distant these past few days. I feel like there's something you're not telling me."

Gabe sighed, running a hand through his hair. "It's not about you, Isabel. It's just... I've been thinking about us, about everything."

Isabel's heart sank. "What do you mean?"

Gabe hesitated, searching for the right words. "I've been so focused on supporting you and being there for you, but I guess I didn't realize how much I was holding back. It's just... seeing you build this studio, seeing you so committed to your work, it's amazing. But it also makes me think about the future and where I fit into it."

Isabel's eyes widened with concern. "Are you saying you don't want to be a part of it?"

Gabe shook his head quickly. "No, that's not it. It's just... I'm scared, Isabel. Scared that you'll eventually leave again, that you'll get swept up in everything and forget about us."

The vulnerability in his voice took Isabel by surprise. She had never seen Gabe so open about his fears. The realization that his emotional distance was rooted in his own insecurities hit her hard.

"Gabe," she said softly, reaching out to him, "I never wanted to make you feel like you were second to anything. My decision to open the studio, it's not about leaving or abandoning what we have. It's about creating something meaningful and making a life here—together."

Gabe's eyes met hers, filled with a mixture of hope and apprehension. "I know you're committed, Isabel. I just... I need to know if we're in this for the long haul. I need to know that I'm not just a temporary part of your journey."

Isabel took a deep breath, her heart aching at his words. She understood his fears now, and she knew she had to address them honestly. "Gabe, I've been afraid too. Afraid that I might not be able to balance everything, afraid that I might let you down. But what I've realized is that this studio, this new chapter in my life, it's not meant to pull us apart. It's meant to be part of our shared future."

Gabe's expression softened, though the tension remained. "But how can I be sure?"

Isabel took his hand in hers, her touch tender and reassuring. "By making a promise to you, and showing you through my actions. I'm not asking you to be a part of my dreams just because of this studio. I'm asking you to be a part of my life, my journey, all of it."

Gabe's eyes searched hers, seeking the sincerity he needed to believe. Isabel could feel the weight of his doubts pressing down on her, but she remained steady. This was the moment to prove that their relationship was more than just a series of coincidences and temporary fixes.

"I want to be with you, Gabe," Isabel said, her voice unwavering. "I want us to build a future together, to face our fears and dreams side by side. If you're willing to take that leap with me, I promise I'll do everything in my power to make it worth it."

Gabe's eyes glistened with emotion as he absorbed her words. The silence between them was charged with a profound sense of understanding and hope. Slowly, he reached out and drew her into a gentle embrace. The warmth of his body against hers was a balm to her anxious heart.

"I want that too," Gabe murmured against her hair. "I want us to build something together, to make it real."

Isabel felt a surge of relief and joy as she held him. The fears and doubts that had clouded their relationship seemed to dissipate in the embrace of their shared commitment. They were both taking a leap of faith, but it was one they were ready to make together.

As they pulled back slightly, Gabe's gaze was filled with renewed hope. "Let's take this one step at a time," he suggested. "We'll face whatever comes our way, together."

Isabel nodded, her heart swelling with gratitude and love. "Together," she echoed.

The night was peaceful, the stars twinkling overhead as they stood together on the porch. The studio, now fully open and vibrant, seemed to glow with the promise of new beginnings. Isabel felt a renewed sense of purpose and connection, knowing that her future with Gabe was not just a possibility but a reality they were both committed to.

They lingered on the porch, savoring the quiet moments of togetherness. The final test had been met with honesty and vulnerability, and it had strengthened the bond between them. Isabel knew that their journey was far from over, but with Gabe by her side and a clear sense of direction, she felt ready to embrace whatever came next.

As they finally turned to go inside, Isabel looked back at the studio, its lights casting a warm glow in the night. The path ahead was filled with challenges and opportunities, but she was no longer facing them alone. With Gabe's unwavering support and the strength of their shared dreams, Isabel felt a deep sense of contentment and anticipation for the future.

Together, they stepped into the studio, ready to face the next chapter of their lives with courage and love. The journey ahead was theirs to explore, and Isabel was prepared to embrace it with open arms and an open heart.

The studio was quiet, save for the soft hum of the air conditioning and the occasional creak of the wooden floorboards. Isabel and Gabe entered the space, and she could feel the palpable shift in their relationship, a renewed sense of connection mixed with lingering uncertainties.

Isabel moved toward the large window overlooking the street, the moonlight casting a serene glow across the room. She paused to admire the view, her thoughts a whirl of the emotions from their conversation. Gabe followed her, his footsteps tentative, as if he were still unsure about the path forward.

"Do you remember the first time we talked about this place?" Isabel asked, breaking the silence. Her voice was soft but carried a note of reflection.

Gabe nodded, stepping closer. "Yeah, you were so excited, so full of dreams. I was just trying to keep up with your enthusiasm."

Isabel turned to face him, her eyes searching his for the reassurance she desperately needed. "I was so sure then, so confident. And now, I still am, but I'm also afraid."

Gabe's expression softened as he approached her, reaching out to gently take her hands in his. "Afraid of what?"

"Afraid of letting you down," Isabel confessed. "Afraid that this dream, this new chapter, might come between us. I want it so much, but I don't want it to overshadow what we have."

Gabe's grip tightened slightly, and he looked deeply into her eyes. "Isabel, I know this studio is important to you. And it should be. It's a part of who you are and who you want to be. But so am I. And I need you to understand that supporting you doesn't mean I'm any less part of your life."

Isabel's heart ached at his words. She could see now that Gabe's fears were not just about their future, but about his own place within it. He had been trying to give her space to pursue her dreams, but in doing so, he had created a distance that he wasn't comfortable with.

"I've been so focused on making this work," Isabel said, her voice trembling slightly. "I didn't realize how much I was unintentionally pushing you away."

Gabe's thumb brushed against her knuckles, a tender gesture of affection and understanding. "It's not about blame, Isabel. It's about us figuring out how to make everything fit together. I want to be part of your dreams, not just as a supporter, but as a partner."

Isabel nodded, feeling a mix of relief and resolve. "Then let's work on that. Let's find a way to balance it all. I need you to be honest with me, and I promise to do the same."

Gabe's eyes held a trace of gratitude. "I can do that. I want to do that. I want us to be on the same page, facing the future together."

They shared a moment of silence, the weight of their conversation settling into a quiet understanding. The room around them seemed to breathe with a new sense of possibility. Isabel felt a renewed connection with Gabe, a bond strengthened by their willingness to confront their fears and uncertainties.

As they stood together, the soft moonlight bathing the studio in a gentle glow, Isabel realized how much she had grown. The journey had been fraught with challenges, but it had also been filled with moments of profound connection and self-discovery.

Gabe's hand found hers again, and he drew her close. "How about we take a walk?" he suggested. "Get out of here for a bit, clear our heads."

Isabel smiled, appreciating the gesture. "I'd like that."

They left the studio, stepping into the cool night air. The street was quiet, the occasional sound of distant laughter carrying on the breeze. They walked side by side, the silence between them now filled with a comfortable ease. The night sky, dotted with stars, seemed to mirror their newfound clarity and hope.

As they strolled through the familiar streets of the island, Isabel reflected on their journey. The fears and doubts that had clouded their relationship were beginning to clear, replaced by a deep sense of commitment and mutual understanding. The studio, once a symbol of her dreams, now also represented their shared future.

Gabe squeezed her hand gently, pulling her from her thoughts. "You know, I've been thinking about what you said earlier. About making it all fit together."

Isabel looked up at him, her heart swelling with affection. "What did you come up with?"

Gabe's eyes were filled with warmth. "I think we need to approach it as a team. We need to support each other's dreams while also making sure we don't lose sight of what's important to both of us."

Isabel nodded in agreement. "I couldn't have said it better myself. It's about finding that balance and making sure we both feel valued and heard."

They continued their walk, the conversation flowing easily between them. The night was filled with laughter and shared dreams, a testament to their growing bond. Isabel felt a deep sense of peace, knowing that their relationship was on solid ground and that they were both committed to making it work.

When they finally returned to the studio, the early signs of dawn were beginning to light the sky. The studio, with its warm, inviting glow, seemed to welcome them back. Isabel and Gabe stood together, the quiet strength of their connection evident in their shared smiles and the way they moved easily around each other.

"I think we're ready for whatever comes next," Gabe said softly, his gaze fixed on Isabel.

Isabel's heart was full, and she smiled up at him with a sense of gratitude and love. "I believe that too. We've faced a lot, but we've done it together."

Gabe's expression was one of unwavering devotion. "And we'll continue to, no matter what."

As they stood in the studio, the first rays of sunlight filtering through the windows, Isabel knew that their journey was just beginning. The path ahead was filled with possibilities, but with Gabe by her side and a renewed sense of commitment, she felt ready to embrace it all.

Together, they faced the new day, their hearts aligned and their futures intertwined. The studio, now a symbol of their shared dreams and efforts, stood as a beacon of hope and a testament to their love. The final test had brought them closer, and as they moved forward, they did so with the confidence that their bond was strong and enduring.

With each step they took, Isabel felt a deep sense of anticipation and excitement for the future. The challenges and uncertainties were no longer daunting; they were opportunities for growth and connection. And with Gabe by her side, Isabel knew that they could face whatever lay ahead with courage and love.

The dawn's first light streamed into the studio, casting long shadows across the wooden floor. Isabel and Gabe stood close together, their earlier conversation having bridged the gaps that had formed between them. As they looked around the space, the weight of their shared dreams and challenges seemed to settle comfortably between them.

Gabe broke the silence with a soft, thoughtful voice. "You know, this place feels different now. It's more than just a studio. It's become a part of our story."

Isabel turned to him, her eyes reflecting both the warmth of the morning sun and the depth of her feelings. "It really does. It's a testament to everything we've been through and everything we're building together."

Gabe's gaze was steady, and he reached out to gently brush a strand of hair from Isabel's face. "I've been thinking a lot about what's next for us. About how we can keep moving forward while staying true to ourselves."

Isabel felt a rush of gratitude and affection. She had been so caught up in her fears and uncertainties that she hadn't fully appreciated the depth of Gabe's commitment to their future. "What do you have in mind?"

Gabe's smile was gentle but filled with purpose. "I think we need to be more intentional about how we share our lives. I want us to create spaces where we can be open with each other, not just about our dreams but also about our fears and challenges."

Isabel nodded, feeling the truth in his words. "That sounds wonderful. I think it's exactly what we need. We've been so focused on making things work that we might have forgotten to nurture our connection."

Gabe's eyes softened with affection. "It's easy to get caught up in the day-to-day and lose sight of what really matters. But I want to make sure we never lose that connection. It's the foundation of everything else."

Isabel took a deep breath, her mind racing with the possibilities. "Let's start with something simple. How about a weekly check-in, where we can talk about our dreams, our challenges, and just how we're feeling?"

Gabe's smile widened, and he pulled her into a warm embrace. "I'd love that. It's a way for us to stay connected and make sure we're always on the same page."

As they held each other, Isabel felt a profound sense of peace. The morning sun bathed them in a golden light, and the studio, with its mix of hope and history, seemed to echo their commitment to one another.

The sound of distant waves crashing against the shore reached their ears, a soothing reminder of the island's timeless beauty. Isabel and Gabe stepped outside, the cool morning air invigorating their senses. They walked hand in hand along the shoreline, the gentle rhythm of the waves mirroring the steady beat of their hearts.

Isabel glanced at Gabe, her thoughts turning to the future. "I've been thinking about how we can make the studio more than just a space for photography. I want it to be a place where people can come and find inspiration, just like I did."

Gabe's eyes lit up with enthusiasm. "That sounds amazing. What if we hosted workshops or community events? It could be a way to bring people together and share our love for photography."

Isabel's heart swelled with excitement. "I love that idea. It's exactly the kind of community involvement I've been dreaming about. We could create a space where people feel welcomed and encouraged."

They continued their walk, their conversation flowing easily between them. The more they talked, the clearer their vision for the future became. They saw the studio not just as a workspace, but as a hub for creativity and connection.

As the morning turned into afternoon, Isabel and Gabe returned to the studio, their minds buzzing with new ideas. The space felt alive with potential, and Isabel could almost see the future taking shape before her eyes.

They spent the rest of the day brainstorming and planning, their shared excitement creating a sense of unity and purpose. The challenges they had faced seemed distant now, replaced by a renewed sense of hope and determination.

As the sun began to set, casting a warm glow over the studio, Isabel and Gabe took a moment to reflect on their journey. The studio, now a symbol of their dreams and efforts, felt like a true reflection of their relationship—grounded in love, trust, and shared goals.

Gabe looked at Isabel, his expression a mix of affection and determination. "I'm really proud of us. We've come a long way, and we've done it together."

Isabel's eyes were filled with gratitude. "Me too. It hasn't always been easy, but it's been worth it. We've grown so much, and I'm excited for what's to come."

They shared a tender kiss, the evening air filled with the promise of a new beginning. The studio, with its warm light and the soft hum of possibilities, seemed to embrace them in its gentle glow.

As they stood together, the future stretched out before them like an open road, filled with opportunities and adventures. They knew there would be challenges ahead, but they faced them with a renewed sense of confidence and love.

Isabel and Gabe had weathered the storm of uncertainties and emerged stronger, their bond deepened by their willingness to confront their fears and support each other. The final test had brought them closer, and as they looked toward the future, they did so with a sense of excitement and optimism.

Together, they would build their dreams, navigate the challenges, and cherish the moments of joy. The studio, with its promise of creativity and connection, stood as a testament to their love and their commitment to one another.

As the first stars appeared in the evening sky, Isabel and Gabe knew that they were ready for whatever lay ahead. Their hearts were aligned, their dreams intertwined, and their love strong enough to face any challenge.

With a final glance at the studio, Isabel took Gabe's hand, and they stepped out into the night, ready to embrace their future with hope and determination. The journey ahead was filled with possibilities, and they were ready to take on the world—together.

The days following the conversation in the studio were marked by an almost palpable shift in the air. Isabel and Gabe poured their energy into planning their future, their shared enthusiasm transforming the studio into a vibrant space of creativity and community. Yet beneath their outward optimism, a subtle tension lingered, reflecting the delicate balance they were striving to maintain in their relationship.

One evening, as they worked late into the night, the studio illuminated by the soft glow of desk lamps, Gabe's demeanor shifted. He was focused, his brow furrowed in concentration, but there was a distant look in his eyes. Isabel, absorbed in her own tasks, noticed the change and felt a pang of concern. She put down her paintbrush and approached him quietly.

"Hey," Isabel said softly, her voice breaking the silence. "Is everything okay? You've been really quiet."

Gabe looked up, his gaze meeting hers. "Yeah, everything's fine. Just... thinking about the future, I guess."

Isabel nodded, her eyes searching his face. "About what specifically?"

Gabe hesitated, choosing his words carefully. "It's just... I'm afraid. I'm afraid that things might not work out the way we're hoping. I've seen too many dreams falter, and I don't want to lose what we have."

Isabel's heart ached at his admission. She walked over and placed a hand on his shoulder, feeling the tension beneath his shirt. "I understand. I have my own fears too. But we've come so far. We've faced challenges before, and we've always found a way through them."

Gabe looked at her, a mixture of vulnerability and hope in his eyes. "It's not just about the challenges, though. It's about us. About me letting go of my fears and truly committing to this."

Isabel took a deep breath, her own fears surfacing as she considered his words. "I've been thinking about what we talked about—the weekly check-ins and being open with each other. I think it's more important than ever now. We need to be honest about our insecurities and work through them together."

Gabe's expression softened, and he reached out to hold her hand. "You're right. I want us to succeed, not just in the studio but in our relationship. I want to be open with you, even when it's difficult."

Isabel squeezed his hand, feeling a surge of warmth and resolve. "We can do this. We just need to keep communicating and supporting each other. I believe in us."

They shared a quiet moment, their hands intertwined, each finding solace in the other's presence. The uncertainty of the future remained, but it was now tempered by a renewed commitment to face it together.

As the days turned into weeks, Isabel and Gabe continued to pour their energy into the studio, transforming it into a hub of creativity and inspiration. They hosted workshops, community events, and shared their love for photography with others. The studio became a place of connection, mirroring the deepening bond between them.

One afternoon, as they were preparing for a new exhibition, Gabe received a phone call. His expression grew serious as he listened, and Isabel could sense the shift in his mood. When he hung up, he turned to her with a troubled look.

"What's wrong?" Isabel asked, her concern evident.

Gabe took a deep breath. "It's work. There's a potential opportunity in another city. It's a big promotion, but it would mean relocating."

Isabel's heart sank at the news. She had hoped their future would be rooted in the island, but the prospect of moving felt like a wrench thrown into their plans. She forced a smile, trying to keep her emotions in check. "What are you thinking?"

Gabe looked conflicted. "I don't know. It's a great opportunity, but I don't want to make any decisions that might jeopardize what we've built here."

Isabel felt a pang of anxiety, her thoughts racing. "We should talk about this more. It's important that we consider how it affects both of us."

They spent the evening discussing the potential move, weighing the pros and cons. Isabel's mind was filled with doubts, but she also knew how much this opportunity meant to Gabe. The conversation was emotionally charged, each of them grappling with their own fears and desires.

As they talked, Isabel realized that the conversation mirrored the challenges they had faced earlier in their relationship. It was a test of their commitment and their ability to navigate uncertainty together. She felt a renewed sense of determination to make their relationship work, no matter what obstacles they encountered.

Later that night, as they sat together on the studio's balcony, the cool breeze a soothing balm, Gabe spoke softly. "I've been thinking about what you said earlier. About us needing to communicate and support each other. I want to make sure we're both on the same page."

Isabel looked at him, her heart swelling with affection. "I want that too. We've come so far, and I believe we can face anything as long as we're together."

Gabe's eyes were filled with gratitude and love. "I agree. Whatever happens, I want us to face it together. We can make decisions that are right for both of us."

Isabel nodded, feeling a deep sense of peace. The future was uncertain, but she knew that their love and commitment to each other would guide them through whatever challenges lay ahead.

As they embraced, the night sky above them seemed to hold endless possibilities. The studio, with its warm light and the promise of their shared dreams, stood as a testament to their journey. They had weathered many storms, and their love had only grown stronger.

The final test had brought them to a place of clarity and resolve. Isabel and Gabe knew that the path forward would require courage and compromise, but they were ready to face it together. Their commitment to each other was unwavering, and their love had become a beacon of hope and strength.

With a renewed sense of purpose, they looked toward the future with optimism and determination. The studio, now a symbol of their shared dreams and efforts, would continue to be a place of inspiration and connection.

As they held each other close, the promise of their future felt as vibrant and hopeful as the morning sun. They were ready to embrace whatever lay ahead, knowing that their love and commitment would guide them through any challenge.

Together, they would build their dreams, navigate the uncertainties, and cherish the moments of joy. The journey ahead was filled with possibilities, and they faced it with a heart full of love and a spirit of resilience.

The days following Gabe's potential job offer were a whirlwind of emotions. Isabel and Gabe found themselves in a delicate dance, balancing their personal aspirations with their shared dreams. Every conversation seemed to amplify their uncertainties, but it also revealed their deepening commitment to one another. The studio continued to thrive, serving as a refuge and a reminder of the life they were building together.

One crisp autumn evening, as the sun dipped below the horizon and the sky turned a fiery orange, Isabel found herself alone in the studio. The soft hum of the air conditioner and the distant sound of waves crashing on the shore were the only sounds breaking the silence. She wandered through the space, admiring the photographs and paintings they had displayed. Each piece told a story, reflecting their journey and their shared passion.

As she stopped in front of a large, framed photograph of a sunset over the island, she heard the familiar sound of the studio door opening. Gabe walked in, carrying a stack of paperwork. His expression was serious, and Isabel could sense the weight of the decision that hung over them.

"Hey," Isabel said, trying to keep her voice steady. "How was your day?"

Gabe set the paperwork down on a nearby table and took a deep breath. "It was productive. I spoke with the company again. They're offering a significant promotion with a lot of potential. But it means moving away."

Isabel's heart sank at the words. She had hoped for a different outcome, but the reality of Gabe's opportunity was becoming more apparent. She took a step closer to him, her gaze meeting his. "I understand how important this is to you. But it's also important to me that we think this through carefully. It's not just about the job; it's about our life together."

Gabe nodded, his eyes reflecting a mixture of hope and worry. "I've been thinking a lot about what you said. I want to make sure that whatever decision we make, it's the right one for both of us. But I also don't want you to feel like you're sacrificing your dreams for mine."

Isabel's eyes softened as she reached out to take his hand. "It's not about sacrifice. It's about finding a balance. We need to be honest about what we want and what we're willing to compromise on."

They spent the next hour discussing their options, weighing the pros and cons of Gabe's job offer and how it would impact their relationship and future. Isabel spoke candidly about her fears of moving away from the island and the life they had built, while Gabe expressed his concerns about missing out on a significant career opportunity.

As the conversation deepened, Isabel found herself grappling with a mix of emotions. She realized that her feelings about the move were intertwined with her fears of leaving behind the stability and community she had come to cherish. She was torn between her love for Gabe and her desire for the life she had envisioned on the island.

Gabe, too, was conflicted. He felt a strong pull toward the opportunity in the city but was deeply committed to making their relationship work. He wanted to ensure that his decision wouldn't drive a wedge between them.

By the time they finished their discussion, it was late, and the studio was bathed in the soft glow of the evening lights. They sat together in silence, their hands still clasped, as they contemplated the future. The decision they faced was daunting, but it was clear that their love for each other was the foundation on which they would build their future.

As they prepared to leave the studio, Gabe turned to Isabel with a determined expression. "Whatever happens, I want us to face it together. I want us to make decisions that reflect our commitment to each other."

Isabel smiled, feeling a surge of warmth. "I want that too. We've come so far, and I believe in us. We can make it work, no matter where we end up."

They embraced, finding comfort in each other's presence. The uncertainty of their future remained, but their shared resolve to face it together gave them hope. The studio, with its vibrant energy and the memories they had created, stood as a testament to their journey and their love.

Over the next few days, Isabel and Gabe continued to explore their options, seeking advice from friends, family, and mentors. They weighed the impact of the potential move on their personal and professional lives, and each conversation brought them closer to a decision.

One evening, as they sat on the balcony of their home, watching the sun set over the island, Gabe took a deep breath and turned to Isabel. "I've been thinking a lot about what we've discussed. I want us to make this decision together, based on what's best for us both."

Isabel looked at him, her eyes filled with emotion. "I appreciate that. It means a lot to me. I want us to move forward with a clear understanding of our goals and how we can support each other."

Gabe nodded, his gaze steady. "I agree. Let's take the time we need to make the right choice. We don't have to rush into anything."

They shared a moment of silence, their hands intertwined as they watched the sky change colors. The decision they faced was significant, but it was clear that their love and commitment to each other would guide them through.

In the following weeks, Isabel and Gabe continued to build their life together in the studio, creating new memories and strengthening their bond. They explored different possibilities for their future, finding a balance between their individual aspirations and their shared dreams.

As the deadline for Gabe's decision approached, they felt a sense of clarity and resolve. They had faced their fears and uncertainties together, and their love had grown stronger as a result. The future remained uncertain, but they were ready to embrace it with optimism and determination.

On the day of Gabe's final decision, Isabel and Gabe stood together in the studio, their hearts full of hope. Gabe took a deep breath and made his choice, one that reflected their shared commitment and their vision for the future. They knew that the road ahead would be challenging, but they were ready to face it together.

As they looked around the studio, filled with the vibrant energy of their shared dreams, they felt a sense of accomplishment and pride. Their journey had been marked by challenges and growth, but their love had been a constant source of strength and inspiration.

Together, Isabel and Gabe faced the future with a renewed sense of purpose and a deep appreciation for the life they had built. They knew that whatever lay ahead, they would face it with courage, love, and unwavering commitment.

The final test had brought them to a place of clarity and resolve, and they were ready to embrace the next chapter of their journey together. The studio, with its vibrant colors and creative energy, stood as a symbol of their shared dreams and their enduring love.

The decision day arrived with a heavy air of anticipation. Gabe and Isabel spent the morning going through the last of their discussions, each of them wrestling with their own blend of hope and apprehension. Gabe's decision would shape not just their individual futures but also the path of their relationship.

As the clock ticked toward noon, Isabel took a deep breath and stood by the window, watching the sky gradually clear after a morning of light rain. The studio, their haven, was bathed in a gentle, diffused light that seemed to hold its breath, as if waiting for the verdict. The walls, adorned with their collective dreams and memories, reflected the weight of the moment.

Gabe walked in, his expression a mix of determination and vulnerability. He had been up early, wrestling with the final pieces of his decision. Isabel could see the strain in his eyes, the way his jaw tightened with every thought he processed. It was clear that whatever choice he made, it would come with its own set of sacrifices and compromises.

Isabel turned to face him, her own heart heavy. "Are you ready?" she asked softly, trying to keep her voice steady.

Gabe nodded, taking a seat at the small table where they had spent countless hours discussing their dreams. He gestured for Isabel to join him, and she did, sitting across from him. The intimacy of the moment was palpable, their shared space feeling like a cocoon that wrapped around them both.

"I've been thinking about everything we've talked about," Gabe began, his voice firm but gentle. "I've considered my career opportunities, our life here, and what it means for us both."

Isabel reached out and took his hand, squeezing it lightly. "I know this isn't an easy decision. Whatever you choose, we'll face it together."

Gabe took a deep breath, his gaze locking onto Isabel's. "I've decided to accept the promotion. It's a big move, and I know it means leaving behind the life we've started here. But I believe it's the right step for my career, and I want us to have the opportunities it could bring."

Isabel's heart sank, but she forced a smile, trying to mask the sting of his words. "I understand. It's a significant opportunity for you, and I want you to be happy and fulfilled in your career."

Gabe's eyes softened, and he reached out to gently touch her cheek. "This doesn't mean I want to leave you behind. It means I'm taking a step forward, and I want you by my side. But I also know it's a big change, and it's going to require both of us to adjust."

Isabel nodded, her emotions swirling. "I'm willing to try. I want us to make this work, even if it means facing new challenges. But I also want us to be honest with each other about what this move means for us, both personally and professionally."

Gabe smiled, a mixture of relief and affection in his eyes. "We've always been able to face challenges together. This is no different. We'll find a way to balance our dreams and make this new chapter work."

They spent the rest of the day preparing for the transition, their conversations now focusing on practicalities and future plans. The weight of the decision had been made, but the road ahead was still filled with unknowns. They talked about moving logistics, potential job opportunities for Isabel in the new city, and how they would maintain their connection to the island that had become such an important part of their lives.

As the evening approached, Gabe and Isabel found themselves back in the studio, which had become a symbol of their shared dreams. They looked around at the photos and paintings that had become part of their story, each one a testament to their journey and their love.

Gabe took Isabel's hand and led her to the center of the studio. They stood together, surrounded by the vibrant colors and creative energy that had defined their time there. "This place will always be special to us," Gabe said softly. "It's where we found our way back to each other."

Isabel nodded, her eyes misting over. "Yes, it's where we discovered what really matters. Our love, our dreams, and our ability to face the unknown together."

Gabe pulled her into a tender embrace, and they stood there for a long moment, finding solace in each other's presence. The studio, with its warm light and creative spirit, felt like a haven that had helped them through their most challenging times.

As they pulled away, Gabe looked at Isabel with a mixture of hope and determination. "We have a lot of work ahead of us, but I believe in us. We'll navigate this transition and continue to build the life we've dreamed of."

Isabel smiled through her tears, feeling a deep sense of resolve. "I believe in us too. Whatever the future holds, we'll face it together."

The evening turned to night, and they shared a quiet dinner in the studio, savoring the last moments in the space that had become their sanctuary. They talked about their plans for the move, the people they would miss, and the new experiences that awaited them.

As they finished their meal, Gabe took Isabel's hand and led her to the window. They stood side by side, looking out at the island that had been their home. The night sky was clear, and the stars twinkled brightly, a reminder of the vast possibilities that lay ahead.

Gabe squeezed Isabel's hand and said softly, "The future may be uncertain, but I know we'll make the most of it. Together."

Isabel nodded, her heart full of mixed emotions. "Together," she echoed. "We'll face whatever comes next with love and courage."

With that, they turned away from the window and began the process of packing up their lives, ready to embrace the new chapter that awaited them. The studio, with its vibrant memories and creative energy, would always hold a special place in their hearts. It had been the backdrop to their journey, a place where they had discovered their true selves and their commitment to each other.

As they left the studio for the final time, Gabe and Isabel knew that the road ahead would be filled with challenges and opportunities. But they also knew that their love and their shared dreams would guide them through. The future was uncertain, but it was a future they were ready to face together.

As the sun dipped below the horizon, casting a warm golden glow over the island, Gabe and Isabel stood outside the studio, the weight of their decision heavy in the air. The transition to a new chapter was imminent, and the bittersweet mix of excitement and trepidation hung between them.

The soft rustling of the trees and the distant hum of evening crickets provided a soothing backdrop to their moment of reflection. The studio, now bathed in twilight, stood as a testament to their shared journey—a sanctuary where dreams had been forged and futures envisioned.

Isabel glanced at Gabe, his profile outlined against the fading light. The lines of his face seemed etched with both resolve and uncertainty. She reached out, gently touching his arm, and he turned to face her, his eyes reflecting the fading light.

"I know this isn't easy," Isabel said quietly, her voice trembling slightly. "Leaving behind everything we've built here... It's hard to imagine."

Gabe nodded, his gaze steady but filled with a mix of emotions. "It is hard. But it's also a chance for us to grow, to challenge ourselves in new ways. I want us to make the most of this opportunity, even if it means facing new uncertainties."

Isabel took a deep breath, her thoughts swirling with the possibilities and challenges ahead. "It's a leap of faith. We're stepping into the unknown, but we're doing it together."

Gabe squeezed her hand reassuringly. "Yes, together. And no matter where we go, we'll carry a piece of this place with us—the memories, the love, and the lessons we've learned."

As they walked away from the studio, Isabel felt a mix of sadness and anticipation. The island had been a cocoon for their love, a place of comfort and familiarity. Leaving it behind felt like stepping into a new world, with all its uncertainties and possibilities.

The drive to their new home was filled with a quiet, contemplative atmosphere. Gabe and Isabel navigated the winding roads, each turn bringing them closer to their future. The journey felt symbolic, a transition from their past to their future.

When they finally arrived at their new city, the bustling energy and diverse landscape presented a stark contrast to the serene beauty of the island. The city was alive with activity, its lights shimmering against the night sky, and the hum of life seemed to pulse through every street and building.

Isabel's heart fluttered with a mix of excitement and anxiety as they unloaded their belongings. The new apartment was spacious and modern, a blank canvas ready to be filled with their new memories. Gabe's enthusiasm for the move was palpable, and he worked with a sense of purpose, unpacking boxes and arranging their new space.

As the days passed, Isabel began to adjust to her new surroundings. The city was vibrant and full of opportunities, but it also felt overwhelming at times. She missed the tranquility of the island, the familiar faces, and the comforting rhythm of her old life.

Gabe, too, was adjusting to his new role and the demands of his job. He was passionate about the opportunities ahead but found himself missing the slower pace of life they had enjoyed on the island. Their days were filled with new routines, and the evenings were often spent talking about their experiences and their hopes for the future.

One evening, after a particularly challenging day, Isabel sat alone on the balcony of their new apartment, gazing out at the city lights. The view was impressive, but it felt distant and impersonal compared to the intimate beauty of the island. Gabe joined her, sensing her melancholy.

"Thinking about the island?" he asked gently, sitting beside her.

Isabel nodded, her eyes reflecting the city's glow. "I am. It's hard not to miss it. Everything here feels so different—so big and bustling. I'm still trying to find my place in all of this."

Gabe took her hand, his touch warm and reassuring. "I know it's a lot to take in. But remember, we're not just leaving behind the island—we're carrying everything we've learned and built with us. We're making a new home here, together."

Isabel looked at him, her eyes filled with gratitude. "You're right. We have each other, and we have our dreams. We can build something new and meaningful, even if it's different from what we had before."

Gabe smiled, his eyes reflecting a shared sense of hope. "Exactly. We'll create our own space in this city, just as we did on the island. And we'll do it together."

Their conversation was a reminder of their shared commitment and the strength of their bond. The city, with all its challenges and opportunities, was now their canvas. They were ready to paint it with their dreams, their love, and their shared experiences.

As they continued to settle into their new life, Isabel and Gabe found comfort in the small, everyday moments that brought them closer. They explored their new neighborhood, discovering hidden gems and forging connections with new friends. Each day was a step toward making their new house a home, and each night was a celebration of their journey together.

The transition was not without its difficulties, but it was also filled with moments of joy and discovery. Isabel found solace in her photography, capturing the vibrant energy of the city and the beauty in its diversity. Gabe embraced his new role, finding fulfillment in the challenges and successes it brought.

Together, they navigated the complexities of their new life, supporting each other through the highs and lows. Their love, tested by distance and change, grew stronger as they faced each new day with hope and resilience.

In the quiet moments, as they looked out at the city from their balcony or shared a meal in their new home, Isabel and Gabe reflected on their journey. They had taken a leap of faith, leaving behind the familiar for the unknown, but they had done so with a shared sense of purpose and commitment.

The future was still unfolding, but Isabel and Gabe knew that whatever came next, they would face it together. Their love, forged in the beauty of the island and strengthened by their new experiences, would guide them through the challenges and triumphs that lay ahead.

As they continued to build their new life, they carried with them the lessons of their past and the promise of their future. Their journey was a testament to the power of love and the strength of their bond, a reminder that no matter where life led them, they would always have each other.

Isabel's heart raced as she walked through the vibrant city streets, a jumble of excitement and apprehension swirling within her. The evening had unfolded with its usual hustle and bustle, but now, as she stood on the edge of their new apartment's balcony, she found a rare moment of stillness amidst the city's vibrant chaos. Gabe's earlier words echoed in her mind, stirring a mix of hope and uncertainty.

The city lights below shimmered like a thousand tiny stars, a sharp contrast to the peaceful expanse of the island they had left behind. Each flicker seemed to hold a promise, yet the enormity of their new life was still settling in, an unfamiliar weight on her shoulders.

Gabe's footsteps approached, his presence a comforting reassurance. He stepped out onto the balcony, joining her in the quiet. The warmth of his hand on hers was grounding, a reminder of their shared journey.

"I've been thinking," Gabe said, breaking the silence. His voice was gentle, almost hesitant, as if choosing his words carefully. "About the future, and about us."

Isabel turned to him, her eyes reflecting the city's glow. "What about it?"

Gabe took a deep breath, his gaze steady. "You know, moving here, starting over—it's a lot. We've both been adjusting, and I've noticed how much you miss the island. I want you to know that it's okay to feel that way."

Isabel's heart swelled at his words. "I do miss it. The island was... a part of us. But I also know that this city holds new opportunities and new beginnings."

Gabe nodded, squeezing her hand gently. "Exactly. And I think we're making the right choice by embracing this new chapter. But I want to make sure we're not just moving forward because it's expected of us. I want us to be sure that we're both ready for this."

The sincerity in his voice made Isabel's heart ache. She had been so focused on the logistics of their move, the practicalities of settling in, that she hadn't fully confronted her own feelings. This city was a symbol of their new beginning, yet it felt so different from what she had known.

"I've been so focused on making this work," Isabel admitted, her voice trembling slightly. "I didn't stop to think about whether I was truly ready or if this was what I wanted."

Gabe's eyes softened with understanding. "It's okay to have doubts. It's okay to question. What matters is that we face those doubts together. We're in this as a team, and we should be honest with each other about how we're feeling."

Isabel felt a wave of relief wash over her. The weight of her doubts, which had been simmering beneath the surface, felt lighter now that she had voiced them. "I appreciate that, Gabe. I guess... I guess I need to find a way to balance my feelings about the island with the opportunities here."

Gabe wrapped an arm around her shoulders, drawing her closer. "We will. We'll find our rhythm, our balance. And we'll do it together."

As they stood together on the balcony, the city lights stretching out before them, Isabel felt a sense of calm settling over her. The future was still uncertain, but with Gabe by her side, she felt more equipped to face whatever lay ahead. The transition from the island to the city was a journey of growth and change, and she knew that their love and commitment would be the guiding light through the challenges.

The following days were filled with new experiences and discoveries. Isabel and Gabe explored their new city, finding hidden cafes, vibrant markets, and charming neighborhoods that began to feel like home. Each outing was a small adventure, a step toward making their new life their own.

Despite the excitement of their new surroundings, Isabel still found moments of reflection. She often visited the nearby park, a tranquil escape from the city's bustle, where she would sit and think about the path she had chosen. The park became a place of solace, a reminder of the quiet beauty she had left behind and a space where she could reconcile her past with her present.

One afternoon, while sitting on a park bench, Isabel's phone buzzed with a message from her mother's old friend, Mrs. Thompson. She had been meaning to reach out to her, and the message was a gentle reminder of her connection to the island. The message read:

"Dear Isabel, I hope this finds you well. I wanted to let you know that the island has been busy with preparations for the annual festival. It's a special time, and I couldn't help but think of you. If you ever want to visit or catch up, I'd love to hear from you. Best wishes, Mrs. Thompson."

Isabel's heart fluttered with a mix of nostalgia and gratitude. The island, despite being miles away, was still a part of her life, woven into her memories and connections. She typed a heartfelt response, expressing her appreciation and updating Mrs. Thompson on her new life in the city.

As she hit send, Isabel felt a renewed sense of connection to her past. The island might have been a chapter closed, but it was a cherished part of her story, one that had shaped her in profound ways. Her journey had brought her to a new city, but it had also deepened her understanding of herself and her place in the world.

Back at their apartment, Gabe noticed the change in Isabel's demeanor. She seemed more at peace, her earlier doubts replaced with a quiet determination. He joined her on the balcony, where they sat together, their fingers intertwined.

"You seem more settled," Gabe observed, his voice gentle.

Isabel smiled, leaning her head on his shoulder. "I think I'm starting to find my balance. The city is overwhelming at times, but I'm learning to embrace it. And knowing that the island is still a part of my life gives me comfort."

Gabe kissed her forehead, his eyes reflecting his pride and love. "I'm proud of you, Isabel. You've navigated this transition with strength and grace. And no matter where we go, we'll always have each other."

The evening settled around them, the city lights twinkling like a thousand promises. Isabel felt a deep sense of contentment as she looked out at the view. The city was a vast and vibrant landscape, full of potential and possibility. It was their new canvas, and together, they were ready to paint it with their dreams and aspirations.

As they embraced, Isabel realized that the journey was not just about the physical move from the island to the city but about the emotional and personal growth that came with it. The challenges and uncertainties had brought them closer, deepening their bond and strengthening their resolve.

The future was still unfolding, but Isabel and Gabe faced it with hope and determination. Their love, forged through trials and triumphs, would guide them through the next chapters of their lives. And as they continued their journey together, they knew that whatever came next, they would face it with courage, love, and a shared sense of purpose.

The city, with all its possibilities and challenges, was their new home, and with each passing day, they were creating a new chapter in their story—one filled with promise, adventure, and the enduring strength of their love.

Isabel's gaze lingered over the cityscape, her thoughts drifting back to the island. The contrast between the quiet, predictable rhythms of her past and the pulsing vibrancy of the city stirred an unease she couldn't shake. It wasn't just about the place; it was about her. Could she truly let go of the parts of herself that belonged to the island, and would she ever fully embrace this new life?

Gabe, as if sensing her inner conflict, leaned against the balcony railing beside her. His voice, low and calm, broke through the silence.

"You know, I've been thinking..." His words trailed off, hanging in the air like the humid evening breeze. Isabel waited, sensing that whatever he was about to say carried more weight than his usual musings. "I've been thinking about how much things have changed for us."

Isabel nodded, her throat tightening. She wanted to respond, to tell him that she felt it too, but she wasn't sure how to find the right words.

Gabe hesitated before continuing, his eyes searching the horizon. "I don't want you to feel like you have to choose between the island and the city. Between who you were and who you are now."

Isabel turned toward him, surprised by his directness. "What do you mean?"

He exhaled slowly, as if preparing himself for the vulnerability that was about to follow. "When we left the island, I thought it would be the best thing for us. A fresh start. But I've realized... maybe I was wrong. Maybe I was trying to pull you into my vision of our future without thinking about whether it was really what you wanted."

Isabel felt her heart lurch, his words cutting through the haze of her doubts. She had been so focused on trying to make this new life work that she hadn't fully acknowledged her lingering attachment to the island—and Gabe had seen it all along.

"It's not just about the place, Gabe," she whispered, her voice barely audible. "It's about us. I'm afraid that if I don't make this work, I'll lose everything. I'll lose you."

Gabe's face softened, a mixture of tenderness and regret crossing his features. "Isabel, you won't lose me. I'm not going anywhere. But I can't help but feel like you're still holding onto something. And maybe you need to let go, or maybe... maybe we need to find a way to reconcile both parts of your life."

His words hung in the air, and Isabel felt the weight of the moment pressing down on her. He wasn't just talking about the physical move; he was talking about the deeper emotional journey she had been on—the journey she had tried to navigate alone.

"I don't know how to do that," she admitted, tears stinging the back of her eyes. "I've been trying so hard to figure it out, but I'm scared. I don't know if I can find that balance."

Gabe stepped closer, wrapping his arms around her in a gesture that was both protective and reassuring. "You don't have to figure it out on your own. We're in this together, remember? But you need to be honest with yourself, and with me."

Isabel rested her head against his chest, listening to the steady rhythm of his heartbeat. For the first time in weeks, she allowed herself to really feel the full weight of her emotions—the fear, the longing, the uncertainty. She had been so focused on proving to herself that she could move forward that she hadn't given herself the space to truly reflect on what she needed.

"I'm sorry," she whispered. "I've been pushing so hard, trying to make everything work, and I've been ignoring how I really feel."

Gabe pressed a kiss to the top of her head, his arms tightening around her. "It's okay. We'll figure it out, one step at a time."

They stood like that for what felt like hours, the city humming around them but feeling a world away. In that moment, Isabel felt something shift inside her—a small but significant change. She didn't have all the answers, and she didn't know what the future would hold, but for the first time in a long time, she allowed herself to embrace the uncertainty without needing to control it.

Later that night, as they lay in bed, Gabe's arm draped protectively over her, Isabel found herself thinking about the journal she had discovered—the journal that had revealed her mother's regrets, her struggles, and her secret hopes. There had been one entry in particular that had stuck with her, an entry that had made her heart ache with its vulnerability:

"There are moments in life when we are forced to choose between what we think is right and what we truly want. I thought I was doing the right thing by leaving, by creating a new life for myself. But in the end, all I ever wanted was to go back, to find that piece of myself I had lost. I just didn't know how."

Isabel hadn't fully understood the depth of her mother's words until now. Her mother had been searching for the same thing she was—a way to reconcile the past with the present, a way to move forward without losing sight of where she had come from.

In the quiet darkness of the room, Isabel made a silent promise to herself: she wouldn't repeat her mother's mistakes. She wouldn't let fear and doubt drive her decisions. She would find a way to honor both her past and her future, and she would do it with Gabe by her side.

The final test wasn't about the city or the island—it was about trust. Trust in herself, trust in Gabe, and trust in the journey they were on together.

The next morning, as the sun rose over the city skyline, Isabel woke with a sense of clarity she hadn't felt in months. She looked over at Gabe, who was still sleeping peacefully beside her, and smiled. This was their new life, full of unknowns and challenges, but it was also full of possibilities.

And for the first time, Isabel felt ready to face whatever came next.

15

Chapter 15: Reunion at the Lighthouse

The drive to the lighthouse was a quiet one, punctuated only by the gentle hum of the engine and the occasional rustle of the wind through the open windows. Isabel sat beside Gabe, her thoughts a whirlwind of anticipation and apprehension. The lighthouse had always been a place of solace for her—a symbol of her mother's hidden past and, now, a beacon for her own journey of self-discovery.

As they approached the lighthouse, the landscape began to change. The cityscape faded into rolling hills and lush greenery, and the air grew cooler and more invigorating. The lighthouse stood tall against the horizon, its white and red stripes stark against the blue sky. It had been restored in recent years but retained its old-world charm, embodying the timeless beauty Isabel had come to cherish.

Gabe parked the car and they walked up the familiar path that led to the lighthouse. The sea breeze carried with it a sense of renewal, as if the lighthouse itself was welcoming Isabel back to a pivotal moment in her life.

Reaching the lighthouse, Isabel paused, her hand resting on the worn stone of the foundation. She closed her eyes, letting the memories wash over her. The lighthouse had been a constant presence in her childhood, a symbol of her mother's enigmatic past. It was here that Isabel had felt the weight of her mother's secrets and the longing for answers. Now, she hoped to find closure and a new beginning.

"Are you sure you want to do this?" Gabe's voice broke through her reverie, filled with genuine concern.

Isabel turned to him, her eyes shining with a mix of hope and resolve. "Yes. I need to. There's something I've been holding onto that I need to let go of here."

They climbed the narrow spiral staircase of the lighthouse, the worn steps creaking beneath their weight. Each step felt like a step toward the resolution Isabel had been seeking. At the top, the door to the lantern room creaked open, revealing the panoramic view of the ocean and the coastline. The sunlight poured in, casting a warm, golden glow over everything.

Isabel stepped out onto the small balcony, her breath catching as she took in the breathtaking view. The sea stretched out to the horizon, its waves sparkling under the sunlight. The lighthouse seemed to stand as a guardian of the past, the present, and the future.

Gabe followed her, and they stood side by side, taking in the scene. The silence between them was filled with unspoken words and emotions.

"I used to come here a lot," Isabel began, her voice carrying the weight of her emotions. "When I was a child, my mother would bring me here. She said the lighthouse was a place of peace, where she could think and find clarity. She had a secret—something she never told anyone, not even me."

Gabe nodded, his gaze fixed on her. "And you think this place holds the answers you're looking for?"

"I don't know," Isabel admitted. "But I feel like it's where I need to be. It's where I can connect with my mother and understand her choices. And maybe... understand my own."

Isabel took a deep breath, her heart pounding in her chest. She had spent so much time trying to reconcile her past with her present, and now she wanted to make sure that her future was shaped by truth and authenticity. The lighthouse had been a symbol of her mother's hidden love story, and Isabel wanted to honor that by sharing her own feelings with Gabe.

"I've been thinking a lot about what my mother might have felt," Isabel continued, her voice trembling slightly. "She must have struggled with her own choices, with her past and her present. And I realize now that I've been doing the same thing. Trying to move forward without fully understanding where I came from."

Gabe reached out, taking her hand in his. "Isabel, you don't have to do this alone. We've been through so much together, and I'm here for you. But you need to let go of the past to embrace the future."

Isabel looked at him, her eyes filled with gratitude. "I know. And I want to. I want to be honest with myself and with you."

With a deep breath, Isabel turned to face Gabe fully. The setting sun bathed the lighthouse in a warm, golden light, creating a perfect backdrop for this moment. "Gabe, I've been holding back my feelings for so long. I was afraid of making the wrong choice, of repeating the mistakes of the past. But I realize now that I need to take a leap of faith."

Gabe's eyes searched hers, his expression a mix of hope and vulnerability. "Isabel, I don't want you to feel pressured. I just want you to be true to yourself."

"I am," Isabel said softly. "I love you, Gabe. I've felt it for a long time, but I was too afraid to admit it, even to myself. I was holding onto the fear of losing you, of making a mistake. But I don't want to live in fear anymore. I want to build a future with you."

Gabe's face softened, and he pulled her into a tender embrace. "Isabel, you don't have to be afraid. We've already faced so much together. We can face whatever comes next, as long as we're honest with each other."

As they held each other on the balcony of the lighthouse, Isabel felt a profound sense of peace. The lighthouse, once a symbol of her mother's hidden secrets, had now become a beacon for her own journey toward love and self-acceptance. The past and the future seemed to merge in this moment, and Isabel felt a renewed sense of clarity and hope.

The sun dipped below the horizon, casting a serene twilight over the landscape. Isabel and Gabe stood together, wrapped in each other's arms, ready to embrace the new chapter of their lives. The lighthouse stood as a silent witness to their love and commitment, a symbol of their shared journey and the promises they had made to each other.

As the night fell and the first stars appeared in the sky, Isabel knew that she had found the clarity she needed. The lighthouse had guided her back to herself, to her love for Gabe, and to the future they would build together. She felt ready to move forward, with the past as a source of strength and the future as a canvas for their shared dreams.

And as they descended the lighthouse together, hand in hand, Isabel felt a sense of completion—a sense that she had finally found her place, both within herself and in the life she was building with Gabe.

Descending the winding staircase of the lighthouse, Isabel and Gabe moved slowly, their steps synchronized in a rhythm that spoke of their shared resolve and new understanding. The lantern room, once a place of isolation and reflection for Isabel, now felt like a sacred space of revelation and connection. Each step they took together felt like a reaffirmation of the promises and feelings they had just exchanged.

Outside, the cool evening air wrapped around them like a gentle embrace. The lighthouse, now a dark silhouette against the twilight sky, seemed to stand as a steadfast guardian of their renewed commitment. The ground beneath them was still damp from the earlier rain, and the scent of the sea mingled with the earthy aroma of the wet grass.

Isabel glanced at Gabe, her heart swelling with a mixture of gratitude and love. "Thank you for being here with me, Gabe. For understanding and for giving me the space to find my own truth."

Gabe squeezed her hand gently, his eyes reflecting the last light of the setting sun. "I wouldn't want to be anywhere else. This journey has been as much about finding you as it has been about finding myself. We're in this together."

They reached the base of the lighthouse and walked toward the nearby bench, a small wooden structure overlooking the cliff. It was a spot Isabel had frequented in her childhood, a place where she had often come to think and dream. Now, it felt like the perfect place for a moment of calm after the emotional intensity of their earlier conversation.

Sitting down, Isabel leaned back, looking out over the ocean, the waves catching the last rays of the sun. Gabe sat beside her, their shoulders touching in a comfortable, reassuring proximity.

The silence between them was peaceful, filled with a mutual understanding that spoke louder than words.

"I used to come here and imagine my mother sitting on this bench," Isabel said softly. "I'd picture her looking out at the sea, thinking about her own dreams and regrets. I never really understood her then, but now, I feel like I'm starting to."

Gabe turned to face her, his expression thoughtful. "It's incredible how places can hold so much meaning, isn't it? They become repositories of our memories and emotions."

Isabel nodded. "Yes, and this place has been holding a lot of my mother's secrets, too. Finding that journal and learning about her past has been overwhelming, but it's also given me a sense of closure. I feel like I understand her better now."

Gabe took a deep breath, his gaze never leaving hers. "It's a profound feeling, to finally see the person you've lost in a new light. It's like connecting the dots of a picture that was previously blurred."

Isabel turned to him, her eyes reflecting the twilight. "I've realized that my mother's secrets were not just about hiding things from me; they were about protecting me. She wanted me to find my own path without being burdened by her past."

Gabe's fingers lightly brushed against hers, his touch warm and reassuring. "And now, you've found your own path. You're not bound by the past; you're creating your future."

The breeze picked up slightly, carrying with it the salty tang of the sea. The first stars began to twinkle in the sky, and Isabel felt a sense of calm settling over her. The lighthouse, standing tall and resolute, seemed to echo the sentiment of their new beginning.

As the evening deepened, Isabel took a deep breath and turned to Gabe. "I want to make the most of this new start. I'm ready to take risks, to embrace the future with you. I want to build something real and lasting."

Gabe's eyes sparkled with affection. "And I'm here, ready to build that future with you. We've come through so much, and now it's time to move forward, together."

They shared a quiet moment, letting the serenity of the lighthouse and the beauty of the night sky envelop them. The past, with all its pain and uncertainty, seemed to fade into the background, leaving them with a clear view of their future. The lighthouse had served as a metaphor for their journey—a beacon guiding them through the storms and leading them to a place of clarity and commitment.

As they stood up to leave, Isabel felt a renewed sense of purpose. The lighthouse, which had once been a symbol of her mother's hidden past, now represented the promise of her own future. The secrets of the past had been unveiled, and the path ahead was clear, illuminated by the light of their shared hope and love.

Walking hand in hand back to the car, Isabel and Gabe shared a comfortable silence, the weight of their recent revelations giving way to a sense of peace. The journey they had undertaken together had brought them closer, forging a bond that was stronger and more resilient.

The drive back to town was quiet, with only the gentle hum of the engine and the occasional rustle of leaves breaking the silence. As they approached the city lights, Isabel felt a sense of contentment. The lighthouse had given her the clarity she needed, and she was ready to face whatever came next with Gabe by her side.

They arrived at the edge of town, the lights of the city twinkling in the distance. Isabel looked at Gabe, her heart full. "Thank you for being my lighthouse, Gabe. For guiding me through the storm and helping me find my way."

Gabe smiled, his hand resting gently on hers. "And thank you for trusting me with your heart. Together, we'll make sure that our future is as bright as the light from that lighthouse."

As they made their way home, Isabel felt a sense of closure and excitement. The journey had been long and filled with challenges, but it had also been filled with moments of profound connection and understanding. The lighthouse had played a crucial role in their story, serving as a symbol of hope and renewal.

Isabel knew that their future was still unwritten, but with Gabe by her side and the past finally laid to rest, she felt ready to embrace whatever came next. The lighthouse had been a beacon of hope, and now, as they moved forward, Isabel felt a sense of peace and optimism about the journey ahead.

The drive back to town was a quiet one, the peaceful stillness between Isabel and Gabe carrying the weight of their shared revelations. The twilight gradually gave way to night, the stars emerging in the sky like tiny beacons of light. Isabel looked out the window, lost in thought, while Gabe occasionally glanced at her, his face reflecting a blend of contentment and contemplation.

When they arrived at the edge of town, the warm glow of the city lights contrasted sharply with the cool, calm darkness they had just left behind. Isabel took a deep breath, feeling a sense of finality and promise in the air.

As they parked and stepped out of the car, Gabe reached for her hand, his grip firm and reassuring. "You know, it's remarkable how places can change over time, but they can also stay the same. This lighthouse, for all its years, still holds its light for those who need it."

Isabel nodded, squeezing his hand. "It's like a reminder that no matter where we go, there's always a place that can guide us home.

Tonight has been so much more than I ever expected. It's given me a new perspective on my past and a clearer vision for our future."

Gabe smiled, his eyes reflecting the light of the nearby street-lamps. "And it's given me a new appreciation for what we have. For how we've grown together and how much we've learned from each other."

They walked through the quiet streets of their small town, the cool night air carrying the faint scent of flowers and the distant murmur of late-night activity. Their conversation was soft, punctuated by moments of comfortable silence. Each glance and touch between them spoke of a deeper understanding and an unspoken commitment.

As they reached Isabel's house, the front porch light was a warm beacon welcoming them home. Gabe held the door open for Isabel, and she stepped inside, feeling the comforting familiarity of her surroundings. She turned to him, her heart full of gratitude and love.

"Gabe, I know I've said it before, but I want you to know how much tonight means to me. It's not just about finding answers about my mother; it's about discovering new possibilities for us, too."

Gabe stepped closer, his gaze steady and sincere. "I feel the same way. Tonight has made me realize how much I value what we have and how much I want to build our future together."

Isabel's heart fluttered as she took in the sincerity of his words. "I've been so focused on my past and my fears that I forgot to fully embrace the present and the future we can create. But now, I feel like I'm finally ready to move forward."

Gabe's hand gently cupped her cheek, his thumb brushing softly against her skin. "And I'm ready to move forward with you. No more looking back, just moving forward together."

The intimacy of the moment felt profound, and Isabel leaned into his touch, feeling a sense of peace and certainty. "There's something about tonight that feels like a new beginning. Like we're closing one chapter and opening a new one, full of hope and possibilities."

Gabe's smile widened, his eyes reflecting the depth of his feelings. "I agree. We've been through so much, and we've come out stronger. Now, it's time to embrace what's next and make the most of every moment."

They shared a tender kiss, the warmth of their connection contrasting with the cool night air. The kiss was gentle, filled with the promise of a future built on understanding and love.

As they pulled away, Isabel looked into Gabe's eyes, her heart swelling with emotion. "Thank you for being here, for supporting me, and for loving me. I don't know where we'll go from here, but I know that as long as we're together, everything will be okay."

Gabe's expression was soft and affectionate. "I feel the same way. We've found something special, and I believe in us. We'll face whatever comes our way, side by side."

They spent the rest of the evening talking about their dreams and aspirations, their conversation flowing effortlessly as they shared their hopes for the future. The previous weight of their past struggles seemed to lift, replaced by a sense of excitement and anticipation.

As the night wore on, Isabel and Gabe eventually said their goodbyes, promising to see each other soon. Isabel watched him leave, her heart full of warmth and hope. The lighthouse had been a symbol of guidance and revelation, and now it stood as a testament to their journey and their future.

When Isabel closed the door and turned back into her home, she felt a profound sense of peace. The lighthouse had provided clarity and closure, and she was ready to embrace the new chapter of her life. The past was no longer a burden but a part of her story that had led her to this moment of renewed hope and love.

With a contented sigh, Isabel prepared for bed, her thoughts filled with the promise of tomorrow and the future she would build with Gabe. The journey ahead was uncertain, but she knew that with love and commitment, she and Gabe could face whatever came their way.

As she drifted off to sleep, the image of the lighthouse remained in her mind—a symbol of the light that guided her through the darkness and toward a future filled with possibilities. The path ahead was bright, and Isabel was ready to walk it with the person who had become her anchor and her beacon of hope.

The sun rose over the island the next morning, casting a golden hue across the landscape and filling Isabel's room with a warm, inviting light. The serenity of the dawn mirrored her own sense of newfound clarity and hope. Isabel awoke with a feeling of peace that had eluded her for so long. The previous night's events felt like a turning point, a moment of reconnection not just with Gabe but with herself.

She made her way to the kitchen, where the smell of freshly brewed coffee filled the air. The house was quiet, a peaceful contrast to the emotional whirlwind of the past few days. As she sipped her coffee, her mind wandered back to the lighthouse, the scene of her revelation and Gabe's heartfelt confession. The place had become more than a mere landmark; it had transformed into a symbol of her journey and transformation.

A soft knock at the door pulled her from her thoughts. Isabel opened it to find Gabe standing there with a bouquet of wildflowers, a smile on his face. "Good morning," he said, holding out the flowers. "I thought you might like these."

Isabel accepted the bouquet, her heart swelling with affection. "Good morning. These are beautiful. Thank you."

Gabe stepped inside, and they shared a warm embrace. The simple act of being close to each other felt grounding, like coming home after a long journey. Gabe's presence was comforting, a reminder of the bond they had rekindled.

"I was thinking," Gabe said as they settled at the kitchen table, "about how much has changed since we first started talking again. It feels like everything is falling into place."

Isabel nodded, her gaze meeting his. "It does. It's as if everything that happened before was leading us to this moment. I feel like I'm finally understanding my past and my place in it."

Gabe reached across the table, taking her hand in his. "And I'm so grateful to be part of this journey with you. It's been incredible to see you open up and confront everything you've been through."

Isabel smiled, squeezing his hand. "It's been an incredible journey for me, too. There's something so special about how we've grown together through all of this. I feel more connected to you than ever before."

They talked over breakfast, their conversation flowing naturally as they shared their thoughts and plans for the future. Gabe spoke of his dreams, his hopes for their relationship, and his excitement about the life they could build together. Isabel listened with a full heart, feeling a deep sense of belonging and partnership.

After breakfast, they decided to take a walk along the shore, enjoying the crisp morning air and the sound of the waves gently lapping against the sand. The beach was tranquil, with only a few early morning joggers and the distant cries of seagulls breaking the silence.

As they walked hand in hand, Isabel looked out at the horizon, her mind filled with reflections on her journey. The lighthouse stood tall in the distance, its beacon a constant reminder of the clarity and direction she had found.

"This place," Isabel said, her voice soft but filled with emotion, "has been a part of my life for so long, but it's only recently that I've truly understood its significance."

Gabe glanced at her, his expression attentive and caring. "How so?"

Isabel paused, taking a deep breath. "When I first came back, I was so focused on my past, on the things I couldn't change. But being here, facing everything, and finding out more about my mother—it's helped me see that the lighthouse represents something much bigger. It's about finding light in the darkness, finding direction when you're lost."

Gabe nodded, his eyes reflecting the morning sun. "It's incredible how places and memories can hold such powerful meanings. And it's even more remarkable when you can share that understanding with someone you care about."

They continued walking, their conversation drifting to lighter topics as they enjoyed each other's company. The connection they shared felt natural and effortless, a testament to the bond they had built through their trials and triumphs.

As they reached the end of their walk, Gabe stopped and turned to face Isabel. "There's something I've been meaning to ask you."

Isabel looked at him curiously, her heart fluttering with anticipation. "What is it?"

Gabe took a deep breath, his eyes searching hers. "Would you consider making this place—this island—our home? I know it's been a journey for you, and I've seen how much it means to you. I want to be here with you, to build a life together."

Isabel's heart leapt at his words. She had imagined a future with Gabe, but hearing him voice it made the prospect feel even more real. The idea of building a life together on the island, a place that had become so significant to her, felt both comforting and exhilarating.

"I would love that," Isabel said, her voice filled with emotion. "This place has become a part of me, and I can't imagine my life without it. And I can't imagine my life without you."

Gabe's face lit up with a radiant smile. "Then let's make it happen. We'll create a home here, together."

They shared a heartfelt kiss, sealing their promise with a gesture of love and commitment. The future stretched out before them, full of possibilities and dreams to be realized.

As they walked back to Isabel's house, their hands intertwined and their hearts aligned, Isabel felt a profound sense of peace. The lighthouse, once a symbol of her search for answers, had now become a beacon of their shared journey and future.

The day continued with a sense of joyful anticipation. Isabel and Gabe began to make plans for their future, discussing their vision for the island and their new life together. Their conversations were filled with hope and excitement, each idea and dream strengthening their bond.

As the sun set, casting a golden glow over the island, Isabel stood by the window, looking out at the lighthouse. It was a fitting end to a day that had been filled with love, revelations, and the promise of a shared future.

With Gabe by her side and the lighthouse as a constant reminder of their journey, Isabel knew that she was finally where she was meant to be. The past had led her to this moment, and the future was wide open, filled with love and the possibility of new beginnings.

The lighthouse stood tall and steadfast in the distance, its light shining brightly as a symbol of their journey and the love that had guided them through. And as Isabel and Gabe prepared to embrace their future together, they knew that they had found their way home.

The night fell gently over the island, draping the landscape in a soft, velvety darkness. The lighthouse stood as a solitary sentinel, its beam cutting through the night sky with a steady, reassuring rhythm. For Isabel and Gabe, the lighthouse had become more than a beacon; it was a symbol of their journey and the love they had rediscovered.

As they arrived at the lighthouse, Isabel and Gabe walked hand in hand, their footsteps soft on the gravel path. The world seemed to slow down around them, the sounds of the island settling into a tranquil hush. The lighthouse's light cast a warm, golden glow over the scene, creating a halo that enveloped them in a comforting embrace.

Isabel paused at the entrance, taking a deep breath. The lighthouse had always been a place of mystery and reflection for her, but now it felt like a sacred space where the past and future converged. Gabe stood beside her, his presence a steady source of strength and support.

"This place," Isabel said, her voice filled with emotion, "has meant so much to me over the years. It's where I've come to find answers, to confront my past. And now, standing here with you, it feels like the perfect place to start our new chapter."

Gabe nodded, his gaze fixed on the lighthouse. "I couldn't agree more. It's become a symbol of our journey and everything we've overcome together."

They stepped inside the lighthouse, the familiar scent of aged wood and sea salt greeting them. The interior was just as Isabel remembered, with its spiral staircase leading up to the beacon room. The space was both cozy and majestic, filled with the echoes of past generations who had tended the light.

As they climbed the stairs, the sense of anticipation grew. Isabel could feel her heart pounding in her chest, not just from the climb but from the emotional weight of the moment. The lighthouse had been a place of solitude and introspection, but now it was becoming a symbol of their shared future.

At the top, they reached the beacon room. The light itself was a marvel, its beam slicing through the darkness and casting a warm, soothing glow over the room. Isabel and Gabe stood side by side, looking out over the island and the vast, star-studded sea beyond.

Isabel turned to Gabe, her eyes reflecting the light of the beacon. "This place has always been about finding direction and clarity. It's where I've faced my fears and found my way. And now, it feels like it's the perfect place to share everything with you."

Gabe took her hands in his, his expression tender and sincere. "I'm here with you, Isabel. Through everything we've been through, I've learned that what matters most is the love and connection we share. This place is a testament to that."

Isabel's heart swelled with emotion. She could see the depth of Gabe's feelings for her, his commitment and love shining as brightly as the beacon itself. The lighthouse had been a symbol of her past struggles, but now it was becoming a beacon of their shared future.

"Gabe," Isabel said, her voice trembling slightly, "there's something I need to tell you. This lighthouse, this island—it's been a part of my journey, my search for meaning. And now, it feels like the right place to take the next step in our lives together."

Gabe looked at her, his eyes filled with understanding and affection. "What is it?"

Isabel took a deep breath, her emotions welling up inside her. "I've realized that my mother's secrets and the struggles I've faced have brought me here, to this moment with you. I've been so focused on the past, but now I see that the future is what matters most. I want to build that future with you, here on this island, in this place that has become so meaningful to me."

Gabe's face lit up with a radiant smile. "Isabel, I've wanted nothing more than to build a life with you. This place, this island, it's become a part of our story, and I can't imagine my life without it—or without you."

They shared a heartfelt embrace, the warmth of their connection filling the space around them. The lighthouse's light continued to beam, casting a steady glow over the island and the vast ocean beyond.

As they stood together, Isabel felt a profound sense of peace and fulfillment. The lighthouse had been a symbol of her past struggles, but now it was a beacon of their shared future. The journey she had embarked upon had led her to this moment, and she felt ready to embrace the next chapter of her life with Gabe by her side.

The night deepened, and the stars shone brightly above, reflecting the light of the beacon. Isabel and Gabe remained at the top of the lighthouse, their hearts aligned and their future intertwined. The lighthouse stood as a testament to their journey, a symbol of the love and commitment that had guided them through their trials and triumphs.

As they descended the staircase, hand in hand, Isabel and Gabe felt a renewed sense of hope and excitement for the future. The lighthouse had become more than just a landmark; it was a symbol of their love and the life they were about to build together.

The island was bathed in moonlight as they walked back to the house, their hearts full of dreams and possibilities. Isabel felt a deep sense of gratitude for the journey that had brought her here and for the love that had blossomed in the most unexpected of places.

With each step, she felt more confident in the path she had chosen and in the future she was building with Gabe. The lighthouse, with its steady beam and unwavering presence, had become a guiding light in their lives, a symbol of the love and connection that would continue to guide them as they moved forward together.

As they reached the house, Isabel and Gabe knew that their journey was far from over. The future held countless adventures and challenges, but they were ready to face them together. The lighthouse had shown them the way, and with love and commitment as their compass, they were prepared to embrace whatever lay ahead.

The night was filled with the promise of new beginnings, and as Isabel and Gabe prepared to embark on their shared future, they knew that their love would continue to shine as brightly as the beacon in the lighthouse. The island had become their home, and the lighthouse had become a symbol of their love—a love that would guide them through every step of their journey together.

As the night wore on, the island seemed to envelop Isabel and Gabe in a cocoon of tranquility. They made their way down the winding path from the lighthouse, their hands entwined, feeling the warmth of their connection. The moonlight danced over the gentle waves, casting a silvery glow that mirrored the light of the beacon.

When they arrived at the house, the quiet inside was a stark contrast to the vibrant celebration of their love earlier. Isabel paused in the doorway, her heart full, yet brimming with anticipation for what lay ahead. Gabe, sensing her lingering thoughts, pulled her gently inside and led her to the living room where a soft fire crackled in the hearth, its light flickering warmly against the walls.

As they settled into the comfortable embrace of the sofa, the intimacy of the moment deepened. Gabe looked at Isabel, his eyes reflecting the firelight, and said, "You know, I've been thinking a lot about the lighthouse and everything it means to us. It's more than just a landmark. It's like a living part of our story."

Isabel nodded, her gaze fixed on the dancing flames. "Yes, it's become a symbol of how far we've come. It's also a reminder of how our pasts shape us, but don't have to define our future."

Gabe took a deep breath, his expression thoughtful. "I've been meaning to tell you something. This place, this island—it's been a dream of mine for a long time. But it wasn't until you came back that I realized it wasn't complete without you. You've helped me see that the dream isn't just about a place, but about sharing it with someone who means everything to me."

Isabel's eyes softened with emotion. "Gabe, I feel the same way. This place was part of my journey, a journey I didn't even know I was on until I came back. And now, it feels like it's all coming together in a way I never imagined."

The fire crackled softly, filling the room with a soothing rhythm. Isabel leaned her head against Gabe's shoulder, feeling a profound sense of peace. The struggles and uncertainties of the past seemed to melt away in the warmth of their shared love and the promise of their future.

After a few moments of comfortable silence, Gabe spoke again, his voice barely above a whisper. "Isabel, I want to build a life here with you. I want us to be a part of this island's story, just like it's become a part of ours. But more than that, I want to build a life together, where we support each other and face everything—both the challenges and the joys—side by side."

Isabel's heart swelled at his words. She looked up at him, her eyes shining with tears of joy. "I want that too, Gabe. I want to build our future here, where we can be ourselves and create something beautiful together."

Gabe gently cupped her face in his hands, his eyes searching hers for a moment. "Then let's take this leap together. Let's make this island our home and build the life we've always dreamed of."

Isabel nodded, her heart brimming with happiness and determination. "Yes, let's do that. Let's make this our forever."

They sealed their promise with a tender kiss, the warmth of their love mingling with the fire's glow. The world outside seemed to fade away as they embraced, their connection deepening with each passing moment. The lighthouse's beam continued its steady watch over the island, a silent witness to their vow and the future they were about to create.

As they pulled away, Gabe took Isabel's hand and led her to the window. The view outside was breathtaking—a landscape bathed in the gentle light of the moon, the sea stretching out endlessly. The lighthouse's beam cut through the night sky, a guiding light that seemed to affirm their decision.

"This is our place," Gabe said, his voice filled with a sense of finality and hope. "And this is where we'll start our new beginning."

Isabel looked out at the view, her heart swelling with a sense of belonging. The island, with its beauty and serenity, felt like the perfect backdrop for their new life. She squeezed Gabe's hand, feeling a surge of gratitude and excitement.

"Yes," she said, her voice steady and filled with conviction. "This is where we'll build our dreams, our future. And I'm so grateful to be doing it with you."

They spent the rest of the evening talking about their plans and dreams, their excitement building with each shared thought. The future was filled with possibilities, and they were ready to embrace it with open hearts.

As the fire slowly died down, Isabel and Gabe felt a profound sense of contentment. They knew that their journey together was just beginning, but they were ready to face it with the love and commitment they had found in each other. The lighthouse, with its unwavering light, had become a symbol of their shared future—a future filled with hope, love, and endless possibilities.

They eventually retired to bed, their hearts and minds filled with the promise of a new day. The island was their home now, and the lighthouse stood as a steadfast guardian of their love and dreams. As they drifted off to sleep, Isabel and Gabe felt a deep sense of peace and fulfillment, knowing that their journey together was just beginning and that their love would continue to shine as brightly as the beacon that guided them.

As the first light of dawn filtered through the sheer curtains of their bedroom, Isabel and Gabe lay entwined in each other's arms, the warmth of their love a comforting cocoon. The events of the previous night felt like a dream, but the reality of their decision to build a life together on the island was as solid as the ground beneath them.

Isabel awoke first, her mind already buzzing with thoughts of the future. She took a moment to savor the tranquility, the gentle rhythm of Gabe's breathing beside her. The lighthouse's beam had guided them to this moment, and she could hardly believe how far they had come.

Gently slipping out of bed, Isabel padded to the window and looked out at the island, now bathed in the soft morning light. The lighthouse stood resolute, a silent sentinel over their new beginning. She felt a swell of gratitude and hope, her heart full as she thought about the life they were about to create.

Gabe stirred behind her, sensing her movement. He stretched and rubbed his eyes, then saw Isabel standing by the window, her silhouette framed by the morning light.

"Morning," he murmured, his voice husky with sleep.

"Morning," Isabel replied, turning to smile at him. "I was just thinking about everything we talked about last night. It feels like a new chapter is about to begin."

Gabe rose from the bed and joined her at the window, wrapping his arms around her waist from behind. "It does. And I couldn't be more excited about it. We have so much ahead of us."

They stood there for a few moments, savoring the peaceful start to their day. The world outside was waking up, the soft sounds of nature blending with the distant calls of seabirds. The lighthouse's steady beam had dimmed for the day, but its light continued to symbolize their shared path forward.

"We should start making plans," Isabel said, her voice filled with resolve. "There's so much to do, but I feel ready to take it on."

Gabe nodded, his eyes reflecting his enthusiasm. "Absolutely. Let's start by figuring out how to set up the photography studio and how we can integrate it into the island's community. I want this place to feel like home for both of us."

They spent the morning discussing their plans, making lists, and brainstorming ideas. Gabe's excitement was contagious, and Isabel found herself buoyed by his energy. They talked about how they could turn the studio into a place that not only showcased their work but also became a hub for local events and gatherings.

As they made their way downstairs for breakfast, Isabel felt a renewed sense of purpose. The lighthouse, the island, and their shared dreams were now intertwined with their daily lives. They had overcome their past challenges and were now looking forward to building a future together.

The kitchen was filled with the comforting aroma of freshly brewed coffee and sizzling bacon. Gabe cooked while Isabel set the table, their easy camaraderie a testament to the bond they had formed. The mundane tasks of preparing breakfast felt different now—like part of a larger, meaningful journey they were embarking on together.

"Do you ever think about how different our lives could have been if we hadn't come back to the island?" Isabel asked, her tone thoughtful as she stirred the coffee.

Gabe looked up from the stove, a smile playing on his lips. "All the time. I think about how much we've grown and changed. Coming back here was like finding a piece of ourselves we didn't even know we were missing."

Isabel nodded, her eyes reflecting the light of the morning sun. "It's strange how sometimes we need to go back to our roots to truly understand who we are and what we want."

They enjoyed a leisurely breakfast, talking and laughing as they planned their day. The sense of unity and shared purpose was palpable, and both felt an overwhelming sense of gratitude for the path they were on.

After breakfast, they set out to explore the island once more, this time with a fresh perspective. They walked hand in hand, discussing ideas for the studio and imagining the future. The island was full of potential, and they were excited to make their mark.

As they walked, they came across familiar faces from the community, who greeted them warmly and expressed their support for the new photography studio. The islanders' enthusiasm was encouraging, and it reaffirmed their belief that their decision to stay and build a life together was the right one.

The afternoon was spent meeting with local suppliers and exploring potential locations for the studio. They were both invigorated by the possibilities and eager to get started on their new venture. The island seemed to embrace their plans, its natural beauty and welcoming spirit a perfect backdrop for their dreams.

As the sun began to set, casting a golden hue over the island, Isabel and Gabe returned to the lighthouse. They stood together on the cliff, looking out over the sea, the sky painted with hues of orange and pink.

"This is where it all started," Isabel said softly, her voice filled with emotion. "And now it's where our new beginning begins."

Gabe took her hand and squeezed it gently. "It's perfect. We've come full circle, and I couldn't be happier to be doing this with you."

They stood there in silence, taking in the beauty of the sunset and the promise of their future. The lighthouse, with its steadfast light, seemed to offer a silent blessing to their new life. It was a symbol of guidance and hope, a reminder of the journey they had undertaken and the love they had found.

As darkness fell and the stars began to twinkle in the night sky, Isabel and Gabe knew that their journey was just beginning. The lighthouse's beam once again cut through the night, a beacon of their dreams and their future together.

They returned to the house, their hearts full and their spirits high. The night was filled with the sound of their laughter and the warmth of their shared love. As they settled into bed, they felt a deep sense of contentment and excitement for the future.

The island was no longer just a place—they had made it their home, and the lighthouse stood as a testament to their love and their dreams. Together, Isabel and Gabe were ready to face whatever came next, knowing that their love and their shared vision would guide them through.

With the lighthouse's light shining softly in the distance, they drifted off to sleep, their hearts full of hope and anticipation for the life they were about to build. The journey ahead was filled with promise, and they were ready to embrace it together, with the lighthouse standing as a constant reminder of their love and their future.

As the evening settled over the island, the soft murmur of the sea and the gentle rustle of the trees created a peaceful backdrop to Isabel and Gabe's growing sense of unity. They had spent the day planning and dreaming, and now, as night fell, they stood on the cliff overlooking the ocean, their hearts full of anticipation.

The lighthouse, a steadfast guardian of the shore, cast its beam across the water, its light piercing the darkness and illuminating their path forward. Isabel and Gabe felt a profound connection to the lighthouse, as if it symbolized their own journey—a beacon of hope guiding them through uncertainty and towards a shared future.

Gabe reached out and took Isabel's hand, pulling her gently toward him. The intimacy of their touch was comforting, a silent affirmation of their commitment to each other. They stood close, the warmth of their bodies mingling with the cool evening air.

"I keep thinking about the lighthouse," Isabel said softly, her gaze fixed on the rotating beam. "It feels like it's been guiding us all along."

Gabe nodded, his eyes reflecting the light from the lantern. "It's more than just a structure. It represents our journey, our struggles, and our triumphs. It's been here through it all, just like we've been for each other."

Isabel turned to face him, her eyes searching his. "Do you ever wonder if we're making the right choice? Moving here, starting over..."

Gabe's expression softened, and he cupped her face gently in his hands. "Every time I look at you, I know we are. You've brought so much light into my life, just like this lighthouse. It's not just about where we are but who we are together."

A tear slipped down Isabel's cheek, and Gabe wiped it away with his thumb. "I've been holding onto so many fears, so many doubts. But standing here with you, I feel like I can face anything."

Gabe kissed her forehead tenderly, his touch reassuring. "We've faced so much already, and we've come out stronger. This is our chance to build something beautiful, something that reflects who we are and what we've been through."

Isabel nodded, feeling a sense of peace wash over her. The lighthouse, standing strong against the elements, symbolized her own journey of growth and healing. It was a reminder that even in the darkest times, there was always a light guiding her forward.

As they walked hand in hand along the cliff's edge, the night air filled with the sound of their footsteps and the distant calls of seabirds. The stars above were scattered like diamonds, their light reflecting off the tranquil surface of the ocean.

They reached a small, secluded area on the cliff, a spot that offered a panoramic view of the island and the sea. Gabe spread out a blanket and they sat down, the softness of the fabric contrasting with the rugged terrain. The blanket was adorned with a simple pattern of stars, reminiscent of the night sky above them.

"I've been thinking about the photography studio," Isabel said as they settled onto the blanket. "I want it to be more than just a place to showcase our work. I want it to be a space that brings people together, a place where they can find inspiration and connection."

Gabe smiled, his eyes filled with admiration. "I love that idea. It's about creating a space that reflects our values and our vision for the future. We can use it to tell stories, to share our experiences, and to connect with the community."

Isabel leaned against him, feeling a sense of contentment. "It's amazing to think about how much has changed. I never imagined I'd find this kind of happiness again, let alone with someone who understands me so deeply."

Gabe's arm tightened around her, and he kissed the top of her head. "You deserve all the happiness in the world, Isabel. You've been through so much, and you've come out stronger and more beautiful than ever."

They sat in silence for a while, simply enjoying each other's presence and the beauty of the night. The lighthouse continued its steady rotation, its light a symbol of their enduring hope and commitment.

As the evening wore on, Isabel and Gabe talked about their plans for the future, their dreams for the photography studio, and the life they wanted to build together. Their conversation flowed effortlessly, filled with laughter and shared visions.

Eventually, they fell quiet, wrapped in the serenity of the moment. The lighthouse's beam cut through the darkness, a constant reminder of their journey and their shared path forward. The light seemed to embrace them, its warmth a comforting presence.

"I feel like we're standing at the beginning of something wonderful," Isabel said softly, her voice filled with emotion. "Like we're about to embark on the most amazing adventure of our lives."

Gabe's eyes shone with love and determination. "We are. And we're doing it together. No matter what challenges come our way, we'll face them as a team."

As the night deepened, they lay back on the blanket, gazing up at the stars. The lighthouse's beam continued its rhythmic sweep, a symbol of hope and guidance.

Isabel felt a deep sense of peace and fulfillment. The lighthouse, with its unwavering light, had guided her to this moment of clarity and commitment. It stood as a testament to her journey and the love she had found with Gabe.

In the quiet of the night, with the stars twinkling above and the lighthouse shining in the distance, Isabel and Gabe knew that their future was bright and full of promise. They were ready to embrace the challenges and joys that lay ahead, knowing that they had each other to lean on.

As they drifted into a peaceful sleep beneath the stars, the lighthouse's light continued to shine, a beacon of their love and their shared dreams. Together, they faced the future with hope and anticipation, ready to build a life filled with love, creativity, and connection.

16

Chapter 16: Epilogue: A New Beginning

The ocean stretched out before Isabel, its waves gentle and rhythmic, mirroring the steady beat of her heart. She stood at the edge of the shore, the cool breeze brushing her cheeks, and felt a sense of peace she hadn't known in years. Willow Creek had become home again, but it wasn't the place that had transformed her—it was the journey she had undertaken to find herself.

Isabel breathed in the salty air, her gaze shifting to the lighthouse on the horizon. The place that once held so many of her mother's secrets had now become a symbol of light and truth for her. The discovery of her mother's love affair, her regrets, and her unspoken wishes had been painful, but it had also opened the door to understanding. Isabel had learned that her mother wasn't hiding out of shame or fear of judgment—she had been protecting her daughter, sparing her the weight of her own struggles so that Isabel could have a chance at a different life.

But in uncovering her mother's past, Isabel had found a way to heal her own wounds. She no longer felt the need to run, to shield herself from vulnerability. She had allowed herself to grieve, to feel the fullness of her emotions, and in doing so, she had embraced the one thing she had always feared the most: love.

Gabe had been there through it all. From the awkward first encounter to the night of the Festival of Lights, he had seen her at her most guarded and her most open. Their relationship had grown slowly, tenderly—like the island itself, shaped by time and the elements. Isabel glanced behind her toward the small house they now shared. It was modest, but it was filled with light—just like their connection.

In the months since they had confessed their love to each other, both Isabel and Gabe had continued to grow as individuals. Isabel had opened the photography studio, turning her passion into something tangible. It wasn't easy at first—she faced doubts, fearing she would fail, fearing she didn't deserve happiness. But every step she took was a step toward building something new, something hers. Her photos were more than just images; they were a reflection of her own journey. Through her lens, she captured moments of raw emotion and beauty, much like the way she had learned to appreciate the complexities of her own life.

Gabe, too, had found new purpose. He had taken over the local inn after his father retired, reshaping it into a place that reflected his own warmth and hospitality. The once quiet and brooding man had opened up, not just to Isabel but to the community. He was more engaged, more present, and his laughter had become a regular sound in the inn's lobby as he entertained guests and welcomed old friends.

They had each found their place in Willow Creek, but more importantly, they had found it together. Isabel marveled at the balance they had achieved—how their relationship wasn't built on grand gestures or dramatic declarations, but on quiet moments of understanding, mutual respect, and shared vulnerability. They didn't need words to communicate their love; it was in the way Gabe brushed a strand of hair from her face or the way she rested her head on his shoulder as they watched the sunset.

For the first time in her life, Isabel felt grounded. She wasn't running anymore—not from her past, not from her emotions, not from the people who loved her. And in that stillness, she had found freedom.

Of course, there were challenges. Building a life together wasn't always easy. There were moments of doubt, disagreements, and uncertainties about the future. But what had changed was their ability to face those moments with trust and honesty. Gabe had taught her that it was okay to lean on someone else, that asking for help didn't make her weak. And Isabel had shown Gabe that it was okay to open up, to let others see his heart.

Together, they had created a partnership where both of them could be fully themselves. Their love wasn't about filling empty spaces or healing old wounds—it was about supporting each other as they grew. They didn't complete each other; they complemented each other.

Isabel smiled to herself, thinking about the journey that had brought them here. It hadn't been easy, and there had been times when she wondered if it was worth the risk. But now, standing at the edge of the water with the life they had built together behind her, she knew that every step had been worth it.

They had both grown individually, too. Isabel's confidence had blossomed with each passing day. She was no longer the woman who second-guessed every decision or worried about what others thought. She had learned to trust her instincts, to believe in her own strength. Her photography studio was thriving, not just because of her talent, but because she had poured her heart into it.

She had connected with the community in ways she hadn't expected, capturing their stories through her lens and helping them see the beauty in their everyday lives.

Gabe had found his own sense of purpose. Running the inn gave him a reason to engage with people, to be part of something bigger than himself. The walls that once surrounded him had come down, brick by brick, as he allowed himself to open up. He was no longer the man who hid behind silence and solitude; he was part of the heartbeat of Willow Creek.

Their growth, both individually and as a couple, was woven into the fabric of their lives. They had learned to face challenges together, not as a way to fix each other's problems, but as a way to stand beside each other, knowing they were stronger for it. Their love wasn't just about passion—it was about partnership, respect, and the belief that they could weather anything as long as they faced it together.

As the sun dipped below the horizon, casting a golden glow over the water, Isabel felt a deep sense of gratitude. She had found more than love in Willow Creek—she had found herself. And with Gabe by her side, she knew that whatever the future held, they would face it together, stronger than ever.

The path ahead wasn't without its challenges, but for the first time, Isabel wasn't afraid of what lay beyond the horizon. She was ready for whatever came next—because now, she knew that home wasn't a place. Home was the love they had built, the life they shared, and the person she had become.

The morning sun filtered through the curtains, casting a soft glow over the room. Isabel stretched under the warm covers, savoring the moment of peace. The sound of Gabe humming softly in the kitchen brought a smile to her lips. It was a routine she had come to cherish: waking up to the comforting smells of coffee and freshly baked bread, the quiet presence of the man who had become her rock.

Her eyes wandered to the small desk by the window, now cluttered with sketches and photographs. Opening her own photography studio had been a dream she wasn't sure would ever come true, yet here she was—thriving, creating, and capturing the world through her lens. The studio was nestled in the heart of Willow Creek, a small, cozy space that had quickly become a hub of activity in the town.

Isabel slid out of bed, wrapping herself in a light cardigan before padding softly toward the kitchen. Gabe was standing at the stove, flipping pancakes with a practiced ease, his eyes lighting up as she entered.

"Morning, sleepyhead," he greeted, leaning in for a kiss. "I was just about to come wake you."

"Is that coffee I smell?" Isabel asked with a grin, moving to pour herself a cup.

"Of course. I know better than to start your day without it," Gabe teased, setting the pancakes on a plate and sliding them toward her.

Their mornings together were filled with quiet contentment, a rhythm they had both settled into over time. After so much upheaval, the simplicity of their daily life felt like a gift. There were no grand gestures or dramatic declarations—just the steady pulse of love and partnership that carried them through.

The photography studio had taken off in ways Isabel never expected. Initially, she thought it would be a slow process, a hobby she might turn into a small business. But Willow Creek had embraced her work, and before long, she found herself busier than she could have imagined. People came from neighboring towns for

464 - EMMA DREAMWEAVER

portrait sessions, weddings, and family photos, drawn not just by her talent but by the authenticity she brought to her craft.

The studio had become a reflection of Isabel's journey—each photograph she captured told a story, much like her own. Whether it was the joy in a bride's eyes, the quiet bond between a father and daughter, or the laughter shared between friends, Isabel had a way of capturing the moments that mattered most. It wasn't just about the technical skill of photography anymore; it was about seeing the beauty in everyday life, in the connections between people.

Gabe had been her biggest supporter throughout the process. He had spent countless hours helping her renovate the space, turning it from an old, forgotten storefront into a vibrant, welcoming studio. The two of them had painted the walls together, hung her work in carefully chosen frames, and set up a gallery where clients could see the magic she created.

But Gabe wasn't just a silent partner in her work—he had found his own sense of fulfillment in running the inn. After taking it over from his father, he had put his heart into revitalizing the place, transforming it into a warm, inviting space that reflected his own personality. Where the inn had once felt like a relic of the past, it now had a fresh, modern charm. Guests flocked to Willow Creek, not just for the beauty of the town but for the hospitality Gabe offered. His easygoing nature, paired with his deep connection to the community, made him the perfect host.

They had found their rhythm as a couple, balancing their personal ambitions with their shared life. In the evenings, after the hustle of the day had quieted, they would sit on the porch of their home—another small project they had tackled together. The house, once an empty shell of possibilities, was now filled with the love they had built. They had made it their own, painting the walls with colors that made them feel grounded and at peace, hanging art-work and photographs that reflected their journey together.

The community had embraced them, too. Where once Isabel had felt like an outsider, now she was part of the fabric of Willow Creek. She was invited to town meetings, festivals, and dinners. People stopped her on the street to ask about her latest project or to thank her for capturing a special moment in their lives. It was a far cry from the isolation she had once felt, and each day, she was reminded of how far she had come.

One morning, as they walked through the town square hand in hand, Isabel and Gabe paused to watch the children playing in the park. The sound of their laughter filled the air, a reminder of the simple joys of life. Isabel's heart swelled with gratitude for the life they had built—one filled with love, purpose, and community.

"I never thought I'd feel so settled here," Isabel said softly, glancing up at Gabe.

He smiled, squeezing her hand. "I always knew you would. You just needed time to see it for yourself."

She leaned her head on his shoulder, watching the children chase each other through the grass. "I'm glad I stayed," she whispered. "I can't imagine being anywhere else."

Neither could Gabe. They had both grown so much since the day Isabel had returned to Willow Creek, unsure of what she was searching for. Together, they had found not just a home, but a life that was full—of love, of purpose, of joy.

Their new life wasn't perfect, of course. There were still challenges, moments of doubt, and days when the weight of their responsibilities felt overwhelming. But through it all, they had learned to lean on each other, to trust in the strength of their partnership.

As they walked back to the studio, Isabel felt a deep sense of contentment. She had faced her past, confronted her fears, and found the courage to open her heart again. And in doing so, she had built a life she could be proud of—a life she wanted to share with Gabe for the rest of her days.

In the end, it wasn't the grand gestures or dramatic moments that defined their relationship. It was the quiet, steady love that grew between them in the midst of their everyday lives. And that, Isabel knew, was more than enough.

The ringing of the phone jolted Isabel from her thoughts as she sat in the studio, editing the latest batch of wedding photos. Her heart sank as she glanced at the caller ID—an unfamiliar number. She hesitated for a moment, then picked it up.

"Isabel Prescott?" a serious voice asked.

"Yes, this is she," Isabel replied, bracing herself.

"This is Jim from Willow Creek Utilities. I'm afraid we've got some bad news about your studio. The storm last night caused a significant power surge, and it looks like it's damaged some of the electrical wiring in the building. We'll need to shut off power for a few days to make repairs."

Isabel's stomach tightened. She had a full schedule of clients lined up, including two major portrait sessions that couldn't be postponed. The studio was her lifeblood, and any disruption meant potential loss of business and trust. She immediately felt the familiar pang of anxiety creeping in, her mind racing with worst-case scenarios.

"Thank you for letting me know," she replied, her voice steady though her heart was anything but. "I'll figure something out."

As soon as she hung up, Isabel buried her face in her hands. The old doubts resurfaced, whispering that she wasn't cut out for this, that she had taken on more than she could handle. But before those feelings could take root, a pair of warm hands rested on her shoulders. She looked up to see Gabe standing there, concern etched in his face.

"What happened?" he asked softly, crouching down beside her.

Isabel explained the situation, feeling the pressure build as she recounted the details. "I don't know what I'm going to do. I have deadlines, clients, and no power for the next few days. It's a disaster."

Gabe listened quietly, his thumb gently rubbing the back of her hand. When she finished, he didn't offer platitudes or tell her not to worry. Instead, he said, "Let's figure this out together. You're not alone in this."

His words, simple and steady, were like a lifeline. The old Isabel would have shouldered the burden by herself, trying to fix everything alone. But now, she understood the power of leaning on someone she trusted. Gabe had been there for her through the toughest moments, and she knew they could weather this storm too.

They sat down together, brainstorming solutions. Gabe suggested moving some of her upcoming shoots to the inn, where there was still power. The large, open lobby could be transformed into a temporary studio space, and the natural light streaming in from the windows would make for beautiful photographs.

"I can rearrange some of the furniture, make it look like an intentional setup," Gabe offered. "Guests love that kind of personal touch."

Isabel smiled at his practicality and optimism. The idea wasn't perfect, but it was a solution. And more importantly, she wasn't facing this challenge alone.

Over the next few days, the inn became a hub of activity. Isabel's clients arrived, curious about the new location but thrilled with the results. The makeshift studio offered a different kind of charm, and Isabel found herself capturing some of her best work in that improvised space.

Though there were still moments of stress and uncertainty, Isabel felt more at ease than she would have in the past. She knew that whatever challenge arose, she and Gabe would face it side by side. Their relationship had been tested, and it had grown stronger each time.

When the studio's power was finally restored, and Isabel was able to move back into her own space, she reflected on how far they had come. The crisis, which once might have sent her into a spiral of self-doubt, had instead strengthened her resolve. More than that, it had shown her the depth of the partnership she and Gabe shared. They didn't just share the good times—they faced the difficult moments together, trusting in each other's strength.

As she packed up the last of her equipment from the inn, Isabel looked at Gabe with a sense of gratitude. "We made it through," she said, a smile tugging at her lips.

Gabe grinned, wrapping his arms around her. "Of course we did. We always will."

And in that moment, Isabel knew that whatever the future held—whether it was more challenges or new opportunities—she and Gabe would face it together, with the quiet, steady love that had carried them this far. Their resilience wasn't just in their individual growth, but in the unwavering trust they had built in each other. It was that trust, more than anything, that would see them through whatever came next.

As the golden hues of the late afternoon sun bathed the island in its warm embrace, Isabel and Gabe sat on the porch of the studio, looking out over the horizon. The soft hum of the sea filled the air, mingling with the gentle rustle of the wind through the trees.

It was a moment of calm, one that spoke of endings but, more importantly, of new beginnings.

Isabel leaned back in her chair, feeling a contentment that once seemed so far out of reach. The storm that had swept through her life when she first returned to the island had settled, leaving behind the kind of clarity that only comes after a long, hard journey. The studio was thriving again, but more than that, she had found her footing in both her work and her personal life. For the first time in a long while, she wasn't running from her past—she was embracing it and moving forward.

"I've been thinking," Gabe said, his voice breaking the quiet but not disturbing the peace. "Maybe we could start offering photography workshops at the studio. You've got such an incredible eye, Isabel. People would pay to learn from you."

Isabel smiled at the idea. A year ago, she might have dismissed such a suggestion, too afraid to put herself out there, to expand beyond what felt safe. But now? Now she saw the possibilities.

"That's not a bad idea," she mused, glancing over at him. "We could bring in people from the mainland, maybe even host retreats for artists. The island is the perfect place for that kind of thing."

Gabe nodded, his face lighting up with excitement. "Exactly. And who knows? Maybe this place becomes something more than just a photography studio. Maybe it becomes a creative hub, a place where people come to recharge, to find inspiration."

Isabel's heart swelled at the thought. It wasn't just a business idea—it was a vision for the future. A future that she and Gabe could build together, rooted in their shared love for the island, for creativity, and for each other.

"I like that," she said softly, her gaze drifting back out to the horizon. "I like the idea of making this place more than just a studio. It could be a space for connection, for growth—kind of like how it's been for me."

They sat in companionable silence for a while, both lost in their thoughts. Isabel knew that the path ahead wouldn't always be easy. Life had a way of throwing unexpected challenges, as they'd already seen. But with Gabe by her side, she felt ready to face whatever came next.

"I've been thinking too," Isabel said after a moment. "I want to travel more with you. See the world beyond this island. But this time, not as an escape. I want to go places because I'm curious, because I want to experience life. And then, we'll always come back here—because this is home."

Gabe smiled, his eyes soft with understanding. "I'd love that. We could take the camera, capture moments from our adventures, and bring them back to share with everyone here. Maybe even start a gallery."

"A gallery," Isabel echoed, feeling the excitement bubbling up inside her. "A place to showcase not just my work, but others' too. It would be a way to keep expanding, to keep creating new things."

Gabe squeezed her hand gently, his thumb tracing small circles on her skin. "The future looks good, Isabel. I don't know what it'll bring, but I'm excited to find out—with you."

Isabel leaned her head on his shoulder, closing her eyes and breathing in the salty sea air. For so long, she had been afraid of the future, afraid of stepping into the unknown. But now, it felt different. The fear was still there, but it was accompanied by hope, by the anticipation of all the things they could create together. They were no longer defined by their pasts or held back by their insecurities.

"I'm excited too," she whispered, her voice filled with quiet determination.

They sat there, wrapped in the warmth of each other's presence, watching the sun slowly dip below the horizon. The future stretched out before them, vast and full of promise. Together, they had faced the storms, and together, they would continue to chart their course—wherever it might lead.

As the first stars began to twinkle in the sky, Isabel and Gabe smiled at each other, knowing that whatever tomorrow held, they would face it with open hearts and the certainty that this—this love, this life—was the beginning of something beautiful and new.